Novels by Jennifer Roberson

Historical Novels

LADY OF THE FOREST
LADY OF SHERWOOD
LADY OF THE GLEN

Fantasy

"Sword-Dancer Saga"

SWORD-DANCER
SWORD-SINGER
SWORD-MAKER
SWORD-BREAKER
SWORD-BORN
SWORD-SWORN*

"Chronicles of the Cheysuli"

SHAPECHANGERS
THE SONG OF HOMANA
LEGACY OF THE SWORD
TRACK OF THE WHITE WOLF
A PRIDE OF PRINCES
DAUGHTER OF THE LION
FLIGHT OF THE RAVEN
A TAPESTRY OF LIONS

THE GOLDEN KEY
(with Melanie Rawn and Kate Elliott)

Anthologies
(as editor)

RETURN TO AVALON
OUT OF AVALON*
HIGHWAYMEN: ROBBERS AND ROGUES

*forthcoming

Lady of Sherwood

Jennifer Roberson

Kensington Books

http://www.kensingtonbooks.com

KENSINGTON BOOKS are published by

Kensington Publishing Corp.
850 Third Avenue
New York, NY 10022

Copyright © 1999 by Jennifer Roberson
Map by Elizabeth Danforth

Library of Congress Card Catalogue Number: 99-071791
ISBN 1-57566-475-5

First Printing: November, 1999
10 9 8 7 6 5 4 3 2 1

Printed in the United States of America

In memory of my grandfather,
SAMUEL JEROME HARDY
April 23, 1902–December 30, 1997
Gentleman, scholar, and true lover of books,
and my mother
SHERA HARDY ROBERSON
March 5, 1928–April 9, 1999
Any success I enjoy is a reflection of her.

Lithe and listen, gentlemen,
That be of free-born blood:
I shall tell you of a good yeoman,
His name was Robin Hood.

—from *A Little Geste of Robin Hood*
and his Meyne
(ca. 1400s)

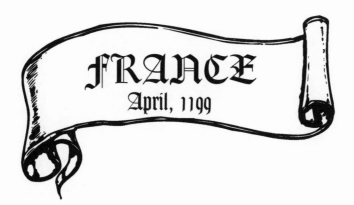

FRANCE

April, 1199

Prologue

The devil lay dying in France.

Ah, but no. Not he.

"My lord," someone said quietly. "My lord king."

The devil was king. Or was it the king was a devil?

"My lord king."

They called him so many things. The man with the heart of a lion. Malik Ric. Son of Eleanor, son of Henry. Eldest surviving son of all named the Devil's Brood, for temperament that, in a hound, might be beaten out, or drowned.

Unless that hound be bred for war.

Dying.

Richard, King of England by the grace of God; Duke of Normandy and Aquitaine, Count of Anjou.

Dying.

"My lord—"

How could it be that *he* could die?

"My lord."

And then a second voice, less quietly; and with markedly less patience: "He cannot hear you. He hears nothing now. Give him peace."

But peace required a man, a warrior, unafraid of others, unafraid of the enemy; unafraid, for that matter, of God, whom he served so well on Crusade in the lands of the Infidel.

But death? No. Not he.

"My lord king."

Almost, he laughed. That first voice, so polite, undaunted by the other more querulous tone, would not recede. There was an answer it demanded, for all it was soft.

"Who?" the voice asked. "Who shall be king?"

Were he his father, he could have spoken any one of three names. And so his father *had*, at one time or another: three sons were left after the deaths of two others, a *triptych* of male heirs from which he must choose one: Richard, Geoffrey, or John. Henry had, in the end, selected the one most fit for keeping the kingdom whole: Richard, the warrior-prince. Who, as sovereign, attempted to perform the service most desired by the Church: to retrieve lost Jerusalem from the Infidel.

But Henry's surviving eldest, as prince or king, sired no sons of his own. On no woman, be she his lawful wife, or whore. He had never intended to let it go so far; but then, he never intended to die, either. Oh, someday; it came to them all. But the greatest warrior in Christendom was not so old that he could not survive three decades more, or more even than that. Surely in so much time he could get a son on a woman.

But time ran out, as did a man's seed. And his he had spent in flesh other than his queen's. In flesh other than a woman's. And so he had no sons.

Who then *could* be king?

"My lord?"

Geoffrey, his next oldest brother, was dead. John, his youngest brother, lived. But so did Geoffrey's *son* survive: Arthur, Duke of Brittany. And there were those in England, those in this tent, who argued it should be Arthur. Not John. Not Lackland. Not Softsword, reckoned unfit. Arthur.

He stirred, and wished he had not. The wound had putrefied; now poison ate his flesh. The man with the heart of the lion was brought down by the sting of a bee: a single bolt loosed from a crossbow in a paltry, pettish defiance, nearly spent in its flight, had nonetheless made a target of his royal shoulder. Insignificance, claimed the king, brushing away the others who would see him to a physician. He had treated it so, insignificantly; had mocked it even as he saluted the crossbowman's impertinence—and now the wound killed him.

"My lord king."

They would say those words to another. It was to him they looked now, this moment, to tell them who it should be.

There was a time men said the old king had too many sons, despite the necessity. Tumultuous, brilliant sons, each in his own way gifted; and each as incapable of being ruled by a father who was king, a mother who was queen, brilliant and brutal sovereigns who set them at one another whenever they were not, as children, united against both parents.

But this man, this king, this devil who lay dying, had sired no sons at all. And so the choice lay now between a brother others hated, and the boy-duke in Brittany.

"My lord, we beseech you—"

"God's Rump," he muttered. "You will hag-ride me to death."

It struck them all into silence, into immobility; they had believed him beyond the sense to form words, let alone a sentence. And a sentence of less decorum than a priest might prefer in the presence of death.

He smelled the ordure of that priest, called the odor of sanctity; he smelled the stink of his own wastes, the foulness of the flesh that ate itself inside out, sapping away his strength as he had sapped the walls of Acre. Acre had fallen at last, and now so would he.

Too soon. Not enough time. There were things left to be done. But he would do none of them. Jerusalem, gone. France, in Philip's control.

"My lord king." The voice tried yet again. "If you would be so kind as to consider the circumstances—"

He twitched a minatory royal finger; the voice broke off at once.

If he would be so kind as to consider the circumstances. By Christ's holy name, he had *created* the circumstances! And he was certain they said it behind his back, and perhaps just beyond the tent-flap. No doubt even his mother would damn him for failing his duties. For leaving her with John.

It would have to be John she supported, surely; Eleanor would give over nothing to the Bretons, who controlled her politically naive grandson in the name of his dead father. Not Eleanor of Aquitaine, who cherished politics the way merchants coveted coin.

"My lord."

At him again. Well, he could not fault them; the line of succession was not so straightly drawn as one might wish, to keep a kingdom whole.

He drew breath. They stilled, awaiting his decision.

"Mercardier," he expelled; it was nothing they expected.

They stirred, murmuring among themselves. But he had named a name, and they summoned the man who bore it.

Rustling: someone drew aside the tent-flap. He heard the quiet word spoken, and then the creak of leather, the scrape and chime of fittings as the mercenary entered. He was armed, of course, even in the presence of his king; Mercardier was bodyguard as much as hired sword. But even he had not been proof against that indolent crossbow bolt, slicing down from the walls of Châlus. Behind which, it was claimed, treasure lay hidden, treasure that had brought Christendom's greatest warrior at once to lay claim, who always needed money.

The mercenary was, like his liege, a large man. He bore the marks of his employment in the seams of his face, the notch in his nose, the line in an eyebrow where once dark hair had grown, bisected now by a scar.

"Mercardier." Difficult now to speak.

The mercenary then did the service he offered no man save his king, and God. He knelt.

"Are they here?" the king asked.

"No, my lord." Mercardier's French-accented voice, ruined a decade or more before by shouting through the din of battle, rasped unevenly in the tent. "There has been no time."

No time. And less of it now, with the king dying. Yet one should reckon that men would therefore hasten. And it was not so very far from France to England.

"Have you sent for them, Mercardier? My matched boys?"

"I have, my lord king. But—" Even Mercardier forebore to say it. Time. Running out.

"I would have—would have Blondel here, to play. And Robin—" He stirred; the bee stung again, poisoning the wound afresh. "I would have my Robin here. He will give me the truth, where no other man will."

Unfair, that, to Mercardier, who knew the truth as well as any and divulged it in his face. But Mercardier was a man of few words under any circumstances.

The rough voice repeated, "They have been sent for, my lord king."

No more than that. But Richard understood the brevity of the answer. No one was certain where Blondel had gone, the Lionheart's favored minstrel; and as for Robin—

"England," Richard gasped. "Nottinghamshire. Go there, Mercardier."

"They have been sent for, my lord king."

"Go there, Mercardier!"

"But—"

But. Unsaid was the truth: if Mercardier left, he would not be at his liege's side as the king expired.

Harder to speak now. "—trust you," Richard managed. "I trust you to see it done. Fetch my Robin here, to me."

Even as the big mercenary opened his mouth to answer, another man's voice slid smoothly into the break. "My lord, if you can send for a lute-player and a man retired from your service, surely you can see it clear to name an heir for England."

The Lionheart laughed. It was little more than a breathless display of teeth, a gritting and grimace against the pain. Through the haze of fever and weakness he saw Mercardier yet kneeling, massive shoulders weighted down by something other than armor.

"John," he said at last, and heard the sharply indrawn breaths. Some were pleased, no doubt. Others perhaps less so, who knew and detested the youngest of Henry's sons. "John—*and* Arthur. Geoffrey's boy."

It shocked them all. Even Mercardier blinked. But there was sense in it; surely they could see that. As Henry had sons to pit against one another in a contest designed to see who was strongest, ablest, cleverest, so Richard might do the same with a brother and a nephew.

Deathbed folly, they believed. He saw it in their eyes. But he was not yet done.

"England for John," he said. "Let him be king in name. And if he is strong enough, he will be king in truth."

"But—Brittany," someone said. "Arthur—?"

"The wherewithal," Richard said, "to wrest it away from John. My lands. My money. John shall have the kingdom. Arthur, the means to take and keep it." The king stretched fever-blistered lips in a rictus that was not a smile. "If he dares."

There. It was said. Was done. His eyes sharpened. "Mercardier," he said. "I have set you a task. See it through. Go to England and fetch Robin. I'll have him serve me once again before John becomes his liege."

"Yes, my lord king." The mercenary rose, bowed, took his leave of the tent and of the dying man in it.

The Lionheart released a pent breath that did not, despite his efforts, drown out the drone of the priest. *God's Holy Arse, but it will be good to see Robin again!*

ENGLAND

April, 1199

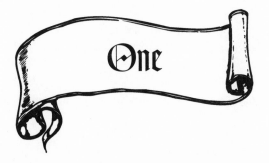

One

The hall lacked the amenities and luxuries of royal palaces, of castles built by nobles, but it was a solid and comfortable manor house nonetheless. Its mistress was diligent in her quest to keep it clean and neat, and warm. Even on days such as this, when hours of drizzling rain turned stone silver-slick and dyed dark all the wood.

The aromas of fresh bread, roasted pork, and the pungency of new cheese masked the mustiness of damp walls and rushes. Spring, nearing, was invoked with religious fervor, but the nights were yet cold. Ovens heated for baking, and fires laid in for roasting lent warmth to the hall, though just now it was mostly empty despite the comfort it offered to chilled bones and empty bellies. Only one person was seated at the table, but she did not eat.

The whispering of servants gathered near a screened corner of the hall died away. They watched the woman at the table, and waited. Expectantly.

Perfect silence, at first. And a meticulous, overstudied stillness.

Then she began to fill it.

Simple tapping: one finger against the expanse of trestle table in the center of the hall. The brief pressure of fingertip, the faint splintery scrape of fingernail. But what began in seeming idleness—*tap . . . tap*—took on the attributes of command: no one in the hall was unaware of the sound, nor of what it portended.

Except the man, the men, who should be present and were not; whose absence prompted the expectancy among the servants as well as the tapping itself. She was mistress of the manor, but not necessarily of her temper when pressed beyond patience. Not since Sir Robert, styling himself Locksley in place of Huntington, had become something akin to master of the manor.

Akin, but not master in truth; Ravenskeep was hers, and had been since her father's death. Since King Richard had been magnanimous enough, upon his brief return to England following his captivity and ransoming five years before, to declare her able to govern her own life, rather than being suffocatingly governed by the Crown in such things as the management of her lands, the dictates of her heart, and the disposition of her hand.

—tap—tap—tap—

Offering suggestive accompaniment, her stomach abruptly growled.

—tap—tap—

*—SLAP—*As the palm of her hand came down. And the thrashing of chairlegs shoved through rushes to scrape against stone floor as the mistress of the manor rose abruptly.

Dust motes rose from disturbed rushes. Marian of Ravenskeep turned to the serving woman standing nearest. "Is it possible," she began with infinite and dangerous clarity, "for a man who has fought for his king and his God in the land of the Infidel to have absolutely no awareness of *time?*"

Joan knew better than to smile. "But he isn't alone, Lady Marian. There are—" She paused.—"Distractions." Four of them, in truth: Little John, Will Scarlet, Much, and Brother Tuck.

"They are none of them blind," Marian declared, "to not notice the sun has set!" Even on such a day as had lacked it, mostly.

"Well," Joan conceded, "no. Unless . ." And she stopped, closing her mouth tightly.

"Unless." Testily, her mistress took it up. "Unless they have gotten themselves so drunk in some Nottingham tavern that they *are* become blind."

"But they may well be just outside the gates," Joan said. "Or even outside the very door."

Marian flung out an arm, stabbing the air with a rigid hand. *"That very door?"* Her arm dropped. "Well then, shall we see?"

Joan held her silence as Marian marched the length of the table, the length of the hall, and unlatched the door. She jerked it open, letting in the post-sunset murk of a rainy day now drying, and illumination from freshly lighted torches smoking in damp sconces and cressets, all of which underscored the emptiness of the door and the courtyard beyond. The gate beyond the courtyard was closed, and seemingly neither Hal nor Sim was being hailed to open it.

Marian turned: her stiff spine and upright stance mimicked a guardsman's pike. "Not outside the door," she said with precise enunciation, even as her breath became visible on the air, "nor, apparently, just outside the gate." She shivered, wrapped her fur-lined leather overdress more tightly around her wool chemise. "Just *inside* the tavern, I should venture."

"Well," Joan said, "you could begin eating without them." She paused. "You have before."

"But he *promised.*" Temper transmuted itself into less perilous exasperation; this was not the first time supper had cooled before the mouths and bellies arrived, but one in an endless litany. It was not always taverns that delayed them, but other vastly important activities such as seeing whose arrow could strike the bull's-eye closest and most often, or whose wrestling had improved enough to give Little John, once called the Hathersage Giant, more of a challenge. If such could be said of a man who won every time. "He stood right there"—a poking finger indicated the appropriate spot just inside the door—"and promised he would be home. By sunset." She cast a despairing glance at the table, filled with meat pies, wheels of cheese, platters piled with pork, loaves of bread, tankards of ale. "We have spent most of the day preparing this meal. I have spent at least half of it praying my bread would not fall." Then another expression crossed her face, one of startled realization. "Do you suppose they *knew* I was going to cook?"

"Lady Marian," Joan said soothingly, "they always eat your cooking without complaint. And, after all, no one told them you were to cook." The woman cast a quelling glance at the other servants as they giggled behind their aprons. "I made certain of it."

"But they prefer Cook's cooking." Marian grimaced ruefully. "*I* prefer Cook's cooking. But that is no excuse. Not when one has promised." Her slow-blooming, evocative smile suggested imminent repercussions. "Therefore, I shall have to go and fetch them all home. Like children. Which men—*some* men—mimic with surpassing regularity." She scowled at the table laden with cooling, congealing food. "Even men who are knights, former Crusaders, and heirs of powerful earls, and should certainly know better."

"But how will you find them?" Joan inquired, hiding a smile. "One tavern in all of Nottingham?"

Marian considered that a foolish question. "A red-haired giant, an overplump friar, a simpleton boy, a perpetually scowling peasant, and an earl's son?" She paused for irony. "Together?"

"Ah." Joan nodded solemnly; everyone in Nottingham knew that particular ill-matched grouping.

With a final sulfurous glare at the table, Marian stalked out of the hall, out of the door—and into a very large man.

She staggered back even as he caught and steadied her with a huge hand. "John—?" she began, readying chastisement, but knew better even as she said it. None of them was here. Not even Robin, who had promised.

In torchlight she saw the glint of steel, the dull shine of worn leather rubbed smooth by time and hard usage. She realized then he was not so tall as Little John—likely no man in England was—but immensely wide through the shoulders. Leather and mail added bulk.

Marian could not help the thought as she looked into the flame-painted face, saw its unshaven scruff and the hard, pitted flesh beneath.

This is a cruel man. But she dismissed it as premonition, and urgency superseded it. "What is wrong?"

He blinked dark eyes and released her arm with alacrity, as if suddenly acknowledging their differences in gender and rank. Had he expected insipid pleasantries prior to the meat of the matter? He should know better; his masked expression hid nothing of an edged intensity, a brittle facade of self-control. And Marian, who had lived with the same herself, had fostered it *in* herself, recognized it at once.

Her mother, dead. Her father, dead. Her brother, dead. She understood loss. Now there was no one left to lose.

Except Robin.

"Who is it?" she blurted, abruptly certain, and as abruptly frightened. "Who is dead?"

Taken aback by her vehemence, he murmured something in harsh-voiced French. Marian heard *Le roi*—and the abrupt catch of his breath, a brief curse. He began again. In English. "Sir Robert of Locksley."

She shivered again, this time from the ice in her blood. Not Robin. Not *dead*. Not the only one left in and of her life. And who was this man to bring her word?

The accented voice was a rough growl. "He is summoned. To France. At once."

Summoned. Summoned. Not dead.

It gave her the strength to speak steadily, to stand with strength again. "Who summons him?"

The face was implacable. *"Le roi."*

"The king," she murmured, baffled. "The king summons him?"

"To France. At once."

The moment of panic and shock had passed. This time, *this* time, there was no word of death, of one more loss, of another body to be brought home. She could manage pleasantries now, and simple conversation.

"He is not here." Marian gestured to the open door behind her. "Will you come into the warmth of the hall? Will you sit at table with me?" She smiled wryly; there was enough food for a king's army—though she thought this man and Little John might account for half the table.

"Non." And again, in English. "No. Where is he?"

"Nottingham," she answered; annoyance rekindled. "Though he should be here by now. He is late coming home—"

He cut her off curtly. "Then I will go there."

"Wait." She caught his arm as he turned, gripped hard, though she doubted he could feel it through hauberk, mail, leather, gambeson, and the fierce knotting of rigid muscle. "What is it? What has happened? Why does the king want Robin?"

Something moved in the dark, hard eyes. "To be there."

Robin had once been a soldier for his king. The question had merit despite the stranger's blatant unwillingness to offer explanation. And she believed she knew the answer: the king always had need of more men, nearly as much as money. "To fight."

His mouth tightened. "To watch."

It baffled her utterly. "To watch what?"

His teeth showed briefly in a grimace of anger, and grief. "To watch the king die."

Even as Marian's hands flew to seal her mouth in shock, the gate behind the man was shoved open; Sim had, it seemed, been hailed after all, for there he was. Into the courtyard, laughing, singing, cursing—and, in one case, praying—spilled a red-haired giant, an overplump friar, a simpleton boy, a perpetually scowling peasant, an earl's son.

And also one other: a slender, graceful man of tumbled golden curls and bright blue eyes, cradling a lute-case. Tardiness and broken promise now claimed an explanation.

"Alan," she said in surprise; they had none of them seen Alan of the Dales for more than two years. And then she forgot all about the minstrel even as the big soldier turned toward the gate.

"Robert of Locksley!" he roared.

The accented thunder of a battlefield bellow shut off the laughing, singing, cursing—clearly a Nottingham tavern *had* been involved—at once. The revelers stopped dead in their tracks, staring. Marian saw Robin unhook an arm from around Tuck's cowled neck and push through the others to stand before them even as they pulled themselves together, frivolity forgotten. She marked the sudden stiffening of his body, the shock in his face.

Disbelief, emphatic and unfeigned. "Mercardier?"

"In the name of the king," Mercardier declared, bass to baritone, "you are to come to France."

"France!" That was Will Scarlet, truculent as usual, especially after too much ale. "What's in France for *us,* then?"

Marian pitched her voice over them all, and their murmurings. "Robin," she said clearly. "You must go with him."

Robin looked from the soldier to Marian. What he saw in her face, in Mercardier's, leached the color from his own.

"Ya Allah," he murmured, stunned, using an invocation she had believed banished in the years since his return. He began to stride toward them, no sign of drunkenness in his gait. "What has happened?"

"A man's pride," Mercardier said harshly in his ruined voice. "He took no thought for his safety, nor for the wound after the arrow pierced him."

Robin's expression was stark as his step faltered briefly, but something moved in his hazel eyes that spoke of undercurrents. "His safety, I believe, was *your* duty, Mercardier."

So, they knew each other. Well enough to dislike one another. But then, Robin had been the king's favorite, and such men encountered much dislike by men lacking royal favor. Or men overzealous in their own royal service. Marian, standing so close to the king's man, was aware of the tension that abruptly immobilized him. And the hostility that was so palpable she very nearly smelled it.

She had experience with men who wished to fight simply because fighting did not require thinking, or an awareness of painful truth. "Stop this," she said sharply, before it could begin. "The king is dying. You owe this time to him, not to your pride."

Pride. Which Mercardier's words implied might cause the death of that king.

Robert of Locksley, once a prisoner of the Infidel, had learned how to set aside such things as pride, as hostility, as personal preferences. He did so now. But Marian, who had learned to read him very well in five years, even such things as level intonations and the set of fair eyebrows, saw the bitterness in his eyes as he strode directly past Mercardier and climbed the steps into the hall.

Her hall. And his. As she had declared it so.

Her king. And his. As God and Henry II had declared it so.

The Lionheart, dying?

No. Other men died. Weaker men died.

To most of the men in his service, Richard Coeur de Lion was legend, not man. And legends did not die.

"You will stay the night, of course," she said to Mercardier; best to depart at first light, rather than sleeping on wet ground. "I will see to the arrangements."

"We go tonight." The peremptory tone halted her. "We go now."

She felt stiff and cold, and powerless. "Is there so little time as that?"

"Madame," Mercardier said curtly, "even now he may be dead."

Legends did not die. But men did.

And kings.

Two

Marian found Robin upstairs in the bedroom they shared. She had half expected to discover him packing feverishly, a duty she planned to lift from him; and clearly he had begun, for one of the big chests was open and clothing spilled forth. But he was no longer digging through folded shertes, tunics, and hosen to select what he thought best to take. Instead, he stood very still near the foot of the bed, mimicking the wood of its testers.

She stopped, noting the brittle tautness of his posture, and waited.

When he saw her at last, when he could form the syllables of words and make sense out of incoherency, he said what she had at first believed: "He cannot die."

She waited.

"Not *Lionheart*," he added, as if she might not know to whom he referred. As if, by hearing the infamous sobriquet, Death might yet be startled away and the warrior-king defended.

She did not say what was obvious: that the king would not have sent for him in such a way otherwise; that Mercardier would not have come himself in such haste and hostility. She said nothing at all, simply waited. There were times a man needed to understand a thing for himself before he permitted a woman entry into his grief. And this was indeed grief, plainly visible in the carnage of his face as he slowly admitted the truth.

"One moment," he said dazedly. "One moment, and all is changed." He looked at her. This time he saw her. "One moment the world is as it is. The next, it is something entirely different. Something it has never been before."

Marian nodded mutely as tears welled into her eyes.

"And *we* are made different," he said bleakly. "On the instant. What we know, what we were, is banished by that instant, razed like a castle under siege, until nothing recognizable is left. The world is unmade."

His world had been made and unmade and made again many times, in war, in captivity, in its repercussions. But this was somehow different. She saw it in his face, in his eyes, in the sluggish quality of his voice, as if he were drugged out of pain but remained aware of it nonetheless, waiting for it to seize him once again.

"One moment," he said, "Richard is alive, and the world is whole, and full. The next . . ." He shook his head. Pale hair stirred against his shoulders. "The next I am summoned to France to see what is left of the man, if he be living yet. So I may witness the world turn itself inside out."

Marian drew a breath. "He wants you to leave at once. Tonight."

Robin nodded. "Mercardier is not a man to waste time."

"Nor should it be wasted," she said, "when a king is dying."

He shut his eyes and flinched. Visibly.

Marian did not know the king. She had met him, once, five years before, when he had come home briefly following his ransoming. When he had looked upon the woman who had won the heart of the man King Richard knew as soldier and confidant, who had gotten drunk with Coeur de Lion; the man who had sung with Coeur de Lion, who had killed with Coeur de Lion in the land of the Infidel, in the name of God. She did not know the king, but she did know the man who had done all those things *with* the king, and she was fully cognizant of the pain such bald honesty caused.

To lance the wound, she said, "I have ordered Sim to saddle your horse."

"A single moment," he said, "and nothing is the same."

Marian bent and retrieved a sherte from the floor. "I will do this," she told him. "Go and eat what you can before that soldier sees to it you never eat again."

"Mercardier." His voice was less drugged, more distinct. As was the dryness of irony. "Not a duty he would cherish, this. Fetching me?" His mouth twitched briefly, then stilled. "But he would see to it where another man might speak of failure, not wanting to set eyes on my face again."

Marian gathered up other clothing, began to place it on the bed so she might select what was needed. "What is he to the king?"

"Captain of his mercenaries, bought men from Aquitaine. But more. They are brothers in many ways, Richard and his captain. More so than ever Geoffrey was, and certainly than John. They are very like in their taste for battle, in the ordering of war."

"And he hates you," Marian said. "Why?"

He was silent a long moment. "Because one day, at Richard's insistence, I wrestled the king. And defeated him. Mercardier has never forgiven me."

She knew better. "There is more than that."

Robin sighed deeply. "Of course. There is always more." He moved at last, to stop her from sorting his clothing. To touch her hand, to grip it, to pull her close. To set a stiff face into her hair as he embraced her. "One moment," he said, "and the world is forever changed. But there is one constancy in my life that I will never allow to change. You."

Marian, offering assuagement in the warmth of her body, the tightness of her arms wrapped around his neck, thought of how she had been certain, upon Mercardier's arrival, that she had lost yet another she loved. And how in that moment the world had turned itself inside out.

But in this moment, as they clung to one another, the world did not move at all. Time was theirs to rule.

Too briefly, Marian reflected. But better one moment than none.

William deLacey, Lord High Sheriff of Nottingham, had sentenced himself this day to his own dungeon. But he was in no danger of being executed or of remaining imprisoned; he inhabited the dungeon cell because it contained money.

The chests of coin were of varying sizes, wood bound by brass, and locked. The sheriff had seen to it that only two men had keys: himself, and his seneschal, Sir Guy of Gisbourne. Who had, five years before, become more than merely steward of Nottingham Castle, but also the sheriff's son-in-law, by marrying Eleanor, the last and least of deLacey's daughters.

Just this moment the sheriff was unconcerned with the chests, stacked into uneven columns against damp stone walls, and equally unconcerned with Gisbourne and Eleanor. His attention was wholly commanded by a large cloth he had unrolled from its oiled casing and spread upon the one piece of furniture in the cell: a crude oak table. The cloth itself was unprepossessing, neither of lustrous silk or fine-woven linen, but it represented everything of his shire that was vital to the realm, so that England, embodied by her sovereign, might thrive.

The cloth was Nottinghamshire's Exchequer, divided like a chessboard into painted squares. Parchment writs served as vouchers for expenses, and wooden tally pieces were placed into an area called the *receipt*, representative of tax payments made to the sheriff. Twice a year it was his responsibility to make an accurate accounting of his shire, and to carry that accounting—and all collected monies—to the Royal Exchequer via Lincoln to London. A preliminary session took place after Easter each year, and it was this session which concerned the sheriff now.

At Michaelmas, in late September, he would be required to *square up* his account, to give a final summary of the expenses and profits of Nottinghamshire by indicating various squares on the Exchequer and explaining what had been done about money—coin spent, and coin collected—in the king's name. It was an exhaustive process, as every sheriff in England was required to attend the sessions. From this final accounting at Michaelmas the king himself was paid, campaigns were funded, the administration of all of England was underwritten, including the payment of sheriffs. Accounts were required to be accurate and absolute; and it was known by all the sheriffs that writs of expenditures, in the days of Holy Crusade, far too frequently outnumbered tally pieces. William deLacey, who would rather hang criminals than account for the king's coin, detested Easter and Michaelmas.

He heard the key scrape in the lock. Gisbourne. And so it was; and so Gisbourne let himself into the dungeon and imprisoned them both. For now the wealth of Nottinghamshire—pardon, the *king's* wealth—was safe.

DeLacey grunted and stepped away from the table. Gisbourne, a short, compact, dark man, bent and placed a stack of wooden tallies into the *receipt*.

"And?" deLacey asked ominously.

Grimly, Gisbourne took a packet of parchment from his purse. He untied it and began parceling out the writs into various squares representing cities, towns, villages, manors. No one in England was spared a share of taxes. But neither was England spared expenses.

"And?" deLacey repeated.

"There are more tallies to come," Gisbourne said. "I have men out now going from village to village to collect the taxes as yet unpaid, but it will take time."

"I do not have a surfeit of time," the sheriff reminded. "Tell the men to be ruthless. I must have a full accounting before the preliminary session."

Gisbourne's mouth barely moved. "Yes, my lord."

"See to it."

"Yes, my lord."

The sheriff glared at the writs strewn across the Exchequer. "It would be much simpler if everyone simply paid the tax collectors on time. Then it would spare me the need to send soldiers to the villages, and spare the peasants the attentions of those soldiers."

"So it would, my lord."

Attention recaptured by the colorless tone, deLacey studied his steward. Gisbourne was being more down-mouthed than usual. "Is this something I should concern myself with?"

Dark eyes flickered. "No, my lord."

"Eleanor, is it?"

Gisbourne was startled that his business was so obvious, but hid it instantly. "The child is ill, my lord."

"Which one?"

"The girl."

Gisbourne's daughter. Or the girl *presumed* to be Gisbourne's daughter; the sheriff was well aware Eleanor was more than indiscriminate when it came to her pleasures. Rumor had it Gisbourne had sired neither the girl nor boy, though Gisbourne himself claimed them.

"Will she live?"

"The chirurgeon believes so, my lord."

"Well, then. Tend my business, Gisbourne, and the chirurgeon will tend his."

"Yes, my lord."

William deLacey let himself out of the cell, resolving to visit the mews. He had acquired a young hawk from the Earl of Huntington, and wished to see how its training progressed.

* * *

Mercardier gave Marian and Robin little enough time to exchange farewells. The mercenary, already mounted, waited at the opened gate. He said nothing, but the intensity of his stare and the grimness of his mouth made it plain further delay would not be tolerated. As Robin led his horse toward the gate, Marian walked with him.

Conscious of the king's man, they exchanged a chaste kiss, though Robin's hand lingered a moment in her hair; and then he was mounting, gathering rein as he swung a leg across the saddle. She had packed him clothing, adding to it a wrapped parcel of cheese and bread; Robin had strapped on dagger and sword. There was nothing left to be done save leave.

"I will be home as soon as may be," Robin told her, gripping her hand a moment, and then he rode out.

She watched them go: one large, mail-clad mercenary atop a huge bay horse, a younger, slighter knight in simple leather and wool, mounted on a gray. The latter wore no mail, but was no less competent, she knew—or less dangerous—than the mercenary captain he rode with. Robert of Locksley had been soldier, Crusader, and king's man also, in the days before the Turks had captured him on the same field where her father died. Before he had come home to England much older in spirit than when he left, if only two years greater in age.

Sim closed and latched the gate. The sound of hooves against court-yard cobbles altered into silence beyond the gate, where stone became dirt track. She would not see or hear him again until he returned.

Until a king was dead.

Marian turned abruptly and strode across the bailey to the hall. Inside there was warmth, food, companionship. Even music; Alan was playing his lute. The melody was simple, his tenor voice pure in accompaniment. She paid little enough attention to the lyrics. Instead, she took her seat at the head of the table, intending to eat and drink—but discovered a sudden inability to move.

The table was no longer empty. Men gathered at it now, the men she had expected to gather at it two hours before, when she had supervised the placing of platters and tankards, the treasured bowl of salt. All men save one, who now rode to France.

It was Will Scarlet who poured a pewter goblet of ale and thumped it down upon the table next to her hand. "Drink," he said. " 'Twill put color back in your face."

She had not known she lacked it.

"Eat." That was Little John, shoving a platter of pork in her direction. The pile was already denuded, ravaged by male appetites. " 'Tisn't a war, is it? He won't die."

Marian looked at them all. At Scarlet, scowling in perplexion; he did not understand her mood. At Little John, with a bush of red beard concealing half his face, but not the blue eyes that were, she saw, plainly worried. For her. At Much, working on a bulging mouthful of cheese— he would never learn proper manners—and at Tuck, whose plate was full of food yet untouched. Alan she gave the merest glance; his head was bent over his lute as he fingered the strings.

"What happens," she asked, "when the king dies?"

Will Scarlet grunted. "They name a new one, don't they?"

"A son," Marian said. "The eldest son, as Richard himself was the eldest of Henry's surviving sons."

Tuck's expression suggested he understood the implications better than the others. "But Richard Plantagenet has no sons."

"Aye, well." Little John looked from Tuck to Marian, shrugging massive shoulders. "They'll find someone."

"The Count of Mortain," she said. "Prince John."

"D'ye think it matters to us?" Will asked roughly. "This king, that king . . . means naught to folk like us." He paused, grimacing. "To you, maybe." She was a knight's daughter, while they were all of them so far below that as to be nonexistent.

Marian drew breath. "Five years ago," she said, "you robbed a tax shipment."

"For the king's ransom," Scarlet declared. "And 'twas Robin's idea, wasn't it? The son of an earl!" He shook his head, lifting a tankard to down a gulp of ale. "Naught to us. The king forgave us all our sins." He grinned at Tuck. "Like a priest."

"That king," Marian agreed, even as Tuck murmured that he was a friar, not a priest, "who may be dead even as we speak."

Scarlet fixed her with a scowl. "D'ye think after five years Prince John would recall a thing about us?"

"Not Prince John." It was Alan, stilling his strings to look at them all. "The sheriff. He will remember."

Scarlet hooted briefly. "*You*, maybe—you tupped his daughter and got caught for the pleasure. But he's naught to do with the rest of us."

"He would have hanged you," Marian said, "for murdering those Normans—"

"They murdered my wife!" he cried, red-faced in sudden anger.

She raised her voice. "—and Tuck was nearly excommunicated because of the sheriff. Much nearly lost a hand to him, for picking pockets—"

"Teach him to be better at it, then," Scarlet muttered, still angry.

"And Alan he would have hanged, too, for certain—indiscretions." The minstrel grinned, amused by her word choice. "And me . . ." She sighed. "Me he would have married."

"Hanging's worse," Little John declared, then colored as she fixed him with a scowl. "Well . . . 'tis. With the one, you're dead—"

"—and with the other, you might as well be," Marian finished glumly, taking up the tankard Scarlet had given to her.

"And it may not be Prince John named at all." Alan smiled blandly as they turned to stare at him. "There's Arthur."

"Who?" Scarlet demanded.

"Arthur of Brittany. Geoffrey's son." The minstrel shrugged. "Traveling as I do, I hear things. And since the king has never sired an heir, nor named one, there are those who whisper we might be better off with Arthur."

"He's but a boy," Tuck protested.

"But he has his grandmother." Alan fingered a flurry of brief notes. "Eleanor of Aquitaine. 'Tis one way to be Queen of England again."

"She's an old woman," Scarlet declared, clearly dismissing the possibility.

Marian smiled. "Eleanor of Aquitaine is not a woman to let age keep her from anything she wishes."

"Then you believe she will fight John?" Tuck inquired.

She thought about it. "One is her son, one is her grandson. Blood means something."

"Blood never kept the Plantagenets from fighting amongst themselves before," Alan observed lightly. "Old King Henry might have had his sons killed any number of times, for their . . ." He paused, savoring it. "Political 'indiscretions.' "

Scarlet shook his head lugubriously. "Has naught to do with us, does it? They are *royal* folk."

"Look beyond yourself," Marian suggested sharply. "Look beyond the immediate world. The sheriff was Prince John's man before—"

"The sheriff is his *own* man," Tuck interrupted forthrightly. He should know; he had been in William deLacey's service five years before. "He serves himself."

Alan asked, "And if serving himself suggests he should serve Prince John?"

Marian glanced sharply at the minstrel. She had always believed Alan of the Dales a feckless if handsome man, full of charm because it was a coin he could spend with impunity, never beggaring himself. But he had said it earlier: he heard things, traveling. And though feckless, she doubted he was a fool. Not beneath the charm wielded with such skill.

Much spoke for the first time. "Pardon."

It silenced them all. Much had grown out of boyhood into awkward adolescence, gaining inches if not flesh and conversation, but he remained odd and unpredictable. And yet there were times Marian believed he understood far more than any credited him.

Scarlet hawked and spat into rushes, then had the grace to color as Marian cast him a pointed glance of annoyance. " 'Twas the Lionheart's pardon," he said. "The sheriff has let us be."

"While the king lived," Tuck said uneasily.

"What, d'ye think the pardon dies with the king?" Little John asked in alarm.

"Would even Prince John dishonor his revered elder brother's memory?" Alan asked mockingly.

Marian, who had herself been subject to Prince John's lewdness and temper, knew better than to answer. Not if she didn't want half the men at her table to spend the rest of the night in disputation.

She caught Much's expectant eyes on her, waiting for her to assure him his world would remain intact. And moved to comfort, as she so often was with him, she fell back on something Will Scarlet had said. "Likely no one will think of us," she said. "They are royal folk, and we are not part of their world."

Scarlet grunted vindication. Little John's eyes brightened and he reached for his goblet. Much shoved more cheese into his mouth. Tuck began to eat at last, cutting into a meat pie, but his expression suggested he had not yet settled the question for himself. Alan of the Dales, eloquent hands gentle on his lute, merely shook his head slightly.

Marian avoided his glance. She did not wish to see the irony in his eyes. Instead, she reached for and began to tear apart a chunk of bread, knowing she would get little sleep that night. Robin was gone, the king was dying, and whether the Sheriff of Nottingham served Prince John, Arthur of Brittany, or the Lionheart's memory, he would, as Tuck suggested, always first serve himself.

Three

"God's Rump," the king swore. "but you're a canny, brave fighter for all you're no more than a stripling youth!" Robin staggered under the Lionheart's friendly embrace. "Crashing your horse through fallen walls, trampling the Infidel, lopping off Saracen heads—Jesu, but you'll make a man of it Robin!"

He had made a man of it already, but compared to the king he was a stripling youth; most of them were, measured against Coeur de Lion. Robin, helm tucked under left arm and mail coif slipped, grinned as the king grinned back, then laughed aloud in sheer exultation as Richard cuffed his skull as a father might a son. Even Mercardier's glowering expression could not suppress his high spirits. He had fought for his God, his king, his country, and come out of it alive.

Alive, intact—and clearly the king's latest favorite.

He had not looked for it, had not asked for it, had in no way invited it. But the king's exuberant affection for those he liked was as instant and overwhelming as Greek fire; no one stood in its way, nor attempted to beat it back. One simply gave way—and let it burn itself out.

But the King was abruptly distracted, called away by others to tend to royal matters, and Robin was left to himself. Horseless now, he stood upon a pile of shattered stone, aware of victory and justified satisfaction. Acre's walls were broken, its Saracen soldiers defeated, its people engulfed by the armies of the Third Crusade. In his right hand he gripped his bloodied sword. He recalled it might be needed again, for Acre was only the first victory: Jerusalem yet lay before them.

Robin knelt, set down his helm, then wrapped the edge of a dead man's robe around his bloodied blade, tending it assiduously so it might serve him again.

Behind him, the bulk of Mercardier blocked the sun. "He will knight you for this."

Still kneeling, Robin twisted to look at the captain of the king's mercenaries. He felt intensely vulnerable, crouched upon the stones with his spine inviting attack. Broken stonework gritted beneath his boots.

But Mercardier did not attack. He simply spat blood, shook his head slightly, and moved away.

Knighted. By the king. In honor of courage, of skill, of victory.

Robert of Huntington, titled Locksley in honor of the manor and holdings bestowed upon him by his father, the earl, as he departed on Crusade, shivered under the glare of the Saracen sun. He had dreamed of it. And now it would be true.

He gathered helm again and rose, unsullied steel blade glinting. All around him Infidel bodies lay tumbled, embraced by blocks of fallen stone. Smoke drifted on the air, mingling with the moans of the wounded, the wailing of the women, the crying and shrieking of children. Beneath his sherte, padded gambeson, mail, and surcoat, he sweated. Itched. Longed for a river in which he might cool himself, cleanse himself, but the only rivers within reach were those of blood.

"He will knight you for this," Mercardier had said.

What more might a man ask in this life?

"Wine," Mercardier said, and tossed the goatskin at him.

Blinking away the dazzle of flames and memory, Robin gathered up the skin bag. He lifted it in a brief salute of gratitude to the mercenary, then unstoppered it. The wine was thin and sour, but served to wash down the cheese and bread Marian had packed.

They had ridden until the forest encroached so vigorously that moonlight dimmed, shielded from the track by a lattice of arching limbs. It had left them with no choice but to stop for the night, and so they had, settling in among the trees with horses groomed, grained, and hobbled. He and Mercardier had not yet managed to find the peace of sleep. Instead, they shared the meager fire, food and wine, silence.

And the knowledge that a man they served, a man they each worshiped, was dying.

"Unfair," Robin murmured.

In shadow, Mercardier's face was expressionless. "That you have no bed? No woman?"

Tension crept into his shoulders. "That a man such as he should be taken from us when we need him so badly."

Mercardier grunted. "He believed the treasure at Châlus would provide the means to mount another crusade."

"*Is* there treasure?"

For a moment the mercenary was silent. When he spoke again, his harsh voice scraped. "The man is the greater treasure."

No one doubted that. "And the Lionheart's captain? What becomes of him?"

"My disposition," Mercardier said, "is at the whim of the king."

"And if, dying, he makes none?"

"He will."

Robin took a pull from the skin, then stoppered it and tossed it back. "And what of England? What disposition does he make for her?"

Mercardier laughed softly, though there was little enough of humor in it. "That I know of . . . none."

It startled him. "None?"

"None before I left him."

"*None?*"

"Surely he will. When he must."

"When he must," Robin echoed.

"And whom he must," Mercardier said.

"And will that be whim as well?"

In Norman French—which Robin understood perfectly; and which Mercardier knew—the mercenary cursed him and the day of his birth.

"It matters," Robin said sharply. "England is not your country, Mercardier. But she is mine. And it matters."

Mercardier, Aquitaine-born, spat. "John will not have you in his bed."

Tension redoubled. It seemed rumor become issue would not be set to rest. Not in six years or sixty. With effort, Robin forced irony into his tone. "Nor was I in Richard's."

"He would have put you there!"

Knowing the man's devotion to the service and comfort of his king, Robin was not certain if the mercenary hated him for being wanted, or for not answering the summons. "He gave me leave to make a choice."

Mercardier swore. "And the minstrel?"

"Blondel chose one way. I, the other."

"Matched boys, he called you. He said it even as I was sent to England to find you."

"And so we were," Robin agreed: both young, both slender, both so fair as to be nearly white-haired beneath the pitiless glare of a sun much fiercer than that of England. "But even if Blondel and I had been sons of the same womb instead of merely of happenstance, our inclinations were very different."

"Therefore?"

"Therefore I served the king as well as I might in all things." Robin paused. "Save his bed."

Mercardier expelled breath through his nose with all the vigor of doubt. "If that is true, why did you let it be said?"

He shrugged, feeling the scrape of bark beneath his cloak and clothing.

"A man may hear the falsehood, and believe it. A man may also hear the truth, and disbelieve it."

"And a man might put his sword to another's throat to convince him to believe."

"What—should I do so to you? Here and now?" Robin laughed softly, careful not to indicate the sheathed sword lest the motion be misconstrued. "And a man might die for it."

"But you are a knight!" Mercardier said it with a contemptuous flourish. "A knight, the son of an earl, a Crusader in the king's army. Surely if the Turks could not kill you in battle—or in captivity—no one else may."

He had found ways to live in battle and regretted none of them. He had found ways to survive captivity and regretted all of them. But the latter he would speak of to no one, save Marian. "You would have preferred I died?"

"Than to have the king waste money on you? *Ah, oui,* so I would."

"And if you had been the captive?"

"I would have died before I could be," Mercardier declared. "They would never have taken me."

Robin believed that assertion very likely, in view of the mercenary's sheer physical power and military experience. "The king would have ransomed you."

The captain spat. "I am not an earl's son."

"You are the king's boon companion," Robin said. "Brothers in arms, and temperament. No man in the army was closer to him than you."

Mercardier's expression remained masked by shadow. "But I am not a nobleman. Only a soldier."

"And that means far more to the king than noble birth. You know that to be true, Mercardier."

"In war." The tone was rough. "But in peace, what am I? What need is there for such as I?"

And so the truth, and fear, was known. Robin wondered if Mercardier realized he had betrayed himself. And it was a valid thought: what place *was* there for a soldier who lost his king and commander? Noblemen, men of consequence because of wealth and holdings, returned home, as he had, to take up other duties. Men like Mercardier fought for coin, went where coin was offered. But men like Mercardier also occasionally found leaders they served out of respect and admiration, out of a kinship in spirit, as the captain served Coeur de Lion.

"If it be John," Robin said, thinking it through. "If it be John, there will still be a war to fight. Against the King of France."

Mercardier shrugged massive shoulders. "Philip is a fool."

"But a rich fool, and wiser perhaps than John." Robin frowned into the dying firelight. "Wiser in the ways of the world than Arthur of Brittany."

"And do you say I should go to France? To serve Philip?"

With care, Robin ventured, "It is a possibility."

Mercardier grunted deep in his throat. "So, is there a possibility I may kill you before dawn."

Robin said dryly, "Then I shall have to pray I do not startle you in your sleep."

Mercardier's tone, surprisingly, was equally dry. "Keep yourself out of my bed, and I shall not be startled."

Robin was surprised into sudden laughter; it was not like Mercardier to wield the weapon of irony in conversation, least of all in threat. Perhaps after all the rumor was set to rest, and hostility in abeyance. "Given a choice, I would be home in a proper bed, and with the woman who shares it."

"Some of us," the captain retorted, "are not so fortunate as to have a home, a proper bed, and a woman in it."

Locksley, grinning, wrapped his cloak around himself and stretched out on the ground near the fading fire. No one, he reflected, was as fortunate as he. Because no one else had Marian.

Come morning, the kitchen was the most popular place in the household. Marian had long grown accustomed to seeing nearly everyone who lived and worked at Ravenskeep coming into the big room to break their fast only to linger near the warmth of the huge hearth; occasionally she had to shoo them out again if the morning was particularly cold, so they might begin their work. This morning the day was not so chill, the kitchen not so crowded.

Until the messenger came into it and gave her his news.

He was young, slim, ruddy-haired, clad in a doublet bearing the triple leopards of the king. He came from Huntington Castle, he said; sent by the earl, he said. His task was to find Sir Robert of Locksley, and he had gone to where he believed Locksley was: at his father's castle. The messenger had the next morning been sent on to Ravenskeep, for the earl had made it abundantly clear his son did not keep to castles, but to the manor house and bed of a wanton woman. Which the messenger was required to state with *precision;* it was his price for being hosted the night at Huntington Castle.

Shocked, Marian stared. She was aware of the hush in the kitchen as Cook and the others waited to hear her response.

After a moment of pain commingled with anger, she carefully set down the mug of steaming cider, incongruously aware of the scent of cloves and cinnamon, so she would not hurl it at the man.

The messenger colored and lowered his eyes, shamed. "Lady," he said, clearly wanting to complete his business and leave before she *could* hurl the cider at him, "I am sent to bring word to Sir Robert that he is to attend the king in France."

She would give him no cause to think of her as anything but what she was: the daughter of a respectable knight, who had died fighting for his king, his country, and his God in the land of the Infidel. She knew well what the earl thought of her; what no doubt the residents of Nottingham believed of her: a woman who lived with a man outside of wedlock. Surely she tarnished her father's memory with such lewd behavior.

But her comportment was her own to tend—she had lost her reputation five years before, when Will Scarlet abducted her from Nottingham and carried her away into Sherwood Forest—and she would see to it the royal messenger had no just cause to speak of her as a woman lacking courtesy. "Will you break your fast with us?"

He ducked his head in brief salute. "My thanks, lady, but I was given food at the castle."

Of course. The earl would want him to say his reception lacked for nothing.

"Your message was brought last night," she said. "By a king's man called Mercardier."

It startled the messenger. "Mercardier? Here? But then—" He broke it off, alarmed. "The *king*—"

"The king is dying," Marian said. And added, very gently, "Mercardier apparently knew how best to find Sir Robert."

It was a rebuke, and he acknowledged it with a flicker of brown eyes. His face reddened again.

"They left for France last night," she said.

"Then if you will excuse me, lady, I shall take my leave as well." He bowed, turned as if to leave, then paused. "Lady," he said diffidently, "perhaps there is explanation in that the earl is ill."

"Explanation?"

"For—what he said. And bade me say."

Marian smiled faintly, glad she was able. "Ill or no, he would say the same. *And* expect you to repeat it."

He nodded, bowed again, was gone.

With exceptional control, she took up the mug. The scent of cinnamon and cloves faded as the liquid cooled. She contemplated its surface a moment.

Joan, who had come in with the messenger, spat into the rushes. "That for the earl!"

Marian smiled sourly. "Ah, but he is ill."

"As he should be, with that black soul." Joan paused. *"Has* he a soul?"

"Then perhaps I should go and see," Marian said lightly.

Joan was astonished. "What, go there? To Huntington? But, Lady Marian—why? He will only speak evil things of you!"

"Of me, yes," Marian agreed. "But also *to* me, which is somewhat preferable to having them said to others."

"You'll beard him!" Joan began to grin. "You'll beard the old fool in his own den, so you will." She exchanged gleeful glances with Cook and the others. "Aye, Lady Marian, you'll shut his mouth for him in good time."

"Oh, I think not. But surely I can inquire as to his health, and whether I may be of aid in any way." She handed Cook the cooled cider. "After all, I was reared to be kind to less fortunate souls."

Joan was transfixed. "What will you do?"

"Visit the earl," Marian answered serenely, "and offer him my company in his hour of need."

William deLacey was most displeased. He was a man capable of adjudicating all that happened within his shire without quibble or hesitation, seeing to it that the folk in this portion of the king's realm did as they were meant. It was a duty he took seriously and performed most assiduously, satisfied that no doubt could be attached to his acceptance of responsibility.

But he doubted himself, his sanity, when his daughter made her presence felt within his world.

DeLacey, outside the mews, carefully placed the young hawk onto its weathering block so as not to tangle the jesses, then took his daughter's arm and marched her away before she could disturb any of the birds. And he knew she would; she had that look in her eye.

DeLacey muttered a brief prayer for patience, then plopped her down on a bench in the shade of an outbuilding wall. "What is it *this* time?"

"What it always is," Eleanor answered. "Gisbourne."

DeLacey's eyes narrowed. "And?"

His daughter attempted to look demure and sound hesitant. She was convincing in neither effort. "He will not do his duty by me."

This was wholly unexpected. The sheriff stared. "You come to me with this? This?" It was preposterous. "Good Christ, Eleanor, this is not my responsibility! You would have me order your husband to sleep with his wife?"

"It is God's law," she said, "that a man should service his wife."

DeLacey barked a harsh laugh. "Like a prize bull, is that it? Christ, Eleanor—this is between you and Gisbourne. It belongs in the bedchamber, not in my hall."

"God's law," she repeated.

"I am the king's servant," he countered. "Not God's. Seek a priest if you wish to involve the Lord."

She fixed a steady gaze on him. "You gave him his position. You gave him *me.*"

"Because you were with child!" deLacey shouted, not caring who heard. "God only knows whose child it is—certainly not Gisbourne's, if I am to believe *this* folly—"

"The minstrel's," Eleanor, interrupting, replied evenly. "The one who forced me."

It well could be, deLacey reflected. The child was nearly five years old, fair-haired and blue-eyed, while his mother was brown in both. But Eleanor's mother had also been fair, so he could not swear the child who bore Gisbourne's name was of the minstrel's begetting.

"Forced you," he said in disgust. "You know what is said of that."

"But you silenced them," Eleanor reminded him, "by marrying me in all haste to the first man you could find." Her mouth twisted in disdain. "Surely there was someone else—"

He cut her off. "I had planned to marry you to the Earl of Huntington's son. But after you and the minstrel were discovered, the chance for that was gone."

"He forced me," Eleanor said. "And so did you. Forced me to marry Gisbourne."

"Would you have been more content had I sent you to the Marches where you could have wed a wild Welshman?"

"Well," she said thoughtfully, "perhaps he might have had more appetite for his marriage bed."

His own appetite was for departure. He found a reason, and told her. "I have business with the earl," deLacey said. "If you are wanting for your husband's affections, perhaps you might offer him more than the edge of your tongue."

Four

The Earl of Huntington watched as his steward, Ralph, carefully sanded the parchment, then sealed it with wax. Ralph neatly pressed the earl's signet ring into the ruby dollop, removed it, inspected the impression, let the wax dry. It was the third such letter he had drafted for his master this afternoon; two others, sealed, lay on the table. They bore names already inscribed on them: *Eustace de Vesci* and *Henry Bohun,* lords of Alnwick and Hereford. Ralph inked the quill again, and with a clear, tidy hand inscribed the third and last letter: *Geoffrey de Mandeville,* who was Earl of Essex and the king's Justiciar.

The Earl of Huntington's mouth crimped. It was likely de Mandeville would lose the latter position, to be replaced by another. Such things were common when the crown passed from one royal head to another.

Ralph, gathering up all three letters, looked to his master for orders. The earl nodded. "See to it," he rasped hoarsely. "As soon as may be."

"My lord." Ralph bowed himself out of the sickroom.

And so it begins. Again. The earl coughed, then pulled testily at the bedclothes, settling them higher about his chest. He detested being ill at this time, when all of England would soon be in turmoil. He had no time for such things as fevers and recalcitrant lungs when great works required doing, such things as he now embarked upon. He and the others had been in close contact years before, when John, the Count of Mortain, had threatened his captured brother's throne. Richard's ransoming had brought him home again to England, where he had chastised John for his folly, sold suspended offices to find money for renewed warfare, and then was gone again. John had since behaved himself, but the earl knew that would soon change. Once Richard died, in all likelihood John would become king.

Unless he and men like him, men of powerful titles and wealthy houses, took steps to ensure John did not become king. And that if he should, to do what was necessary to protect certain interests John had never endorsed as his own.

England was, the earl believed, on the brink of disaster. Such times required haste and hard decisions.

He closed his eyes and would have given himself over to rest, save someone knocked briefly at the door, then opened it. Ralph again, though the letters were not in evidence.

"My lord," the steward said, "the sheriff is here. Shall I tell him you are indisposed?"

"DeLacey?" The earl frowned. "What does he want?"

Ralph deferred his unnecessary answer with a courteous question. "Shall I show him in, my lord?"

Huntington considered declining—he found William deLacey frequently tedious—but in view of events, perhaps it would be best to see the sheriff. It was time to learn men's hearts and minds, so they could be made use of—or controlled in other ways.

"Have him in," he told Ralph. "Bring wine, and water."

"My lord." Ralph bowed himself out.

In a matter of moments deLacey was shown into the earl's room, and a page brought wine and water. The sheriff, silvering dark hair windblown from his ride, brought the scent of horse and the chill of dampness into the room. Huntington coughed.

DeLacey was unctuous. "My lord, may I tender my most felicitous wishes for a hasty recovery?"

The earl eyed the man, then waved him into the chair beside the small table still holding inkpot, quill, wax, and parchment. He saw the sheriff note the signs of recent scrivening, though he smoothed his face into a mask of solicitude.

"You may tender more than felicitous wishes," the earl said plainly. "You may tender me your opinion."

The sheriff was clearly startled by the blunt invitation, but offered immediate acquiescence. "Of course, my lord. On what do you wish me to offer an opinion?"

"Your heart," the earl declared.

DeLacey blinked. "My lord—?"

"You are Richard's man," Huntington stated. "You have paid him for your office so you belong to him."

Color moved thickly in deLacey's face. Brown eyes flickered momentarily before becoming opaque in poor light. "So I am, my lord," he said tonelessly, "and so I did."

"Therefore I require assurances of your heart, deLacey. Is it Richard's as much as your money is his?"

Clearly at sea, the sheriff took great care with his words. "I am of course loyal to the Crown, my lord—"

Huntington interrupted. "I am not speaking of the Crown just now. I am speaking of Richard Plantagenet."

DeLacey surrendered prevarication and careful courtesy. "Of what are we speaking, my lord? Am I Richard's man? Yes; as you pointed out, I paid him to retain my office when he might have stripped me of it. But I was certainly not alone in this; he demanded it of many when he returned from imprisonment. Do I resent it?" The sheriff's mouth hooked briefly. "I resent the necessity, but not the man who demanded it."

"You supported the Count of Mortain, I believe, when last he was here."

DeLacey opened his mouth. Shut it. Began again. "My lord, may I be frank?"

"If you would not waste my time."

William deLacey said, "I owe my office to the king's pleasure. Only a fool endangers it by rebelling against that pleasure."

"And if the crown is contested?"

A brief startled frown marred the sheriff's brow. "Contested, my lord? In what way? Prince John will not attempt to overset his brother." Unspoken was the knowledge John had once tried precisely that while the king was imprisoned in Germany, and had failed abysmally.

The earl gazed penetratingly at the other man. "There is the boy in Brittany."

"Arthur? Yes, of course—but what has he to do with my office?"

"Your office may become his pleasure."

DeLacey made a brief dismissive sound—he knew of no reason they should speculate without cause—then sealed his mouth closed. A muscle twitched along his jaw. Curiosity was rampant, but his lack of response confirmed his unwillingness to commit himself, or be led into hasty—and potentially incorrect—conclusions.

Tedious betimes, but never a fool. Huntington smiled. "So you may well wonder. But the succession is muddy at best. There is neither law nor precedence requiring a childless king's youngest brother to inherit before the king's nephew, if that nephew be sired by the next oldest brother."

"Geoffrey," the sheriff murmured, thinking swiftly.

"Were Geoffrey alive, he would be heir, as Richard has no sons. But though Geoffrey is dead, he *did* sire a son. And there are those who will argue Arthur has more right to the throne than John."

The sheriff's face had taken on a peculiar waxy pallor as he came to realize what the true point of discussion was. "My lord earl . . . may I ask *you* to be frank?"

And now the moment was here. Huntington relayed the truth without embellishment, without emotion. "The king is dying in France. He may already be dead. Therefore England is at risk."

It confirmed deLacey's suspicions as well as his concern for his personal welfare. "But he will name an heir!"

"If he is able, he will. According to the royal messenger, the king had not yet done so."

Even deLacey's lips were pale. "My God. My God."

"Therefore I ask you again: are you Richard's man? Or your own?"

DeLacey, his breathing quick and shallow, took up the pitcher of wine and poured his cup full. His hand trembled.

"Is it so terribly difficult," Huntington inquired icily, "to know your own mind? Or do you predicate every decision on how best it serves yourself?"

DeLacey drank deeply, then set the cup down with a decisive thump. Wine smeared the rim of his upper lip. The edge of his hand removed it. "Arthur of Brittany is a boy."

"His mother is no fool. And there is, as always, his grandmother to consider. Eleanor of Aquitaine may wish to be queen again."

"John is her son."

"If you are a woman, Sheriff, and you have the appetite to rule as well as the wherewithal to do so, whom would *you* support?"

DeLacey's answer was immediate. "John would never permit her to rule."

"Even so. Therefore we are left with a choice: John, who is a man grown somewhat acquainted with rulership—and who is not so incapable of ordering a realm as his enemies might suppose—and Arthur, who is yet young but surrounded by ambitious and powerful women, among them one who has already been England's queen." And France's, but France was, at this particular moment, unimportant. Only *after* England embraced a new king would the matter of France take precedence again.

"But if the king names an heir before he dies . . ."

"If. And even then there is no certainty his choice may keep the throne. Kings have lost them before."

"I must think," deLacey blurted.

"Indeed," the earl said. "I suggest you do so. With all great haste and diligence, for time is not precisely a collaborator in this matter."

The sheriff rose. He steadied himself with one hand pressed against the table. "My lord, may I inquire as to *your* heart?"

"You may not," Huntington replied imperturbably. "But you may leave. After you have poured and presented me with water."

Grim-faced, deLacey performed both duties. Then he backed out of the chamber with a stiff inclination of his head.

Huntington drank deeply, bathing an unhappy throat to prevent an explosion of coughing. Then, still gripping the cup in both hands, he smiled satisfaction at the closed door now empty of the sheriff.

It did not matter which way the man jumped, any more than it mattered how the frogs in the lily pond leaped. What mattered was *knowing* which way—and when—deLacey intended to go, so as not to trip over an obstacle when least expecting it.

With movements abrupt and discourteous, William deLacey snatched leather gloves out of the servant's hand and tugged them on. Even as the servant attempted to settle his cloak over his shoulders, the sheriff swore and yanked the fabric away, pinning it himself even as he clumped in heavy riding boots out of the hall into the stableyard. He shouted for his horse; it was brought immediately. DeLacey caught rein and stirrup leather and prepared to swing up, but the clatter of incoming horses briefly distracted him. With one foot hovering and a horseboy poised to offer him a leg up, he paused long enough to recognize the first rider and immediately set his foot down again. He paid no attention to the horseboy now deprived of duty, and curtly told the other at his mount's head to tend it yet.

She was cloaked and hooded, but tendrils of black hair had escaped captivity to frame the rim of her hood and the face within. Roses lived in her cheeks. She had not yet seen him, did not yet know he was there, and thus her expression was open and enchanting. For a moment deLacey wished he might permit her to remain ignorant of his presence—it would retain the expression and grace—but he had no time for it.

He stepped to her horse and caught the rein before the scurrying horseboy did. "Marian."

Her attention had not been on the man, but on the boy. Now she saw him, and he marked how the grace transmuted itself to stiffness, how the set of her mouth tightened into displeasure. Blue eyes were chill as she gazed down upon him, making no effort now to dismount, because to do so would put her into his arms. Behind her came a companion, one of the Ravenskeep women, whose startled expression gave far more away than Marian's measured mask.

He had no business with her, but it amused him to avail himself of her. Her choice was to stay on the horse, or allow him to aid her. So he made that his business.

Plainly annoyed, Marian eventually dismounted with his assistance. This close, he smelled her perfume: a tracery of roses and cloves. She was petite, delicate, fragile—and yet a woman of tougher temperament he had never known.

Except perhaps Eleanor of Aquitaine, whom he had met once, and briefly. But Eleanor was a queen, a woman born to rule men. Marian wished, apparently, to rule herself.

"A question," he said.

Marian waited for him to release her gloved hand. When he did not, she tugged it free. Her mouth was a tight seam now, her jaw sharp as steel. In five years her beauty had matured, but the absence of innocent girlhood did not trouble him. Now he would learn if it troubled her.

"A question," he repeated. "Has he married you yet?"

The pallor of her features was transmuted to blazing color. He thought she might strike him a blow in the face, but she forebore.

"A fair question"—he caught her arm as she made to move beyond him to the steps—"since you have arrived at his father's home. It is my understanding you are denied that particular pleasure. Therefore I assume he *has* married you, and I should wish you happy?" Marian attempted to snatch her arm out of his grasp. She failed. That much he could ensure; he was far stronger than she. And then, with a polite smile, he relinquished his grasp. At *his* whim. "By your silence, Lady Marian, I assume the answer is no. Why then are you here?"

"The earl is ill," she answered tightly.

"So he is. But not so as you might fear he will die, thereby permitting entrance into a place that is expressly denied to you." He studied her pointedly. "Unless you have come to relinquish your claim on his son? Surely even you would do so, if only so the boy might see his father again. It is a sad state of affairs when a man's affection for a woman turns him from his father."

"And his legacy?" she asked tartly. "Oh, Sheriff, do not bestir yourself on Robin's behalf. He lives as he wishes. He lives *where* he wishes."

"And forfeits a title. A castle."

"And he would gladly trade both if it would keep the king alive!"

She meant to go past him. He caught her arm again, trapped it. Swung her to face him, so roughly her hood slid off her head to puddle across her shoulders. "You know about the king?"

"Robin is even now on his way to France." Bleakness flickered in her eyes as her arm went slack in his grip. "The king sent for him."

DeLacey released her. The earl knew. Locksley knew. *Marian* knew. How many others?

Prince John? He was in Brittany, visiting his nephew, Arthur.

The king was dying, and *John was with Arthur.*

"My God," the sheriff murmured. "John will have him killed."

"Robin?"

"No . . . no, of course not. Locksley has nothing to do with this." DeLacey scowled at her, then tempered it into casual concern as his thoughts worked it out. "You became a ward of the Crown on the death of your father."

"I was," she said guardedly. "The king released me of that."

"And pardoned murder, thievery, rape, and other such activities as might earn a man a hanging." His smile now was cold. "If John becomes king, as he is certain to do, he may have other ideas. Pardons may be revoked. Unmarried daughters of dead knights may have their lands— and the disposition of their *hands*—claimed by the Crown."

Color flared in her face again. "And will that be your advice to the new sovereign?"

"That shall be for the ears *of* the new sovereign, whomever he may be," deLacey answered smoothly. "But my advice to you is to consider that your circumstances may be about to change."

Before she could speak again—if indeed she meant to—he turned once more to his horse. This time he permitted the boy to offer him a proper leg up, and swept his cloak across the saddle as he settled and slid his right foot into the stirrup. The reins were supple in his gloved hands.

William deLacey smiled, inclined his head to her with all lordly courtesy, and rode out of Huntington Castle. There was much to do, far more than had been on his plate an hour before. Knowledge of Richard's imminent death altered everything. The world would be unmade, then remade in another king's image.

He had told the earl nothing of his thoughts, his preferences. But he knew very well his only chance to retain his office and power was to support Prince John. Arthur of Brittany was a boy; he would be surrounded by ambitious women, and Bretons who had neither love for nor under- standing of England. But John, John was eminently preferable. The Count of Mortain and the High Sheriff of Nottingham had already established a rapport.

Now was the time to solidify it.

Marian offered the earl's steward nothing but courtesy—yet seasoned it with consistency. She would see the earl, she said. Repeatedly. To offer him comfort.

Ralph's expression suggested that her presence would offer no such thing to the earl, though he said nothing of it. Merely explained the earl was ill and could receive no visitors.

"He has received the sheriff," she countered calmly.

"Lady, I do apologize, but I fear—"

She interrupted. "You fear nothing save your master's displeasure. And indeed he shall be displeased when he sees me. But admit me, and I vow by the time I leave, the earl's displeasure will be mitigated."

Ralph's suspicion led him out of courtesy into demand. "How?"

Joan, bearing the bundle of things Marian had ordered brought for the earl's pleasure, blurted a shocked exclamation that a fellow servant would so far overstep his duties as to question her mistress.

"Convey my request to the earl," Marian repeated. "Tell him I am aware of the king's illness, and what it means to my circumstances as well as his own . . ." She paused. "And those of his son."

Something flickered in Ralph's eyes. After a moment he briefly inclined his head and directed them to wait. Still clad in cloaks, still bearing as yet unaccepted gifts, Marian and Joan waited.

"Will he see you?" Joan murmured.

"Oh, yes."

"How can you be certain, Lady Marian?"

"He is ill. He needs an heir."

Joan whispered it. "But—my lord of Locksley has repudiated his father."

"All things change when a king dies."

"*All* things, my lady?"

Marian felt the pinch of grief. "When old King Henry died ten years ago, my father yet lived. But the new king, the warrior-prince who dedicated himself to regaining Jerusalem, summoned knights to serve him. And my father died for it."

"But that was Holy Crusade, my lady!"

"Of course it was. But my father died nonetheless." Marian brushed a strand of hair from her face. "And now the warrior-king is dying, and a new king shall have the ordering of the realm, the ordering of our lives.

And I cannot promise you anything of those lives shall remain as they are."

Ralph was back. "The earl will see you."

Marian smiled at Joan and gave her the second basket even as a page appeared to gather up their cloaks. "I should not be long."

Five

The day dawned befogged, but promised yet to be sunny, lacking the clouds and drizzling rain of the previous days. Robin felt an unexpected lift in his spirits—until he recalled why he and Mercardier were on this road.

Dulled again into an abrupt and pernicious sense of futility, he watered his horse, then hastily saddled it and mounted, settling the cloak around his shoulders and pinning it haphazardly into place even as he urged the gray to move. Mercardier already waited on the edge of the road a few paces from the small clearing they had inhabited for the night, wreathed in layers of thinning fog. Robin, annoyed by the pinch of guilt—he felt rather as if his father waited for him—expected to be reprimanded for tardiness, but he found Mercardier distracted, at pains to identify a rider coming their way.

Fog yet obscured him. The slap-and-dig of galloping hooves into wet track became more apparent as the rider neared, as did his haste and the raspy, rhythmic breathing of his mount. At last the fog thinned and peeled away, stirred to recoiling by the motion of horse and rider, so that Robin and the captain caught their first glimpse of the man who rode so swiftly.

His quartered crimson tabard, flapping in the wind of his passage, was mud-spattered, soiled with his mount's lather and froth. It was not until he was nearly on them that his badge came into hazy view and was thus identified: the triple leopards of England.

"No," Robin murmured. And inwardly: *It is come.*

Mercardier spurred his horse into the center of the road into a pocket of fog, shouting at the rider to stop in the king's name. The rider, wind-ruffled and red-cheeked from the efforts of his gallop, pulled up sharply. His expression was grim, tense, focused on his task. His sliding, muddy-legged mount fretted at its bit, grinding steel in massive teeth as it fought for footing.

Oh, my lord . . . oh, Richard . . .

"Gerard!" Mercardier blurted.

The messenger, focusing now on the man who stopped him, blurted a startled and heartfelt oath in French. He reined in his blowing horse with unthinking expertise. "Captain—"

Mercardier cut him off. "What news?"

As fog stirred and thinned about them, as equine exhalations set spumes of steam into the air. Gerard's gaze flicked to Robin, who read the answer in the messenger's expression. *"Le roi,"* Gerard said breathlessly. *"Morte."*

Robin shut his eyes. But closed lids did nothing to shield him from the truth, the piercing anguish of acknowledgment.

Richard Plantagenet. Coeur de Lion. Richard, King of the English. Malik Ric, as the Saracens called him.

Not Richard.

Not Richard.

Not the warrior who had knighted him at Acre after they took the city, who brought him into his inner circle of counselors and boon companions, who ransomed him from the Turks before even his father could.

The Saracens would say, *what is written is written.* But he could not countenance such loss. Could not comprehend what such absence would mean to the world.

The world that was, in one moment, utterly unmade.

Mercardier, with startling alacrity, heaved himself out of the saddle and fell to his knees in the muddy, fog-laden road. With no grace, merely a surfeit of grief, of seemingly incongruous piety, he bowed his head and crossed himself, then began to murmur a prayer in hoarse-voiced French.

Not Richard.

Robin's eyes, painfully dry because nothing in his youth had permitted tears, locked on to those of the messenger. His sluggish mind told him he knew this man, that this man knew him. And Gerard, acknowledging it, wore the face of bitter acceptance.

"We are sent," Gerard said in his accented English; he, too, was a man of Aquitaine, of Eleanor and Richard, duchess and titular duke. "Many of us, so many of us, to carry word. To London. To France. To Brittany. To all the great houses, the great men of England."

"My father," Robin murmured blankly.

Gerard's expression acknowledged that. He knew Sir Robert of Locksley. Knew who and what his father was. "My lord," he said. "The king is dead. It is my duty to carry word."

Mercardier, done with prayers, surged so quickly to his feet that his horse shied back, prevented from leaving the road only by dint of a mailed hand clenched upon his rein.

"Who?" his ruined voice scraped. "Who was named? Prince John, or Arthur of Brittany?"

Gerard's face was pale and taut. "Both."

"Both?" Robin demanded, shocked out of sorrow into politics and the necessity of understanding the implications.

"The king wishes—" Gerard broke it off, began again. "The late king wished the strongest to inherit."

He understood at once. He knew Richard better than most, and understood.

So did the mercenary. They stared at one another, tense and grim, knowing what the king had done and what it meant.

"I am for France," Mercardier declared abruptly, turning to his horse.

Of course he was. Richard was there. Richard must yet be served.

"Where?" the captain asked, swinging a leg across the broad rump of his mount.

"They will take him to Fontevrault Abbey," Gerard answered. "To be entombed at his father's feet."

Robin grimaced. Fontevrault was in Angers, in Richard's French domains. England lost even the body of her king, as it had lost his father's before him.

As Mercardier settled into the saddle and gathered reins, he nodded once, decisively. "Then that is where I shall go." His gaze was grim as he looked at Robin. "And you?" He paused, and the tone acquired an undertone of contempt. "The king now has no need of his matched boys."

Wincing inwardly—Mercardier wielded words as well as his sword— but permitting none of it to show, Robin looked at Gerard. "Where are you bound?"

"To Huntington. To Nottingham."

To the earl, and the sheriff. Neither of whom would permit such news to paralyze mind or body, nor halt the plans they would plot.

"Go elsewhere," Robin suggested. "I will carry the word to my father, and to the sheriff."

But Gerard was experienced in such things as might affect the governance of a realm in the wake of a monarch's death. His face was oddly calm as he shook his head. "It is my task. A service for my lord king."

There was no service Sir Robert of Locksley might offer a dead king. But there yet remained living companions, and the woman he loved. He said no word to the mercenary who now lacked a master, to the late king's courier. He simply wheeled his horse upon the track and set it to full gallop, cloak rippling in the wind, and ignored Mercardier's curses as the mud flew up behind.

Just outside the earl's bedchamber door, Marian inhaled a deep and steadying breath. Ralph had at long last taken her cloak, so that she faced the earl in dry and decent clothing. Hastily she smoothed back from her face the tendrils of hair loosened from twin braids, tucking them beneath gauzy coif and narrow fillet. There was no complaint to be made of her bearing and apparel, but she did not doubt the earl would find something.

Ralph knocked briefly, then unlatched and opened the door. His face was expressionless as he allowed her into the chamber, redolent of the sickbed and the cloying scent of beeswax candles only the rich and powerful could afford.

Just inside, before comment might be made—and to be certain of self-control—she dipped into a deep and respectful curtsey. The door behind her thumped closed as she rose from the floor, and Marian realized she was to face the earl quite alone.

She invoked whatever strength might be had from such powers as God, her will, and her conscience, then looked up on a spurt of self-confidence to meet unfriendly eyes.

Huntington's body was a narrow bundle beneath heaped covers of rich cloth and a quilt of pelts, propped up by layers of pillows. She had not seen him to speak to in several years; he was older, whiter of hair and thinner of flesh. The aging face with its bony prow of nose was pale save for mirrored spots of color burning high in withered cheeks. She could not be certain if it was born of fever or fury, for the look he cast upon her in no way mimicked courtesy.

Marian folded her hands against the doubled girdle of her kirtle and drew another steadying breath. She brought her battle to Huntington's field, where he knew the terrain far better than she. She dared not give him even a single blow that she could not blunt or turn with one of equal measure. "I came," she said plainly, "against your express wishes. To see if indeed you were ill."

Huntington did not reply, though his eyes blazed at her.

"You *would* lie," she said, discounting his affronted expression, "if you believed it might profit you."

Huntington said nothing.

"And a father might send a lie to his son in hopes the son would come."

The earl stirred then, a brief, angry spasm beneath bedclothes and pelts. His voice was raw from coughing. "I sent neither lie nor truth to my son. The king sent a messenger; I in turn sent him."

She picked her way carefully, but steadily, avoiding pitfalls with meticulous attention. "As it is true, it may be argued a sick man *should* send word to his son."

His tone, despite his weakness, was peremptory. "What word I send or do not send is my concern."

"He is your son."

"He lives elsewhere."

"Many sons do."

"Many sons do as their father wishes. If they hope to inherit."

"Your son does not bind himself to that duty."

"Fools and madmen," he said, "turn their backs on duty."

"And on titles and great estates?"

"By God," he ground out, "you dare much—!" And lost the balance in a bout of harrowing coughing. His narrow shoulders jerked within the folds of his heavy robe.

"I dare it," she said when he was done, giving him no latitude even in illness lest he use it against her, "because it matters to me what becomes of him."

He drank water from a cup held in trembling hands, then rebutted her. "Because it matters to you that he should inherit an earldom."

"Yes."

He thumped the cup down on the bedside chest. "So that you might become his countess."

"No."

Contempt and disbelief were manifest.

"I have a manor," she explained matter-of-factly. "I have lands. I have *myself*. I need no man to give me anything."

"You come now to see if it is true that I ail, so you may judge for yourself if there is profit in it for you and how soon it might be yours."

Marian shook her head.

The earl's words were clipped. "You know the king is dying. You know also that his successor may not be so generous as to let you keep your lands. You may believe and declaim you need no one but yourself, but I daresay if Prince John or Arthur of Brittany scruple to claim your lands, to bestow upon some unwitting man your unwed and tainted hand, you would seek whatever rescue you believed my son could offer."

From somewhere Marian dredged up a calm smile. "You believe I wish to marry him."

He said nothing, believing it implicit. He would not waste time and voice on unnecessary confirmation.

"He has asked," Marian said, "more times than I can count. And each and every time I have refused. What need, my lord? He loves me without benefit of wedlock. He lives with me without benefit of wedlock. My reputation, as you have observed repeatedly, was quite ruined five years ago . . ." She paused. "And there are no bastards requiring a marriage to gain legitimacy as your grandchildren."

The earl's tone was bitter. "You are a deceitful woman. You fancy yourself clever, I do not doubt, to say you do not want what you very badly need, but you are too young for cleverness, and of the wrong sex."

With effort she governed her temper. "Would you say the latter," she wondered acidly, "to Eleanor of Aquitaine?"

He pulled himself up against his pillows, glaring at her furiously. "You dare compare yourself to *her?*"

With edged and brittle honesty, Marian asked, "How could I, my lord? She had two husbands, while I have none. She had, they say, countless lovers—while I have but one. She bore eleven children, albeit few survived. While I, my lord of Huntington, am like to bear none."

"None," he echoed sharply.

"Three times in as many years," she said simply, "I have miscarried. In two years I have not even conceived."

It struck him into silence. He gazed upon her, rapt in her expression, in the rigidity of her posture. She saw him weigh out the words she said, the meanings of those words, the implications that some men might draw from those words. He knew now, she saw; was clever enough, had heard enough, to realize what she intended. And because he knew it and yet feared it could not be true, he said nothing, no word; made no exclamation, offered no sign of his opinion, lest he yet startle or drive her into the withdrawal of what he most wanted. He simply lay propped against his pillows, fever in eyes and cheeks, and waited to learn he had won the field with nary a battle begun.

Marian met those hostile eyes and did not waver from the course she had set herself in the endless, senseless hours of empty bed and sleepless night. "A man needs an heir, my lord. And his son an heir after him."

Age-creased lips parted slightly. He took care to let his hands remain still upon the bedclothes, but she saw the minute trembling in the loose flesh of his throat. Disbelief. And burgeoning hope. "Does my son know this?"

So many times she had thought to tell Robin, to give him the truth of the miscarried children. But they had each of them been barely begun, and she not even aware of their presence in her body until the cramping and bleeding came upon her. Each time she had, with only Joan's assistance, tended what needed tending, that he might be spared. Let him believe her barren; and for all she suspected that might indeed be true, after two years.

She would not be Eleanor deLacey, forced to wed Gisbourne because she had conceived, and she would not make Robin into Gisbourne, forced to marry because *she* had conceived. Will Scarlet's notorious abduction of her from Nottingham Fair had quite ruined her reputation, and with no children conceived and carried to term, there was no need of marriage. In a world where women had no choice in their disposition unless they be queens, and then rarely, it was her only freedom: to tell the man she loved she would not marry him.

"No," she told his father. "He knows nothing of this."

"Then I will do you this kindness," the old man said hoarsely. "I will grant here and now, within this chamber and of this moment only, that he loves you as you say, and has asked you to marry him. And so I ask in return, granting these things: why then would he leave you?" He paused, honing the edge. "Or has he already left you, and this merely a shabby attempt to salve your pride?"

A wave descended upon her. Marian was cold, cold *and* hot, all at once, and so angry so abruptly that she trembled with it. After a long moment, and with pronounced precision, she said, "If you wish an heir, my lord, I suggest you find a kinder question to ask."

"Of you?"

"Of him. He is *your* son, my lord . . . make no assumptions concerning what shapes his actions, lest you shape in him an answer you cannot bear."

After a tense moment, the earl assayed a slight—and infinitely brief—smile. "Well said. Perhaps there is a measure of cleverness in you after all."

"I might thank you for that," she replied coolly, "were I to respect the source."

Sallow face mottling again with angry color, he waved a curt hand. "Get out."

Marian held her ground. This time she employed a tone that mimicked his own, when he declared how a thing should be. "I have given you the key. Use it wisely. There will be no impediment from me as you seek the lock it fits, but neither will I refuse him should he ask me again to marry."

"Get *out*—"

As he descended again into coughing, this time she went.

Six

DeLacey had ample opportunity to work his way through the myriad mazes of personal possibilities and political probabilities on the ride back to Nottingham. By the time he made his way through the tangled skeins of city streets, clattered his way into the castle bailey, and leaped down from the saddle to toss reins at a hurrying horseboy, he knew what he would do. And thus he did it as soon as he reached his private solar, stripping gloves from his hands and dumping cloak onto the floor. A servant had followed to divest him of such accoutrements, to clean the floor of smears and clumps left by muddy boots, but the sheriff merely waved him out again. Let the gloves, cloak, and brooch lie scattered on the floor. Other matters were of far greater import than the tidiness of his dwelling.

If he would *keep* that dwelling.

He found ink, a quill, and parchment, gathering them together with sealing wax, sand, and signet. He sat down heavily into the weighty chair, yanked it forward one-handed with a screech of wood on stone as he dragged parchment before him, and hastily uncapped the ink. For a moment he stared into space, retrieving the form of the letter he had composed in his head. Then he began to write swiftly and steadily, commiting himself, pausing only to reink the quill when it sputtered and scratched its way into indecipherability.

'*Good my lord,*' he began, adding flourishes, titles, and appropriate salutations in thick, uneven letters, '*it grieves me to hear of such dire news as the grave illness of your gracious brother, our lord king. May God grant he recovers. But if you will in turn be so gracious as to pardon the need for plain speech in this unhappy time, permit me to remind you of the thoughts and hopes we have shared in the past.*'

He paused, considering phrasing again. Then dipped the quill in the inkpot and continued.

'*It is naturally my concern, as a loyal officer of the Crown, that you be adequately served by men you may trust. Be assured of my constancy, good my lord, in believing you an able and honest servant of God, of England, and England's people.*'

Enough, deLacey reflected. John was no fool, nor politically naive. He would know the sheriff worked to save his office, to align himself now with the man he judged most likely to hold England. But he would also know the sheriff recalled those former discussions in infinite—and potentially dangerous—detail, and a shared passion for opportunity best able to serve personal interests.

John would need powerful allies in England. He had years before angered many wealthy barons who, at one time, conspired to keep him from claiming England for his own while the Lionheart dwelled in his German prison. The man called *Softsword* and *Lackland* needed certainties and assurances that other men supported him, now that the throne could come to be contested. Sheriffs were not earls and dukes and counts, but they were nonetheless the abiding power within the individual shires.

"Money," deLacey murmured. "It comes to coin. Taxes collected, taxes delivered. A realm is governed by the coin that is spent, not merely a king's whim and wishes."

Such taxes as those due for accounting at the preliminary session and to be followed by another at Michaelmas, sitting below in his dungeon.

Smiling grimly, deLacey signed his name. Then dropped the quill and rose from his chair to pace the chamber, considering again potential repercussions of the course he had set.

"Time," he muttered. "John is in Brittany, with Arthur . . . will he yet be there to receive my message? Or will he depart for France? For England."

Abruptly he sat down again and drew up fresh parchment, sharpening, then reinking the quill. Twice he copied over his initial letter, changing nothing, then sanded, folded, and sealed all three sheets as individual letters.

Best to send word to multiple places in hopes of reaching Prince John sooner rather than later.

They had left behind Huntington Castle and were nearly to the Nottingham road when Marian reined in sharply. Joan, less handy with a horse, rode a little beyond, then laboriously turned her mount back. "Lady Marian? Lady?"

Marian sat slack in the saddle, reins gripped in gloved, numb hands. "What have I done?"

"Lady?"

She pressed reins and hands hard against her face, speaking into leather-clad palms. "What have I *done?*"

"Lady—" Joan wrestled with the horse, who wanted to be heading home again. "What *have* you done, then?"

Marian's horse, undirected, wandered to the edge of the track and began idly to graze.

Oh, God. Oh, God. She shut her eyes tightly. "Oh, God."

Joan was now clearly alarmed. "Lady Marian!"

She had thought it through. Worked it through. Knew the course, had selected the course, was certain of her choice. But now, in the light of day, with all the words said to the earl, she knew also the edges of panic crowding into her mind.

"No," she said, catching her breath. "His decision. *His* decision. Not mine. Not mine." She released a gust of breath. "Not mine."

"Lady."

"I merely give him the chance, the choice." She nodded. "Yes. It must be so. Let it be *his* choice. He will make it. One way or another." She looked at Joan. "I have given him the freedom to make that choice, with no obligation attached."

Joan was mystified, but she held her tongue.

"It must be so," Marian repeated. "He will stay, or he will go. But the choice will be his, without obstruction or distraction."

"Lady Marian," Joan ventured. "Whose choice about what?"

"Staying," she said. "Or going. As it should be. It isn't mine to make. He should have opportunity to reconsider that he will be an earl, with attendant power and great holdings, responsibilities. Obligations to the name."

Realization dawned in Joan's broad face. "Lady," she said, "Oh, Lady Marian—he does love you!"

Marian laughed breathlessly. "I know it, Joan. I do know it. But he must have a *choice*, do you see? He must have the choice presented to him again." She gathered up slack reins, took control of the horse, who sullenly gave up ripping chunks of mud-rooted grass from the ground to be turned back onto the road. Marian punctured the air with a forefinger. "He has not thought *truly* about what will happen when his father dies. He does not know, has no conception. He has never lost a father, to know how it feels." She prodded her horse into motion with determined heels. "I do know, Joan. And I have made the proper choice."

Joan let her stolid horse fall in beside Marian's better mount. "Are you certain, lady?"

"Oh, yes." The moments of panic had passed. Her course was clear again, and her doubts disciplined. She took a deep breath, held it, then released it on a gust of relief. "Yes."

Robin's horse was fresh. The messenger's mount was nearly blown, would require rest soon, and water, before Gerard was on his way again as swiftly as before. Therefore Robin did not doubt he could reach his destination first.

But not Nottingham. Not Huntington.

Ravenskeep. To warn the others. Then it would not matter whom the messenger told, or in what order.

Mentally, Robin revisited his companions, contemplating transgressions that would merit punishment. Alan of the Dales would hang for tupping the sheriff's daughter. Robin knew Eleanor had been the instigator, but perception was all. Alan had been accused, arrested, and thrown into Huntington Castle's dungeon, intended to stand trial for forcing deLacey's daughter; upon which verdict, no doubt, he would have been hanged with all expediency. The minstrel escaped that fate only because Sir Robert of Locksley, of his own volition and for his own reasons, bribed the dungeon guards to release him.

Will Scarlet, once called Scathlocke, had murdered several Normans. It mattered little to such men as the sheriff, or Prince John—whose men they had been—that the Normans had raped and killed Scarlet's wife. Will and his wife were Saxons, poor and powerless peasants. Scathlocke/ Scarlet would hang as much for that as for abducting Marian from the Nottingham Fair. And Little John, by wholly unfortunate circumstance, had been implicated in the abduction. He, too, would hang.

Much would not. Much had killed no one, abducted no one, raped no one. But he *had* picked the sheriff's pocket and would, according to law, forfeit a hand.

Tuck was undoubtedly safe from hanging, or from having a hand chopped off, but his vocation was now tainted. He would never see the priesthood, would never serve God in any capacity beyond his limited purview, set forever apart from cathedral or abbey, apart from his order. Additionally, William deLacey would undoubtedly invent a fitting punishment for a man who thwarted the sheriff's plan to marry Marian.

And if such transgressions were not enough, all of them, at Robin's devising and behest, had stolen money from the Lord High Sheriff, bidden by Prince John to redirect the tax shipment intended to help pay King Richard's ransom to John himself, in Lincoln. The party of soldiers guarding the shipment had been foully murdered. But the sons and heirs of powerful earls, the beautiful heiress-daughters of honorable knights killed on Holy Crusade, would have transgressions overlooked.

Such men as peasants and outcast monks, charming minstrels and simpleton pickpockets would not enjoy the same privilege.

Robin, who had ordered no one killed and had been present during the robbery, knew William deLacey himself had murdered his own guard. But there was no proof. Even his word as the son of the Earl of Huntington was suspect: he had distanced himself from his noble father to reside with an unwed woman and a pack of pardoned outlaws. Perception, again, was all.

The wind of his passage whipped Robin's cloak over his back, tugging at the heavy silver brooch pinning his right shoulder. His clothing was liberally daubed with mud. Already one eye had suffered its share of clogging insult; he scrubbed an arm across the side of his face to rid himself of the worst of the mud. He tasted it now, gritting in his teeth. Eyes watering, he leaned to spit—and saw the trunk of a tree fallen across the track.

"Ya Allah—" The horse gathered himself powerfully, leaped the trunk and the shattered spears of broken limbs. Robin, half blinded but well versed in horsemanship since childhood, rode the effort well enough for a man taken unawares. It was only as the rope came singing up from the ground into thrumming tautness that he recognized the trap. Retreating from Arabic into stolid Anglo-Saxon English, he cursed the men who had set it.

He was taller than they had planned for. The rope, instead of cutting into his throat, caught him across chest and shoulders. It canted him awkwardly and abruptly backward in the saddle, tangling cloak and hair.

Stripped instantly from the saddle as if he weighed no more than a dandelion stalk, Robin was unhappily aware of air, of the horse running out from under him; that the cloak now blinded him utterly—and that his landing was going to hurt.

He came down flat and hard onto muddy track and tree. A limb dug hungrily into his back, another jabbed into one shoulder. Then his skull and tree trunk collided with an audible thud.

Stunned and completely bereft of breath, he lay sprawled slackly, seeing darkness and sparks of light. His lungs labored but offered no air. He was aware of vagueness, of senselessness teasing at the edges of consciousness, and panic. He could not *breathe*—

—and then he felt hands upon him, cruel and ruthless hands, and knew he could do nothing to prevent them from commiting whatever indignity they wished to commit.

In this case, the hands worked swiftly and neatly. His purse was cut away, the brooch jerked from his cloak, his sword and knife appropriated. The hands had no care for him beyond what he offered; the tugging at his hips when they pulled the sword from its sheath was not gentle. By the time he had air in his lungs again, by the time he could do more than lie sprawled helplessly and inelegantly across the ground with his head against the tree, gulping wool-barriered air through the cloak wound around his head, the hands were gone.

He heard shouting: something about his horse. *Charlemagne*—? Robin assayed sight again, and freedom, by dragging the enfolding cloak away from his face and shoulders, and discovered as he levered himself hastily up on one elbow that the thieves had not departed. He froze, tantalized by the view of the tip of his own sword drifting perilously near his throat.

He wheezed then as lungs spasmed at last into normal activity. He felt the prick of blade, the cut, the trickle of blood. He raised one hand a matter of inches, wanting to block the blade, but realized the folly in that instantly as a second prick of honed steel drew additional blood.

Men surrounded him. All carried longbows, though the foremost among them gripped Robin's sword. Two of them spilled out the contents of his purse into ready hands, anticipating coin; a third tossed the heavy silver brooch into the air repeatedly as if estimating its weight and worth.

He *knew* these men.

And now that he was unwrapped from the cloak, they knew him.

Adam Bell smiled broadly. "Locksley," he said in surprise, then broke into laughter. "Well met!"

The others came closer. William of Cloudisley, with his mane of brown hair; Clym of the Clough, sandy-haired, a squint in one blue eye; even Wat One-Hand, who had, from muttered complaints of recalcitrant horses, lost the gray entirely.

Robin stared up at Adam Bell. Now that he could breathe again, he could also speak. But he would offer them nothing of fear, of hesitance. Only casual courage; it would do more to annoy them. "The sword, if you please?"

"Ah. Forgive me." Bell, slight and dark as a Welshman, though his eyes were pale brown, moved the tip aside and grounded the blade next to his own booted foot even as his mouth twitched. "Come and have a cup of ale with us."

Robin sat up, frowning ferociously as he picked dollops of mud out of the vicinity of his right eye. "No time," he said, wincing as muscles protested the importunance of tree limbs; he would be badly bruised before morning. "I must go on to Ravenskeep." He gazed balefully at Wat One-Hand, summoning the tones of his noble father. "You have lost me my horse when I have the most need of him."

Clym of the Clough, never friendly and frequently openly hostile, was predictably outraged. "And d'ye think we'll let you leave us so soon?"

"Why not?" Robin countered. "You have my purse, my brooch, and my weapons. Have I not paid my toll?"

"I think *not*," Clym retorted, in heavy good humor since he had the upper hand. "You've a father who's an earl, d'ye not? You may not be worth the ransom paid for King Richard, but you'll bring us a silver mark or twenty."

Robin, affronted, looked at Adam Bell. "You would not."

The outlaw shrugged.

Robin surged to his feet, then stilled abruptly as longbow strings were swiftly drawn. "In God's name, we broke bread together at my hall! We robbed three lords together!" Three lords who were, in fact, his father's friends, and men he knew well. "We were brothers in arms!"

"*And* you robbed the sheriff of the tax shipment." Adam Bell nodded; Sir Robert of Locksley, knighted by the king, had become Robin Hood, outlaw, in the name of that king. "But you were pardoned, aye? We were not."

"You're not one of us," Clym declared. "Never were."

Handsome Cloudisley smiled winningly. "The earl will pay a considerable amount for his only son."

"There is no time," Robin said sharply, dismissing elaborate dances. "I must get to Ravenskeep and warn the others."

"Warn the others?" Wat echoed, baffled.

"What others?" Clym growled.

Alarmed, Cloudisley demanded, "Warn them about what?"

Adam Bell, who gazed steadily at Robin for a long moment, without further comment returned his sword and knife.

The others were plainly shocked. And, as plainly, disagreed with Bell's decision, making loud complaint.

Robin sheathed the weapons at once, safing the sword and settling the belt so the weight hung properly. "There is a messenger coming," he said crisply. "A king's courier. Let him pass unmolested."

That earned him additional enmity from Clym. "Why should we do any such thing? Because *you* say so?" He spat into leaves. "You're naught to us, Locksley."

"Because the word he carries will alter the realm," Robin answered plainly, slipping again into the tone of command. "The king is dead in France. We will have a new king—once they sort out who it is to be." He knew better than to ask for purse or brooch back; they would be kept as toll. "My task now is to reach Marian and the others to warn them, to give them time before the sheriff is told."

Bell's eyes were knowing. "The pardon."

"King Richard's," Robin said only; nothing more was required.

Adam Bell nodded thoughtfully. Clym of the Clough, eventually comprehending the implications, began to laugh, displaying poor teeth.

Cloudisley's arched brows rose high onto his forehead. "He'll have you yet, will he, our lord high sheriff?"

"Not *him*," Clym declared, laughter spent. "He's a father, hasn't he, who'll pay for another pardon."

One-handed Wat watched Robin speculatively. "Why should it matter to you what becomes of the others?"

Bell wanted other information. "How did the king come to die?"

Robin opened his mouth to answer, then could not prevent the brief gust of air that escaped in wry acknowledgment of irony. "During a siege," he said to the four outlaws, "to capture treasure from a French castle."

It struck all of them dumb, that the King of England might be killed even as they might be killed, laying claim to wealth belonging to another man. Robin saw startled looks exchanged, flickers of disbelief, and then the slow shaking of heads. Adam Bell, once a respectable yeoman, jerked his mouth sideways. "He'd have done better to die in battle against the Saracen."

"Or in England," Clym muttered.

"Who's to be king?" Cloudisley asked.

Bell said, frowning, "Likely John, aye?"

"Or Arthur," Robin answered. "Whichever of them can claim and hold England against the other, accepted and acknowledged by the barons, anointed in London." He looked at Adam Bell. "Do you see now why I cannot waste more time?"

Bell did. "Go," he said, gesturing for the others to let him pass.

Robin took two long steps upon the track, then, struck by inspiration, paused and turned back. "The courier carries news of the king's death and should not be molested," he said casually. "But now that I am afoot, I should not be averse if he were *delayed* somewhat."

Adam Bell grinned and bowed with a flourish. "You may depend upon it, my lord."

That much time bought, Robin set out at a steady, swift pace.

Seven

Marian adored Ravenskeep. It was not a castle such as the Earl of Huntington had caused to be built, nor a lavish manor such as those owned by the titled and truly wealthy, but it was a comfortable and familiar home. The lands were lush and green, the livestock well tended, the two-story, half-timbered house kept as snug as possible against the cold and damp, and its larders well provisioned. It was not a vast holding, but enough to comfortably support a few tenants and servants, a man, his wife, a son and a daughter, and to pay tribute to the Crown in the form of one knight, a horse, and appropriate equipage. The knight, his wife, and his son were now dead, leaving only the daughter, but she was determined to see that Ravenskeep remained what it had been in her father's day.

As Marian rode up the muddy lane toward the walled courtyard and manor house, she grimly recalled the sheriff's words: *'Unmarried daughters of dead knights may have their lands—and their hands—claimed by the Crown.'*

It was said as coy observation, but also implication and as much for threat. She knew better, now, than to trust deLacey, no matter what the issue. He was liar, manipulator, ruthless opportunist.

Marian laughed briefly, curtly, aware of the startled glance Joan cast her. No. It wasn't true she could never trust deLacey. There was indeed one thing about him into which she could place complete and unwavering trust: that he would always serve himself.

And so I am become what I dislike in him: a manipulator. For she would use William deLacey as and how she must—just as she now used the Earl of Huntington—to keep Robin safe, her lands, and even the others who would likely never thank her, for they would as likely never realize the nature of their danger.

Alan, she thought. Alan would. A man such as he, a minstrel wholly dependent on the tastes and tantrums of others, who knew how to charm and seduce women—and who had himself been used by Eleanor deLacey to his detriment—would fully understand the seriousness of their circumstances.

The sheriff had also said, *'Pardons may be revoked.'*

It was time, Marian feared as she approached the thick-planked gate, that she sent away from Ravenskeep the very people she most wished to remain.

He was not, Robin discovered to his annoyance and chagrin, currently disposed physically or temperamentally to walk the remaining miles to Ravenskeep. The abrupt and forced departure from his saddle and the resultant collision with the tree and its pernicious limbs had accounted for any number of offenses to flesh, muscle, and bone. His skull throbbed, the backs of his ribs and thighs were bruised and abraded, and his spine appeared to have been twisted in some way either in midair or upon landing, because he believed he might do better without one altogether than with the spine he currently had.

It would have been worse, he knew, had the ground been packed hard, but while the mud had somewhat softened his landing and prevented him from shattering into bits, it had not precluded him from bringing with him a share of its presence. Mud clung liberally to cloak and clothing; what did not coat his clothing adhered stickily to boots, accumulating additional clumps and layers until he could not feel his footing.

Robin slipped, slid, cursed, stopped to kick off clumps, cursed some more, then squished his way off the track to seek a deadfall limb that would serve to break the suction and free his boots of weight. He tried skirting the track along the narrow verge between vegetation and roadway, but the grass was too thin to provide purchase and the growth too thick to permit passage.

When, after several more steps, using a stick did not prove sufficiently effective—the heavy mud sheathing merely renewed itself—he attempted to scrape off the coating against a deadfall tree. And while the efforts allowed him the opportunity to walk unimpeded for perhaps six steps, the pauses to rid himself of mud took more time than actually walking in it.

Sourly, Robin reflected he might do better to depart the road and retreat into Sherwood to try the deer trails used by outlaws, but he had not himself been an outlaw in Sherwood long enough to learn them. And having already made the acquaintanceship of such ruthless folk once this day, Robin did not relish the risk of repeating it.

He stopped again, scowling back along the track the way he had come. Mercardier was gone, bound for France and his dead king. Short of Adam Bell holding the king's messenger overnight, which was unlikely, Robin thought it probable no enforced delay would keep Gerard and his news from reaching the earl and sheriff first. Which left him with but one solution. And that solution presented itself in the guise of a man on horseback.

Robin, standing along the verge as the man—likely bound from Nottingham and for Lincoln—approached, considered his predicament and the possibilities.

He had no coin with which to buy the horse, even if the man were willing to sell it; which was, Robin felt, a supremely unlikely event in view of the condition of the road, quite apart from the business that put the man *on* the road. Additionally, he no longer claimed a cloak brooch that might be presented in lieu of or as promise of payment, and wore no rings. His sword and knife were quite plain; but he could never surrender the weapons the king himself had presented upon Robin's release from the Saracens. Lastly, his word as the son of an earl, which he did not wish to offer, would be doubted even if he did so; sons of earls did not generally walk on muddy roads. Heirs of Huntington most assuredly did not. And nothing about him suggested he might be believed if he *did* claim to be an earl's son and heir, even Huntington's: he was filthy, bruised, and—he felt gingerly at his throat where his swordtip had cut— probably smeared with dried blood.

Of course, he could tell the truth. *I was accosted by outlaws and robbed* . . . whereupon the man might briefly commiserate but would no doubt be on his way hastily in hopes of escaping the same fate, thus leaving

Robin still horseless and still afoot and the royal messenger still bound for individuals Robin did not wish him to reach.

I was accosted by outlaws and robbed—and now I must reach men who were once declared outlaws themselves so that I may keep them from being declared so again.

Sighing, Robin allowed the rider to pass with only brief nods exchanged—a merchant, he thought, not a fighting man—and then he picked up from the side of the road the fist-size stone he had already marked in his mind as best.

Thinking regretfully of such historic paragons as Alexander, Roland, and Charlemagne, whom he had idolized in childhood, he squinted at the stone. "This is not particularly heroic—" He aimed for the meat of the man's back so as not to crack open his skull, and let fly. "Or knightly," he added, wincing sympathetically as the stone found its target. "But it ought nonetheless to be effective . . ."

The man, upon being thunked in the back by a hurled stone, cried out in shock and outrage and immediately wheeled his horse around. Robin had already discounted a sword: the merchant had none. But he did have the horse. Howling his fury, the aggrieved victim set heels to his mount and rode Robin down.

At the last moment Robin leaped aside—but only after he caught the reins and yanked the horse offstride. The horse, vigorously protesting such rude handling, jerked his head aside.

Robin, slipping and sliding and cursing again, withstood the tension in his overstretched arm, set his weight, and jerked back. Whereupon the horse, as insulted now as its rider, embarked on a vigorous tug-of-war in the middle of the muck-laden road.

The horse would win, of course; short of using a sword or ax to hack the animal's legs to bits, no man could win such a lopsided confrontation, especially in such poor footing. But in the meantime the merchant was utterly nonplussed by the turnabout of affairs—he had clearly expected to knock his attacker down, not place control of his mount into the attacker's hands. He leaned haphazardly forward in an attempt to yank the reins out of Robin's hands, and thereby conveniently changed the distribution of weight in the saddle and altered his center of balance.

Robin, winding rein around one wrist and praying the horse would not bolt, caught hold of the merchant's nearest ankle and thrust the leg upward. Hard.

The rider, much as Robin had himself not so long before, came off in a tangle of cloak and flailing limbs. By the time he unwrapped and levered himself up on one elbow to sputter his outrage, Robin was treating the stranger to a view of the tip of his sword.

His mouth twitched; had *he* appeared so undignified and indignant when Adam Bell greeted him the same way? "The balance of your day may now be somewhat rearranged—I would suggest a bath and clean clothes—but you are alive and whole. Be thankful for the small blessings of life—"

"Blessings! " the man erupted. *"Blessings?"*

Robin continued despite the interruption. "And be grateful also I haven't the time to make you feel more indisposed and uncomfortable— and possibly more humiliated"—he arched an ironic eyebrow—"than you presently are." Whereupon Robin saluted the red-faced man with the sword, stepped back, sheathed it deftly, then turned and, suppressing an indecorous wince of pain, swung up onto the snorting horse.

"Outlaw!" the merchant howled, scrambling up awkwardly from the oozing track. "You're a bloody outlaw—"

"Muddy," Robin corrected with precise enunciation, gathering reins as he anticipated his own bath and clean clothes.

"—and I'll have the sheriff on you!"

Robin ignored the threat. "There will be a man along behind me," he said helpfully, "likely within the hour, or perhaps two. You might relieve him of *his* horse, should you find the wherewithal—" Somehow he did not believe the merchant's aim and execution would be as effective as his. "And then nothing much be lost except the shine on your boots." He smiled: and thus even more time would be put between Gerard's arrival at Nottingham and Huntington, and Robin's at Ravenskeep.

Giving the muddy, angry man a helpless shrug, Robin set heels to his stolen mount and set off yet again for Ravenskeep. He had no doubt that by the time his victim was found, was admitted, and complained to the sheriff, the number of thieves who had set upon a poor, helpless merchant would have increased from one to twenty.

Marian had just stepped down from the saddle when Hal, near the gate, hallooed that another horse was coming in. She thought nothing of it—people arrived when and as they would—until Hal added that the horse was lacking a rider.

On the ground now, handing the reins to Sim, Marian turned sharply. Joan's horse was in the way; impatient, Marian slapped the firm rump to shift the horse, then squeezed by. And stopped short, stricken, as she saw the muddy-legged, lathered, froth-spumed horse Robin had departed on the night before.

"Catch him!" she cried, even as Hal stepped out and did so. She left her own mount in Sim's competent charge and went at once to the big gray Hal was examining. She caught a stirrup and looked at the saddle, searching for blood. She ignored the horse as he turned his head and attempted to rub hard against her. Hal murmured an apology and took a tighter grip on the bridle. "No blood—" Marian said tautly.

"Nor injury," Hal confirmed. "To the horse," he added quickly, belatedly recalling her concern lay elsewhere. "This big boy could have had him off, Lady Marian."

"Robin doesn't *come* off that easily."

"Any man may," he reminded her.

It was true. It was also true men came off because other men assured it. "I'm going back out," she said abruptly. "Take Joan's horse, and bring this one. If Robin is afoot, he'll want Charlemagne. If he's hurt—" She looked at the man. "If he is hurt, I'll send you back for aid and stay with him myself."

Hal's voice was diffident. "You'll be wanting more than me if he's—"

Marian cut him off curtly. "I have no *time* for more than you."

"And what about us?" demanded another voice: Little John's deep bass.

Marian looked over her shoulder. Hal's shout and her own raised voice had brought the others out from the hall into the courtyard. She saw their curious expressions change to sharp concern as they marked the riderless horse. Tuck crossed himself, murmuring a prayer. Everyone in Nottingham knew Charlemagne belonged to Huntington's son.

"No time," she repeated. But mostly because none of them, save Alan and nimble Much, rode better than poorly. Then, as she saw the expressions of stunned disbelief, she flapped a hand. "Come after, then," she relented, if impatiently. "Sim—"

Sim was there with her horse, aiding her to mount. Joan was saying something, remonstrating that a lady should not go unaccompanied into possible danger, but Marian had less time for that than she did for poor riders. With a glance for Hal, who was mounting Joan's horse even as he pulled Robin's gray close enough for leading, Marian gathered reins and turned her mount sharply. It was entirely possible she would find him walking, bereft of horse but safe, yet she knew there was an equal chance Robin was injured. The sheriff and his soldiers had not yet tamed Sherwood's outlaws.

But Much was faster. Even on foot, Much was faster. He darted past her, past the horses, and was through the gate. Marian, understanding the boy's fear, followed at a hard long-trot preparatory to a gallop, mind fixed wholly upon hasty departure and hastier discovery of what had become of Robin—but as she rounded the open gate, she very nearly collided with Much, who had inexplicably stopped short, and another horse.

Her mind registered that she did not know the horse, even as it registered she *did* know the rider. But only after she eventually recognized him beneath the mud and grime. "Robin?"

He was as startled to find her piling out of the courtyard and nearly into his horse, with Hal riding Joan's behind her leading a riderless gray. She wanted to question his disheveled appearance and the circumstances; clearly, he wanted to question her haste. But both of them instead were somewhat occupied with sorting out various equally startled horses, who snorted and sashayed and cast white-rimmed, wary eyes upon one another as they bared large teeth in potent promise. Charlemagne, completely out of temper, kicked at Marian's horse, which promptly protested with a ringing squeal and high-flung head, and Hal's horse, borrowed from Joan, took an instant dislike to the one Robin rode. It was only after they had all spent long minutes wrestling with discommoded horses, averting an equine war by the narrowest of margins, that anyone was able to complete a civil sentence.

"You're all over mud," Marian managed at last.

Robin, scowling, leaned forward to smack the flat of an admonishing palm down across his borrowed mount's head. "Where are you going in such haste?"

"Stop it!" Marian muttered to her own fractious mount, before the gelding might begin hostilities anew. "Looking for you," she answered when she could. "Charlemagne came in—"

"Thank God!" Robin said fervently, looking the big gray over with avid eyes. "I feared he might be taken by someone else."

"—and I was worried," she finished dryly. Then, with a bland expression, thinking of Hal's observation, she inquired: "Did he throw you?"

It provoked, as she meant it to. "He did not throw me, nor did I fall," Robin explained with precision. "It was a trap."

"*What* trap?"

"Adam Bell," he answered. "And the others."

"Adam?" She was startled. Robin and Bell had parted in amity years before. "Why would they set a trap for you?"

"Not for me specifically. For anyone. It happened to be me." Robin peeled away a smear of mud on his chin, still studying the mud-splattered gray Hal ponied. "I suspect they would have stolen him, had he not taken himself away."

Marian had no time for the horse Robin so valued. Her concern was for his rider. "Did they hurt you?"

Robin shrugged out of the loose, unpinned cloak, hoisted a leg across the saddle, and jumped down. "They *robbed* me," he elucidated, pulling the mud-weighted cloak from the saddle. "Of my pride, if nothing else. Much—" He turned to the young man, handing him the reins of the borrowed horse. In that moment he had no attention for anyone else, speaking clearly and with a glint in hazel eyes. "Take him into Nottingham. To the castle; you can get in safely?" Much nodded, eyes alight, and Robin smiled broadly. "Make your way to the stables and put him with the sheriff's personal mounts."

Marian was astonished. "Is that *deLacey's* horse?"

"No. He belongs to the poor fool I stole him from." Robin slapped the horse on the rump as Much set out for the Nottingham road, smiling. Marian knew that look; he plotted something. Something to do with the borrowed horse, that would plague deLacey.

She refused to be put off from her line of inquiry. "You stole the horse? I thought you said Charlemagne was stolen."

"Charlemagne broke loose, or he *would* have been stolen—although perhaps they would have given him back in light of the news." Robin shrugged. "Once Adam and the others let me go—"

"*After* they robbed you."

He nodded, flinging the cloak across one shoulder. "I was on foot, and needed a horse badly, so . . ." He shrugged, much as a little boy who is helpless to justify proscribed actions.

"Robin." Marian, sighing inwardly, climbed down out of her own saddle and turned to fall in beside him, even as Hal, leading Charlemagne, brought up the rear with a bemused expression on his face. She thought of Huntington then, thought of telling Robin his father was ill, but something within her shied away from it. Not yet. Later. Let him be put at ease first, let him bathe, eat, sleep; she could tell from the way he moved he was in some pain. For now she would speak of other things. "I understand not *wishing* to walk a muddy track, but why did you need a horse so badly you saw fit to steal one?"

"Because of you," Robin said.

"Me!"

And he added, as the others joined them, "Because of them."

"Why us?" Will Scarlet demanded. "What's you stealing a horse got to do with any of us?"

Robin's expression, as he slid an arm around Marian's waist, was bleak. "The king is dead," he said, "and even now a messenger is on his way to carry word of it to the Sheriff of Nottingham." He looked at each of them. "None of you is safe."

With Marian's help, Robin stripped slowly out of mud-caked clothing in the tiny chamber serving as a bathhouse. As his battered back came into view, she drew in an audible breath of empathy, which he appreciated— *everything* hurt!—then spoiled it by murmuring of carelessness, stupidity, and a man's stubborn pride.

Somewhat aggrievedly, he asked, "Why are you blaming me? I didn't do this to myself!"

One well-placed palm pushed him toward the oak half-cask Joan and others had laboriously filled with steaming water. "You were far more concerned with the welfare of your horse and how Much should leave a *stolen* horse in the sheriff's own stables." Marian poked his spine as he dawdled, and he winced. "You left with Mercardier, bound for France—get in, Robin—but your horse, apparently disinclined to go, came back without you. Do you have any idea what thoughts went through my mind . . . and will you please get in *before* the water turns cold?"

"I never have any idea what thoughts go through your mind." He climbed into the cask gingerly, hissing as bruised flesh recoiled from heated water.

"I was concerned."

Robin gripped the cask rim. "So was I."

Her tone was somewhat testy. "What had *you* to worry about?"

"My reception . . ." He twitched as cool fingers investigated a particularly sore abrasion. "Here," he finished. "Marian—"

"Sit," she commanded. "Mother of God, Robin, what did this to you?"

"A tree."

"A *tree?*"

"It is somewhat chastening," he confessed, sinking down onto the bathing stool, "for a king's knight to be defeated by vegetation." And then he went very still, recalling that the king who had knighted him was no longer alive.

After a moment Marian bent and encircled his neck from behind with both slim arms. Her chin rested gently atop his mud-weighted hair. "I am so sorry."

He closed his eyes. The arms around his neck were comforting, familiar, beloved. Strands of her hair stuck to his damp skin. He smelled her welcome scent, felt her breath in his own hair.

"I know you loved him," she said quietly. "All England loved him. But England has loved kings before, and shall again."

"Perhaps not the next one," he said grimly, thinking of what he had said to the others in the hall, how he had explained that new kings were not always committed to supporting what dead kings commanded. Thinking, too, of Much's abruptly bloodless features, of Scarlet's crude curses, Little John's furrowed brow, Tuck's distraught silence—and Alan's ironic smirk—he said, "They will do better at Locksley."

Marian unwound her arms, taking up the ladle so she might pour water over his sore shoulders. "If they will go," she agreed.

"They must. You know the sheriff will come here."

She did know, and said as much as she emptied the ladle.

He shivered beneath the water. "Can you do without them?"

"I did without them before they came." She took up a ball of soap and gently began to lather his shoulders. "And did without you, as well."

He smiled, recognizing the banter that masked her worry. "Marian—"

"Later," she said. "Close your eyes, forget everything but that the warmth of the water can soak the ache from your bones, and let me tend you."

He had dreamed of this as he stole the horse from the merchant. He had recalled this as he shared a campsite with Mercardier. He thanked God for this as he closed his eyes, forgot everything but that she was with him, and let her tend him.

Alan found Marian in the kitchen the next morning. He had for once left his lute elsewhere and was unencumbered save for the mane of golden curls tumbling across doublet-clad shoulders. Surprised by his appearance, she left off directing Cook in the preparation of Robin's favorite breakfast, which she wanted him to eat before she sent him to his father. Unexpectedly, Alan did not tease, nor seek to charm out of habit as he leaned against the wall in casual negligence, arms crossed. But she sensed a subtle tension in him.

"What is it?" she asked.

" 'Tis no hardship for me," he told her matter-of-factly. "I am a minstrel—my life is upon the road, and music buys me a meal most nights and a roof over my head. I can move on from here today, if necessary, and may well do it."

Marian frowned in perplexion.

Alan shrugged. "But the others are not so fortunate."

She studied his face, trying to read it. She could not; Alan had learned years before how to present a bland mask to the world. Testing his intent, she said, "He has offered all of you shelter at Locksley."

"For which Tuck is grateful—he is a generous, trusting soul and would do well anywhere—but what of the others?"

"What *of* them?" Marian was exasperated; she could not divine his point. "They have been offered a home, Robin's home, as I offered all of you mine five years ago."

His expression was serious, the bright blue eyes quiet but oddly anticipatory. "The sheriff is no fool. If they are not here, he will go there."

"What would you have us do?" she asked. "All of you are family now. Should we put you out and lock our doors behind you because England has a new king? Because the sheriff will use it as an excuse?"

"He will."

"I know it," Marian said. "As you do; you know best of all what is in William deLacey's mind."

Alan's expressive mouth twitched wryly. "Because I was in more than his daughter's mind?"

"What would you have us do?" she repeated, ignoring the crudity; Alan of the Dales enjoyed provoking shock. "Send you to London? To France?" She shook her head. "With King Richard dead, there is no Crusade, and thus no room for you all to become anonymous soldiers in a large army, or minstrels, or friars, lost among your brethren." Marian spread her hands. "What else may we do save what we have done?"

"Send us," Alan said, "into outlawry."

She was stunned.

"Much is a thief," the minstrel declared plainly. "He has remained so despite his place here with you, cutting the occasional purse in Nottingham, no matter how often you told him it was wrong." Marian's face grew warm; she knew it for the truth. "He is a simpleton," Alan continued, "doing what he knows best. Sending him to Locksley village will not alter his habits."

"Why are you telling me this?" she asked, giving up; perhaps annoyance might win a direct answer. "Is it merely to put me out of sorts, or is there a purpose in it?"

Alan's gaze was level. "Five years ago it was a simple thing to offer all of us shelter. We were pardoned, and none of us—save for Much, who doesn't understand—of a mind to be outlaws beyond what we became so briefly in the name of King Richard's ransom. But now . . ." The minstrel shook his head, stirring hair against shoulders. "We will be *un*pardoned, exactly as you fear, and sheltering men who would be hanged, maimed, or imprisoned is not the same."

Marian understood at last what Alan was doing: providing opportunity, a chance for disengagement, because of them all, only she and Robin *had* opportunity. "No," she said simply. "We will not turn our backs."

A flicker in his eyes acknowledged she had found him out. "He is an earl's son. And you a knight's daughter."

"An earl's son who has, as you yourself just admitted, stolen from the king, and who has repudiated his father." Inwardly she winced; that repudiation might well soon be altered. "As for me, I may not have stolen the money, but there are other reasons for the sheriff to treat me unkindly. Turning our backs on those we consider family would gain us nothing."

Alan's brilliant smile was abrupt as he adorned himself once again with the persona of charm and insouciance. "Ah, well, it shall make a lovely ballad . . . how a Crusader knight and his lady fair gave succor to lowly outlaws."

Marian sighed. "The world is not a song, Alan."

"The world *is*," he rebutted. "And 'tis my task to find the words and music for it."

"Alan." She stopped him as he reached the door, touching his arm briefly. "Alan, there are things such as beliefs, convictions—and people—worth the risk."

His infectious grin was wide and warm. "And ballads," he said, too brightly, "well worth the making and singing despite royal resprisal."

There was—nothingness. No thought, no feeling, no impetus to react. Merely nothingness, as if the words had no bearing on his life. And yet Robin knew they should. Knew once perhaps they had, and might yet again. Someday.

But for now: nothing. And no appetite as he sat at table, attempting to eat what she had presented him.

Marian sat on the other side of the table. "I am sorry."

She had said that several times during the past three days. Sorry the king was dying. Sorry for his worry. Sorry the king was dead, and for his grief. Sorry now that his father was ill.

But am I? he wondered.

"I've ordered a horse for you." Marian's brief smile was slight. "Charlemagne, unless you believe him too taxed by his adventures of yesterday."

"No," he murmured, and wondered if he referred to his horse's condition or denied his father's illness.

"Perhaps I should have told you yesterday, when you first came home. But you were so muddy and tired, and when I saw the bruises . . ." She let the implication stand proxy for the words.

For five years his life had been what he had made it since breaking with the earl. Peace such as he had never anticipated, living at Ravenskeep with frequent trips to Locksley to oversee his holdings. A quiet life livened only by such things as a fox amidst the henhouse, a wolf stalking the lambs, the festivals of spring and Nottingham's fairs, occasional intercourse with taverns, though never with tavern bawds. After the perils and brutalities of the Crusade, after cruel captivity, after seeing his king won free from his own kind of captivity in a foreign king's court, Robin had welcomed the quietude others might name tedium.

Now Richard was dead, John would likely be king, the sheriff would come hunting outlaws—and his father was ill.

"One moment," he said.

"One moment?" she echoed.

"One moment, and the world is never the same." He stood up then over the remains of his breakfast, pushing the bench away from the heavy trestle table set in the center of the modest hall. She rose as well, rounding the table to set his tunic aright. "If for nothing else, I should see if Gerard has arrived at last."

It baffled her. "Gerard?"

"Tell the others," he said, fixed on the task. "Tell them to go now. I will ride straight to Huntington by the Nottingham road—it is faster, and I may be able to delay the sheriff should he have heard the news and set out—but the others had best take themselves into Sherwood at once, then make their way to Locksley." His tone and manner were briskly casual, yet clearly in command; his mind worked swiftly, envisioning potential problems and creating resolutions. "By now such things as pardons may bear no weight until a new king is named, and he will hardly concern himself immediately with what Nottingham's sheriff does."

She understood him then. He saw the shift of color in her face from milk-and-roses to corpse-candle white, the puckering of her brow; felt the tension in her hands as they rested on his chest.

"I trust you," he said. "And so do they."

Marian nodded mutely. Robin kissed her, and left her.

The earl felt he should be angry. Possibly even outraged. The woman dared to meddle in his life, dared to suggest an agreement made between them, as if she were an equal; dared to promise it was solely within her purview to deliver the son to his father, or to lure him away forever from title, heritage, legacy. Even from blood, and power.

But the earl was not angry. Offended, yes, entirely so—but not outraged. He recognized realities and the necessities of life, those within his own life as well as in hers. Robert had inexplicably chosen to estrange himself from his father and everything the earl represented. For all Huntington believed his son a fool to do so, a romantic idealist shaped too much by his mother's soft hand and softer mind, he knew there was a measure of himself in the boy. Were they not similar in the tenacious stubbornness that made forgiveness of one another impossible, Robert perhaps would have come back years before.

Perhaps. And yet forgiveness was not possible. But cooperation, given the right circumstances, indisputably was.

Huntington considered the facts. His son loved an unsuitable woman. The earl had himself *wed* an unsuitable woman—in temperament, though not in wealth and blood—but he had had the good sense not to love her. He understood the value of such comportment, the power won from self-control. His son never had.

"All of them dead," he said aloud, recalling other sons. "All of them save for Robert. The last—and the least."

But all he had. Now.

There was a measure of compensation, a degree of relief, and an inchoate sense of righteousness: the woman Robert bedded out of wedlock could not conceive. There were no bastards of her, nor would be. But there might be grandchildren yet, and a grandson more suited than his recalcitrant father to hold the title, to command the wealth, the lands, the castle. It required merely that Robert be made to see his duty, to marry a *suitable* woman capable of giving him children. Sons, preferably.

But to convince or perhaps seduce Robert to such duties required careful voyaging. No enticement had served to keep the earl's son with him, and Huntington doubted that any offered since, had any *been* offered, would have retrieved his heir.

With a curious flash of insight, Huntington admitted that just as no enticement existed that might induce *him* to repudiate his title and the honors of it—certainly not a woman!—there was every possibility, difficult as it was to comprehend, that Robert believed his stance equally valid. A man committed to principles in place of political realities was unpredictable in the ordering of convictions, the disposition of his commitments. Such a man could never be properly used as a weapon in the war, because he refused duty, rejected responsibility, in the name of selfishness.

Gripping a goblet in trembling fingers, the earl mused thoughtfully, "But a man may make a principle *of* political reality and thereby control another, should he be clever." And very, very careful.

He considered it thoroughly, swathed in bed linens and coverlets against the pernicious chill that had invaded aging bones. And when Ralph came to him and announced his son had arrived, Huntington, with an uncommon thrill of anticipation, acknowledged the unsuitable woman had provided precisely the opportunity she had promised.

Now was the time to seize it.

But what had she said? *". . . make no assumptions concerning what shapes his actions, lest you shape in him an answer you cannot bear."*

Huntington was not a fool. He accepted advice from even the crudest of sources, if in his judgment that source provided the answer.

'I have given you the key,' the woman had said. *'Use it wisely.'*

And so he would.

"Have him in," he told Ralph. "Send my son to me."

In the gloom of a dying day, Brother Tuck was plainly startled as he pushed from knees to feet. "But I cannot," he blurted. "I am not a priest."

Marian drew breath, measured it out again as if she fed forty hens with but a handful of grain. "I do not mean it as confession."

"Then—what?"

Now that he asked her, now that she was required to explain it, to put words to the emotions that had brought her to the oratory, Marian was mute.

"Lady."

She had told him a thousand times to call her by her name. But Tuck was devotedly circumspect in all matters.

Marian sat down upon one of the small benches Will Scarlet had made. The oratory had been used only rarely prior to the arrival of Robin and the others, but Tuck had made of it a place reflecting the purpose for which it had been built.

She shook her head. Then bowed it. She intended neither prayer nor supplication, merely expressed the inability to choose the proper words. And Tuck, at last, understood.

He sat down on the bench beside her, and listened.

She told him everything. And then spoke of her fear.

"I did it," she said, "because it needed doing. I cannot claim him; Robin isn't mine. He is himself, belonging to no one. It is *his* will, *his* choice, *his* future at stake." She drew in a trembling breath. "But he has gone to Huntington, and I have had time to think again, to consider what I have done. To know now I was a fool."

"Lady—"

"I am *afraid*, Tuck. For myself." She felt the prickle of shame. "I am not a good woman."

" 'Good' is defined by many things," he declared with such certainty that she nearly gaped at him. "It is," he insisted. "And only God can judge whether our 'goodness' is"—he smiled—"good enough."

"But how can I be considered 'good' when I want nothing more than for Robin to reject his father outright and come back to me?"

"Regret is natural," Tuck said. "But your intent was to give Robin the opportunity to choose. Were you a 'bad' woman—however you wish to define it—you would never have gone to the earl in the first place."

Marian scowled. "I was a fool to do it."

"We test ourselves," he said gently, "with everything we do. All those choices we devise for ourselves, and the choices we make."

"This is *my* test, then?"

"One of them," he agreed.

"And if I am afraid of this test?"

Tuck's expression was solemn. "You should be."

She had not expected that of him, but rather comfort and sympathy. Startled, she stared into the sincere brown eyes.

"There is always fear in any undertaking that includes risk." Tuck explained. "And surely this does. Have you not given his father the means to win him back?"

Marian thought about it. "I told him I would not interfere. It is Robin's decision. But his father *may* win him back."

"But that will not be your doing."

The tone was bitter. "No?"

"There is some difference," Tuck said, "between a woman who leaves the door unlatched, and the woman who orders her husband out that door."

Marian frowned.

"I am not *blind,*" he said. "Nor deaf. Nor am I dead."

She gazed at him in some perplexity; none of the men she counted as friends was making sense this morning.

Tuck's face reddened. "A religous vocation does not necessarily make a man ignorant of . . ." He struggled with it a moment. "Of *compassion.*" His expression suggested that was not the word he intended to use, but nothing else was forthcoming.

Ah. "No," she said, smiling.

"It is risk," he agreed, seemingly relieved he need not explain himself more fully with regard to what he did and did not understand of men and women. "But even pledging oneself to God invites a measure of risk." Tuck leaned toward her, speaking in a confiding whisper. "The devil, you know."

"The devil?"

"But give him the opportunity, and he shall mislead." Tuck nodded once. "That is risk."

"The devil," she said dryly, "may be but a babe compared to the earl."

Tuck recoiled. "Never say so!"

Marian sighed. She should have known better than to say such to a monk, trained from the day he took his vows to be a literalist. She thanked him briefly and rose, feeling no more content than when she had entered, but before she could leave the oratory, he called her name.

Her name. Not her title.

Marian turned back, hand on the latch of the narrow wooden door.

"The choice he makes," Tuck said, "will be his own. He has had two decades with his father, and five years with you. But he is not his father's son, and he is not his woman's puppet. You have said it: he is himself. Whatever decision he makes will be born of his own heart."

"Duty," she said faintly, thinking of the earl.

"Duty," Tuck agreed. "To his father. To you. And to himself."

Marian said, "And to his king. His country."

Tuck's eyes were bleak. "His king is dead."

Nine

The Earl of Huntington looked upon his son and was disgusted, though he let none of it show. Robert's fair hair was untidy from the ride, tangled against his shoulders, and he wore clothing best left to peasants. There was nothing of elegance, of his station, about the sherte or crude hosen. The boots were terribly worn, and the tunic of plain brown wool displayed woody slubs in the weave that bespoke poor wool and a poorer hand at the loom.

His son had come home from Crusade in 1194 vastly changed by war, and by captivity. The fey, feckless boy had been transformed into a man who was wholly a stranger, and while the earl applauded self-control—he disliked frivolity and effusiveness—he felt there was a distinct difference between keeping one's own counsel and turning oneself to stone. There had been times he feared for his son's sanity; and, in fact, was convinced the Saracens had ruined him utterly. Robert had always been difficult to manage, but after Crusade he was impossible.

Now, still abed, the earl stirred in vague discontent as his son gazed upon him. Robert was yet a stranger. Five additional years, albeit spent in England, in peace, had wrought additional changes. Some measure of healing had occurred; Robert seemed less brittle than before, less unpredictable. His eyes were not so haunted, his face not so gaunt, his movements not so constricted by concern for what his captors might require of him, or punish. He was markedly self-contained and plainly no more enamored of being under the castle roof he detested than he had ever been, but clearly he had come with no thought for anything beyond his father's health.

And that was a weapon the earl intended to use.

There was, Huntington noted in mild surprise—he had forgotten—the faint pale tracery of a scar curving along the underside of his son's jaw. He had seen other scars once, the permanent whip-weals in his back, but had noted no others. Now, as he lay in bed and Robert stood beside it, the earl could mark such inconsequential details as white-blond lashes, the clean arch of eyebrows, the molding of nose and cheekbones that echoed his mother's features; and also such things as the grimness of his mouth and tension in the jaw—and unfeigned startlement in hazel eyes as he realized that indeed his father was ill.

"Did you think it was a lie?" the earl rasped.

Robert's face blanked itself. The honest reaction was gone, banished by a mask his father recognized. His tone was perfectly courteous, but utterly lacking in emotion. "My lord?"

"Do not prevaricate," Huntington said testily. "I see it in your face. You believed it a ruse?"

He was so fair that even the faintest tinge of color gave away his emotions. But the mask remained intact.

The earl grunted. "We have not been comfortable together for many years, Robert. I will feign no confusion, beg no explanation. We are very different men."

He considered that. Then relaxed the mask enough to reveal an ironic wariness. "So we are, my lord."

"Oh, do sit down!" the earl snapped, and gestured peremptory direction.

Robert glanced around, found the indicated chair at a table, and dragged it over. After a momentary hesitation, he seated himself, though somewhat gingerly and without any of his habitual grace, as if he hurt. He was quite stiff, the earl noted, poised to depart the chair—and possibly the chamber—the instant he decided it was necessary.

"You will recall," Huntington said, "that it was not I who asked you to come."

Robert opened his mouth immediately. Reconsidered. Shut it, and held his silence.

"You have been most plain with regard to your feelings for me," the earl said. "You have rejected my roof, my hopes, my heritage. You have made a life apart from the one I intended for you. In five years you have not come here once." He looked steadily at his son. "And yet you come now because you fear I am dying."

"No," Robert said.

"Then why?"

It was apparently too much to ask: his son stood up abruptly. "Perhaps I should not have come."

"That is not an answer," Huntington pointed out. "Make a *proper* one, Robert. Tell me the truth." He twitched a hand briefly in a suggestion of supplication. "Let it be your truth, if you will, and I shall listen; I have already said we are two different men. That should suggest I give you the latitude to be yourself, rather than what I would have you be." He grimaced. "You have won that much of me."

Color seeped into the face again. "She said you were ill."

"And so I am."

"She said I should come."

"And so you have."

"She said . . ." But he closed his mouth on it.

"She said a great deal," the earl observed at last.

His son held his silence, though his eyes narrowed slightly.

He waits for me to attack the woman, so he may defend her. "Would you have come," the father asked with devastating simplicity, "had she not suggested it?"

It was not a question the son had expected. He frowned slightly, briefly, turning over the words in his mind as if he sought a weapon within them. He found none. Now the pale brows knitted beneath tangled locks of windblown hair.

"Would you have come," the earl repeated, "had she not suggested it?"

There was no bitterness in the eyes, no resentment in the expression, only fresh consideration as he revisited the inquiry. Robert was beginning to measure *himself* now instead of his father.

The earl followed up the advantage. "I have never sent for you. Not once. Not in five years. Nor did I send for you now."

Color moved again in the face, staining flesh anew. The high cheekbones burned.

"I have asked nothing of you. Commanded nothing of you. Demanded nothing of you—" He raised a silencing hand before his son could interrupt to dispute the matter. "In five years."

Now the answer was different. There were no grounds for dispute. "You have not," Robert confirmed with obvious reluctance.

"Nor do I do so now. Save for one thing."

The faint smile was bitter.

Huntington stirred beneath the bed linens. With one aching hand he groomed the coverlet. In a muted voice, he said, "Tell me what you would have me be."

This was unexpected. His son stared at him, plainly taken aback.

And again: "If you could make me into the father you would have preferred, what man would I be?"

His son remained mute, and rigid as the chair.

"Tell me, Robin. The truth. How could I have done better?"

At the name his mother had bestowed and others used freely, lids flickered briefly. Something moved in the hazel eyes, something kindled, blazed, then was abruptly extinguished. He was not yet weaned. Not yet won.

"I have been true to myself," Huntington explained. "I have done what I believed necessary for the good of the family. Means and methods do not always agree with the designs and desires of others; they did not agree with you."

"They did not."

Huntington drew in an uneven breath. "If I have wronged you, Robin, I do apologize."

So profoundly shocked was his son by the statement that he was entirely incapable of speech. He blanched white as the finest bed linen. Eyes transformed themselves to opacity. Even his lips, as they slackened, were pale.

"It is my deepest regret," Huntington said, "that we have lost so many years."

After a moment Robert managed speech. *"All* of them."

Protest rose to the earl's lips—surely not all of them; had there not been a time when he and the boy were in accord?—but he swallowed it and deferred. "All of them?"

His son rose. Somewhat unsteadily he wandered to the deep-cut window embrasure and stood there, his back to the room, to his father. His arms were folded against his chest as if he hugged himself. And perhaps he did. He seemed oddly reduced, undone by the admission. He set his brow against the stone.

Even his words were sluggish. "I wish . . ."

The earl waited.

"I wish you might have said this to my mother."

Huntington asked, "How do you know I did not?"

Robert turned. His body trembled with avid tension. "Did you?"

The earl said nothing.

"Did you?"

"I did not," Huntington said. "That, too, I regret. And so I make amends to you. For you . . . and for her."

His son yet hugged himself. He collapsed against the wall beside the embrasure, wincing slightly, and stared into the pallor of candlelight. There was, the earl saw, a sheen of tears in his eyes.

The time is now. "Forgive me," Huntington said, "but I tire easily. Perhaps you will come back later?"

Robert, yet lost, stared at him blankly.

"Later," the earl said, and reached for wine with trembling hands.

Robert, stirring laggardly from his reverie, hastily took up the cup from the bedside table and set it into his father's hands. Fingers briefly brushed. The earl reflected it was the first time they had touched one another in more than two decades.

"Send Ralph to me," Huntington said hoarsely.

"You should rest."

The earl sipped wine; indeed, that much was true. The weakness was unfeigned. "And so I shall . . . but there is a matter Ralph must tend first."

"Let me."

Huntington considered it, let the consideration show; then smiled faintly and shook his head. "Ralph is more familiar with the household and with my business."

Then came the words he had sacrificed dignity for: "Ralph has been more of a son than I."

The earl gazed into the cup and forbore to offer answer, which was answer of itself.

The door thumped closed. Huntington bared his teeth in a brief, feral grin, and drank to his victory.

William deLacey, deep in his dungeon, left off his labors over the Exchequer cloth and cast a murderous glare at Sir Guy of Gisbourne, who stood in the door he had just unlocked and opened to announce a visitor. Belatedly. "Where is he?"

Gisbourne raised his brows. "In the kitchens, of course. He has ridden hard on his errand; I sent him there for food and drink."

"It might have waited," deLacey said between his teeth. "It *should* have waited until after he had given his message to me."

"You said you were not to be disturbed." Gisbourne paused. "You said it twice."

The sheriff lost the remains of his patience. "I am *always* to be disturbed for the king's messenger, you fool!" Particularly as it was very likely the word the man carried was of the king's death. But then, Gisbourne was not aware of that. So far as deLacey knew, only he, the Earl of Huntington, and the miscreants at Ravenskeep were privy to the news of Richard's impending death.

"Fetch him to the hall," the sheriff said in irritation, folding up the painted cloth. "I shall meet him there." He stowed the Exchequer behind one of the coin chests, then stomped out of the cell with Gisbourne in tow, taking care to lock the door before he put the key into the pouch at his belt. As steward, Gisbourne had a complete set of keys that fit every lock within and without the castle, but deLacey preferred to carry a few of the most vital on his person. "Did he indicate any manner of haste?"

Gisbourne's breathing was loud as he followed deLacey up the stairs. "He had ridden hard, my lord, and had little breath left to speak. Beyond asking for you, he said nothing—although . . ."

"Although?"

Gisbourne's tone sounded abashed. "He did insist it wasn't necessary that he should be fed immediately."

"But you saw to it he was ushered into the kitchens regardless."

"Your orders had made it clear—"

"My orders are that I should be apprised of any royal messenger at any hour of the day or night!"

"And I know that," Gisbourne observed with stolid persistence. Then added, "Now."

DeLacey stopped so short upon the stair that Gisbourne nearly slipped. The sheriff looked over his shoulder, considering the entertaining possibility of shoving his steward down the stairs so he might never have to deal with his exasperating truculence again. But Gisbourne was by nature uniquely suited to his stewardship, and deLacey needed him until he could find another.

There was also the small matter of Gisbourne being his son-in-law, and the father—well, save for one, possibly—of the sheriff's grandchildren, though he doubted Eleanor would care if her husband lived or died. He had insisted upon the marriage as much to annoy his daughter as to deflect the shame of her out-of-wedlock pregnancy.

DeLacey, still stopped upon the stairs, reconsidered the setting for the meeting. "Bring the messenger to my solar instead."

"My lord?"

"This may be better done in private." He began climbing again. *Better done in private so I might consider how best to react with only a single man as witness.* Because no one knew, nor could one surmise, how the politics would play themselves out over the next few months.

DeLacey grimaced. The king was dead. Long live the king.

John, surely.

Or possibly Arthur.

"Money," deLacey muttered. "Money bought Richard out of imprisonment. And money shall make us a new king."

"My lord?"

"Never mind, Gisbourne. Just send the messenger to me at once."

The truculence and slyness had vanished. Gisbourne, too, was working out the potential ramifications of the royal messenger's unexpected visit. "Yes, my lord."

John. Surely.

But possibly not.

DeLacey wondered what sort of reception the erstwhile Count of Mortain would give his letter offering support.

"Money," he muttered again.

This time Gisbourne was mute.

When Much arrived beside her, Marian was engaged in trimming back rose canes weighted with voluminous blossoms. The postern gate was nearly obscured by a tangle of canes and stems, and Will Scarlet had already complained of thorns snagging and shredding his tunic whenever he used the gate; his fear now, he said lugubriously, was that an eye might be next. Marian took the hint.

Much was taller now than she, though she thought it likely he weighed less. His growth had come quickly, too quickly for grace; and that had always been Much's gift. He was all pimples and knees and elbows and spindly bones, and would remain so until his body became reacquainted with itself; though, from the look of him, there existed the possibility that physical symmetry might not reoccur until the next century.

Marian eyed him, marking a tangible if subtle anxiety, but knew better than to ask him directly what was on his mind. Much was far more likely to answer that sort of question when she asked an entirely different kind on a completely separate topic. But then, so were most of the men she knew.

As she worked on a notably woody cane, Marian took care to keep accusation or irony from her tone. "Did you put the stolen horse in the sheriff's stable?"

Much nodded.

But tactics failed as her normal nature reasserted itself. "Foolishness," she murmured, thinking an ax might be better for this particular cane.

"Robin said."

"I know Robin said. But Robin, much as I love him, isn't always right." She caught a glimpse of disbelief on the pimpled face. "Well, he isn't! I realize he's your hero, but—"

"Lionheart," Much said; his tone implied nothing more was required to make *his* opinion known.

Marian sighed. "I suppose in his way he is a little like the Lionheart. But even the king can be a fool occasionally, and let pride defeat him." She felt the wrench within her heart; England's hero-king was gone. "You might have been caught, Much—"

"No."

"*Yes*. You were caught once, were you not?—and right in front of me!"

His face reddened with shame. He recalled it as well as she: their first introduction in Nottingham, as the sheriff caught the simpleton boy attempting to steal his own purse. Much had nearly lost a hand for it; and still might, if deLacey had cause to catch him again. Or if the pardon were revoked.

But she knew his shame was not inspired by his thievery. It was because he had been caught, and right in front of her.

She gave up temporarily on the one defiant cane and turned to others less inclined to defeat her efforts, dropping them to the pile at her feet. A new tactic occurred. "If *Robin* told you not to steal, would you stop?"

"Didn't steal," he declared. "Horse already was stolen."

Marian grimaced; in point of fact, he was correct. "Setting aside that horse for the moment, what about the purses you cut in Nottingham?—and don't lie, Much. I know you still do it."

He refused to meet her eyes. Instead, he gazed very hard at the pile of discarded canes from under a swathe of lank hair.

"I know you stole for the king," Marian said patiently. "For the Lionheart, when he was imprisoned in Germany. So did Robin and the others when they took the tax money. But that time is past, Much. There is no need for such. You have a home with us."

"Not now," he muttered.

She stopped cutting roses. "What do you mean?"

His mouth was mutinous. "Locksley."

Now Marian understood. "I know, Much . . . but it isn't safe here. Not now. Not until we know what the sheriff might do. You are all of you better off away from Ravenskeep."

Much glared at her. "Home."

It was, she knew, the ultimate compliment, that he cared so much about Ravenskeep and the others. They had become a family. "It need not be forever," she told him. "Perhaps only a few weeks. But it is the only choice, for now. You will be safe there."

"Here."

Marian shook her head. "Everyone is going. Will, Tuck, Little John—even Alan, if he chooses to stay awhile."

"Robin?"

Inwardly she flinched. "Robin will undoubtedly spend time at Locksley. It is his manor, his village."

His eyes were fixed on hers. "Marian comes?"

She sighed. "Marian stays."

"Marian comes!"

"I will visit," she said. "But Ravenskeep is my home, my responsibility. I cannot simply leave it."

He mimicked her slyly: "Only a few weeks."

Marian attacked the enemy cane again with renewed determination. "I will visit," she repeated "But I must *live* here."

Much considered that. "Robin there. Marian here." He scowled. "Not family in two places."

No, it was not family with Robin there and Marian here, and she did not know how to explain to him precisely how she would manage, because she was not certain she could. She had been completely honest with Robin in saying she had done well enough without the others, even without him—but that had been before she had fallen irretrievably in love with him.

Husbands died, making widows of their wives. Lovers died, or left. She had managed alone since her father's death. But she could not envision, now, living without Robin.

The stubborn cane at last succumbed to her knife when she least expected it. But Marian, watching in a detached sense of shock as blood gushed from her gashed palm, was certain no physical wound could hurt as much as the wound left behind by a person's death or departure.

Ten

Robin wandered out onto the sentry-walk skirting the curtain wall of the castle. It was necessary to get *out* of the huge hall, *out* of the heavy stone chambers; his spirit was not made to be housed within the gloom, but to soar with the sun. He wondered how much of that had to do with the imprisonment he had endured in the Holy Land. He would have thought he'd had his fill of the sun on Crusade, where men in armor collapsed from the heat of it. But England boasted a much gentler sun, where gray days pervaded, and men need not wince beneath a nearly physical oppression.

He smiled at a quick-striking memory: Once, giving way to whimsy just before supper, he had told Marian that riding to war in the Holy Land had gained him tremendous sympathy for the haunch of meat searing over the kitchen fire, and perhaps they ought not eat it after all. But she merely said she was very hungry, thank you, and would not let *his* overrefined sensibilities deflect her from her goal, which was to fill her mouth and belly with succulent boar, and the Saracen sun be damned. Her view had appalled Brother Tuck—it was unlike Marian to swear— but amused everyone else once they got over the surprise.

Robin grinned, then stopped to lean against the wall, hooking elbows over its rim. Just now the day was not gray, but blue; the rain at last had gone, the ground was drying, and his skin reveled in the pre-spring light. It occurred to him that he was very, very lucky. There was Marian, with whom he would be content anywhere in the world, even among, he believed, the Saracen; there were *two* halls he felt comfortable in, one of which was his; there was enough money to live. And in the spirit of comradeship, the kind forged in war and shared danger, there existed bonds with men whom others might name worthless, but he counted as friends.

There even seemed to be a wholly unexpected chance he and his father might yet understand one another, or at least find a degree of respect for one another's opinions and inclinations.

And that was miracle in itself, that he could even consider a peace between them. For more than two decades they had been at war. He was not the kind of son the earl wanted, but for years it hadn't mattered. There were older brothers, an old*est* brother who would be earl in his father's place. Young Robert—Robin, to his mother—was but a third son, and insignificant. He did not matter. And so his mother had had the tending of him, encouraging flights of fancy. The earl, well satisfied with his two oldest sons, did not interfere. Young Robin had known him only as a cold, austere, and overly precise man who was to be called at all times under any circumstances *my lord Father,* and who was to be obeyed without question. Without even an inkling of a question.

Robin had rebelled. Frequently.

His father punished him, of course. His brothers took pleasure in it: the youngest of them, their mother's favored child, was out of favor with their father. Alice, Countess Huntington, had despaired, urging him to do as his father wished; and yet she had also given her son the freedom to let him dream his dreams in private, in his head, where his father could not find him, nor his brothers.

And then his brothers and mother had died. First Henry, the middle son, of a fever that swept the countryside one summer. Then William, the oldest, the heir, who fell from his horse a year later and cracked open his skull. His mother, bearing a late child two years after that, had bled too heavily of it. Neither she nor the girl survived.

And then there was only Robin.

And now there was only Robin.

Without conscious thought he blurted, "He is dying." And *knew,* abruptly and with all the certainty of his soul, that it wasn't borrowed trouble, it wasn't a flight of fancy.

Merely truth.

He had said it to Marian: one moment, and the world changed.

The king was dead. The earl was dying.

He wants me back.

Because there was only Robin.

An earl without issue, or an earl with a living, legitimate, but disinherited son, surrendered his lands, title, and wealth to the Crown on his death. The Earl of Huntington, who had worked so hard to keep John from becoming king when Richard was imprisoned, would never countenance John gaining his lands.

Robin felt the stone beneath his hands. It was cold. It was dead. It was not anything he aspired to, nor would have built, particularly at the cost of razing Huntington Hall, which he had loved. But his father had razed the hall, his father had built the castle, and now his ether required a son to inherit all of it.

Will Scarlet, coming in from the stable, changed his course when he saw her. "What have you done?"

Marian, who believed it obvious, paused in the courtyard and turned her palm toward him.

His brows shot up. He stepped close and took her hand into his own, noting the bloodstained skirts. "Christ, were you gutting a stirk?"

Dryly, she said, "Cutting roses."

He glanced up sharply from her hand, judging her expression. She knew he suspected she was attempting to blame him by mentioning the roses. She wasn't, but it hurt nothing to let Will think so. Or at least to debate the issue inside his thick skull.

He scowled and swore beneath his breath; unlike Little John, who swore and then apologized if she were present, Scarlet was indifferent to her maidenly sensibilities.

Marian smiled wryly. *Except I am no maiden.*

"You're bleeding all over the cobbles," he accused, having some governance over the manor's appearance; Scarlet was the closest thing to a steward Ravenskeep had. "You'd best come inside where this can be tended."

"Yes," she agreed mildly, closing the hand up tight. "I was bound for the hall."

"Well, come on, then." He took the knife from her other hand and gave it to Much. "Here. Be useful, boy." He clamped thick fingers around her wrist.

She gasped and stiffened. "That *hurts,* Will!"

" 'Tis supposed to," he retorted, unrepentant. "Best to keep the blood *in* your body, aye? Come along."

"There is no need to drag me . . ." And indeed he did drag, leading her swiftly to the hall as Much followed along behind in possession of the knife that had done the deed.

"It might want stitching," Scarlet declared.

"But *you* won't do it!" Marian blurted in alarm.

He cast her a sulfurous, sidelong look. "D'ye think I can't?"

"Oh, I think you can . . . but do I want you to?"

He grunted. "Better than bleeding to death."

"When was the last time you stitched a sherte? Or hemmed a chemise?—ouch! Or embroidered cambric? Or—"

"Never *mind* all that," he said brusquely, interrupting. " 'Tis different stitching flesh."

"Yes," she agreed breathlessly as he practically hurled her up the steps toward the open door. "That was my point."

"But if you're set against my stitching, I *could* just slap a red-hot knife blade against it. Cautery'll work."

Marian winced as she caught a toe crossing the threshold and nearly tripped. "I am not certain one is preferable to the other."

"Spider webs," he announced. "Mud, grass, spider webs, all mixed together. 'Tis good for wounds."

"Will, could you loosen your grip—"

"And let you bleed more?"

"—a little?" she finished. But she reflected he was right; the bleeding had stopped. Then again, her hand felt so numb from the pressure of his fingers she wasn't certain she would notice if it hadn't.

"Joan!" Scarlet bellowed. Marian winced. "Kitchens," he said succinctly, and dragged her there down the length of the hall. He cast her a quick, sidelong glance. "Or maybe the barn."

"Don't you dare liken me to a cow, Will Scarlet!"

"Pig," he countered. "You were bleeding like one."

She opened her mouth to protest, then realized he meant none of the crude tone. Once, he might have; once he would have left her to bleed. They had met under less than ideal circumstances: Will Scathlock, called Scarlet, had kidnapped her from the Nottingham Fair and hauled her away like a side of beef into Sherwood Forest. He had, by doing so, single-handedly ruined her reputation. But he had also set into motion events that led to a rescue by Sir Robert of Locksley.

Marian supposed one day she should thank Will for that.

"Joan!" he shouted again, as Cook and her helpers gathered around to express varying degrees of shock, concern, and dramatic suggestions as to how to stop the bleeding, save her hand, save her arm, and save her life.

"I'm not going to *die*," she snapped.

"Might," Scarlet said, and turned to mutter at Much as Joan arrived to inspect the wounded hand.

"Oh, lady!" she cried. "How did you do this?"

Marian shot a pointed glance at Will. "Practicing castration."

He bared his teeth at her, but the flesh at his eyes tautened enough for her to know the blow had landed. Then he was muttering at Much again, but she lost interest in that as she attempted to pry his fingers from her wrist.

He let go. Blood gushed anew from her palm.

Cook exclaimed about the resultant state of her floors, then clapped both hands over her mouth as she realized Marian might not appreciate such tactlessness; Marian herself, meanwhile, was somewhat astonished by the amount of blood running through her fingers.

Joan promptly tore off her apron and wrapped cloth around the hand. Scarlet wore a look of triumph.

"Very well," Marian muttered.

"Oh, best to let it bleed now," he said lightly, nearly snickering. "Wash the choler from your spirits. 'Tis a bit tainted by bad temper."

She scowled at him. He grinned back.

"Spider webs," Joan said succinctly, then jerked her head toward one of the spit-boys. "Take Tom to the barn and look." To one of the girls, she said, "Go and fetch my sewing basket. I'll need a needle and the strongest thread we have."

Marian said, "Stool—?"

"Oh, good Christ." Will heaved a sigh. "You'll not swoon on us, will you?"

"Of course not," she shot back. "No more than you would if I used *you* for embroidery practice!"

Joan was horrified. "You'll not have *him* do it!"

Scarlet was instantly affronted. "I know how!"

"And you might know how to hem a sherte as well," Joan said, undeterred by his glowering expression, "but that doesn't mean the hem will be straight when 'tis finished!"

Much inspected Marian's hand, marking the line of the deep cut where it sliced crosswise athwart her lifeline. "Crooked anyhow."

Marian wobbled.

"Stool!" Scarlet bellowed. "Sweet Jesus, but it's a swooner!"

"I am no such thing. It is merely that all of you are standing so close—" But the stool arrived, the spider webs arrived, and Joan's sewing basket, and no one paid the least attention to her protest. Will simply shoved her down on the stool, then held up a belaying hand to the others as he bent over the wounded palm. The bleeding had slowed again, but only because his other hand remained clamped around her wrist.

He peered at her hand, then nodded at Joan as if to indicate she should set about stitching. "Much," he said lightly, "—*now.*"

Joan shrieked as Much, one hand wrapped in a thick wad of borrowed apron, pressed the red-hot blade of the knife against Marian's palm.

She shot to her feet so fast the stool fell over entirely. But its services were no longer required; Scarlet had his revenge.

"See?" he announced, as the world grayed out around her. "Women always swoon."

William deLacey offered the royal messenger—Gerard, he said— courteous welcome, apologized for his steward's misunderstanding, invited him to drink good wine, invited him to be seated. But Gerard declined wine and chair and simply said, with no little urgency: "Lord Sheriff, it is my duty to give you the news that the king has died in France."

There it was. Confirmation.

Coeur de Lion. Dead.

DeLacey promptly expressed the expected shock by thrusting himself from his chair even as he cried out a stricken denial. Gerard assured him the news was true. After a moment, when he judged it time to recover his powers of speech, the sheriff collapsed into his chair and slumped there, murmuring a prayer for the soul of Richard's poor widowed queen, Berengaria, and also for England as well, now sadly lacking her warrior-king.

Such sentiments addressed, deLacey next applied himself to conjuring an appropriate tone of loss and bewilderment. "But what shall we do? How shall the realm continue?" He paused sharply, as if he had only just now realized there was more to learn. "But the king has no son!"

Gerard's mouth tightened fractionally. "No, Lord Sheriff."

"Forgive my indelicacy . . ." He waited for indication he might continue; when it came, he asked, "Was the king alert enough before he died to name an heir?"

And so Gerard explained matters, such as he knew them. By the time he had finished, deLacey had no better idea of what faced him than he had before. But he conveyed nothing of his irritation to the messenger, merely thanked him for his sad news and gave him good wishes for his continued journey.

Whereupon Gerard, hesitating, spoke of outlaws.

"Outlaws!" DeLacey was genuinely surprised; royal messengers had always been sacrosanct. "They attacked you?"

"They did not precisely attack," Gerard explained, at pains to be precise. "Rather, they detained me."

"*Detained* you?"

"Then sent me on my way." The messenger's expression was troubled. "It struck me as a jest, Lord Sheriff."

"A jest."

"Or perhaps a game."

"But they did rob you."

"No, my lord. Not of my purse, my ring, or my horse. Only—of time."

"This is preposterous," deLacey murmured. "Why should they stop a royal messenger to begin with, and then, when they do, why merely detain him?" He looked piercingly at the man. "Did you tell them the message you carry?"

Gerard, plainly offended, replied sharply. "My duty does not lie in discussing such things with outlaws." He paused, then went on with a diffidence deLacey suspected was false. "Perhaps you might learn why they detained me once you have caught them."

DeLacey scowled at the subtle suggestion as to how he should tend his duty. "Indeed." He rose, indicated the door. "As you have already eaten, I'll not keep you any longer."

Gerard took the hint and bowed himself out.

"Huntington." DeLacey tapped fingers against the chair arm as he sank down again. "You'll be bound to the earl next, I'll warrant . . . and in the meantime, I think I shall make it *my* duty to hold the tax money here until we know just who shall be king in Richard's place."

But there was another duty, also, a puzzle to be solved. He pondered it, sorting out possibilities. A particularly astonishing one presented itself to him, but he dismissed it instantly as wholly ridiculous.

Until it presented itself again.

DeLacey swore. It was indeed possible. They had done worse before.

But why? Why now? Why detain a royal messenger who carried word of the king's death?

DeLacey swore again, with more vehemence. He lacked information, and he knew of only one way to gain it. Only one way to *dependably* gain it, where highborn accent and manners might otherwise obfuscate, and a woman would apply her beauty to intentionally mislead. Other men might fall prey; other men *had*, including Sir Guy of Gisbourne. William deLacey would not.

The sheriff departed the chair, the chamber, even the hall, and went out to have his horse fetched up from the stable.

Eleven

Marian came to awareness in a haze of pain so intense her body was soaked with sweat.

"When she wakens," someone was saying, "give her the poppy syrup. She'll want it."

"Salve," someone else said. " 'Twill help the hand heal."

"Privacy!" That was Joan. "Let her be, will you? I'll have the tending of her."

Marian opened her eyes and found them all gathered around the bed she shared with Robin in the room under the eaves. The bed was empty, save for herself. But the room was filled with men.

"My poor lady . . ." Joan sat on the edge of the bed and wiped her brow with a cool, damp cloth.

Marian felt all her muscles knot themselves one upon another. Her hand was afire beneath bandaging. "Will . . ." she croaked.

"Had to," he said before she could even ask him. " 'Twould take months to heal with stitches, because you'd always be using your hand even when you meant not to."

"Then why—?" It took too much effort to finish, though he seemed to understand the incomplete question well enough.

"Distraction," he told her. "You'd be thinking about Joan and her needle and her thread. So Much could get the knife blade on you before you knew."

"Whoreson," she said.

Brother Tuck and Joan drew in simultaneous gasps of shock. Little John was equally astonished, though less noisy about it; Will Scarlet grinned, and Alan began to laugh.

"Why are *all* of you here?" she asked, still sweating.

"You screamed," Tuck answered.

"Screamed?"

"I heard you clear out in the sheep meadow," Little John said.

Marian was appalled. "Out there?"

"Well, I *was* coming in," he explained. " 'Twasn't so far as all that."

Alan's eyes were bright. "I see they have perverted you, Lady Marian. Such fine speech for a knight's daughter!"

She squeezed her eyes tightly closed. "Hurts—"

"Poppy syrup," Scarlet said sharply.

"Much went for it," Little John said. "And a spoon."

She opened her eyes again. "Did I swoon?"

"Screamed, swore, and swooned," Scarlet confirmed. "Alan's right. You're no more the fine lady."

"I wasn't that," she managed, "the moment after you stole me from the fair."

Little John smiled, but it faded quickly. "Should we send for Robin?"

"No," Marian answered at once. "His father is truly ill. This is . . ." She gazed upon the bandaged hand. "This is inconvenience."

The giant did not look convinced. "He'd want to know."

"He *will* know, John—when he's back of his own time."

Joan pressed the cool cloth against her damp brow. "Lady, no need to spend your strength on talk."

Marian intended to answer, but she held her tongue as she and everyone else heard the pounding on the stairs. Much burst into the little room, stoppered vial in one hand and spoon clutched in the other. But he had no time for that. "Sheriff!"

Alan swore with considerable inventiveness in French and English.

"How far?" Little John asked sharply.

"Soldiers with him?" Scarlet demanded.

"Manor road," Much answered. "Alone."

The red-bearded giant bobbed his head. "That's something."

"But I shall fetch my lute and go regardless," Alan said, turning hastily to the door. "He may be after parts of me I'd rather be keeping."

Marian frowned, working it out despite the nagging pain. The sheriff was coming alone. He was not there to arrest any of them. The pardon yet stood.

"All of you save Alan," Marian croaked. "All of you return to what you were doing. Let him see you industrious."

"But there's you," Little John protested.

She smiled briefly "He is hardly coming to arrest *me*."

Scarlet lifted brows. "How do you know that?"

"The pardon was for stealing the tax shipment," she said. "But the sheriff wants Alan for something entirely different, and it is unrelated to the theft or the pardon."

"So we are safe," Little John declared, though there was a note of doubt in his tone.

"For now," she agreed. "He doesn't know *we* know the king is dead. He is here to talk, not arrest. Give him no reason to doubt your intent."

Alan was gone, but no one else moved.

Marian sat up, cradled the injured hand against her breasts, and moved to swing her legs over the edge of the bed, provoking an alarmed remonstration from Joan. Tuck said something as well, but she could sort out none of it through the grayness in her head. From very far away she heard a pinched voice. "Must I shoo you from my room like a stubborn cat?"

"I'm staying," Tuck declared. "What better duty would I have than seeing to your welfare?"

Scarlet, muttering, slipped out. Little John, catching hold of Much's tunic, dragged the boy from the room and aimed him down the stairs, but not before she saw the pallor of Much's face and the worry in the giant's eyes.

Marian collapsed against the pillows. "What *does* deLacey want?"

Tuck produced the vial and spoon Much had brought. "You'll not be seeing him to find out, Lady Marian. We'll send him away."

But Marian knew better. William deLacey was not a man to be sent away from anywhere he wished to be. "If the pardon *is* revoked—"

"Then the others will be safe at Locksley," Tuck soothed. " 'Tis why Robin suggested it, aye, lady? But if the sheriff were bent on capture, he'd have brought soldiers."

If she thought about deLacey and the safety of the others, she diverted some of the pain. "I don't trust him," she said tightly. "Not him."

Tuck unstoppered the vial, tipped it to pour a spoonful of its contents, handed the vial to Joan. "Lady, take a swallow of this. You need to rest. The hand will heal more quickly."

The sweat was drying now, but she felt as if a coal had taken up residence in her palm. She focused on the sheriff so as to distract herself. "I should speak with him."

Tuck insisted, and at last she allowed him to pour the syrup into her mouth. It tasted sickly sweet, and had a sharp pungency. Marian swallowed, then asked for water to wash it down. Tuck provided it.

She plucked at the bandaging shielding her hand, trying to peel away the wrappings. When Joan questioned her, Marian answered, "I want to see it."

" 'Tis whole," Joan assured her. "I'll not forgive him for burning you that way with no warning, but I swear, lady, the hand is whole. There'll be a scar across your palm, but you'll have the use of it."

"Later," Tuck suggested, urging the invasive fingers away from the cloth. "Sleep, Lady Marian. We'll keep the wolf of Nottingham from our door."

Our door. Weakly, Marian smiled. It pleased her they all felt so comfortable at Ravenskeep. When she had first offered them her roof five years before, she had not been certain any of them would accept; nor, if they had, that any of them would remain. But only Alan had gone at last, as was required of itinerant minstrelsy. Not for him was the patronage of a high lord who'd give him a permanent place in his household. Alan had forfeited such when he'd slept with William deLacey's daughter. It was vital he not be known, lest the sheriff have him taken, and thus he limited himself to inns along the roadways. But everyone else had stayed on at Ravenskeep.

The first shock of the wound and cautery was passing. Marian felt weak, shaky, and oddly restless because the body was so offended, but she was also aware of an element of relief. The others were safe. And Robin was elsewhere. It was entirely possible deLacey's mission, whatever it might be, was rendered futile before he even appeared.

Marian therefore allowed herself to relax. The poppy syrup, given leave to do its work without the hindrance of too-busy thoughts and an overabundance of worries, overwhelmed her senses and carried her away.

Ralph met him as Robin came in from out of doors. In his haste to see his father, he hadn't marked how the steward's hair was beginning to gray. Ralph was no longer young, but he retained the quiet competence and trustworthiness that made him indispensable to the Earl of Huntington. "Sir Robert, forgive me, but I am laying in stores for the larders, as the earl is expecting guests. Shall you be staying on?"

Robin had originally intended to ride to Locksley and visit overnight before continuing on to Ravenskeep after seeing his father. His realization upon the sentry-walk that the earl was likely dying had made him reconsider. But—guests? "Should he have anyone in when he is so ill?"

"He did send for them, Sir Robert. He expects to see them regardless."

"Who is coming?"

"The earls of Alnwick, Essex, and Hereford." Ralph smiled faintly. "Old friends."

Old friends—and equally old conspirators. Robin was stunned. "In God's name," he blurted, "what does he plan *now?*"

Not a muscle twitched in the steward's calm face. "Forgive me, Sir Robert, but—"

" 'But' nothing, Ralph! If he's having those three lords in, he is plotting something. You know it. Don't prevaricate with me."

Ralph said diffidently, "I trust Sir Robert recalls I am his father's man."

Sir Robert did recall. He would get nothing from the steward that was not in his father's interests—or under his father's control. "Have they been here in the last five years?"

"They are your father's friends, Sir Robert—"

"Friends and peers," Robin said curtly, aware of a rising sense of apprehension. "That I know, Ralph. Answer the question."

"They have each of them been here."

"Together?"

Ralph's expression suggested he preferred not to answer. Which was answer in itself.

Robin scowled. "The last time Eustace de Vesci, Henry Bohun, and Geoffrey de Mandeville were here together in my father's company, they planned to stop John from taking the crown while Richard was imprisoned. Well, Richard is no longer imprisoned; Richard is *dead*—and John is very likely to be king." There was no confirmation in Ralph's face or eyes, merely immense patience. "Damn you," Robin said, furious, "do you realize what this could do to him?"

"My lord earl sets his own course. Always."

"Even if it kills him?" Frustration and futility welled up. Robin scraped a stiff-fingered hand through his hair and yanked at it as if the offense to his scalp might somehow alter the moment. "Do you not see, Ralph?— if John *does* become king, such plotting is treason. My father will be executed, his title and lands forfeited to the Crown . . ." He cast a beseeching look at the steward. "Is this what you wish him to risk?"

"He will forfeit his title and lands only if he has no son to inherit them." Ralph's voice was steady. "He risked you, and lost you, Robin. There is no reason he should not now risk a title and lands you have no wish to inherit."

He did not miss the slip into familiarity. "And if John is stopped and Arthur of Brittany becomes king instead?"

Ralph's tone was dry as chalk. "Then certainly the earl will retain his title and holdings. Treason is not treason if your side wins."

Robin shook his head, muttering a particularly vehement army oath he had learned on Crusade.

"He believes it vital for the welfare of the realm, Sir Robert," Ralph insisted. "Just as you did when you went on Crusade."

Ya Allah, but Ralph was as skilled with words and intonations as his father! "I did not risk being charged with treason."

"You risked being killed, and very nearly were." The steward shrugged. "Battles are fought in many different ways on many different grounds, my lord. You did what you felt was best for England and her king. Your father does as well."

"By plotting treason against a prince?"

"That prince plotted the same against his own brother."

Robin began to wonder if beating his head against the wall might lead him to comprehend. As it was, he was firmly convinced his father, Ralph, and various earls had gone completely mad.

Or perhaps he should beat *their* heads against the wall.

"Last time he meant to marry me to John's bastard daughter," he said darkly. "What is he plotting for me this time?"

Ralph's surprise was unfeigned. "But you have no part in this, my lord."

"I am here, am I not?"

"But not at his command."

Robin felt very near to grabbing handfuls of Ralph's tunic and slamming him into a wall. "Damn you, speak plainly with me! You know he desires something of me. Now that I am here, he will plot his plots and involve me in them." He scowled. "What does he want of me?"

"Merely to be," the steward said, "what you were born to be."

He wanted to laugh, but it was unconnected to humor. "I was born a third son. I was never meant to be heir."

"That is true," Ralph agreed quietly after a moment.

"Did he send word to Marian so that she would urge me to come?"

"Not through me."

"Did you send word to her in my father's place?"

"I did not."

He scowled. "Then how in the name of all the saints did she find out?"

"A messenger arrived from the king. You were summoned to France. But you were not here, and he was sent on to Ravenskeep."

"Where Marian received the message." Robin nodded; he had been en route to France with Mercardier. "And so she learned my father was ill."

With great care so as not to shade his tone with anything other than simple truth, Ralph explained, "She was not sent for, nor was she brought. She simply came of her own accord."

It was preposterous that Marian should do such a thing, and yet wholly like her. She knew she was not welcome at Huntington Castle. Yet the earl was ill, and so she came.

Robin studied Ralph's emotionless face. "Did he receive her?"

"He did."

That was startling. "What did she and my father speak about?"

"I was not privy to the conversation."

"Well, then," Robin said, "perhaps I should go and ask the same question of someone who was."

"Wait!" Robin turned back as Ralph clutched at his sleeve. "Wait, Robin. He truly is ill—"

"I've seen that."

"—and like to die." Anxiety, unmasked, now carved lines in Ralph's face. "No matter what he does now against John, he will be dead before he could be charged with treason and executed."

"What has this to do with Marian?"

"A personal plea," Ralph said in desperation, "from me, if you would grant it. Please, my lord, let this go. If you must know, could you not ask your lady? It was she who came here. She who precipitated the conversation. Ask *her.*"

After a moment Robin nodded. "Very well. But I think I shall speak to him nonetheless about the guests he is expecting, and their business."

"My lord," Ralph said, releasing the sleeve with alacrity, "that is your decision."

Robin was unmollified. "It is somewhat encouraging that you allow me at least one."

A wave of color flooded the steward's face. "My lord—"

Robin turned to go, already planning what he would say to his father.

"There is one possibility, my lord." Ralph's voice was very quiet. "One solution that may save him from what you consider lunacy."

Robin swung back sharply. "What is it?"

The steward said, "Be his son again. In every way. Then it will matter to him what you think. He may even listen."

" 'May,' " Robin echoed pointedly.

"He is a stubborn man, the earl—"

"In all the ways you may count!"

"—and his son equally stubborn." Ralph's voice firmed out of servitude into opinion. "But if they could be made to work together, instead of against one another, no one in England—neither sheriffs nor princes—could defeat them."

Robin stared at him, then expelled a sharp laugh. "My God, Ralph, but you do serve him in all things! He has well and truly tamed you."

"It is the truth."

"As *you* see it."

"It is the truth."

"Set myself beneath his roof again so I may *possibly* alter his plans?" Robin shook his head. "He will merely use the time to attempt to alter mine."

"Well," Ralph said, "I have already said you are as stubborn as he. I doubt it would be any easier for him to make you believe as you feel you cannot than for you to make *him* do so."

"Then it would be no more than a waste of time."

"He has little left," Ralph declared curtly. "He should do well to waste it in his son's company."

Robin opened his mouth to answer with equal curtness, and then realized there *was* no answer.

Not yet. Possibly never.

"Excuse me, my lord." Ralph was servant again. "I must tend to the larders."

As the steward slipped by him, Robin shut his eyes and shook his head in slow, steady denial.

There were many ways to win a battle. There were fewer ways to win a war. But he felt without a doubt that his father, through Ralph, had found one of them.

Twelve

William deLacey swung down from his horse, tossed the reins in the general direction of the hurrying horseboy, and climbed the steps to the hall door. His pounding was eventually answered by a woman he recognized as having seen a time or two with Marian, though he did not know her name.

"Robert of Locksley," he said brusquely.

She shook her head. "Sir Robert isn't here, my lord sheriff. He's gone to Huntington."

"*Has* he?" Sarcasm was heavy; he knew as everyone did that the earl and his son were not on speaking terms. "Then I'll see your lady." Locksley was preferable—it was he and his companions the sheriff suspected—but Marian would do for an initial salvo.

"I'm sorry, but she—"

He halted her in midspeech with a raised hand. So, they wished to play games. He struck a pose of overly dramatic surprise. "What, is she not here also? Has *she* gone to Huntington?" Marian was less likely to visit the earl than his son. "Hold your tongue, woman—" As she began to protest: "I shall see for myself." He pushed past her, setting her aside rudely.

"My lord! My lord sheriff!" She grabbed for his sleeve and missed. "Please—my lady is hurt—"

"Is she? Sad news indeed." He strode through the hall he had not been invited into for five years. "What has befallen her, I wonder?"

The woman hastened after him. "She is resting—"

"Abed, is she?" He paused at the bottom of the stairs. "And would she be alone? Or is Locksley there with her?" He didn't wait for an answer, but climbed the stairs steadily with a heavy tread. The woman pursued; he ignored her entreaties. "Locksley! Marian!" he shouted. "Roust yourselves . . . you have company—"

DeLacey broke off and stopped short at the head of the stairs before the narrow door, but only because a man stood in his way: a fat and frowning monk swathed equally in the plain black robes of the Benedictine brotherhood and severe disapproval.

"My lord sheriff," Tuck said in tones of rebuke, "the Lady Marian is resting. She is not to be disturbed."

"Hurt, is she?" DeLacey offered the monk a smooth smile. "Ah, well, by now I don't doubt she is bored and longing for company. Let me not tarry, and I'll relieve her of tedium."

He was certain he had found Robert of Locksley, or that the room was empty. But when he realized he could not get by Tuck short of shoving him over the edge of the landing to the rush-strewn floor below—thereby possibly killing him, which would not recommend him as a particularly effective sheriff no matter how tempting—he resorted to something perhaps a trifle more subtle but no less impressive.

He drew his sword with a hiss of steel. "Stand aside, Brother, or you'll be making your confession before God within the hour."

Tuck was astonished. "Lord sheriff! Such behavior is outrageous!"

"Stand aside," deLacey repeated.

Tuck hesitated, and the sheriff took the opportunity to set a hip against the man. It served to buy him room; he pushed by, jerked aside the latch, and stepped across the threshold with his blade raised. He slammed the door shut, latched it, and leaned against it; short of breaking it down, which deLacey believed Tuck would not attempt, no one could enter.

He looked at the bed, grinning, and froze. "My God—"

She was slow to wake, fumbling upright against propped pillows. He saw the mass of braided hair with tendrils loosened around her face, the pallor of her skin, the slow blink of heavy lids across blue eyes gone to black.

"Marian?"

She lifted a hand to push hair out of her face, and winced. He saw then it was bandaged; heard the hiss of pain as she jerked the hand away from her head.

This was not a mummer's dance. He had seen sickness before, and injury, and the effects of poppy syrup.

She recognized him, he saw. Color was slow to bloom, but it did. She was fully and modestly clothed beneath the bed linens, but jerked at the coverlet nonetheless.

DeLacey eventually remembered to lower his blade, though he did not sheathe it. "Well," he said. "Shall I inquire as to whether your appearance is due to the services of your paramour?—ah, no?" Her anger was slow because of the drug's effects, but it arrived eventually. "No, I see not. Injury, is it?"

Marian said, in distracted annoyance, "The wolf is *in* my door."

It astonished him. "Wolf?"

But she merely scowled and offered no answer.

Drugged half insensible, he was likely to get little coherency out of her. But William deLacey also realized he could nonetheless gather up enough odd bits of information that, pieced together, might provide him with some answers.

Two strides, and he was at her bedside. Steel shone dully in muted light as he bent over her. "Lady," he said, "why did Locksley and the others accost a royal messenger on the road?"

She frowned owlishly up at him.

"Why did Locksley and the others detain a royal messenger?"

There came banging at the door, and raised voices. The woman and Tuck, both calling for him to come out, to let them in, to leave the lady alone. He ignored all suggestions, all orders.

"Why?" he repeated.

"Pardoned," she murmured.

"For now," he agreed. "But not irrevocably. Not if they have taken to outlawry again. Not if they are accosting royal messengers on business of the king, certainly!"

She blinked up at him. "Dead."

"The king? Yes. So I have been given to understand. But the news arrived considerably later than it should have." He sheathed his sword and bent closer to her, altering his question. "Where are they? Where is Robin Hood? Where is the Hathersage Giant? Where is that murdering villein Will Scarlet, the simpleton cutpurse, and, in particular, *where is the man who violated my daughter?*"

Marian drew in a deep, unsteady breath, then expelled it. She managed at last to knit enough words together to form two coherent, if lackluster, sentences. "He did no such thing. Ask Eleanor."

He had asked Eleanor. He knew very well Alan of the Dales had not forced his daughter; more likely, she had forced him, though deLacey doubted the minstrel had been unwilling. But it remained his task as father first and sheriff second to arrest and punish the man regardless of the truth. "Where is he?"

Marian smiled drowsily. "Gone."

"And the others?"

The smile broadened. *"Not* gone."

The door behind deLacey burst open, torn off its hinges. He turned, expecting Tuck; found himself faced instead with a very large, very angry John Naylor of Hathersage, now known as Little John of Ravenskeep. DeLacey took a single step backward and fetched up against the bed.

"What d'ye think you're doing?" the giant roared.

DeLacey had asked where they were, knowing it very likely all were already in hiding. But two of them were here: Tuck, and Little John. This was not what he had expected.

The woman squeezed in beside Little John and went directly to Marian, planting her body between his and the bed as she murmured indignant asides regarding lord high sheriffs who had no courtesy and even less right to burst in upon people inside their own homes.

DeLacey set his teeth. There was nothing left for it but to stand his ground and brazen it out. He scowled at the big man. "Why did you detain a royal messenger?"

Little John clearly had no idea what he was talking about, or had in the intervening years become an expert mummer. There was no flicker of recognition in his eyes, nor of guilt. "What royal messenger? We haven't *detained* any royal messenger. Why would we?"

It wasn't a lie, not insofar as the former Hathersage Giant knew. But that did not mean the others were innocent. "Where is Locksley?"

"Huntington."

"Huntington," he repeated, imbuing it with elaborate tones of doubt.

"Aye, Huntington," Little John repeated. "His father's ill, aye?"

Indeed, the sheriff had seen that for himself. And it *was* possible father and son might reconcile in the face of ill health. It occurred to deLacey that if they did so, things would likely become much harder for him. Best to find evidence of misbehavior as soon as possible, so he would have a weapon. Earl's son or no, Robert of Locksley could end up out of royal favor if deLacey presented proof. "Did he and Will Scarlet— and that whoreson minstrel!—stop the messenger on the road?"

"*What* road? *What* messenger?" Little John drew breath to shout. "And *what are you doing* in the lady's bedchamber?"

Immensely frustrated, the sheriff wanted to say, "Making a fool of myself." But not before them. "I am seeking Robert of Locksley. Last I knew, he shared the lady's bedchamber." He raised one elegant brow. "Or have things changed? Is that why he's gone back to his father?"

The huge man pointed at the door. "Get out."

DeLacey cast a glance at the bed's inhabitant. She was tousled, heavy-lidded, and still flushed from the outrage of his presence. For one moment he felt a stab of intense jealousy—she might have been his, once—then buried it beneath an icy self-control. "When Locksley comes back," he said, "send him to me."

Little John was astonished. "D'ye think he'll come because *you* ask for it?"

"He may come of his own accord—or he may not, in which case I shall send soldiers. I am empowered to do so. I am empowered to do anything I believe necessary to maintain the peace of the shire, including ordering sons of earls to attend me in Nottingham." He smiled with sweet implication. "I should think it would be easier, and far less embarrassing, if he rode in himself, rather than being *brought* in." DeLacey stepped to the door as Little John moved aside, then turned back quickly to Marian to rap out a final question when she least expected it. "How did you know the king was dead?"

She seemed puzzled that he should need to ask. "Messenger."

Indeed. Messenger. There it was: the truth. He blessed the poppy syrup even as fury thinned his tone. "I'll have him," he promised. "Huntington's son or no, Crusader knight or no, the Lionheart's boy or no, I'll have Robin Hood. I'll have you all."

Marian's woman turned a furious face to him. "Get *out*."

He was unattended by soldiers in a room hosting the man who was likely the largest in all of England. This time deLacey got out.

The earl had taken himself from bed for the first time in three days. He felt weak because of it, nearly enfeebled, and was angered to see how his limbs shook as he stood up. He wore an overrobe in addition to bedclothes, but pulled the pelt coverlet off the bed to add another layer against the chill. He got as far as the table with its wealth of parchment, inkpot, and quills, and sat down heavily in the chair. He could hear his breath moving noisily through aching lungs.

He supposed they believed him dying. Ralph had been moving about quietly with a peculiarly bland expression for the last several days, and Robert himself had looked more than a little shocked to see his condition. But Huntington knew better. So long as there were duties to tend and a realm to have the ordering of in lieu of a proper king, he would not die. But he had no compunction regarding allowing Robert to *believe* he might die; that, too, was a weapon, and Huntington disdained few.

The earls of Alnwick, Essex, and Hereford would be here in a matter of days. Until that time, he had opportunity to reconsider what he would propose. But he knew very well his mind was made up. There was no other course.

Huntington took up a quill, inspected the nib to judge if it would take ink properly, then dipped it in the pot. He pulled a sheet of parchment to him and proceeded to write out two names: *Mortain*, and *Brittany*. Both princes; one the son of a king, the other a grandson of the same sovereign.

One of them would be king. The other would likely be killed.

Arthur of Brittany was a boy, an unknown entity. John, Count of Mortain, was a man grown and very much known. But nothing about him recommended him to most of England's barons as fit to hold the throne.

His hand shook so hard the ink spilled from the nib. His fine letters were spoiled by the resulting blots. He hissed displeasure between his teeth, until he heard the latch lifted and the door pushed open. His son stood in it.

"Robert," he said in surprise.

"Meddling," Robert eyed the parchment and trembling quill, "will be the death of you. You'll die abed one night of a surfeit of frenzied plotting, or be executed for it."

He set the quill down sharply. "These things must be *done*, Robert!"

"Let someone else do them."

"I have given my life to this realm—"

He was overridden. "Let others do so."

It was preposterous that his son should speak so. "You went on Crusade, Robert. Surely you must know what it means to dedicate oneself to a cause one believes in."

"That," Robert said, "was escape."

"Escape!"

"From you." He hitched a single shoulder briefly and leaned casually against the jamb, as if what they discussed was a matter of whether to hunt boar or deer. "Oh, I did hope there would be glory of it, and the chance to ride with King Richard was enough to feed a starving man's soul, but mostly I went because I could not bear to be beneath your roof anymore."

The earl's head jerked up stiffly. "Is this your idea of kindness to a sick man?"

The smile was excessively dry, as was the tone. "You have never wanted kindness, my lord father, ill or well. All you ever demanded was obedience."

"So a son *should* obey!"

"And a son *shall* obey, so long as his heart does not see a better way."

The earl sat crossways in his chair, gripping the back with one palsied hand. "What have you come to say? That I have been a poor father?"

"I have not."

"Then why?"

Robert yet leaned against the jamb. "To ask you to stop meddling in the affairs of kings."

"If wise men do not, as you say, meddle in the affairs of kings, England may suffer for the man who *is* king."

"You are old, and you are ill."

Unspoken were the words: *"and dying."*

The earl scowled. "Perhaps if I had a son I could trust to work in my place—"

"Oh, do stop it," Robert said wearily, straightening up at last to walk fully into the chamber. "John, or Arthur—what does it matter? The affairs of kings are above us."

"Kings depend on men such as myself. Without us, they are lost. They must have our support, our money, our influence. They may be born to the title, but *keeping* it depends on us."

Robert inspected the great tester bed, noting its dishevelment. "And so you and the others plot treason."

The earl said clearly, "England has no king."

"And therefore it is not treason?"

"Nor will it *become* treason if we take steps to see that the wrong man never gains the throne."

"Surely that is up to Richard."

"Richard is dead. What matters is what living men want."

Robert turned and sat down upon the edge of the bed. "You, my lord father?"

The earl did not miss the irony, but chose to overlook it. "I," he agreed. "And you, if you joined me."

Robert sighed, then shook his head slightly, less in denial than in wry disbelief that this should once again be a subject of conversation. "I came to visit a sick man, not to join a rebellion."

"A rebellion, if you will, of men who have had the governing of the realm in Richard absence," the earl said sharply. "None of us wants the throne, Robert. We merely want to preserve the power of it for the man who will do best by England."

"Arthur of Brittany?"

Huntington's tone was acerbic. "You have met John. Would *you* wish him to be your king?"

Robert ignored the question. "If you lose, you will die."

"We all die," the earl said. "Some of us die for causes, not for complacency."

"Do you think God cares?"

Huntington said, "No more than I care what God thinks of my actions."

"Heresy," Robert said, *"and* treason. Surely you are damned."

"Oh, as to that—I believe you damned me for being your father the moment you were old enough to understand what damnation was."

"Yes," his son said.

The earl, neither surprised nor disturbed, merely smiled. "Then join me, Robert. Join me in hell. But we'll go there knowing we did it for England's sake."

One pale brow arched. "Together?"

"Well," Huntington said with a hint of irony, "it might be the first time we went anywhere together."

The topic was not amusing. But Robert laughed.

Thirteen

Within two days Marian was up and about, albeit with no pretensions to fitness. Her hand still hurt and she found it excessively taxing to be limited to one, particularly when it came to such things as participating in the daily tasks. Joan soon told her to leave the household to her care and merely heal; but Marian demurred until Joan said, in no little exasperation, that she was merely getting in the way.

Rather meekly, Marian took herself *out* of the way by wandering outside to the meadow to gaze upon lush greenery and clustered puffs of white sheep shadowed by wobbly young.

Little John was with them, but came striding up when he saw her. The sun burnished red hair brilliant and shaded his beard with gold. For all he was so huge, his movements were tamed; she wondered how much of that was a natural, if substantial grace, or gained because of wrestling.

She thought of going to meet him, but now that she stood comfortably collapsed against a stacked stone wall beneath the golden warmth of the midday sun, it was far more attractive to stay where she was.

John carried his crook. Seeing the smoothed, mellow wood in his hands reminded her of the tale Robin told of their first true meeting, when the Hathersage Giant, employing a quarterstaff, had tipped Sir Robert of Locksley, king's knight and Crusader, off a log bridge into the water. Marian did not entirely understand what motivated men's mock battles—she had asked her father once, and her brother, receiving no reliable answer—but had learned that men took great pride in such things.

Robin was chagrined to have lost, but not undone by it; and it gave Little John a certain pleasure to know he had defeated a man so far above him in birth and rank.

Marian thought privately Little John would defeat any man, Crusader knight or no. He was not trained in the arts of a knight, but when it came down to sheer physical power, no one in all England could defeat him.

He grinned at her, blue eyes bright. "Too grand a day to spend indoors."

She returned the smile. "You would not say that on a winter's day."

"But the ewes lamb in the spring," he countered. "I know better than to come out in the midst of winter."

"You have," she reminded him.

"Aye, well, if the sheep need me." He nodded his thick-maned head in stolid acceptance.

Marian asked, "Who would you have me set to tending them, when you've gone to Locksley Village?"

He hooked one massive leg across the low wall and perched there, straddling it easily. "I'd sooner stay here."

"Yes," she agreed, undeterred and undismayed. "So would you all. But it will be safer there."

He did not dispute that. "Matthew," he said. "He has a fair hand with the sheep."

"Very well." Marian noted how slender the crook looked in his big hands, and how the freckles upon them were coppery as his hair. "Thank you for seeing to it the sheriff departed my bedchamber."

His face, above the beard, flamed briefly. "He had no right to be there."

"William deLacey does not trouble himself about such things as manners and rights," she said dryly.

He glanced at her briefly, then looked away. "I still say we should have fetched Robin home."

She kept her voice even. "Robin has family business with his father."

"He's no family, the earl," John said roughly. "Robin is best off here."

"We may all believe so," she said simply, "but it is for Robin to choose."

The big man jerked his chin. "He'll be back, so he will."

"I do hope so."

He looked squarely at her. "He isn't daft, is he?"

She took that for the flattery he intended and smiled her thanks. "Family does matter," Marian said. "It must."

"I've none. You've none. We none of us has anyone except one another." He excavated in grass and dirt with the heel of his crook. "We are our own family."

"He must have the choice," she said firmly.

Little John's voice was curiously flat. "Because he has more than the rest of us?"

She did not duck the question, or the answer. "I want him here with no regrets."

"I've none," he declared.

Marian grinned. "Forgive me, John—but I don't share my bed with you."

"Oh, aye," he said with elaborate and mock wisdom. "It does make a difference."

"As well it should!"

"Aye, well ... he could have both." John glanced at her. "The earldom, and you."

Marian shook her head. "Not while his father lives."

The giant shrugged. "No man lives forever."

No man, not even the earl. But such men as earls did not grant errant sons the privileges of heritage if errant sons proved intractable, and Robin was nothing if not impossibly stubborn when it came to principles.

Or to her.

Marian sighed. Little John meant well, but she knew the earl would, unlike the Lionheart, make up his mind about such things as heirs *before* he died.

"Are you ready?" she asked.

"To go?" He bent and spat. "Aye, if you want us to."

"It is necessary. You know that."

"And if the sheriff doesn't come?"

"He will."

Little John sighed. "Aye."

"Much is watching the road."

"Aye."

"He'll bring soldiers this time."

He looked at her from under gold-tipped lashes. "And this time you'll be able to speak for yourself."

Marian smiled as a touch of wind lifted strands of hair from her face. "So I shall."

* * *

Sir Guy of Gisbourne escorted the man into the sheriff's private chambers with solemn alacrity, despite the fact the sheriff was in the midst of a bath. DeLacey, furious, considered reprimanding Gisbourne for it—he had ordered everyone save the woman tending his back to leave him be—but he recognized Gisbourne's revenge. With effort, he received steward and stranger with aplomb, despite the fact he was seated naked on a stool in the middle of a cask filled with steaming water. In fact, the woman had just poured a ladle of water over his head, and he stared at Gisbourne and the man through dripping, water-weighted curls.

Gisbourne's tone was uninflected. "A messenger, Lord Sheriff."

DeLacey considered crossing his legs, but forbore; the cask was his shield. "Tell it to me."

The messenger inclined his head. "I am to present it to you, my lord, not read it. So privacy is assured."

The water was refreshing and relaxing, and deLacey had no intention of deserting it. "I permit you to read it."

"Forgive me, my lord, but the Count of Mortain entrusted it only to you."

The sheriff sat upright on the stool. "The count—?" He flapped a hand at the woman; after a moment, he included Gisbourne in the dismissal as well. "Go. Go." He put out his hand. "Give it here."

The messenger retrieved a sealed, folded parchment from his pouch, and presented it. Even as deLacey broke the wax, the man bowed himself out.

The crisp parchment, introduced to the steam rising from the cask, wilted. DeLacey swore as the ink began to fuzz into damp lines. Lest it soon be indecipherable, he climbed hastily and awkwardly out of the cask and went to the slotted window, standing nude and dripping in the golden glow of late afternoon.

He read the message. Read the signature. Read the message again.

Then he shouted for Gisbourne. For a horse. For soldiers. For clothing, including mail. And such accoutrements as weaponry.

"What is your price?" Robin asked.

His father was stunned. "My price?"

They had changed places since the last time they had met in this room. The earl was in bed once again, and Robin sat at the table. He took up a quill and ran the speckled feather through his fingers, testing against the web of thumb and forefinger the soft but tensile strength.

"To buy a son. An heir."

Huntington was now beyond astonishment. Speechless, he stared as the color rose in his face.

"Ralph has suggested," Robin said, "that you might do well to have a son again. Someone who might . . ." He paused a moment, selecting his words with care. "Mitigate your aspirations."

"Ralph speaks out of turn," the earl snapped.

Robin hitched one shoulder in an elegant half-shrug, noting inwardly that some of the residual soreness left from being stripped out of the saddle and dumped on the ground was fading. "But surely you have one. A price."

"Surely *you* have a price!"

"I do, yes. But I want to know yours."

Huntington glared out of the shadows of the huge bed. "I wish you to join me."

"To overthrow a king?"

"He isn't king yet."

"To keep him from *becoming* king—and to overthrow him should he become it anyway."

"Yes," the earl said grudgingly.

"And what is your price for me to do so?"

"I had rather know yours."

He grinned. "To see if you can afford it?"

"Robert, I do need you."

"To rebel."

His father scowled. "You were always good at that."

Robin laughed aloud. "So I was. Far better than William and Henry."

Those names had not been spoken between them for more than a decade. The earl's face reddened, then faded to match the shade of bleached bed linen. "Then serve me in this."

"To rebel. To conspire. To commit treason."

"In God's name, you robbed honest men!"

"In *Richard's* name," Robin corrected, smiling. "And we robbed the sheriff of taxes John meant to steal for himself. Taxes levied to make up his brother's ransom."

"But you turned thief, Robert. Admit it!"

"Briefly, I did. For the principle of it."

"There is no principle behind thievery!"

"John was stealing his brother's money. I stole it back." He did not elaborate, admitting that he had also robbed the very lords on their way to Huntington; no need to give over additional ammunition to his father.

The earl scowled. "Then consider this another principle: we mean to save England from ruination."

Robin observed the severe and aging face with its proud beak of a nose. "How do you *know* John would make a poor king?"

"Good God, Robert, how can you ask such a thing? You yourself stole the taxes because he intended to misuse them for his own purposes."

"But if he were king, he would hardly steal from himself." He smiled again, if wryly. "And Richard himself forgave him for conspiring to take the crown."

"One Plantagenet forgiving another? What of it, Robert?—they are the Devil's Brood, capable of anything."

"And only one remains." Robin stared blankly at the quill in his hand. "Of all the sons Old King Henry and Queen Eleanor had, only John remains."

"And so we are brought to this pass."

"So we are." Robin stroked the underside of his chin with the feather tip. "No man who is your son would commit himself to another's service without first learning and weighing the price. And so I ask you yours."

"A son should serve his father!"

"In most things, yes. But a son need not commit treason to suit a father's whim."

"Whim!"

"By your words: service. By John's: treason. By mine?" He shrugged. "Whim."

The earl struggled against the bolsters piled behind his back, pulling himself more upright. "Very well. I name this as my price: a grandson."

Robin went still, clutching the quill in stiff fingers.

"I would have a son, a *willing* son, even if only temporarily, as it suits him," Huntington declared. "You see, Robert, you have at last convinced me that you will not be the kind of man I would have you be, the kind of man your brothers would have been."

"Praise God," Robin murmured.

"Therefore I shall not expect it of you, save for the time it requires to sire a son."

Abruptly, he felt emptied of all emotion. All thought. His voice seemed to come from a very great distance. "And you would take him from me, then?"

"Not immediately," the earl said testily. "But he would be raised knowing he is to be earl in my place."

"In his grandfather's place."

"Because his father has rejected that place!"

"You would have me be a sire, but not a father."

"Is that not what you believe *I* was?"

Anger, oddly, was nonexistent. In its place was a cold, abiding detachment. "And you would wish me to perpetuate the folly?"

"I would wish you viewed none of this as folly!" Huntington declared. "In God's name, Robert, I am giving you your freedom!"

"At the price of a son."

"I lost two of them!"

Detachment was abruptly extinguished. Robin threw the quill to the tabletop. "Then you should know how impossible it is to contemplate *purposely* giving one up!"

"I would assume," the earl said acidly, "that the boy's mother would prefer to keep him with her. That I understand; I permitted your mother far more latitude with you than with Henry and William. I am not suggesting the woman surrender the child at birth! Merely that he be raised as my heir, to know who and what he is, and what he shall be. What his reponsibilities are to his country, his king—"

Icily he asked, "Which king, my lord father?"

Huntington glared. "Do not interrupt."

Robin's smile was ghastly. "And I suppose you have the mother selected already? The proper brood mare for the stallion?"

The earl's gaze was pitying. "The woman ruined you."

"Who did? Marian?"

"Your mother. She raised you to believe in love, in chivalry, in *romance.*"

Robin's smile now was genuine. "Praise God."

"It is unrealistic, Robert. The world does not improve itself in the name of romance."

"But it may decline in the name of ambition."

The earl scowled. "I have named my price. Now you must name yours."

Robin sat back against the chair, relaxing for the first time since he'd entered the room. Anger was banished, detachment dissipated. Something within rejoiced: he would defeat his father soundly and win this war. "Marian. As wife. As mother. Received by you properly, publicly—*and* privately—and openly accorded by you all the honor and respect due her as my wife."

A glint of triumph kindled in Huntington's eyes. "Impossible."

Robin thrust himself from the chair so quickly he overset it, ignoring the myriad protests from bruises and stiff muscles. The chair thumped behind him as he stood stiffly, staring in outrage at his father. "How dare you? How dare you attempt to *buy* an heir but insult the woman I would have be his mother?"

"But I do not," the earl said simply. "I would readily accede to all the points you have set me, even to having that woman under my roof, but the terms could never be met."

"How not?"

"Because there must be a child," the earl said. "And she herself has told me she cannot bear one."

Fourteen

Huntington saw the color run out of his son's face. With pale hair and paler face, Robert suddenly put the earl in mind of a corpse. And then he saw the rage kindling in the hazel eyes.

"She told me!" the earl blurted. "This is not a lie—"

"How would I know? *Ya Allah,* but you twist the truth to make it suit your purposes—"

"The woman *told* me!"

"Why should she tell you and not me?"

"Ask her," the earl suggested, aware how constricted his chest felt. "Go to her and ask her. She will tell you the truth of it, Robert: she came here to me and told me there will be no children."

"Why?"

"*Ask* her!" he repeated, at pains to make his son understand this was not his doing. "But she said she would not stand in your way if you wished to come back."

"Come back," Robert echoed.

"To me," the earl elaborated. "She said it was your right to choose." He clutched the coverlet, uncertain why it was so vital Robert understand he had not arranged this, nor made it up. "And so it is. And so I ask you to do so."

Robert's breath ran ragged in his throat. "Choose? Between you and Marian?"

"Between an earldom and a knight's portion, Robert. Between the vast lands of our family and the lesser lands of hers. Between a title, and none—"

"None save the knighthood bestowed upon me by the king himself!"

The earl grasped and wielded the weapon. "Between a woman and no children, and a woman who can bear them."

There was no response, just a fixed, mute stare.

"Robert." The earl disliked the tentativeness of his tone and firmed it. "Robert, I do so swear: I asked her for nothing. *She* came to me. *She* told me this. *She* said you should have the right to choose. *She* said she would not stand in your way, nor interfere with me."

"Easily confirmed." Robert's voice was rusty. "As easily refuted."

Huntington nodded eagerly. "You have only to go to her for that confirmation."

Coldly, "So I shall."

"But—come back." The earl stiffened as his son began to turn away toward the door. He wanted to reach out; with great effort he curtailed the gesture. "Robert, do come back. Whatever your choice."

"Whatever my choice?" He turned. "You would have me stand before you, body and soul, and swear I will have no part of the earldom, no part of vast lands, no part of politics?"

Huntington raised his head, employing his nose as a shield. "You will tell me yourself. Whatever your decision. On your honor as a knight and Crusader."

"Very well," Robert said grimly. "You shall have it as you wish."

"When you have made your choice."

"And how do you know I have not made it yet?"

"Because everything in you cries out to see the woman first," Huntington said crisply. "At this moment the only thing on your mind is to go to her, to question her; what I say here and now means little to you. Do so, Robert. Go to her. Talk with her. See that I have told you the truth. And then, *then*, come back to tell me your choice." He clenched his hands in an attempt to still their trembling; he would not have his son see such frailty. "Predicate nothing on lies, Robert, or incorrect assumptions. Go to her, speak to her, learn the truth. Make your choice then with knowledge as your tutor, not emotion."

"That you will accept?"

"I will."

After a moment Robert said, "Of anyone else I would ask how he would respond, were he in my place, if only to make him consider the issue more keenly. But there is no need with you. I know. To you an heir is everything." He paused and made it telling. "A *proper* heir."

"An heir to whom I may trust all that I have worked to preserve in the name of my ancestors. That is the sum of a man's life, Robert. To preserve what his antecedents have also preserved, and to entrust them to an heir." He spread his hands in direct appeal. "What else is there? A man is born, lives, dies. But he may know immortality only in his sons."

"Then I share your sorrow that I am, now, the only one you have."

"Robert—"

"Does England not play a role?"

"Of course England plays a role! Why do you think I work now to keep the realm whole? The wrong sovereign could destroy her."

"*Your* vision of England."

"As you cherished Richard's vision," the earl declared. "Do you see, Robert—it is so with every man. He makes his choices. None is easy, and he need not always agree with them. But he makes them, because to fail those choices is to fail himself, his name, his family, his country."

"I am going to Marian," Robert said. "That is my choice."

"Go to her," Huntington agreed. "But make your choice only after you have seen her."

"You know what my choice is." He paused, inserting irony. "My lord father."

"If you make it now, before seeing her, you do her a vast disservice."

"Disservice!" Robert shouted. "I do *her* a 'vast disservice'? In God's Holy Name, I have tried to do her every service at my disposal!"

"Then allow her a role in this," the earl said. "Make no choice without asking her what she thinks of it. To do less reduces her to what you believe *I* reduce her to."

Robert came close again. His tone was bitter. "You never gave my mother the right to make a choice. You never permitted my mother any role but the one you defined for her."

Huntington said with devastating simplicity, "Then I ask the son not to make the same mistake the father did."

And he knew his battle—*this* battle, *this* moment—was won. It remained to be seen if he would yet win the war.

Unfortunately, he had the distinct feeling the final arbiter would be Marion of Ravenskeep.

"Damn her," he murmured as his son departed the room. "Has she any wisdom at all, she will tell him it is folly to surrender everything I have—and will bequeath him—for a woman who can bear no children."

But he knew there remained another element. He had said it himself: his wife had raised the youngest of his sons to believe desperately in love, in chivalry, in romance.

"One must be *practical*," he said with some vehemence. "One cannot have the ordering of his life based on romantic ideals. The world puts no trust in such things!"

But Robert did.

"Damn *him*," he said.

Marian heard Much's warning of the sheriff's approach with a sense of calm she didn't understand. Surely she should be frightened, possibly even panicked. But there was no time for such folly now; they were all of them in danger. She simply nodded once and told Much to do what they had all decided was best for him to do.

And so the others would be gathered in secret, and the others would depart. Alan already was gone. Much would tell Will Scarlet and Little John, and they would go. She would tell Tuck—except she saw there was no need. Tuck was coming in the front door, his normally kind and placid face taut with concern. So, Much had met him on the way out.

"It is now," she said.

"Lady, I might remain here."

"No," she said flatly. "I thank you, Tuck, but it us unnecessary. You he will arrest, along with the others." She smiled grimly. "Me he will merely threaten."

"But—"

"Go *now*," she said, using the subtle inflection of command she had learned from Robin. "Take the food we have set aside, and go on at once to Locksley. If you are caught, you endanger all of us."

Tuck's expression was mutinous, but he nodded. "God be with you, Lady Marian!"

She watched him turn back in a swirl of black cassock, and felt the first pang of loss. It was happening so fast. They had expected it, planned for it, and it had come; but now circumstances moved out of their control, colored by the random whim of such men as Prince John, and the malicious revenge of William deLacey.

Marian turned her left palm up. With grave deliberation she picked at the bandage knots and, once undone, freed her hand of the linen. There was no stitching, no blood, no wound. Merely a lurid and very tender purple welt cutting across creases. Will had said in time the scar would pale to silvery white.

"What would a fortune-teller make of this?" she wondered absently, then smiled. "Ah, but I make my own."

And Marian of Ravenskeep went up to her room under the eaves to ready herself for the enemy.

DeLacey led his men down the lane toward Ravenskeep at a steady long-trot designed to cover ground quickly. Dust floured the air, rising in clouds; the days were warm now, the rain past. Sunlight bathed him in a sheen of polished steel, from the fine mail shirt to the helm warding his head. The two-handed Norman broadsword rode at his belt, weighting one hip. He felt grimly jubilant that now, *now,* he could act with impunity and do what he had wished to do for the past five years.

As they rode toward the closed gates, deLacey lifted a mailed hand. One of the soldiers bellowed for the gates to be opened in the name of the Lord High Sheriff of Nottingham.

It was.

At the head of his troop, William deLacey clattered into the cobbled courtyard. Iron rang on stone, bridle fittings chimed; horses stomped, snorted wetly, chewed noisily on severe bits. As ordered, the soldiers formed themselves into a loose semicircle. All wore mail beneath blue tabards, faces hidden behind the dehumanizing nasals of Norman helms. Weaponry included swords, shields, crossbows, and a fierce determination to succeed at their task.

DeLacey reined in his horse and gazed down upon the lone courtyard inhabitant, who stood upon the top step in front of her hall clad in a crimson chemise. A fine golden girdle was double-wrapped around a slender waist to hang low upon her hips, and a golden fillet bound her brow. She wore no coif, and only the merest wisp of veil covered thick braids hanging to her waist. But then, Marian of Ravenskeep had long ago given up any pretensions to modesty.

It annoyed him to be struck first by her beauty, when he had come to disrupt every portion of her life, anticipating the pleasure of it. And there still would be pleasure of it, he knew; but the moment was somewhat tarnished when everything about him responded to her as a woman, not an opponent. He was reminded all over again how she had rebuffed him, despite knowing her father had hoped they would make a match. But that father had reckoned without Robert of Locksley, and without Marian herself, who had grown uncommonly headstrong in her father's absence.

She was worse after he'd died in the Holy Land, deLacey reflected. Once upon a time she'd been a malleable soul.

No longer. Now she stood before her hall, which had been the outright gift of King Richard five years before, who had held her and her lands in wardship following her father's death, and wore an expression of such serene confidence that the sheriff wanted to spit.

Instead, he raised his voice so that all of his men would hear—and everyone else in the hall. "Search it. Every room, every cupboard, every garderobe hole; search the barn, the outbuildings, the cow-byre, the hen-house; search the lady's clothespress, if you will, and be certain she has hidden no man among her smallclothes."

It was crude insinuation, and Marian did not miss it. She was ordinarily quite fair of complexion, but now her cheeks burned red.

He smiled faintly. "When you have found any man I have named to you, bring him out, bind him, tie him behind your horse, and take him to Nottingham Castle. Drag him if you must."

He watched her expression, particularly the eloquent eyes. She was furious that he would order his men to such duty in such rude fashion, but not surprised. Nor was she even slightly concerned about what they might find, which meant she expected them to find nothing.

"Roll casks aside," he said sharply. "Unstopper the wine, unstack the hay, uproot the hearthstones. If there be wooden planking, tear it out. If there be a fire laid, put it out and stir amongst the ashes. Open every chest, every basket. Let *no place* large enough to hold a man be overlooked." He glanced briefly sideways in each direction, then jerked his hand in command.

Two of the soldiers rode their horses up the hall steps toward the open door. Marian, crying out in startled outrage, leaped after each of them. She caught the reins of one, but released it immediately, hissing in pain; she had used her wounded hand. Now the men and their mounts were inside the hall, while others jumped down from their saddles and set about following orders.

DeLacey, still mounted, leaned forward in his saddle and rested the palms of his hands one atop the other over the high pommel, stretching mail-weighted shoulders as he smiled. "Good day to you, Lady Marian."

Her face was white as she cradled the aching hand. "They will find nothing."

"So be it."

"They will destory my hall and my possessions *for nothing.*"

"So be it."

"This is no more than childish revenge!"

"Untrue," he said calmly, rejoicing at her anger. "This is a duty I was given by my sovereign."

"Sovereign?"

From the sleeve of the mail shirt he pulled a folded parchment. With great deliberation he unfolded it, smoothed it, displayed it to her. "A letter," he said, "from Prince John, Count of Mortain, who has claimed the crown as sole heir of his late royal brother."

In angry disbelief she asked, "A letter ordering you to destroy my hall?"

"Authority," he answered, "to do whatever is in my power to secure the realm for John."

"Oh, of course!" she said. "This hall provides a true threat to Prince John!"

"Indeed," he said silkily. "It has harbored criminals."

"They were pardoned."

"But I have *un*pardoned them."

"You cannot! You haven't the authority!"

He waved the sheet of parchment.

She shook her head, coldly certain. "Revoking King Richard's pardon is not yours to do. That is for the new king to do, should he wish to."

"He does. Or will. When I have explained why it is so vital that these men be arrested, imprisoned, and tried for their crimes."

"Prince John was stealing that money for himself, and you know it!"

"But now Prince John is king, and I daresay he would prefer to blame *them* for stealing it instead. Which they did do, if for supposedly honorable reasons. Of course, Prince John is unlikely to view it that way." DeLacey carefully refolded the parchment and returned it to his sleeve. "You see, I do understand why they found it so important to delay the royal messenger with word of Richard's death. How better to give themselves time to plan an escape?"

Marian glared. "They delayed no messenger! And if they had planned it, why would they have been here when you came the other day?"

"To misdirect. And it was cleverly done," he admitted. "Of course, had I brought a troop with me that day, I could be hunting pheasant today instead of men."

A crashing sound emanated from the hall. Marian winced, spun around, then swung back, stiffly desperate, to deLacey. "Stop this! Stop *them!*"

He smiled sweetly. "Have Robin Hood and the others come out of hiding."

"They are not *in* hiding!"

"Where are they?"

"Not here."

He raised his brows. "No?"

Another crash sounded, plus Joan's angry shout. Marian gritted her teeth. "No."

"Then the search shall continue."

"If my father knew what you were ordering—"

He overrode her. "If your father knew his only surviving child was living with a man outside of the marriage bonds . . ." DeLacey shook his head sadly. "How can the poor man rest in his grave?" He paused. "But then, he hasn't a grave, has he? He rotted on the sands of the Holy Land."

"My God," she gasped. "Have you no shame?"

"Have you? I offered honorable marriage—"

"That was a sham! Tuck isn't a priest; that ceremony would have been false."

"I offered you honorable marriage *before* that," he reminded her. "You refused me."

"And this is your revenge!"

"Oh, now, Marian . . . you value yourself too high. I confess I did indeed wish to have you to wife, but once you had been compromised by outlaws in Sherwood Forest, marriage was no longer a possibility. No, this is not revenge. This is duty. This is done to secure the realm for King John."

Outraged squawking came from the direction of the henhouse. Marian glared at him through tears of fury. "They are not here."

"Where are they?"

She shook her head.

"Where?"

She shook her head.

DeLacey spurred his horse forward. She did not flinch, did not recoil, did not move out of the animal's path. Most horses preferred not to trample people, but deLacey had intentionally ridden a trained warhorse. This mount would.

"Where?"

"Not here."

"Then where?"

"Elsewhere."

"A little precision, if you please. *Where* elsewhere?"

There was another angry yell from Joan inside the hall.

"Sherwood!" Marian cried. "And I suggest you take more men with you if you hope to come out of there alive. I daresay the Sheriff of Nottingham has a surfeit of enemies hiding in the shadows!"

He urged his horse forward a single step. The gaping, foam-slicked mouth was perilously close to Marian's face. "Where?" he asked again.

Marian's fist connected sharply and audibly with the warhorse's muzzle.

As the startled horse jerked his head straight up into the air she turned a shoulder and spun out of his way before he might employ snapping teeth or striking hoof. DeLacey swore and wrestled with the reins, trying to keep the stallion under control. From the corner of one eye he saw the vivid slash of crimson chemise and a glint of gold. She was out of harm's way, and grimly satisfied at the havoc she had wreaked.

One hand, trembling with anger, dropped to the hilt of his sword.

Marian saw it. "Oh, do," she said coldly. "And then explain to our new king how you construed his letter as the authority to kill a woman on the steps of her own hall."

With effort he reined the horse to a standstill. Soldiers were coming up from carnage, blood and feathers marring their tabards. "I made you a promise," he said. "I make it again, this moment. I will have Robin Hood. I will have them all. And, if necessary, I will have you as well. And see that all of you hang."

"Get out," she said. "Get out of my hall. Get out of my courtyard. *Get off my lands.*"

"For now," he agreed, icily angry. "But be certain that they will not always be your lands. In point of fact, I believe I shall ask for Ravenskeep as a boon of King John, in recognition of my service." He jerked his head toward the men. "And I shall take immense pleasure in telling you to get off *my* lands."

The two mounted soldiers rode out of the hall. Marian glared at deLacey through a sheen of furious tears. "May you rot in hell."

"So be it," he said easily. "But I am not there yet, and in the meantime I shall enjoy myself."

Before she could offer answer, he gestured dismissal to his troop. He wondered, as he rode out, if she might resort to throwing stones as well as striking his horse, and stiffened his spine against the anticipated onslaught. But no stones flew. Not even curses.

As they rode down the lane toward the Nottingham road, he said one word: "Huntington."

The others likely were in Sherwood. But Robin Hood was not.

Fifteen

Robin swung up into Charlemagne's saddle, gestured at the horseboy to release the rein, and spun the big horse in a tightly bunched circle that set the mount back on his haunches. Iron-shod hooves scraped and slid noisily on cobbles as Robin murmured a quick internal apology, and then he sank spurless heels into the horse's ribs. With a startled grunt and burst of power that mimicked the trebuchets his rider had witnessed on Crusade, Charlemagne launched himself forward.

Footing on slick cobbles was poor, but once free of the castle gates the dirt track began, and the wide hooves dug in deeply. Robin took a deeper seat in the saddle, let himself adjust to the horse's natural rhythm, and bent over the gray neck. He had not asked so much of Charlemagne in months, but now he required it.

He had no doubt that what his father had said of Marian was true. Even the earl would not lie outright about something so significant as Marian's ability to have children when it was a simple matter to confirm it. Huntington might twist the truth for his own aims, but Robin did not doubt that the central issue was fact, not falsehood. It explained why Marian would go to the earl. It explained why the earl would so unexpectedly undertake a new campaign to win his son back and speak of the future. It explained why Marian would urge Robin to visit his father when they had not spoken for five years. It explained everything.

And it explained nothing.

Huntington himself had said it: Robin owed Marian the courtesy of holding her own opinion, of determining her role in his world. He did not *own* her; nor were they married, that he might, by law and custom, have the ordering of her life. He began to suspect now why she had refused him each and every time he had asked her to marry him; though not so highly ranked as he, Marian was nonetheless a knight's daughter and privy to such things as legacies. She was an heiress in her own right. Children were vital to the continuation of names, of heritage, of titles, rank, privilege. She would not be blind to his own position, and the needs of an aging, ill earl who badly needed a son, any son, even one so poor as Robert of Locksley, who was utterly unlike the two dead sons the earl had treasured. Because nothing in this world was so vital as the certainties of inheritance. Certainly Richard's deathbed follies pointed up the need for known heirs, and for clarity in the disposition of titles and holdings.

He had broken with his father five years before, depending on his own Locksley holdings for income and security. He had made the decision not to be an earl's son, to be no more than a simple knight and landowner without benefit of an earldom. But now his father offered it in abundance, offered a future so many others valued for its wealth and power. And Huntington was correct. Kings wore the crowns, sat upon the thrones, levied taxes to pay for the privilege of sovereignty, but it was the peerage of England, her wealthy nobles, who permitted the realm to survive. Without supporters among the majority of such men as the earls of Huntington, Hereford, Alnwick, and Essex, any king of England would find it difficult if not impossible to rule unopposed. And enough opposition could strip a man of the crown, possibly his head. There would always be a king of England—not even the barons would envision anything else—but that king had best not offend too many of his subjects without the support of others already assured.

It had seemed simple enough, and he had posed it to his father: he would wed Marian, and be heir in truth again. Because Ralph had the right of it; it was possible the son might influence the father. But now the simple solution had collapsed. Marian could not have children, the earl would never accept her as his son's wife because of it, and Robin, if he were to sire a legitimate heir to the earldom, would be required to marry another woman.

Surely Marian knew that.

Surely Marian had known that when she went to the earl.

Certainly she had known that when she sent *him* to the earl.

Robin admitted it as he rode: he had assumed there would be children. It had not occurred to him to wonder why none had been conceived, except to believe Marian, unwed and desiring no bastard, had sought the means to keep his seed from taking root, as he had heard of other women doing. Bearing children lay within a woman's purview, was her responsibility; he knew nothing about it beyond the obvious: a man and a woman in carnal congress often produced children. He had simply assumed one day *they* would produce children.

Now he knew they would not. As Marian had known, and had told his father.

His *father.*

Not him.

And so he rode his favorite horse at a full gallop along the road to Nottingham and beyond to Ravenskeep, skirting Sherwood Forest, not knowing if he should be angry, dismayed, hurt, stunned, or grieving that she should tell the father and not the son; that she could not have children; that he would never be a father to a son or daughter; or even if he should and could surrender to all of the emotions, or to none of them.

Perhaps he already had.

Perhaps he would.

Perhaps he never could.

The sheriff's men had followed orders. Holes were hacked in walls, planks pulled up, stones excavated, baskets sliced open, cupboards dismantled, larders emptied, furniture upended and broken. Nothing in the hall remained whole, except for such items as could not be easily destroyed. Marian stood in the middle of the aftermath, pressing her aching hand against her equally aching heart, and was aware of no impulse so strong as the one to weep.

Everything. Destroyed.

As she stood surrounded by the devastation wrought by a single man's command, others began to come into the hall. Sim and Hal, to speak of chickens killed, eggs smashed, a henhouse destroyed. Stephen, to speak of a well urinated into. Matthew, to mention a foal who had been so terrified as to run into a fence and snap its neck. Plus Joan, Cook, and others to explain how food stores were now broken, scattered, or made inedible; how clothing was torn and stained beyond repair; how keepsakes had been smashed and plundered. William deLacey had not physically harmed her, had not so much as touched her hand, but he had ruthlessly violated every other part of her.

In a matter of days King Richard was dying, and dead; John had named himself king; the men she had grown to depend on and care for were banished for their safety; Robin was sent to his father; the Sheriff of Nottingham had come into her home and destroyed it utterly.

One moment, as Robin had said, and the world was turned upside down.

"Lady," Joan said, "what shall we do?"

Marian made no answer.

"Lady Marian, what would you have us do?"

"Do?" she echoed.

"Aye, lady."

"Well," she said, "I suppose we should sort through the broken bits to find anything that can be salvaged. You and the others may begin that."

Joan was plainly worried. "What about you, Lady Marian? What shall you do?"

"I?" Marian felt the slow pulse of anger replacing the dullness of shock. Waves of stunned disbelief, like fog, were burned away by the heat of her kindling outrage. "I shall declare war on the Sheriff of Nottingham."

It shocked them. She sensed the stirring, heard indrawn breaths.

Now the anger turned bitter cold, like morning frost upon metal. If any flesh touched hers, surely it would burn. "I expect none of you to do the same," she explained calmly. "This is my task. This is my war." Grimly, she smiled. "This is *my* Crusade."

"Lady Marian—"

"You may begin," she said, glancing from one shocked face to another. "Waste no time."

"Lady—"

"Begin," she said.

This time they began, as she walked out of the hall.

William deLacey relished the memory of the expression on her face as the mounted soldiers had ridden into her hall; as he displayed the letter. He had believed at one point that treating a woman so might leave him with a feeling of discomfort, distaste, of shame, but he realized with a sense of relief that he felt no such emotion about what had been done at Ravenskeep. At some point in his life, though he could not say when, he had come to despise Marian FitzWalter, and it disturbed him not in the least to cause her trouble. He could curse a man, fight a man, lift live steel against a man. He had no such recourse with a woman, even one he detested. Queens and their causes could be fought for or against on the battlefield, but women such as Marian were inviolate.

Until now.

She had defeated him five years before, had turned her back on his suit despite her father's wishes, had repudiated him in the name of Robert of Locksley. Though he did not consider this revenge in the pure meaning of the word—he acted only in the name of King John—he did take pleasure in knowing that at last he could wage war. Could at last defeat her. Could feel no guilt in the face of simple, abiding dislike. Civilities were no longer needed. He could be honest. He could be plain. He could name her the enemy.

And it would be delicious to make Ravenskeep his own.

"Rider!" someone shouted, and deLacey shook himself out of his reverie.

Indeed, rider, and coming at them in all haste. With equal measures of shock and pleasure, deLacey recognized the fair hair blown back, the determined set of handsome features, the fine gray horse he rode.

How infinitely convenient, that Robert of Locksley should come to him.

The sheriff snapped out a curt order, and was pleased when the men fell neatly and without hesitation into formation. Only a blind man would not understand the implied threat of a road blocked by armed soldiers. Locksley drew rein, easing his horse into a slow canter, and at last, as he halted, turned him sideways so as not to set the gray nose-to-nose with deLacey's own mount. He was frowning, clearly irritated and impatient, echoing the tones the sheriff had heard in the earl.

"Stand aside," Locksley said. "Give me room to pass."

DeLacey smiled. "I think not."

"You have no cause to detain me."

"I am the sheriff. Do I need any?"

"DeLacey—"

"But of course I *do* have cause," he went on smoothly. "A simple matter of a royal messenger stopped upon the road and kept from his duty. A simple matter of a merchant complaining of a horse stolen by a fair-haired outlaw; though I confess I've only just now come to understand your part in that. A simple matter of delay, and of haste, all so you and your outlaw friends might be warned before the new king can revoke the old king's pardon."

Locksley's brows arched. "Has the new king done so? *Have* we a new king?"

"Oh, indeed. The only man who might offer you concern with regard to your peasant friends." DeLacey made a show of removing the parchment from his sleeve, unfolding it, tending its creases; then, with deliberate offhandedness, offered it to Locksley. "Do read it, I beg you."

He did so, though nothing in his expression divulged his thoughts;

Locksley had learned that well enough. He handed the letter back. "I believe you are overzealous in your interpretation of Prince John's—"

"*King* John's, if you please!"

"—desires," Locksley finished, without correcting himself. "Perhaps it might be best if a more detailed letter was secured *before* you endeavor to arrest half the countryside."

"I am empowered by my office—and by this letter—to do what I believe is necessary to secure the realm for King John."

"I should think there are others who pose greater threat than my companions."

"Including your father?" deLacey asked pointedly. "The earl is well known as a man unafraid to set himself against King John."

With equal pointedness, Locksley said, "He set himself against a prince who was attempting to claim a crown yet held by his older brother."

"And now?" the sheriff inquired.

Locksley smiled ingenuously. "Do you know, the last time Prince John and I spoke, he intended me to marry his daughter."

DeLacey laughed aloud. "If that is to be construed as a warning that you are in good graces with our king, let me forestall further false assumptions. I have been commanded by that king to serve him in all things, most particularly in securing any man under my control who might prove disruptive to the king's rule. As you may recall, you were named as an outlaw in John's own presence, as the man responsible for the murder of an armed guard and the theft of tax monies."

Locksley controlled his restive horse with unthinking ease. "And *you* may recall that King Richard himself put an end to such accusations."

"Do you deny that you stole the money?"

Locksley did not. He knew the sheriff, believed dead at the robbery site, had witnessed it. He also knew the sheriff had himself later slit the throats of his dead and dying men to make it look like butchery, but no one had witnessed that.

"You were fortunate Richard returned home when he did," deLacey said flatly. "Else you likely would have hanged."

Locksley's eyes were guileless. "And will you hang me now?"

"Not yet. For now, I intend merely to arrest you."

"On what charge?"

"Accosting a royal messenger."

Locksley laughed. "I did no such thing."

DeLacey shrugged mail-clad shoulders. "That may be true. But until I can be certain, until I have ascertained the truth from the messenger himself—which may take some time, as he is currently riding about the countryside informing others of Richard's death—I shall lodge you in my dungeon, Robin Hood."

"Robin Hood?" Locksley smiled. "Rather, Huntington's heir. Who certainly has no need to rob a tax shipment or accost a royal messenger when he stands to inherit—within a fortnight, perhaps—the wealth and power of one of England's most important earldoms."

DeLacey felt the first twist of dismay in his belly. As he had feared, the earl and his son *had* apparently patched up their differences, and unless the sheriff wished to gain himself a dangerous enemy—no matter how short the earl's remaining life, letters could be written, even letters to John, who needed support from men like Huntington—he was powerless to act.

For now.

But he could still ask a question to which he as yet had no answer. "Where are they?"

"Where are who?"

"Your fellow outlaws, the ones you have been harboring at Ravenskeep."

Locksley's surprise, damn him, was unfeigned. "Are they not there?"

"No, they are not there. I had the manor searched. Where have they gone?"

Huntington's heir was dryly amused. "Perhaps they grew weary of being called outlaws and moved to another shire."

"I would give thanks to God for that," deLacey said, "were I to believe it. You have sent them somewhere."

"But I have been with my father."

Perhaps. Perhaps not. It would bear checking. "Then *she* did it."

Locksley shrugged. "Perhaps you should ask her."

The sheriff gritted his teeth. "Indeed."

"Ah. I see you *have* asked her." Locksley laughed. "Then perhaps you had best search Huntington Castle. I have no doubt the earl would understand you are merely doing your duty."

It took effort not to show his anger. "I will find them. And I will arrest them. And one day I shall arrest *you*."

"Then do so. In the meantime, may I suggest you stand aside?"

This time the sheriff gave the order for his men to move. As Robin Hood rode by, offering a cheerful good day as he set his horse once again into a gallop, William deLacey began to write yet another letter in his head. This one, as the others, would be addressed to King John; this one, *un*like the others, would explain that he, his king's loyal servant, held the tax monies for all of Nottinghamshire in his castle, and that he had legitimate fears that even an earl's son, who had proven perfidious before, might reckon the money his for the taking.

Before his warrior-brother, John had not pursued deLacey's contention that Robert of Locksley had stolen money John wanted for himself. But Richard now was dead and John now was king, and the earl was dying, and if the earl's heir might be proven to be an outlaw in the guise of a nobleman, all the lands and wealth of Huntington would revert to the Crown.

The sheriff smiled grimly. *Let Locksley think he has won.* So long as he believed so, he would be careless. And deLacey knew himself an immensely patient man.

Sixteen

Some distance down the road Robin pulled up yet again in the midst of rising dust. Gentle hands on the reins and a soothing voice quieted the snorting, stomping horse as he listened closely for the sound of soldiers on his trail. Within moments he was certain no one had followed.

Robin muttered unkind words concerning the sheriff, the sheriff's letter, and the man who had named himself king. His choice now, thanks to deLacey, lay in two opposing directions. He could ride on to Ravenskeep, which was precisely what he'd set out to do, or seek the others at Locksley Village. He badly wanted to see Marian, particularly in view of the sheriff's comments regarding a search of the manor, but the latter course beckoned because he felt the others' lives were genuinely endangered. DeLacey was no fool; the sheriff would soon recall, if he hadn't already, that the earl's son was Sir Robert *of Locksley.* The village was his, as was its hall, and that hall, after Ravenskeep, was the likeliest place of refuge for Scarlet, Little John, Alan, Much, and Tuck—if they had even reached it. If they had not, they should be warned away as soon as possible.

And yet if he rode straight to Locksley and the sheriff did turn up to search the hall and village, deLacey would know at once that Robin was indeed involved in hiding the others. So long as the others—particularly Alan, whose capture was personal for the sheriff—remained unfound, Robin and Marian could not be accused of hiding men who were now, apparently, unpardoned and outlawed again, insofar as the new king had in his letter conveniently left such things open to the sheriff's interpretation.

Meanwhile, Robin had done something wholly unexpected even by himself in claiming the protection of his father's name. He despised himself for it, for the abrupt impulse that had put the words in his mouth if only to deflate William deLacey; and yet further reflection suggested such action nonetheless bought him desperately needed time to sort out the next step. So long as he was under the earl's protection, even if only by implication, he and Marian were free to act with impunity unless, and until—and *if*—the sheriff convinced King John to authorize their arrest as well.

Robin did not doubt deLacey would attempt it. But for now, he had time. He had best use it wisely. So he sought, found, and took the first deer track leading into Sherwood's shadows. He, like the sheriff, was hunting outlaws. But he, *un*like the sheriff, had a use for them that did not entail hanging.

When everyone at Ravenskeep had been set to restoring order, from salvaging dead chickens for the cookpot to burying the dead foal, Marian went out into the meadow where Robin and the others had set up the butts. Clumps of straw and grass had been fashioned into rough man shapes, wrapped and stitched in sacking, painted with comically leering faces as well as crimson hearts over the left breast, and were tacked up against rough upright wooden planks. She took with her the bow Robin had made her—shorter, more flexible, requiring less strength than his own—and clothyard arrows he had also painstakingly cut to her measure and fletched with goosefeathers. It was not unusual for highborn women to shoot at the butts, or even to hunt with bow and arrow, though Marian knew few who truly did attempt to bring down game. She had learned to shoot several years before, and had, with Robin's guidance, become a very good shot. But it had been months since she had last taken practice.

She paced out the distance, then stuck a handful of arrows point-first into the ground. She bent and strung the bow, repressing a grunt of effort—it had been too long!—then lifted the bow to draw and test the pull, and the string, which she had coiled and stored away in an oiled leather pouch to keep it pliable.

Pain blossomed in her palm as she gripped the bow.

Marian gasped and snatched her hand from the bow, pressing the curled palm against her breast. She had not thought of her hand, or how it might protest such usage. Pain set her teeth on edge.

But pampering her hand would accomplish nothing.

Marian at last laid down the bow, knelt, took the small meat-knife from the ornamental sheath at her girdle, and began to cut strips of fabric from her fine linen underdress. She bound the strips around the bow's grip and bandaged her hand. Then she rose again, lifted the bow again, drew again, and found it somewhat more bearable.

" 'Twill do," she muttered between gritted teeth.

Marian lifted the slender fillet from her head and tossed it aside. The sheer veil was employed to tie and bundle her braids, which she then stuffed down the back of her chemise. She pulled an arrow from the soil, used the skirts of her crimson chemise to clean the head of clinging earth, then nocked the arrow, lifted the bow, and drew. Her eye would require practice, but was keen enough withal. Marian sighted down the slender length of the arrow, selecting a spot of ground *below* the straw-stuffed man. If she aimed directly at the target, the arrow would fly over by a wide margin.

Her arms trembled slightly. Indeed, too long. Marian relaxed, stilled her breath, focused on the patch of ground.

"William deLacey," she murmured, and loosed.

The arrow hummed into flight. Marian, who had not tended her elbow well enough and paid the price with a stinging slap of string against her bunched sleeve, muttered of incompetency. She was even less pleased when the arrow sailed clear of the target and planted itself in the meadow beyond.

She took up another arrow, cleaned it, nocked it, drew the bow, rotated her left elbow slightly, set right thumb against jawbone, and adjusted her aim.

"William deLacey."

This time the string did not sting her elbow, nor did she miss, though the arrow pierced no part of the outline of the man, only the edge of the sacking. It stuck into the wood planks.

Her hand was afire and throbbing. Marian closed her eyes briefly, reprimanded herself for weakness, waited for the coals in her flesh to burn away into ash, then took up her third arrow. The ritual was repeated.

"William deLacey."

The painted man was wounded, if not killed. Marian smiled grimly and continued.

* * *

The Earl of Huntington, shrouded in bedrobe and pelts as he sat at his writing table, received the Sheriff of Nottingham in his bedchamber. It was somewhat startling to see deLacey in mail and armed, but he was the sheriff, and the safety of the shire was his purview, and such safety occasionally required force, so Huntington dismissed the oddity of appearance and asked him what he wanted.

William deLacey made no effort to be obsequious, though he did not forgo courtesy entirely. "My lord, I must ask a difficult question."

Surprised, the earl arched wispy white brows. "Yes?"

"You are aware your son once stole a tax shipment."

Huntington dropped the quill with a noisy exhalation of exasperation. "I thought that had been settled years ago, William."

"I merely reaquaint you with the knowledge, my lord, because I fear he has returned to his old ways."

"Do you?"

"I do."

"Those are statements, William. I have not yet heard your question."

DeLacey's face colored. "Are you aware that your son stole a horse from a merchant a matter of days ago?"

"Robert did? But why would he do such a thing, William? He owns several horses."

"To me it matters little *why* he did such a thing, merely that he did it."

"Who accuses him?"

"The merchant he stole it from."

"The merchant knows my son, to recognize him? To name him?"

"No, my lord, but—"

"Then how can you be certain it was my son?"

"My lord, he did describe him, and the description suits." DeLacey shrugged. "But, truly, my concerns extend far beyond this horse. There is the matter of the tax money, *this* session's tax money—"

The earl glared. "Do you tell me you have lost it again, William?"

"I tell you no such thing," the sheriff rasped in thinly disguised irritation. "I merely warn you that the stolen horse indicates a willingness on his part to take that which does not belong to him. Moreover, he delayed a royal messenger on the Nottingham road in order to warn his outlaw friends that Richard was dead and the pardon might be revoked."

"Did he? And has it been?"

"He did, and it has."

"And does this revocation also extend to my son?"

"Not as yet, my lord, but now that John is king—"

Huntington freighted his words with a combination of surprise and condescension. "*Is* he?"

DeLacey stopped, took in the earl's attitude, began again. "He says so, my lord." There was a glint of pleasure in his brown eyes. "Have you as yet received no word of King John's ascension?"

He meant to annoy, and he did. Huntington scowled briefly, then cleared his face of all expression. "What has my son to do with John claiming himself king?"

"The money your son stole before was King John's money, my lord—"

"Indeed not," the earl said sharply. "It was tax money collected for King Richard's ransom."

"Your son stole it."

"I saw no evidence of that, William."

"Because the money disappeared when Richard came to Nottingham."

"Did it?" Huntington fixed the sheriff with a penetrating stare. "Tell me, if you please . . . why would my son have stolen money when he stood to inherit an earldom?"

DeLacey said smoothly, "Because, my lord, as everyone knows, he stood to inherit nothing at the time. You had disinherited him."

"Ah, well." Huntington smiled serenely and was pleased to note the sudden stiffening of the sheriff's spine. "Boys are often—boys. Would you not agree?"

DeLacey's breathing was shallow and fast. "My lord, do you mean—"

"I mean that I shall have Ralph send you the price of a good horse before supper tonight, so the merchant's feathers may be smoothed. I mean that my son offers no threat to any tax current shipment, nor will again."

DeLacey's face darkened. "*Rapprochement*," he gritted.

"Indeed," the earl said smoothly. "Every man needs an heir."

The sheriff was struggling to retain some measure of self-control and courtesy. "Then, my lord, may I warn you, as is my duty as a servant of the king, that should any man willingly attempt to endanger or oppose that king to the detriment of the soverign's life and welfare, I shall be forced to use any means necessary to arrest him. Even should he be killed in the doing of it."

"So I am duly warned," the earl said with dry amusement. "Though I doubt at my age I would offer you much of a fight, William."

DeLacey opened his mouth to explain, Huntington did not doubt, that he did not refer to the earl, then clamped it shut again.

The earl waved a hand as he took up his quill again. "You may go, William. Surely, you have more pressing matters to attend, possibly such as hunting down and arresting *actual* outlaws."

He listened to the tautly muttered farewell and the sheriff's heavy tread, the faint chime and scrape of fittings as he stalked out of the chamber. Huntington smiled briefly; then the smile faded as he considered his son's actions.

Robert was not yet truly his to command. And neither was the sheriff. There was only so much a man, even an earl, could do to manipulate the behavior of others.

But if John lost his throne and was replaced by Arthur of Brittany, men such as William deLacey might lose their offices to better men, particularly men suggested by powerful earls.

Huntington sighed, thinking about dead kings, new kings, tax shipments, stolen horses, outlaws, angry sheriffs, and stubborn sons. "I shall have to have a talk with Robert," he concluded aloud.

The deer tracks were narrow and unsuited to a man on horseback, which was why so many outlaws utilized them. Robin himself, five years before, had found such tracks mightily helpful during his brief sojourn in Sherwood, but just this moment he wished the deer were wider so that he was not subjected to so much encroachment by foliage. Despite using an arm as a shield, his face was slapped by leaves and limbs any number of times, his hair snagged, and his thighs had already been poked so frequently he wished he was wearing mail.

In exasperation he pulled up and listened. The noise of his passage had startled birds and small animals away; he thought surely it should have brought outlaws to him by now. But nothing seemed amiss.

Robin sighed, mentioned briefly to God that He might take pity on a poor foolish knight for inviting trouble to attend him when he wore no mail and carried neither sword nor bow, and shouted a name loudly. The forest rang with it.

"They will believe me a madman," he muttered, "or someone setting a trap."

But if that were the case, they had only to pin him with arrows and the trap sprung without result.

He shouted again, and this time the arrows flew.

None touched his flesh. He felt them plucking at his tunic, and one hummed through his hair, which froze the marrow of his bones, but none drew blood. They buried themselves in tree trunks and quivered there.

When he found his voice, Robin raised it once more. "If you are not Adam Bell, I have no need of your assistance."

A man shouted back, "Assistance to take your coin?"

He smiled crookedly. "Clym of the Clough, you have mine already!"

"What do you want with Adam?"

"I'll tell Adam."

"Tell me, aye? I'm the one with the bow."

"Who is with you?"

"Friends," Clym called.

"I have need of friends," Robin said. "I have need of friends to assist other friends."

"Do you, now?"

He thought of insisting they show themselves, as he found it somewhat frustrating to hold a conversation with a forest, but decided not to press the issue. "I have friends bound for Locksley Village. But so is the sheriff. They would do better to go elsewhere."

"Outlawed friends, are they? Would it be the Hathersage Giant?"

"It would."

"Would it be Will Scarlet?"

"It would."

"Would it be a minstrel and a fat friar and a cutpurse?"

"It would."

"And would it be the son of an earl?"

Robin sighed. "Not as yet."

"Ah! Then what should we do with him?"

"Let him ride on to Ravenskeep," he suggested.

"Why should we do that, earl's son?"

"Because you already have his coin, his ring, and his brooch!"

Clym hooted. "But not his horse!"

"Oh, *Jesu*," Robin muttered in sheer disgust.

The foliage beside the track rustled. A man stood there in the shadows, hands wrapped around a bow. Adam Bell grinned. " 'Tis a fine horse, that one."

Robin scowled down at him "You've already left me afoot once."

"But the horse took himself off that time."

"And I would like to take *myself* off—on horseback—as soon as I know you will get word to the others."

"Are they truly outlawed again?"

"The sheriff says so."

"Why are they bound for Locksley?"

"We hoped it would be a bolt-hole if the pardon were revoked."

"But now the sheriff's after all of them."

"And me as well," Robin said grimly, "when he can find his way around my father."

"Ah." Adam Bell leaned and spat. "So for the moment 'tis the earl's son."

The barb went home. Robin retorted grimly, "You use what tools are at hand."

The outlaw grinned. "So you do."

"Will you help them? For their sakes, if not for mine?"

Bell arched a dark brow. "Help them yourself."

Robin shook his head. "You can reach Locksley sooner, and in secret."

"And you? He'd be wanting you as well, our sheriff?"

"Oh, indeed. He is accusing me of detaining the royal messenger, which I did not do—" The outlaw grinned. "And accusing me of stealing a merchant's horse, which I *did* do. He's already promised to fling me into his dungeon."

"Then why didn't he arrest you already?"

"The earl's son," Robin said briefly. "For now, he dare not cross my father."

" 'You use the tools at hand,' " Adam Bell quoted, his peculiarly light-brown eyes bright with amusement. "And a powerful tool it is, being Huntington's heir."

"Huntington's *sometime* heir."

Bell feigned astonishment. "What's this, then? You and the earl are not always in accord?"

"I and the earl are almost never in accord," Robin answered with pronounced irony. "Any more than I and Clym of the Clough."

The outlaw laughed and tamped the heel of his bow against the ground. "So, you'll have us find the others and fetch them away from Locksley."

"Before the sheriff arrives there, yes."

"And you will go on to Ravenskeep?"

"To Marian, yes."

"While your friends stay—where? Here?" Bell smiled. "In Sherwood?"

"Better here in Sherwood," Robin said pointedly, "than lodged in the sheriff's dungeon."

"And will you give us your horse for it?"

"No, I will not give you my horse for it. You lost him once before!"

"Then what? There's a toll to be paid, to pass through Sherwood."

"Defer it," Robin suggested. "I have coin elsewhere, and can fetch it back to you another day."

Bell's expression was smug. "At Huntington Castle?"

Robin exploded. "In Christ's Holy Name, if I do not bring hard coin back, I swear you may *have* the horse! Now, will you do as I've asked? I should like my friends warned before they meet the sheriff, not *as* they do."

"Done," Bell agreed promptly. "Of course, we've got them with us already, so you may as well just bring the coin back here right away."

Robin nearly bellowed it. "They're *here?*"

"Well, not just here, perhaps. Back in the brush a ways, with Cloudisley and Wat One-Hand." Bell hitched his head. "Clym's out there keeping an eye—and an arrow—on you."

"Where are they?"

The outlaw grinned. "Bring the coin, and you'll see them soon enough."

"You are holding my friends for ransom!"

"Ah, well . . . we took the idea from what German Henry did to King Richard." Bell shrugged. "If kings can do it, why not outlaws?"

"And have you proof you *are* holding my friends?"

In silence Adam Bell disappeared into foliage a moment, then returned bearing a lute case and a rosary Robin recognized. He sighed. "What would you have done had I not come looking for you?"

"Looked for *you*," Adam Bell said matter-of-factly. "And I daresay 'twould be easier for us to find you than for you to find us. Unless we *mean* to be found, of course."

"Of course." Robin eyed the foliage, wondering just where Clym of the Clough was with his nocked arrow. "You will keep them safe from harm?"

"Come back with the money, and they'll live to be old."

Robin scowled down at him. "You are ransoming fellow outlaws, Adam."

"Aye, well . . . only because you're willing to pay for them." Bell smiled. "Now, why not be on your way? Sooner there, sooner back. And the toll will be paid, and your friends released."

Glumly, Robin turned Charlemagne around. As he rode back the way he had come, an arrow whisked by his head in an outlaw's mocking farewell, tattering leaves and very nearly his nerves.

Seventeen

William deLacey strode out of the hall of Huntington Castle, down the steps, and into the bailey. He paused there where his men waited quietly with their horses, examined the bailey and sentry-walk, and took note of the fortifications. The earl had done a proper job of having the castle built; it would require siege warfare to get in if Huntington desired no visitors. He supposed John could do it if necessary, though the new king was not particularly known for his military prowess.

Immensely displeased with the way the meeting had gone, the sheriff shook his head. So long as Robert of Locksley remained in accord with his father, there was little deLacey could do. Despite his threats, he knew very well he could not arrest Locksley and throw him in the dungeon while he and his father were in *rapprochement*. It would likely be the end of his office. Of course, if he had evidence that Locksley had turned outlaw again, and the king supported him, then even the earl might have to give ground; and if he had evidence the earl plotted treason, he could kill both birds. But only if he flushed them first.

DeLacey took the reins to his horse and swung up, holding his scabbarded sword out of the way as he settled into the saddle. His men no doubt anticipated riding back to Nottingham with him, but he had other plans.

"Locksley Village," he said curtly. "Locksley Hall. Find them, bring them, and toss them all—without benefit of a ladder—into the dungeons. Until that is accomplished, none of you shall go home."

He saw the startled expressions that altered quickly to consternation, then to studied blankness. They had wives, children, and lovers in the castle, and plans undoubtedly made, but deLacey had no time for such things. His own plans came first.

"When you have them," he said, "come and tell me. I expect to see none of you otherwise." He gathered reins into his gloved hands. *"Now,"* he commanded, and they bestirred themselves at last.

Outside the castle the road split. DeLacey took the turn to Nottingham. His men, setting spurs to flanks, went the other way.

Robin, thinking of Marian, of outlaws, of friends held for ransom, of money needed to free them, of his father's proposition, of the potential for rebellion against the new king, of William deLacey's threats, rode with a clatter into the courtyard of Ravenskeep and jumped down beside the hall steps, thrusting reins at the boy who came up. He ignored the boy's hesitant beginnings of speech and went directly into the hall, seeking Marian, seeking answers.

There he encountered devastation.

He stopped dead in the doorway, astounded. The trestle table was overturned, its planks ripped apart; stones from the floor were pulled up and scattered, leaving holes like missing teeth to mark their absence; the lath-and-plaster walls were cracked and crumbling, as if a battering ram had been used. Or possibly back hooves, were a horse set to kick. Through an oddly attenuated distance descending upon his ears he heard the mutters and murmured lamentations of servants and the crisply angry voice of Joan, who came out from behind a kitchen screen that bore signs of damage as well.

She saw him, hands awkwardly gathering apron folds filled with shattered crockery, and stopped short. "My lord!"

One of the broken cups fell, shattering to bits. Tears abruptly welled up in the older woman's eyes.

He found his voice and used it, though he did not recognize it. "What has happened? Where is Marian?"

"The sheriff happened," Joan said viciously. "As for my lady, she is down at the butts."

It was astonishing in incongruity. "The *butts?*"

Tears spilled over, carving runnels in the dust coating her face. "You'd best go." Joan suggested, and Robin went at a dead run.

He found her in the meadow behind the barn, pulling arrows from one of the straw-stuffed men. His eyes delivered so many images at once that he was unable to decipher them all, merely marked what he saw for sorting out later: arrows clutched in her hands; bow set upon the ground;

the glint of discarded fillet lying in grass; the red of her once-fine chemise stained dark and bestuck with feathers; the dishevelment of her hair, stuffed down the back of her dress; the stark pallor of her face counterbalanced by brilliant patches of color blazing in her cheeks as she turned from the butts and saw him.

He could not move. But she could.

She came up from the target, holding arrows he had made. There was grime on her face, and tendrils of hair hung loose by the right cheek, torn free of one braid by the action of the bowstring. She was unaccountably barefoot; slippers, too, had been discarded to rest in the grass. The hem of her chemise was freighted with dirt. He saw other stains upon the fabric he knew as blood; he had seen its like before. A crude bandage was wrapped around her left hand.

"In God's name . . . *Marian*—" She was mute as he went trembling to her and clamped hands on to her arms. "Marian?"

Still she said nothing. His hands framed her face, cradled it, stripped the loosened hair away so he could read her eyes. The fine bones stood out like ribs of stone beneath skin pulled taut as a drumhead. He felt the tension against his fingers, the coldness of her flesh. Then he gathered her skull in his palms, cupped it, pulled her close, enfolded her. He smelled blood, a fading tracery of roses and cloves, the hint of fear-sweat, now drying, and cold fury. She was stiff in his arms, a woman made of wood.

He said nothing more, merely held her. He recognized this, *knew* this, understood its moods and its needs, the blackness of its face, the poison in its heart. It grieved him to know Marian had made its acquaintanceship. He had, on Crusade. He had, in battle. He had, in captivity. In the depths of darkness and desperation.

Finally she let go of the arrows. He heard them rattle upon the ground as she lifted her arms to return his embrace, to wrap and grip his neck. She pressed against him. Hung on.

He found he was speaking now, though he did not comprehend what he said, merely that he spoke, that he soothed, that he gentled, that he reached through the anger and grief and bewilderment to touch the aching heart within.

When she began at last to cry, cursing herself for it, claiming now that the man, the monster, had won, he told her no man, no monster, had defeated her; and he lifted her into his arms and carried her into the hall past the broken table, the debris of what had been home, past Joan who sharply ordered everyone out of the hall; carried her up the stairs

and across the threshold into the room under the eaves. It, too, had
suffered its share of offense, of destruction, but it was *their* room still, and
would be so again.

There he unfastened and unwrapped the doubled girdle, unlaced
and divested her of the soiled chemise, stripped off the tattered underdress,
washed the dirt and tears from her face, loosed the braids from confine-
ment, heaped blankets upon the floor and lay down with her, avoiding
the overturned bed; to entwine his legs with hers and tangle hands and
arms in the mass of her hair as he shaped himself around the unexpected
strength of a smaller body wracked by grief and outrage. He asked nothing
of her but that she remain in his arms as she wept again, cursing deLacey
and deLacey's soldiers and deLacey's soldiers' horses, describing atrocities,
enumerating losses. But he was peculiarly dull to that beyond distant
disbelief, cut off to the pain and anger, aware only of gratitude that *she*
was unharmed, who was far more vital than a hall, than chickens, than
crockery, than furniture, even than Charlemagne's foal. His true world
was not comprised of such transient things, only of her.

He could be angry later, when he had time. For now reconstruction
of what had been broken began with her bruised and angry spirit, and
when at last she kissed instead of cried, when at last her hands began to
strip him of his clothing as he had stripped her of hers, he knew the
darkness would not warp her, nor the hate, nor the grief.

He would be angry later, when he had the time. For now there
was only the need for restoration, for the reaffirmation of life, of the
overwhelming completeness found always in one another.

Upon the road deLacey met three men, and gave them good day with
all good grace, showing them no sign of consternation or apprehension. He
knew them: Alnwick, Hereford, and Essex, powerful men all and more
than somewhat engaged with the ordering of the realm. That they had
come again together to Huntington as they had five years before told the
sheriff all he needed to know, though he was not privy to their thoughts.
They granted him the brief pleasure of their company, their rote courtesies,
though nothing of value was said, then rode on.

He waited in the road, watching them go, weighing the worth of
information, extrapolating plans undivulged, writing letters in his head.
King John was not yet in England: the crown was claimed from a distance
through the offices of such men as William deLacey, of sheriffs who held,
in their castles, in their keeps, the tax money collected for the imminent
session. For this moment, he and men like him, not earls such as Huntington, controlled England, for without money the realm would fall.

Let Eustace de Vesci, Henry Bohun, Geoffrey de Mandeville, and Huntington himself believe themselves inviolate, safe from discovery, safe from repercussions. He held John's money. He held John's soul. He held John's power.

Now he need only determine how best to use it.

Afterward, Robin had wrapped them in blankets against the chill of drying bodies. She luxuriated there, using the heat of his flesh to warm her own. His face was buried in the crook of her neck, hidden in her hair; his own, so pale where hers was so dark, fell in a tangled curtain across one shoulder. Her hand, upon his back, felt the old weals, the scars left of captivity and Norman punishment, levied by men jealous of the king's favor, believing tales that were not true. There were other nicks and blemishes worn in the flesh as keepsakes of Crusade, the scar along the brow at the root of his hairline, and also the serpent crawling upon the underside of his jaw. Both forearms and wrists were ridged with sinew trained to strength by swordwork; beneath the pale frieze of the fine hair were traceries of old cuts and slices, reminders of battles in the name of God and king.

He had come home from his. Her father had not.

She felt oddly emptied, and yet oddly full. In the storm of fury and weeping, in the recounting of what had been done, she had purged herself of what she now considered a childish trust in the world's ability to right itself, the certainty that men would, when put to it, comprehend follies and transgressions, to apologize for them. William deLacey had altered that certainty, that trust, forever. He had killed the child in her, and given birth to the adult.

Enmity had existed between them for years, but she had never expected this. She had never before witnessed naked hatred in a man's eyes, never realized how fury and frustration could drive a soul to wanton destruction. She had tasted both herself now, in the aftermath of deLacey's cruelty, and understood at last how a man might be moved to kill another.

Or at least to try.

Robin had killed men. Saracens, in battle. And Norman soldiers, when he and the others stole the tax shipment that Prince John was stealing for himself so that he might be king in place of his imprisoned brother.

The brother who now was dead. The prince who now was king.

"We have to stop him," she said.

Robin stirred, shifting within the cocoon of blankets. "What?"

She sat up. "We have to stop him."

"The sheriff?—oh, be certain of that." His tone was coldly vicious. "He and I shall have words at the end of swords by nightfall."

"No," she said thoughtfully. "I mean King John."

He was startled. "Stop *him?*"

"We must."

He sat up. The blanket slid to his lap, exposing one bare hip and thigh. "Stop him from being king?"

Marian wrapped her portion of blanket more tightly around her shoulders. "Poor Robin. Do you fear I have gone mad?"

His answering smile flickered briefly, was gone as he slumped back again to prop himself on one elbow, finding renewed warmth in rearranged blankets.

"We must stop him," she repeated. "He will harm England. Harm her people by taxing them to death. He cares only for himself, for his own pleasures. As you loved Richard, you must surely hate John."

"There is nothing to admire," he admitted, taking up a lock of her hair to feel its texture.

"Then stop him."

"Marian—"

"You said the words, Robin. One moment the world is as it is. The next it is upside down." She touched his face, traced the line of brow, the furrows of baffled concern. "The world is upside down," she told him sadly. "Richard is dead. John is king. William deLacey intends to hang all of you, and to take Ravenskeep for his own."

He sat sharply upright, releasing her hair. "He will do no such thing!"

Marian smiled. "You are fiercer in regard to Ravenskeep than to your possible hanging."

"Richard gave you this manor!"

She nodded. "And John may take it away."

He got up then and stood in the room without benefit of blankets. With the anger in his eyes and the hair spilling free and the body clad only in blistering righteousness, he put her in mind of an avenging angel.

With precisely measured lightness, Marian asked the question she had dreaded, but now needed answered. "Do you mean to join your father?"

Something within him recoiled, as if she had touched an open wound. He did not match her tone but conjured his own, and it was all of darkness. "I do not."

She moistened dry lips. "Not even to be earl?"

"I do not."

"Not even to be a sick father's son?"

"I do not." His eyes were steady, as was his tone. "For no reason, Marian."

A chill passed across her flesh. "But you do not know all the reasons why you should consider it."

"I do."

She searched his face. "Do you?"

He turned from her, went to the overturned bed and righted it with effort. Then he sat down upon the edge of the frame, still naked, and said very gently, "You are not a broodmare."

Her belly clenched into a painful knot. "No. But men may expect children. It is not unreasonable."

"Are you dead yet?"

"No but—"

"Marian." He said it with finality. "My decision was made there upon the floor. I did not come to live with you merely to get children."

"No, but—"

"It is a *part* of life, yes, and one I might otherwise cherish . . . but not all there is."

She sought the faintest trace of falsehood, of words said merely to comfort. "But Robin . . . your father—"

"My father is but one parent, and not one I honor." He smiled faintly. "My mother would understand."

Within she blossomed, rejoicing, but now there were other issues at stake. "He will arrest you, will he not?"

"My father?"

She did not see how he could find humor in the moment. "DeLacey! King John's lapdog. He hates you, Robin." But did not add, *As he hates me.*

Robin's mouth compressed. "If he can, he will hang me. When he knows I have broken with my father, he will move to arrest me until he has evidence that supports my hanging. Or he will manufacture it." He grimaced. "When my *father* knows I have broken with my father, he may well himself command the sheriff to do so."

"Tell neither of them. Yet."

He contemplated her warily. "What are you thinking?"

She shrugged. "That if he will hang you anyway, you should perhaps give him reason."

He rose again, expression abruptly stilled. She knew the look in his eyes.

"Give deLacey reason," she said, "but remove from John the *means* to support his lapdog."

He gazed down upon her. His tone was peculiar. "Lady, do I take your meaning aright?"

 Marian stood up, dragging the blanket with her. She was not so free as he was to be unconcerned with nudity in the middle of the day. "You do, my lord."

Despite the severity of his tone, a light was kindling in his eyes. "Let me be certain we speak of identical matters, if you please: you, a knight's daughter, are counseling me, an earl's son who was knighted by the Lionheart himself, to steal taxes from the sheriff. To steal taxes from the king."

"But never to keep it," she pointed out matter-of-factly. "You are not Adam Bell."

His brows arched up. "Then what would you have me *do* with the money I steal?"

"What you did five years ago with the money you stole then." She smiled to see his expression. "Give it back to the people."

William deLacey was bitter of mood when he arrived at Nottingham Castle, thinking ahead to the letter he meant to write to King John. When he saw Gisbourne coming down the steps to greet him, his mood plunged further.

"My lord," Gisbourne said, "there is someone waiting to see you."

The steward likely would never again allow him a moment's peace with regard to visitors. "Another royal messenger, Gisbourne?"

"Not precisely, my lord. But he is sent from King John."

DeLacey swung down and let the horseboy take the reins. "Sent from King John, but *not* a messenger?"

"Well," Gisbourne said, "he is not leaving. He has come to stay. So no, I believe he is not a messenger, even though he carries word from the king."

The sheriff cast him a withering glance as he climbed the hall steps. "Who is this man? Did you bother to ask?"

As they crossed the threshold and a body loomed up before them, Gisbourne said, "*You* might ask, my lord."

DeLacey stopped short. He was unaccustomed to being accosted within his own hall. He was less accustomed to being accosted by large, strange, stubbled men clad in mail, coif, spurs, wearing a massive Norman sword and carrying a helm tucked into the crook of a thick arm. He was, deLacey reflected, the very image of vengeful demon taking on the guise of a soldier. Except the badge bearing a cross stitched into the shoulder of his surcoat gave lie to the image of a dark-eyed, dark-haired, scarred, and lightly pocked demon: he had fought on Crusade.

Richard's man, then. Perhaps Gisbourne had mistaken *which* king the man had come from.

But Richard was dead. The sheriff owed no loyalty to a dead king. Therefore he had latitude to dismiss courtesies and discourage strangers. "Later," he said curtly.

The big soldier spoke to deLacey's retreating back. "I am sent from King John, my lord."

The accent was French, the voice a harsh rumble, the tone without embellishment. DeLacey turned back. "From King *John?*"

Dark eyes glittered. "It was where my lord Richard asked me to be."

This was unexpected. "Did he? And when did you see him last?"

The stranger did not answer the challenge implicit in deLacey's condescending drawl, but merely the question. "The day they entombed him at his father's feet, at Fontevrault. But I was told by others what he wished for me, where he wished me to be."

It was astonishing. "He wished you to be *here?*"

"At his brother's side. His brother sent me here."

The sheriff stilled. There was something about the tone, something *in* the man, that demanded attention. "Then why is King John, so recently gifted with Richard's loyal man, sending you to me?"

"He is particularly concerned with the security of the tax money," the soldier replied. "I am here to escort the shipment."

Of course he was; it should come as no surprise that John wanted to be certain his money was safe, in view of the loss five years before. But once the tax shipment was taken to the Exchequer session, deLacey surrendered his power. He therefore said smoothly, "We are as yet still collecting the taxes. Peasants are slow to pay. Be certain that when we are ready, the king shall have his money."

Gisbourne said ingenuously, "Despite the outlaws?"

DeLacey, furious, glared, but before he could reprimand his steward, the soldier spoke. "And so the king has sent *me*, Lord Sheriff. I shall be certain the shipment is unmolested on its journey."

DeLacey frowned. *One man? John sends me one man, believing that to be enough when Sherwood is full of outlaws?* But he merely asked, pointedly, "Who are you, that he would expect such capable service?"

"King's man" was the clipped answer. "Captain, once, of Coeur de Lion's mercenaries."

The sheriff stiffened. *"Mercardier?"*

The man did not smile. "That is my name, my lord."

DeLacey rejoiced. DeLacey laughed aloud. DeLacey knew this man; Mercardier was infamous. "Then you are well come!" he said jubilantly. "Well come indeed. There is much for you to attend." He gave the big man his hand in a firm clasp, then clapped one wide shoulder in a friendly buffet. "You are perhaps the greatest boon I might ask of my king." He glanced aside. "Gisbourne, see to it Mercardier is assigned proper quarters—in the castle, if you please—and then he and I shall share a meal in the hall."

"My lord," Gisbourne affirmed, and took himself off.

DeLacey turned the full force of a charming smile on the mercenary. "Come, Mercardier. I have no doubt there are many tales you might tell me of your experiences on Crusade."

There was no answering charm in the big man's face, merely stolid acceptance. "My lord."

A tedious man, no doubt, but useful. And uncommonly competent when it came to killing. Anticipating with pleasure the shock in store for various outlaws, the sheriff escorted the best and bravest of the Lionheart's personal bodyguard into the hall.

Eighteen

Robin wanted nothing more than to stay with Marian, to aid in efforts to restore Ravenskeep, but Adam Bell had given him a task he must complete if he were to free his friends. Once told, Marian had herself ordered him to go at once, seeking hastily and finding amidst the wreckage the small wash-leather pouch of mixed coins she had set aside. He had already beggared himself and not reached the sum demanded, but he added to it Marian's coin, and a silver Celtic cloak-brooch his mother had given him twelve years before. Now he rode near dusk into Sherwood, waiting to be found.

It did not require much time. As William of Cloudisley stepped out of deepening shadows not far from the Nottingham road, Robin was of the opinion he likely had been followed to Ravenskeep and watched. "Where is Adam?" he asked.

Cloudisley grinned and made no answer.

Robin flung the pouch. "Let them go."

The outlaw, catching it, weighed it thoughtfully, then jerked his head toward the foliage. "Come to the fire and have ale with Adam."

"I have no time for ale. Let them go. I've paid their toll."

"Adam expects you."

He set his teeth. "Adam may expect what he likes. I expect to leave."

"You *will* leave, aye?—after you join us for ale. D'ye not wish to see that your friends are well?"

"I have no time—"

"Then you'd best sort that out with the others." Cloudisley leaned on his bow. " 'Tis an invitation you'd do well not to refuse, or Clym will offer you another from the end of an arrow." The handsome outlaw grinned, indicating with a jerk of his head that Clym of the Clough was quite near; not that closeness was required with an English longbow. "And you'll do better on foot. 'Tis hard on a horse, trying to come through here. Leave him."

Robin blessed the foresight that had suggested he leave Charlemagne at home, since he now expected he'd not see this horse again. He dismounted with deliberate slowness so Clym would not be persuaded to loose his arrow, and tied one rein to a limb. It did not surprise him in the least when Cloudisley, moving close, relieved him of meat-knife.

"Where?" Robin asked curtly.

"The track's through there," Cloudisley said. "Move along, aye?"

He moved along, aware of the knife at his back and Clym's presence somewhere nearby, and at last broke out of deer trail and foliage into a compact clearing that served as a camp. A tiny fire smoked fitfully, smelling of oak and resin. Adam Bell was perched idly on a fallen tree, cradling a skin of ale.

Robin halted, sensing trouble. "Where are they?"

Bell shrugged, then tossed the skin across the fire.

He caught it without thought. "Where *are* they?"

"Where you sent them," the outlaw replied.

"*Locksley?*" And then Robin understood. "You never had them!"

"We did. But they paid their toll." Bell indicated the lute case leaning against the log, then dangled Tuck's rosary from one hand. "They'll have them back, once they buy them back."

Astonishment kindled into anger. "If they are at Locksley they may never be able to buy anything back," Robin said heatedly. "Did you think I lied about the sheriff? They are in danger. He means to arrest them all. It will cost Scarlet and likely Alan their lives, and Much his hand!"

"Lying?—likely not." Adam Bell took up another skin and tilted his head back to drink before continuing. "But 'tisn't our concern what the sheriff does, unless he does it to us."

Robin hurled the skin back at the outlaw, then turned on his heel. He stopped short, but only because Cloudisley was there with the meat-knife at his throat. Beyond him, leering with broken teeth, stood Clym of the Clough, arrow nocked.

"Earls' sons," Adam Bell said lightly, "are worth more than fat friars."

Anger flared anew, fed by frustration. All manner of protests and oaths tangled themselves in Robin's mouth, but he made none of them. Nothing he said could convince these men to do anything they wished not to do; they reckoned their actions along such courses as knights and noblemen did not know. It was best to wait, to bide his time, mind his tongue, and watch for opportunity.

Robin eventually turned back to Bell. "A clever trick," he said tightly, trying to keep self-control from fraying further, "but you know as well as everyone else that my father and I are not in accord. I was disinherited; he will pay you nothing for my safety."

"Aye, well, we'll give him the chance to tell us so." The outlaw flung the skin back yet again. "Now sit down and drink with us."

Robin caught the skin but did not move otherwise. "I must go to Locksley."

"If the sheriff has gone hunting them there, he has them already. You can do nothing but be caught and thrown into the dungeon along with them—or so you say." Bell smiled companionably as Cloudisley tied Robin's wrists at his waist with leather thongs, then shoved him toward the fire. " 'Twill be dark soon, and we're not expecting to hear from the earl until tomorrow. You'd best bide with us. Sherwood isn't safe at night, now, is it?"

The Earl of Huntington put off his bedrobe and coverlet in honor of his guests, and met them all in a room not his bedchamber. There was food in abundance, give thanks to Ralph's competence, and fine wine. He himself ate little and drank less, not wishing to display his weakness with goblet and meat-knife, and let Alnwick carry the pointless conversation. Eustace de Vesci, a bluff and impetuous man, was good at such things.

But now the meal was done, the table cleared, and they all of them sat loose-limbed and at ease in cushioned, tall-backed chairs and discussed what they had come to discuss: England's new king, and their role in his rule.

Until they were interrupted.

Ralph was quiet, as always, and certainly aware of the topic, but the earls broke off at once when he came into the room. Huntington, knowing his steward would never consider interrupting without excellent reason, motioned him near immediately.

Ralph bent close. "A caller, my lord. A Benedictine monk. He says he has news of your son."

It was so baffling he did not keep his voice lowered. "What has a Benedictine monk to say about my son?"

"He spoke of outlaws, my lord."

The earl was instantly suspicious. "Was there not a monk involved with my son five years ago? Or, rather, involved with the woman?"

"Indeed, my lord. In fact, he accompanied her here."

De Vesci stirred in his chair, straightening. "I recall that! It was your son's whore, was it not?"

"Marian FitzWalter." That was de Mandeville, more circumspect, who had met her father.

Huntington refused to discuss the woman. "He is an outlaw himself, this monk. Why should I see him?"

"For your son's sake, he says."

Henry Bohun, Earl of Hereford, gestured. "Tend it, Huntington. Your son's welfare is vital."

Said de Mandeville, with a marked degree of dryness, "Especially as you and he have only just come to be speaking again."

Huntington, who had in a wholly unanticipated excess of pride, told them Robert would support them, would in fact join them, wondered uneasily now if he should have said nothing. But he nodded at Ralph and waited impatiently as his steward went to the door and asked the monk to enter.

The earl recognized him at once as the man who had indeed accompanied Marian FitzWalter to Huntington Castle five years before. This time, as the last, the monk was clearly in an agony of anxiety that he might do something wrong in front of four of England's most powerful earls. Huntington, assailed abruptly by a weakness in vision and memory, gripped the chair tightly a moment; had they not played out this scene only yesterday?

But no. The woman was not present. This was now, not then.

"Yes? " he rasped.

The tonsured monk, perspiring from nerves, was a mass of corpulence beneath the black cassock. He cast a stricken glance at the other earls from worried brown eyes, then looked at Huntington. "Outlaws, my lord. Your son is taken. I am sent to say you must ransom his freedom."

Huntington lifted eyebrows. "Must I?"

"My lord!" the monk said, shocked. "They have taken him!"

"Who?"

"Adam Bell, my lord. And his men."

"In Sherwood."

"Yes, my lord."

"They hold my son in Sherwood? Adam Bell and his men?"

"They do, my lord."

"And they send you to me with a request for ransom?"

The monk, Huntington saw, was clearly puzzled by the interrogation; had he expected the earl merely to cough up coin? "Yes, my lord."

"Why *you?*"

"Because they took us all, my lord."

"But you are here."

"I was sent, my lord, to bring you word."

"Of my son's capture."

"Yes, my lord."

"Did you *see* him captured?"

"No, my lord. But—"

"Then how can I know it is true, this tale? How can I be certain this is not some elaborate means to steal my money?"

The monk flushed deep red, then went pasty white. "I was *sent,* my lord—"

"Oh, you may have been sent. You may have sent yourself. But that does not mean there is truth in this mummer's tale." Huntington gestured. "Ralph, show him out."

The steward was startled. "My lord?"

"He is lying."

The monk now was ashen. "*No,* my lord! I swear it is the truth!"

"Then where is your proof?" The earl felt a flutter deep in his chest and stifled a cough. "And what should a good monk swear on, when he has no cross?"

The monk fumbled desperately at his cassock, seeking his rosary and cross; his face flooded with memory. "My lord, they took it!"

"Did they? Why? Was it made of gold or silver?"

The monk's face was running with sweat. "No, my lord . . . my lord, they wanted proof. To show to your son."

Huntington did something he had not done for some time. He laughed.

"My lord!" The monk was astounded.

The earl pulled himself forward in the chair. "You come to me with a tale that my son is taken by outlaws, and that *you* were taken by outlaws, and that they stole your rosary to prove to my son they had you, yet they released you to come here, which you have done, but while my son is given proof of *your* capture, you are given none of his to display to me, his father?" Huntington shook his head. "How am I to believe this? Would you? Would any man with sense?"

The monk said miserably, "It is the truth, my lord."

"It is an abysmal falsehood."

"No, my lord. They told me they would take him."

The earl pounced on that. "*Told* you they would take him."

"Yes, my lord—"

"But had not taken him yet?"

"No, my lord—"

"They *intended* to take him?"

"Yes, my lord—"

But you have no proof that indeed they *did* take him, only that they said they would. Yet you were sent to collect a ransom."

"I was, my lord."

"For a man who may not be held at all."

"My lord, I do swear—"

"I care nothing for what you will and will not swear, you wretched man. This is a lie—" Coughing overwhelmed him.

"*No*, my lord!"

The earl drank wine to still the spasm, then continued hoarsely. "But even if it were not, I would give you nothing. Not for this Adam Bell and his men. Not for yourself, who is as much an outlaw as he."

"My lord!"

Huntington lied with precise enunciation and emphasis, and without compunction. "I disinherited Robert of Locksley five years ago, monk. I have no son. There is no one to ransom."

De Mandeville was startled into speech. "My friend, perhaps you should not act so hastily."

Huntington made a sound of disgust, thrusting himself back into the chair. "It is a lie, Geoffrey. An attempt to deceive me, for money. Well,

I will not tolerate such." He glared at the monk. "Go back into your woods to whatever fool sent you and say you have failed. There will be no money, for there is no son."

"Tonight?"

"Tonight. At once. Now."

The monk crossed himself. "My lord, I do swear on my soul, which is God's—"

"*Is* it?"

"—that I have spoken only the truth."

"Then devise a better one." He gestured at Ralph. "Show him out."

Ralph did. When he and the monk were gone, when the door was shut again, Huntington allowed himself to breathe.

"My God," Bohun said. "What of your son?"

De Mandeville's gaze was sharp. "The son you told us was one of us."

"He is," Huntington said sharply.

De Vesci frowned. "Yet you told the monk he was disinherited."

"Let him believe it, Eustace. Let him say to others that we are no more in accord now than we were last year, or the year before that. I'll not have outlaws believing they may take my son captive in order to cozzen coin."

"But—if he *is* being held . . ." De Vesci did not finish.

Huntington shook his head. "Only a fool would believe it." He lifted a silver goblet and drank deeply of his wine. For the moment, strengthened by anger that he, an earl, should be used so poorly by such benighted fools as outlaws, he did not tremble.

At sunset William deLacey jogged down the stairs into his dungeon which had become of late, he reflected in mild exasperation, a place he visited nearly more often than his bedchamber. One hand clenched the heavy iron key to the cell, which he employed for its purpose with neat economy once he reached the appropriate door.

Inside he took up the Exchequer cloth he had folded away, shook it out, and spread it upon the table. From the pile of leather scroll-cases he took one up, uncapped it, slid parchment out. DeLacey unrolled it, spread it atop the painted cloth, weighted it, and began laboriously to inspect it. He sought one particular name; upon finding it, he smiled.

There was quill and inkpot nearby. The sheriff uncapped the ink, swirled it briefly to mix the pigment, then dipped the quill into it. When he was satisfied the nib carried enough ink but not so much as to sputter and spoil the parchment, he bent over the list and ran a meticulous line

through the name he had sought. Then another, then another, until the inked bar upon the parchment made the name beneath it indecipherable.

DeLacey sanded the parchment, capped the pot, set the quill aside, rerolled the parchment and returned it to its case. That done, he spent a great deal of time going through the casket containing receipts. At last he found the one he wanted, read it, tore it to pieces, and crumpled the shreds into the palm of his hand. Satisfied, he locked the door and climbed the stairs in no haste, rehearsing in his mind the explanation and order he would give to Sir Guy of Gisbourne at first light.

Robin drank ale stolen from a shipment on its way to Nottingham from Lincoln. Robin ate venison that had been poached from the forest, and could cost a man a hand. Robin listened to stories of daring and outrageous robberies, none of which he believed. Robin complained his wrists were tied too tightly; they laughed and tightened the knots, then tied his ankles as well. Robin described each and every one of them in terms most explicitly offensive, save he did it in Arabic and none of them understood. They laughed, drank ale, ate venison, told tales embellished with equally distributed blame and insults, drank more ale, and eventually, as the quarter-moon slid behind clouds, slept. Robin did not.

In the ashen dampness before dawn he slid fingers inside his boot, withdrew the slender knife, and sliced his ankles free. He placed the hilt between his knees with the blade upright, squeezed to keep it there, then cut through the wrist bindings. He reflected wryly that if they caught him, he would explain he merely needed very badly to relieve himself, which was perfectly true.

Sherwood was their home. But he, a solitary and fanciful boy who enjoyed creeping through shadows pretending he was anything but what he was, had grown up on the hem of Sherwood's skirts at Huntington Hall, before his father razed it. He had fought a war in a harsh and foreign land, killed men, been wounded, made ill by recurrent fevers, knighted, wounded again, captured, imprisoned, beaten, ransomed by the king himself, and beaten again by Normans purportedly his fellow knights of courtesy and conscience. He was not alien to darkness, to the forest, to fighting, to killing, to pain, to patience, determination and ruthlessness, nor to the need for stealth.

The fire had burned down to a scattering of jewellike ruddy coals within a ring of stones. The clearing still smelled of roasted venison, spilled ale, and unbathed men who had feasted well. With great care Robin rose, gripping the knife. He waited, lest the shifting of his clothing waken them, but the outlaws slept on. The knots had been secure—even now loops remained around ankles and wrists—but Adam Bell had not searched him further, had not counted on live steel.

He closed his eyes, turned his head slightly, and let the night take him. The coals were banished. When he opened his eyes again the blackness had definition.

One step. Two.

He waited.

One step. Two.

He paused.

Someone beside the fire shifted, muttered in his sleep, flopped over. Robin stood perfectly still and eased his grip on the hilt, twisting his torso slightly toward the clearing. But when there was no alarm given, he eased back again, released pent breath, and ventured another step.

One more.

Two.

He was in the trees.

A twig beneath his right boot snapped. A limb briefly snagged his sleeve. He froze.

Nothing.

One step. Two.

His senses told him a tree was beside him. Carefully Robin bent, then crouched. An outstretched left hand examined the ground. He felt grass, and fallen leaves. Mostly dirt. A few twigs. With exquisite care he found and picked up each twig, then set it aside. When his searching hand told him no more twigs remained and most of the leaves were cleared from a specific area, he let his knees down. Cold ground met them, but no leaves crackled, no twigs broke.

He pressed one hand against the ground, steadied himself, then very slowly rotated into a turn. The tree was now behind him. Robin sat down. He waited. There was no sound of discovery, no noise of pursuit.

Still gripping the knife, he leaned against the tree and prepared to wait for first light, when he could see again.

Marian, having broken her fast at dawn after a night of little sleep because of Robin's absence, was engaged in more repairs to the kitchen when Hal came in and said Sir Guy of Gisbourne had come to see her. Surprised, she got to her feet and wiped her grimy right hand on her apron, taking care with her left. It was still immensely sore, still bandaged but healing.

She was unfit for visitors, but with Gisbourne she did not care. She walked out into hall, thinking inhospitable thoughts about the sheriff's steward, only to stop short, startled, when she discovered him already inside. Apparently he had invited himself in from the courtyard when Hal had gone to fetch her.

Marian had not seen Sir Guy of Gisbourne save from a distance for years. Now, face-to-face again with the short, compact man, she recalled how it was he who had given evidence against her at the travesty of a trial before the Abbot of Croxden, who was, because of William deLacey's elaborate and false tales and manufactured evidence, more than persuaded to declare her a witch. Gisbourne once had proclaimed his love for her, his undying loyalty; both had been extinguished upon learning she refused to return his feelings, and he had summarily sought to discredit her.

Courtesy therefore was not something she was willing to offer this man. Marian waited, resolutely silent, until splotchy color crept into his saturnine face. He cleared his throat, scowling. "You are to pay your taxes."

She had harbored no expectations of what his business might be. But this was astonishing. "I did pay my taxes!"

"We have no record of it."

"I did," she repeated. When he made no reply, she said, "Gisbourne, I counted out the coin myself and sent Hal to Nottingham." Marian glanced at the gray-haired servant who nodded vigorously, clearly as taken aback as she.

"We have no record of it."

"I *paid* them."

Gisbourne bestowed upon Hal a look so pointed that even a blind man could not misinterpret the meaning.

The servant turned white. "I paid them, Lady Marian! I took the money to Nottingham! I gave it over to the collector in the castle bailey!"

Gisbourne declared, "We have no record of it."

"Then your record is false," Marian snapped. "In God's name, Gisbourne, I paid my taxes!"

"We have examined the Exchequer," he explained. "We have inspected the tax roll, and the receipts. Your taxes are lacking."

She felt as if there were no other words in her mouth except four: "I paid the taxes." Then, more emphatically, "Gisbourne, I *paid* them."

"We have no record."

"Look again!"

"We have looked thrice, Lady Marian."

"Look a *fourth* time, then!"

"The sheriff has sent me to collect the taxes."

"He has already collected them, Gisbourne."

"You are to pay me here and now, or forfeit your lands."

She began to understand this was neither poor jest nor nightmare, nor had she taken momentary leave of her senses and imagined everything. Her bones turned to ice. "Forfeit my lands?"

"If the taxes are not paid."

Marian looked at Hal, who trembled with shock. She knew him; had known him for more than two decades. He had been her father's man. She did not doubt he told the truth.

She *did* doubt Gisbourne. Or deLacey. Or both.

"This is a lie," she said. "This is a ruse."

"Lady?"

"I paid them. You know I paid them. DeLacey knows I paid them. This is a ruse. This is revenge." Anger abruptly boiled up into her throat so hot and painful she wanted to spit into his face. "He set his soldiers to destroy everything I cherish within this hall, and now he seeks to take what is left!"

"You are to pay here and now——"

"I can't pay," she said, beginning to shake with outrage. Her stomach churned. "I have no money."

"Then your lands are forfeit."

"They are *my lands*, Gisbourne!"

"But forfeit, unless you pay your taxes."

She found it difficult to breathe through the constriction in her throat. She felt as if she might vomit. "He can't have them. Not my lands. Not Ravenskeep. They were my father's lands. I inherited them on his death."

"They were Crown lands, lady, after your father's death. The Crown held them in trust for you, until you married." He paused. "You have not married."

"The king gave them to me outright!"

"That king is dead."

She had paid the taxes. She had given Robin the last bit of money she had, to ransom Will and Little John and Tuck and Alan and Much. There was not a single coin left in the hall.

"Tell him . . ." Her voice shook. She steadied it with effort. "Tell him I paid the taxes. I paid them this session, and I will pay them next session, and every session after that."

"Lady," Gisbourne said, "we have no record."

"Your record is *wrong.*"

"The record is the record."

"Gisbourne!"

Gisbourne shrugged. "It was the sheriff's command."

"And one you were pleased to follow!"

He smiled. "Indeed, lady."

No money. There was no money. None in all the hall.

"No," she said.

"Then you are in arrears."

For the first time in her life she wished she had a sword, that she might open his belly with it. "Tell him I refuse. Tell him the taxes were paid. Tell him I will not permit him to take my lands."

Gisbourne reached into his sleeve and withdrew a folded parchment. He released it, let it fall to the floor. "So be it, Lady Marian. But if the taxes are not paid within a fortnight, soldiers shall be sent to escort you out of the hall." He paused. "And you will not be permitted to return."

"*My* hall, Gisbourne! *My* lands! Tell him that."

DeLacey's steward laughed. "Tell him yourself, whore. I am his servant, not yours."

Shocked into silence, she watched Gisbourne turn on his heel and stride out of the hall. When he was gone, when the hall was silent again, empty of orders and denials, of threats and sworn certainties, Marian stared blindly at the folded parchment lying at her feet.

"I paid," she said blankly. "Hal—I *paid.*"

"Lady, so did I."

She focused on him then, saw his face then, noted the stricken expression. He was as frightened as she. Ravenskeep was her home, but it was his as well.

Marian held out her hands. They shook as if she were palsied. She still felt ill. She swallowed once, then again, and felt the lump go down. She clenched her hands into her apron, ignoring the pain in her left.

In arrears, the sheriff said. Lands forfeit, the sheriff said.

Whore, Gisbourne called her.

Every mark, every silver penny, had gone to ransom the others.

She had paid the taxes. She had counted them herself. Locksley was Robin's to tend: she tended Ravenskeep. She had *paid* the taxes.

But the sheriff was the sheriff. It was his duty to collect taxes from the shire each session, from every manor, estate, village, and hamlet, to do the accounting, to write amounts and names on the rolls, to sort through the receipts, to enforce the laws of the land with regard to payment and forfeiture.

Forfeiture.

Anger, she knew, was better than terror, or she would be utterly helpless.

"Hal," she said quietly, "saddle me a horse."

"Lady?"

The trembling began to diminish. She focused only on the task. "I am going to Nottingham. I am going to the sheriff. The sheriff and I have something to discuss."

Not long after dawn, Adam Bell and his men awoke to discover their prisoner missing. Robin, crouched low in foliage, did not move except to tense *for* movement. There was shouting, swearing, accusations made, then Adam snapped at them all that they were wasting time; he could not have gotten far; he was a stranger in their forest and knew nothing of its secrets; and they had best catch him soon or lose the sweetest ransom they might ever hope for, unless they, like German Henry, captured themselves a king.

Robin purposely had decided against trying for the horse. While a mount would have carried him to safety more quickly, finding the horse in the dark would have resulted in too much noise. Trying to find him *now* would give away his presence instantly. Better to depend on his feet, slower but far more quiet, than risk discovery in the name of speed. And, for all he knew, the horse had been taken elsewhere by one of Adam's men.

He watched as each outlaw, cursing, gathered up weapons. Cloudisley, Clym of the Clough, and Wat One-Hand went, respectively, north, south, and east. It was sheer bad luck that Adam Bell, former yeoman and the one Robin least wanted to face because of his skill with a longbow, came west, directly toward his hiding place.

Inwardly he cursed and slipped the knife back into his boot. Adam Bell was on him, though he did not yet know Robin was there. Before he could discover it for himself, Robin thrust himself up from the ground and surged at the outlaw.

He caught Bell around the hips and threw him down flat on his back. Robin scrambled upright, sat on the outlaw's belly, saw the shock in the light-brown eyes, and smashed his right fist into the stubbled jaw. Then he was on his feet. Quickly he set one boot against the longbow's belly, grasped one end, and pulled upright against his bootsole with all his might. A sliced string would render the bow temporarily unusable, but Bell likely had another string; better he concentrate on disabling the bow instead.

When it cracked like a broken leg, Robin dropped the broken half and ran. Behind him, Adam Bell, dazed but conscious, shouted hoarsely for aid.

Limbs snatched at Robin, snagged his clothing; vines snared his ankles, dropped him more than once. He scrambled up, spitting out leaves and soil, and ran again, leaping downed trees, beating back branches, pelting his way through hip-high fern, bushes, and other foliage. Behind him he heard more shouts. He heard the thrum of a loosed arrow, the tattered hiss of torn leaves giving way; felt the kiss of its passing as it thudded into a tree beside him. Robin dodged aside, dove through fern, scrambled up again, ran again. An arrow loosed from an English longbow could punch through mail. At this short distance it would likely be driven clear through his body. The only way of defeating one was to avoid it. An archer needed a clear line of sight to take proper aim, and he refused to give any of them that.

He ran, ducking and dodging, swinging around saplings, rolling and bouncing up if he fell, always moving, always cutting an unpredictable course through the trees. He was absently aware of hair being snagged and yanked out of his scalp; of broken boughs stabbing into his legs; of leaves and limbs slapping at his face, against upraised forearms; of the burning in his chest. But he ran.

A creek . . . he splashed through, attempting to stay atop rocks but not succeeding: his boots now were wet. Damp hosen clung clammily to his legs. Slick mud on the other side slowed him briefly, but he leaped free, struck dry soil and grass again, and went on.

He crossed a deer track and took it briefly, using its beaten ground to gain him footing and time, but he did not stay on it. A track offered no protection; better he stick to shielding foliage.

A second arrow rattled through nearby branches. He threw himself aside, rolled through fern, came up, barely dodged a thornbush, swung under a low limb, heard an echoing shout of frustration from lengthening distance. He dove through foliage, fetched up painfully against a lightning-shattered trunk, and lay there, winded, for some time, breathing. Listening. Around him nothing moved. All was still except for the heaving of his lungs.

There were no more shouts, no cursing, no humming of arrows loosed from too close, no rattle through the trees. Only silence.

And then a bird began to sing from a branch over his head, answered by another a few trees away, and he knew he was safe.

Robin sat up slowly, wincing against small wounds now making themselves felt. The knife in his boot had shifted; he pulled it out, resettled it in the other boot; grimaced displeasure in the feel and weight of cold, soggy leather.

Now he had time to sweat. He wiped it from his face with a sleeve, then stood up. Sherwood enclosed him. No man but one who knew the forest intimately would find him, so long as he was very still, or very careful.

Robin nodded, catching his breath, then set out again at a far more decorous pace than his former headlong flight. He blessed the Godsent sense of direction that never failed him—he was "lost" as a child only when he wished to be—and headed toward the Nottingham road. He needed badly to get to Locksley, and stood a better and faster chance if he sought transport on the road.

Even if he were forced to steal another horse.

Early in the morning, not long after dawn, the sheriff was awakened by a servant pounding on his door. DeLacey, struggling up from under linen and confusing dreams, was less than pleased. He called out crossly for the servant to go away, until the servant explained that his soldiers had caught one of the outlaws.

Whereupon deLacey shot out of bed, snatched up a robe, thrust arms into sleeves, and tore open the door. "You're certain?"

The servant bobbed his head. "Aye, my lord. The soldiers brought him into the hall. He's below."

Below. By God, they had *caught* one of them! DeLacey spent a moment hunting up house boots, ran a hand through his hair, then took himself out of his chamber and strode rapidly down to the hall, anticipating all manner of punishment, where he was greeted by the grimy, gasping, blood-smeared face of Much, the miller's son, gripped firmly between two soldiers.

DeLacey stopped short. "The others?"

"No, my lord," one of the soldiers said.

He bit his tongue on a sharp retort. "This is the *only* one you caught?"

"Yes, my lord."

He glared at Much, then shifted attention back to the soldiers, who were clearly tired and as clearly wary of his mood. They had spent more than a day searching for five men and had only caught a boy. "Where are the others?"

"In Sherwood, my lord."

Sherwood. *Damn* Sherwood, who swallowed men whole and almost never gave them up. Anticipation turned to ash in his mouth. He had hoped for Will Scarlet, who had murdered Prince—now King—John's men, and whose escape had embarrassed the sheriff deeply; or for the minstrel, whom he had decided to have castrated while his daughter watched. But the miller's half-wit son was the least of them, and not worth waking up for

"Throw him in the dungeon," he ordered, gesturing dismissal, and took himself back to bed.

Twenty

Robin slipped down through the trees, jumped a ditch by the side of the road, stopped long enough to get his bearings—Nottingham yet lay ahead, and beyond that Huntington Castle—and set out at a good pace for Locksley Village, which lay beyond Huntington at the edge of the forest. He did not walk long; ahead he saw a cart full of cut and bundled wood hitched to a slow-ambling mule, praised Allah before he remembered it was permitted again to thank God in perfectly common English, and broke into a jog.

The woodcutter, persistently hailed, looked over his shoulder, considered, and obligingly pulled up his mule. Robin arrived, markedly less winded than he had been on his race through the forest, and requested a ride. A cart was not so fast as a horse, but was swifter and decidedly more comfortable than feet which were rapidly blistering inside still-wet boots.

"Going to Nottingham," the woodcutter said.

Robin was not. But that was closer to his destination than where he was currently. "I'll hop off at the turning," he said.

The woodcutter shrugged and jerked his head toward the back of the cart; Robin boosted himself onto the back as the mule was told with a slapping of reins and muttered command to move along again.

After several pokes in the back, he rearranged a portion of the piled wood and sat more comfortably, legs and feet dangling off the back. He considered removing his boots to see if there was remaining water to empty out, but decided against it lest his feet protest having wet leather put back on. Instead, he occupied himself picking tangles and twigs out of his hair as well as tree sap, working thorns free of his clothing, and inspecting several scratches on his forearms he didn't remember getting.

Then he heard hoofbeats.

He looked up sharply. The approaching horse and rider were bound the same way as the cart, likely to Nottingham, and therefore Robin, riding on the back and facing the way they had come, had an unobstructed view of the oncoming rider.

He thanked God this time in Saxon, Arabic, *and* French, just to be certain the Deity understood.

Robin grinned. With tangled hair, torn and stained clothing, mud- and dirt-soiled hosen, he was hardly the picture of an earl's heir, a knight, or even a minor landowner. No one would think to find him perched upon the back of a woodcutter's cart, idling his way along the Nottingham road, even a man the sheriff might otherwise have ordered to arrest Robert of Locksley. And perhaps had.

He waited until the rider and his horse were even with the cart and very close, paying no attention to the lowly peasant woodcutter and his disheveled apprentice, and then Robin stood up in the back of the cart.

"Gisbourne!" he bellowed into the steward's right ear.

Gisbourne started visibly. Before his mount could react, Robin flung himself bodily from cart onto horse, straddled the rump quickly, yanked the knife from his boot, slung one arm around Gisbourne's chest to grab the reins, then quietly set the blade at the steward's throat.

"Gisbourne," he said, "I need your horse."

"I am a *knight!*" the steward cried, who had not had time to see anything more of his assailant than a leaping body.

Robin grinned. "So am I."

Gisbourne stiffened, then hissed at the touch of the knife. "You? I think not. Knights don't ride with woodcutters, hold knives at other knights' throats, *nor* do knights steal other knights' horses."

"They do if they need them more than the other knights do. But you are not truly a knight, Gisbourne, just a man whose family bought him the title and sent him into the world, where he became a lapdog to William deLacey."

Gisbourne was outraged. "Who *are* you?"

Robin ignored the question, asking one of his own. "Has the sheriff arrested anyone at Locksley Village?"

"Locksley Village!"

"Answer me, Gisbourne."

"He sent soldiers there."

"Did they arrest anyone?"

"They haven't come back yet."

He relaxed minutely. Perhaps there was still time— But Gisbourne, who felt the lessening of tension, abruptly sank his spurs deep into his mount's sides.

The horse, being told to run in the most emphatic of ways, and being told to stop in an equally emphatic way as Robin sharply reined him in, proceeded to do the only thing left for a horse to do.

He reared.

Robin, sitting bareback atop a slick and abruptly vertical rump, slid off unceremoniously, dragging Gisbourne with him, and landed flat on his back as the horse swung around in alarm. Gisbourne landed atop him. The horse, no more content to have two bodies sprawled against his front hooves than giving him conflicting orders about going or not going, attempted to leave. Immediately.

Like all horsemen who preferred to ride than walk, Robin had not released the reins. The horse, employing far greater weight and power than the man at the end of the reins, backed up frenziedly, dragging him in his panic out from under Gisbourne's body.

As the horse moved, Robin flipped over, doubled up, and dug in his knees, but was pulled flat again onto his belly with an *oof* of expelled air, then onto his side as the horse, responding to the weight that still clung to the reins, sashayed abruptly sideways. Fortunately for Robin, he sashayed sideways into the startled woodcutter's equally startled mule, which responded to the offense by reaching out a gaping mouth to grab a hunk of the horse's shoulder.

Robin, muttering imprecations at the horse, used the distraction to scramble to his feet, whereupon he leaped to grab the bridle and unceremoniously jerked the horse away from the mule.

Gisbourne was on his knees. Robin, standing at the stirrup of the snorting, rolling-eyed and quivering—but newly submissive—horse, suggested he stay there.

The steward, getting his first good look at his assailant, stared at him with mouth agape, patently astonished. "Locksley!"

Robin said lightly, "From one knight to another, I still need your horse."

"That's *stealing!*" Gisbourne shouted, but by then Robin was in the saddle and departing at a gallop.

DeLacey waited as soldiers brought the boy up from the pit dug below the floor of the dungeon. It required the unlocking and peeling back of an iron grate from the stone floor, and the lowering of a crude wooden ladder that the prisoner was required to climb in order to get out, thereby putting himself into the waiting arms—or at the waiting end of sword or pike—of the soldiers fetching him out.

Much was nimble coming up the ladder; he was a cutpurse and quick with hands and feet, so the sheriff knew better than to take no precautions. The boy was grabbed and yanked up at the lip of the hole, shoved unceremoniously against the wall, where his hands were tied behind him. Then he was hauled upright again and positioned before the sheriff, bent elbows clamped in the hard grips of soldiers.

"Tell me," deLacey said.

Much stared at him from beneath lank hair, vacant-eyed.

The sheriff smiled. "Boy, you may be a half-wit, but the *other* half undoubtedly understands questions. Tell me where they are."

Much made no answer.

"Where did they go?" deLacey asked.

This time when Much said nothing, the sheriff brought the back of his gloved hand across the boy's face. Blood burst from his mouth and spilled down his face to drip onto his tunic. He gasped in shock, eyes shying away as if he were cornered prey; and deLacey, who rather considered himself the predator, repeated his question.

Bleeding, Much said nothing.

DeLacey sighed, then struck again. He felt the fragile bones of the nose break. Much stared wild-eyed a moment, and then the pain swamped him. He moaned pitifully, began to cry, and sagged in the soldiers' grasp.

"My men took you near Locksley Hall," deLacey said. "They went into the forest, found you, and took you. The others must have been nearby. I want to know where they went."

Much continued to cry.

"Boy, I can do more than this. I can break every bone in your body. Is that what you wish?"

Great gouts of blood painted Much's face, dripping steadily onto the floor. He was taller now than the sheriff recalled, but quite thin. It would be nothing to shut a wrist into larger hands and snap the bones.

But he had hoped it would not be required.

"Where?" he asked again.

Much, trembling, with tears carving runnels in the blood and grime, said through the blood in his mouth: "Forest."

"Where in the forest?"

"Forest!"

DeLacey shut gloved fingers upon one of Much's ears. "Boy," he said, "I can rip this off your head."

"Forest!" Much shouted.

"Where in the forest?"

"Don't know! Don't *know!"*

Which was entirely possible. Questioning of the soldiers who had caught the boy suggested the outlaws had fled all at once and with no apparent direction in mind. If they had believed themselves safe at Locksley Hall, they might not have thought beyond a roof and a meal.

"Where?" he asked again, pinching the ear more tightly.

Much sobbed. "Ran," he said. *"Ran."*

DeLacey opened his mouth to ask another question, but heard footsteps on the stairs. He waited, watching the boy tremble, as the soldier came down.

"My lord, the Lady Marian FitzWalter is here."

DeLacey released Much's ear and turned sharply. "Marian?"

"Yes, my lord. She insists on seeing you at once."

The sheriff entertained the brief but perversely satisfying image of having her escorted into the dungeon to meet with him, but decided against it. She had been in the dungeon before, had been in the pit before, and likely would not be much intimidated.

Instead, he glanced at the bleeding boy, then stripped off the one glove. "Put him back," he said, and as the rope was cut from Much's wrists and he was shoved unceremoniously toward the ladder, deLacey climbed the stairs. Smiling, he murmured aloud, "I believe Gisbourne delivered my message."

* * *

Marian had been in the great hall of Nottingham Castle countless times. But the last visit had been no more pleasant than this one; Robin and the sheriff had engaged in a deadly swordfight. Then the hall had been thronged with Prince John and his entourage, with soldiers, with Scarlet, Little John, Tuck, and Alan, with the castle servants, while everyone watched in perverse fascination as a lord high sheriff attempted to kill a king's knight.

That one of them had not died was attributable only to the timely arrival of King Richard, ransomed home from imprisonment, whose appearance ended the fight as well as Prince John's plans to take and keep the throne. But the Lionheart, unaccountably jovial in view of his brother's plot, had in short order forgiven that brother certain follies, pardoned Robin and his friends from whatever crimes deLacey insisted they had committed, and declared Marian no longer a ward of the Crown but a free woman with a manor and lands of her own.

Now William deLacey, whose arm she had broken five years before in front of all those people, was trying to take that manor and lands away from her.

She paced. The groin-vaulted ceiling arched high over her head, balanced upon massive stone pillars marching the hall's length like a line of faceless, limbless soldiers. Rushes snagged at the hem of her chemise and summer-weight mantle until she kicked them out of the way, cracking bones the dogs had missed beneath the soles of her shoes. She scowled at the dais with its trestle table and high-backed chair, where the sheriff sat to pronounce sentence upon such people as he declared criminals, subject to punishment. Some men died. Some lost hands, and homes. Some men languished in the dungeon cells. Others were turned out upon the roads to fend for themselves, often becoming outlaws in order to live. And all of their women and children lost a provider, no matter the means.

Marian wondered if outlawry or begging was what deLacey expected of her, stripped of her manor and lands.

"No," she said aloud, kicking away another bone.

"No?" It was deLacey's voice. He came into the hall from a side door, pleasant smile upon his face. "And what are you denying, alone here in my hall?"

"You," she said. "Your efforts. Your attempt to ruin me."

He strolled casually to his chair upon the dais and paused there a moment, one hand resting lightly upon a carved finial. "But I understood you were ruined some time ago, when a certain murderer abducted you from the fair. Then, of course, you further ruined yourself by taking up with a pack of outlaws and a disinherited knight."

"They were—and are—far more honorable than you."

"And do you reward them for it?" He arched brows in delicate implication. "All of them? I had not believed Locksley the type to share his whore, but perhaps your appetite is such that he must."

Ice descended upon her. She felt it sheathing her bones, creeping out to encase her flesh. A lady would not answer the challenge, most particularly not with the sweet venom she employed, but if deLacey claimed she was no more a lady, she would satisfy his opinion. "And how is your arm?" she asked, reminding him sweetly that she herself had broken it with a blow of a crutch. "Did it heal well? Does it ache in the winter, or before a storm? I understand it is far more difficult to recover from injury when one is of an advanced age."

It told. His mouth tightened and the flesh beneath his eyes crimped into a deeper fretwork of lines. But he merely smiled. "Have you brought the taxes?"

"I have brought no such thing," she retorted. "I owe you no taxes. I paid my taxes."

"The rolls show you did not."

"The rolls lie," she said. "Or you do."

"But *I* am the sheriff. It is *I* who determines what has been paid, and what is yet owed. It is *I* who makes the accounting. Do you wish to contest it with me?"

"I do."

He stood behind the chair now, forearms folded upon its back as if he were at ease. And perhaps he was. It infuriated her. "Marian," he said, "this ends. Ravenskeep shall be mine."

It took immense effort not to spit the words at him. "It shall not."

"Then pay the taxes."

"I paid them."

"We have no receipt saying so, nor is your name entered in the rolls."

"Then there has been a mistake."

"The mistake is yours. You neglected to pay your taxes."

"*I paid.*"

"But I am not so cruel as you might claim," he went on. "I have given you a fortnight to pay them. I could take Ravenskeep now, today, yet I give you time to comply."

She opened her mouth to answer, but a shout from behind her

interrupted. "Lord Sheriff!" Marian spun. Gisbourne stood there. As he saw her his face went white, then red, and he fixed his gaze pointedly upon deLacey. "My lord, will you come out?"

The sheriff frowned. "Come out where, Gisbourne? This is my hall. You may speak if I say you may speak."

Gisbourne glanced again at Marian, then away. He seemed nothing so much as distressed by her presence, as if what he had to say would embarrass him before her. "Will you come out, my lord?"

DeLacey considered it, sighed, then assented. As he crossed the hall and passed by Marian, he gave her the flicker of an amused smile. "We may continue our pleasant discourse when I return."

Marian, who had a great deal more to say to him, gritted her teeth. She wished she had a crutch, that she might break his arm again.

Or better yet, his skull.

Upon reaching Locksley, Robin went immediately to the hall, which he found deserted except for the two servants who cared for it in his absence. The woman and her husband said yes, the sheriff's soldiers had indeed come looking for Little John, Will Scarlet, and the others, but none of them was present so none of them was found, though the soldiers had immediately gone into the forest to search for them there.

Robin frowned at that; surely the others should have reached the village before the soldiers arrived. *Unless Adam Bell delayed them longer than I thought.* There was also the possibility that they had spied the soldiers before reaching Locksley.

The husband went on to explain the visit from the sheriff's men had caused some hardship for the villagers because the soldiers had been merciless in their questioning and hasty search but that the bruises would heal and the things broken could be mended. And while Robin was relieved to hear little damage had been done to villagers and property, he was left wondering just where Alan, Tuck, Much, and the others had gone and how they fared.

"Sherwood," he murmured absently when he went back outside to the waiting horse. He had no idea *where* in Sherwood they might have gone, but he believed it likely they had sought shelter in the depths upon discovering soldiers had reached the village first; and at least they *had* discovered it first. He reflected with irony that perhaps it was fortunate they had run into Adam Bell and his men despite the enforced visit and toll. Otherwise they might have been in the village when the soldiers arrived.

Robin, looking at the fringe of forest encroaching on the village outskirts, knew Locksley was no more a safe place now than Ravenskeep or Nottingham. Short of leaving the area entirely, they had no place to go but into Sherwood.

He left orders with the couple to welcome his friends should they arrive, though now he doubted they would, and then took himself back the way he had come on Gisbourne's horse. The others were safe from arrest; so long as he was required to ride past Huntington Castle on his way back to Ravenskeep, he might as well call on his father to acquaint him with his decision regarding Marian, marriage, children, earldoms, and treasonous activities designed to bring down a king.

DeLacey was more than a little annoyed that Gisbourne felt it necessary and appropriate to drag him out of his own hall. But when the steward spilled his news in a rush, he understood. *"Locksley* stole your horse?"

Gisbourne nodded vigorously. "I saw him clearly, my lord. Nor did he attempt to hide himself. He said he was taking my horse, and so he did."

For once Gisbourne had demonstrated good sense in not sharing his news in the hall where Marian would hear. DeLacey did not want her to know—*yet*—that Locksley had stolen Gisbourne's horse, lest she find some way to delay his arrest; and he thought it would be delicious to return with her outlaw lover in chains and parade him before her.

He smiled, anticipating her reaction. And then he laughed, clapping the man on his shoulder. "Well done, Gisbourne! Now we have proof and I have cause. Go back outside and tell the castellan to have soldiers readied; we ride for Huntington Castle at once." He paused. "You as well, Gisbourne. I want the earl to hear what you have to say."

The steward was startled. "I have only just got here! I had to ride a woodcutter's cart all the way in."

"Well, now you shall have a horse to ride instead." He paused. "I trust this time you'll be able to keep it."

"But—" Gisbourne blurted as he began to turn away.

"Yes?"

"Will the earl listen?"

"He shall have to. Have we not an unimpeachable witness, the Sheriff of Nottingham's very own seneschal?"

Darker color flooded Gisbourne's saturnine face. "It is somewhat embarrassing, my lord, that he was able to take my horse. I am a knight."

DeLacey was exasperated. "*Jesu*, Gisbourne, do you think it matters to me that he embarrassed you? You will say what you saw to the earl himself, and I shall arrest Locksley. This is *two* horses he has stolen in less than a fortnight. He has proven himself an outlaw before witnesses, and I shall treat him accordingly."

"My lord—?"

Once again, the sheriff turned back. "What is it?"

"Do you intend to take Ravenskeep from Lady Marian?"

DeLacey, distracted, frowned; what had this to do with the topic? "I do."

"Then I would request that the manor and lands be given to me."

It was astonishing. "To *you!*"

"Yes, my lord. I have a family. I am a knight. I should like to have a knight's lawful portion." His chin rose, thrusting itself against the air. "I deserve it."

"*Do* you?"

Gisbourne said with no inflection, "It would remove your daughter from beneath your roof."

For a moment deLacey was so stunned he could only stare at the man. And then he began to laugh.

"My lord, I am serious!"

DeLacey eventually regained self-control. "But Gisbourne, then she would be under *your* roof. Constantly."

The steward's face was implacable. "She would be there, under that roof. I would be here. Under yours."

Still amused, deLacey said, "I should have you beaten for such disrespect. She *is* my daughter." Gisbourne did not so much as blink. "But I understand, Gisbourne. Oh, indeed I do." He grinned again. "I shall consider it. But first we have to arrest Locksley so the lady has no one to whom she might turn in order to get coin to pay the taxes."

"If she did," Gisbourne said, "you would only find another way of saying she hadn't paid."

"Wise to that, are you?"

"My lord, I am wise to all of your schemes."

DeLacey cocked an eyebrow. "That, Gisbourne, is perhaps not something of which you should boast."

"No, my lord. Of course not."

Satisfied that the warning was heeded, and pleased to contemplate hosting Sir Robert of Locksley in his dungeon, the sheriff went back into his hall to don soldier's gear. He wanted the earl to remember who ruled Nottinghamshire, and by what authority, when he took his son and heir into custody.

Marian was struck by the sheriff's manner as he returned to the hall. Wariness set in when she marked the smile on his face and the glint in his eyes. His body spoke of anticipation and incipient activity, and when he saw her watching him his smile broadened.

"What is it?" she asked.

DeLacey paused long enough to strike a pose of delicately measured surprise and arched one brow. "Are we friends now that you should be privy to my business?" But he overrode any answer she might make. "Outlaws," he answered succinctly. "I regret that we shall have to continue our discussion at another time, but my duty is to the safety of the people of Nottinghamshire."

As he strode by her, Marian inquired acidly, "Including those who are overtaxed, or who have already paid but are accused of not paying?"

"Another time, Marian," he called over his shoulder. "Run along home—" But he turned briefly to bestow upon her a warmly insincere smile. "Though it may not be your home beyond a fortnight." And he was gone before she could summon another retort.

Marian wanted to howl with frustration. She did not know whether to believe him regarding outlaws; it could be a ploy to avoid her. But Gisbourne had been sincerely agitated, and certainly there were outlaws aplenty in Sherwood, and she thought it likely deLacey had told the truth. It made her no happier.

She could leave. But she had not yet said everything she wished to say to the man she had come to detest with unflagging venom. Irresolute and angry, Marian stood in the middle of the hall and scowled fiercely at the high-backed chair and trestle table set upon the dais. "Were I man," she declared, "we would settle this at sword's point."

A harsh, accented voice said, "An honest solution. But more difficult than you might expect."

Marian, startled, turned sharply, one hand pressed to her breast. At first she saw only the shape of the man, the height, the breadth of shoulders, the thick mailed torso beneath its belted surcoat. Then she saw the sword, the wide hand resting upon its pommel, and his face.

Last time she had seen him, little had been visible in the deepening of dusk and the first wash of torchlight. But here in the hall, coif slipped to his shoulders, the stubbled jaw shaved so that the flesh was unshadowed, she marked the man far more clearly. He was a veteran soldier incarnate, with a hard face showing the nicks and blemishes of battle, the pocks of childhood disease, the implacability of dark eyes accustomed to seeing death in all its forms. Silver threaded near-black hair. One heavy, level eyebrow was bisected by the thin slash of a scar.

Mercardier, Robin had named him.

"You went to France," she said, then realized how inane it sounded.

He ignored it. He walked toward her steadily, the hem of his surcoat rippling against the greaves warding his shins. When he was but two paces away, he drew the two-handed broadsword.

Marian tensed to recoil as it hissed from the sheath, but he merely turned it in his hands and offered it to her. She stared at it, then looked into his face.

His tone was rough. "Take it."

"Why?"

"Take it."

When Marian made no effort to do so, he stepped forward with more speed than she would have expected from a man of his mailed bulk, and before she could protest, he grabbed both of her hands and wrapped them around the hilt. She was trapped as he imprisoned them, making certain she grasped the sword lest she drop it on her feet.

And then he released it. The weight was astonishing.

"Hold it," he said curtly. "Do not dull the edge against the stones."

She was a knight's daughter. She had been taught that a properly balanced sword was at home in a trained man's hands, neither too heavy nor too light. But she was a woman, not a man, and this sword, this massive Norman sword forged for a ruthless mercenary whose only code was killing for coin, dragged itself downward despite her grip.

She recalled what her father had taught her: the round end was a

wheel-pommel, for balance; the channel down the center of the blade—
in this case, there were two—was a fuller, and had been inscribed. With
effort—the sword was over a yard in length—she kept the blade from
touching the floor beneath the rushes. Her forearms flexed and trembled.

He stepped closer. One hand caught and lifted the tip, so that the
point rested squarely atop the long leather belt wrapped around his hips.
Were the sword to pierce, it would cut through the wall of his abdomen.
"Now," he said, "settle it."

Marian stared at him.

"Settle it," he repeated.

"Settle what?"

"Your dispute about the taxes. You said you would settle it at sword's
point."

"With the *sheriff*," she explained. "I have no quarrel with you."

"But you do. I am sent from the king to collect the taxes the sheriff
has collected, to escort them to London."

"You?"

"*Oui, madame.*"

It was impossible to hold the sword up any longer. Her arms ached
with it. "Take it back," she said. "And tell me why you insisted I hold
it."

He shifted the tip aside, then stepped forward to close one hand
around the grip even as she gave it into his keeping. "Because you do
not respect the sword, or the means to use it." The big man sheathed
the weapon. "It is easy, no, to say you will kill a man? To say you will
settle a dispute at sword's point? But the truth is different. It deserves
respect, as does the sword."

It occurred to her that perhaps he was mad. But she did not think
so. Robin had once said something very similar about the bow, when he
gave her a lesson. One was to respect a weapon before one should use
it.

"I have cause," she said plainly, "and you are not privy to my business
to know what I should and should not respect."

"The sword is *my* business. As is war."

Marian smiled thinly. "Do you believe a woman cannot have cause
to wage war?"

"All battles are not the same," he said in his accented rasp; she
thought perhaps he was conceding the point, though she wasn't certain.
His eyes were dark and unreadable. "Were you a man, you might indeed
settle it with a sword, had you the courage and the will. But that is more

difficult than you believe, and better left unspoken unless you understand what such things require. Instead, you had best use a woman's weapon."

"A *woman's* weapon?"

"Your tongue," he said; with Robin, it would have been irony. With this man, it was fact as he saw it. "Tell me your dispute."

"You are the sheriff's man." She weighted her tone with contempt. "It serves no purpose."

"I am *the king's* man. And it serves every purpose."

Marian studied him, marking the hardness in dark eyes, the granite of his face. He was, she thought, immense of commitment and immovable in flesh, a dangerous enemy. She found herself very glad he and Robin had fought on the same side.

"My war," she said, "is with William deLacey. Taxes are the excuse. But he has shaped that excuse into a weapon—a sword, if you will, for which he has no respect—and holds it to my throat."   .

"Tell me, madame."

But before she could speak again, deLacey himself came into the hall. He had put off his fine clothing and wore serviceable mail, spurs, and carried a sword. He was taller than Mercardier but considerably slighter when judged against the mercenary's bulk. Abruptly whimsical, she decided deLacey was a dagger, thin-bladed and honed to a sharpness that would cut into viscera before anyone knew. Mercardier was the very weapon he carried: a massive, heavy broadsword designed not to puncture, not to slice, but to batter flesh into pulp and to shatter all the bones.

"Ah, I see you have met," the sheriff said lightly. "Perhaps Mercardier might acquaint you with the expectations of a kingdom requiring taxes of every individual." The light in his brown eyes was pronounced. "In fact, why not inspect the tax rolls yourself, Marian? I shall have Gisbourne escort you before he departs with me; Mercardier shall stand guard, of course, so I need not fear any attempt on your part to add your name unlawfully." He smiled, tugging on a glove. "In the meantime, my duty lies elsewhere."

Marian gritted her teeth against a furious shout as he walked from the hall. And then she became excruciatingly aware of Mercardier's examination of her expression.

Looking at him warily, she wondered if he measured her the way he measured a man before he killed him: with contempt for the puny opponent.

"Place no trust in that offer," she advised with some heat. "If he gives me the means to examine the rolls, then be certain he has had them altered."

Mercardier said nothing.

"You know neither of us," she accused, "to believe without question that he is right and I am wrong."

"What I believe, I believe. Right or wrong does not matter, madame. I am to escort the tax shipment, not enforce its collection." With a slight inclination of his head, he added, "Let us go down, madame."

She said it reflexively. "Down?"

"To the dungeon, madame. The sheriff has locked in the king's taxes, and locked out those who might otherwise wish to steal them."

Marian, who had herself once been locked in deLacey's dungeon, was not pleased to visit it again. But she would offer no hint of that displeasure before this man. "Down," she agreed.

Twenty-Two

Huntington was closeted with Alnwick, Hereford, and Essex when his son came into the chamber. At first blush he was pleased that he would be able to present Robert to the men again; and then he saw him clearly, and was appalled.

"My God, Robert! Have you been wallowing with the pigs?"

Robert stopped short just inside the door, taking note of the chamber's inhabitants. A certain fixed and determined expression abruptly faded into the still implacability the earl found so infuriating.

"Forgive me, my lords," Robert said with careful courtesy. "The past day and night have proven somewhat—discomfiting."

"I should say so!" Huntington snapped. "How dare you present yourself before these men in such a state!"

Geoffrey de Mandeville observed mildly, "He may have good reason."

"He does," Robert affirmed with a trace of irony, and glanced appreciation at Essex. "Nevertheless, forgive me—"

"Have a bath poured," Huntington commanded, interrupting. "And I believe there is appropriate clothing here as well."

There was, of course: Robert had left most of it behind when he departed Huntington Castle for Ravenskeep. But the earl would not speak so specifically; such things were best kept private.

"My lords," Robert said with a slight but correct bow, and took himself away.

"Forgive me," Bohun said lightly when he was gone, "but you might have asked him *why* he was in such a state."

Eustace de Vesci, with eyebrows arched, inquired with amusement, "Is he consorting with outlaws again?"

A sharp retort rose to Huntington's lips, but he suppressed it. Instead, he rose, gathered the robe more closely about his frail body, made his apologies and excused himself from their company. There were questions to be asked of his son, but he would not do it before them.

By the time he reached the bathing chamber down near the kitchens, the earl was out of breath. He was somewhat mollified to learn that Robert had indeed ordered a bath, and was waiting with every appearance of resigned patience as the servants filled the cask. He sat framed within the deep sill of a splayed window, one foot on the floor while the other, bent knee hitched up and wedged against the embrasure, waggled idly. Fair hair was haloed white against the sun-drenched glass. As he saw his father enter, he crossed his arms, leaned more heavily against the dressed stone, and raised both eyebrows beneath a tousled lock of untidy hair.

Huntington took his lead from de Vesci. "Are you consorting with outlaws again?"

Robert's mouth twitched. "Not intentionally."

"How *un*intentionally?"

"As any man does," he answered. "He is robbed."

"You were robbed?"

"*And* taken captive."

The earl sat down abruptly upon a bench as the servants moved in and out with buckets. "Do you mean that corpulent monk told the truth?"

"Tuck." Robert smiled briefly, as if imagining the tableau.

"He came to me and said you were taken, that the outlaws wanted money."

"And so I was, and so they did."

"But—I refused." The earl felt tightness in his chest and rubbed idly at it through the clothing. "I disbelieved him."

"Ah."

Huntington did not care for the noncommittal tone in his son's voice. "Do you blame me for that?"

"How can I? I did not know you had refused until this moment."

"And now you are here."

"Yes."

"So a ransom was not necessary."

"No."

Huntington shifted uneasily. It was simpler to discuss such things with Robert when he was angry, not so cool, self-controlled, and inwardly amused. "How did you get free?"

"On my own. It was not required that a king ransom me."

Huntington took that as insult and attack because he had not immediately paid the Saracens the ransom to free his son from captivity six years before. But only because King Richard had paid it first. "Robert—"

"I am well," he said, as if that was the question his father intended to ask.

It was not, and the earl chafed beneath the mild sting of guilt and implied rebuke. "If you would present yourself to powerful men as my heir and a man who may be trusted with vital information, you would do best to comport yourself accordingly. This includes appearing before noblemen as one of them, not clad as some workman's apprentice!"

"They seemed disinclined to take my appearance as insult."

"But it is insult regardless, Robert. You are not a peasant. You are not a yeoman. You most certainly are not an outlaw—"

"No?"

Robert *was* amused, and at his father's expense. Huntington glared. "We are speaking of your future as an earl."

"I think we are speaking of your pride as an earl."

He was astonished. It struck him that his son obviously felt *he* was very much in control of the situation. The earl found this not only annoying, but disturbing. "How dare you speak to me so?"

"To make you recall that I hold my own opinions. And that they may not always be in accordance with yours." Steam from heated water rose between them. "I am not William or Henry, my lord father, to answer your every whim without thought, to *be* you even if I wear a different face. I am the disobedient son, the youngest and unimportant son, the one you so disliked you left me—praise God *and* Allah!—to my mother. Had my brothers lived, we would not be having this conversation." The tone was infinitely casual. "But they are dead, my lord, and I am after all the only son you have. Now you must listen."

"I '*must*' do nothing!"

"You may choose not to hear me, you may dismiss me, you may believe me a fool, but you must listen."

"I have heard nothing of any value!"

Robert tilted his head slightly, as if listening to an inner voice. "Then perhaps I am not fit to *be* your heir."

Only immense self-control—and the desire not to punish him in front of servants—prevented the earl from stalking across the chamber to strike his son. It was this very attitude, this unflagging and unsubtle intransigence, that had so appalled and infuriated him when Robert was a child. Then it had been a simple matter to beat the boy into submission, or banish him from his sight for weeks on end, but the child was now a man, and was, as he had noted, the only son Huntington had. The line ended with Robert.

Unless the seed in his loins produced a suitable grandson.

The earl rose. "When you are presentable again, come to me and the others. We must speak of important matters."

"Indeed we must," Robert agreed, "though our topics may differ."

Huntington waved away a drifting wisp of steam. "There is only one topic of which to speak, Robert, and that is the future of England and the role you shall play in it, whether as my heir or the sire of my heir."

Robert slid down from the sill and began abruptly to strip off disheveled clothing. "Then perhaps our topics are the same after all."

Huntington had no wish to see again the permanent welts carved into the flesh of his son's back; only peasants and felons were whipped. He departed at once.

Marian followed Gisbourne down the staircase into the dungeon. The dimness she found oppressive and overfamiliar; she recalled with unsettling clarity how she had once before inhabited the sheriff's dungeon, left in a damp pit of a cell with a scattering of straw, a lone malodorous bucket, and rats for company. She suppressed a shudder as she descended, but could not persuade her face to assume an expression other than stark distaste.

Behind her was Mercardier, chopping his steps so as not to overtake her. She was aware of sounds despite the lack of speech: Gisbourne's keys clinking, iron against iron; the echo and scrape of footsteps; the faint metallic song of Mercardier's weaponry and fittings. In the distance, she heard moaning.

"How many are down here?" she asked; the sheriff's steward should know.

Gisbourne reached the bottom of the staircase and moved aside, shrugging. "Thirty-six."

"Thirty-six! Charged with what crimes?"

"Poaching, mostly," he answered as she stepped beyond him. "But cutpurses and murderers, too."

"What do you do with them? You cannot just leave them here!"

"Most often," he said, "we execute them. Or, with poachers, chop off a hand. Punishment, and lesson."

"And what shall they do then but poach again?" she demanded. "In God's name, Gisbourne, how would *you* live if you lacked a hand?"

Mercardier joined them, and Gisbourne ignored her. He led them to a cell even as Marian skirted the iron-grated pit, and unlocked the heavy, studded door. He eased it open, then moved aside so Marian might enter.

It struck her then that he need only shut the door, lock it, and she was imprisoned again, made helpless by the sheriff. But she dared not show nervousness to Gisbourne, who would no doubt enjoy it. Marian moved past him into the cell, and saw the chests and caskets of varying sizes and shapes stacked against the walls.

It astounded her, that so much money could be gathered from rich and poor alike in the name of a king's taxes. When so many of the latter needed it to live, and often turned to poaching in order to eat.

Gisbourne joined her in the cell, opening leather scroll cases. Mercardier stood in the doorway, blocking it.

She waited as the first parchment was removed from its case. Gisbourne unrolled and spread it on the table, weighting the top corners, then motioned for her to inspect it.

Marian looked at the parchment, then at the scroll cases stacked along with the chests of coin. In this cell was contained a portion of the power that allowed a realm to function, the names of every resident of the entire shire. This *was* Nottinghamshire, and England as well, bordered by the confines of a small, dank cell.

"The sheriff is waiting," Gisbourne said. "I leave you with Mercardier; and do recall there are guards."

Marian's mouth twisted. "You consider me a thief?"

"Perhaps not yet," he answered, "but you are certainly a whore. And whores cannot be trusted to behave honorably."

It took her breath away, that such hatred could be so blatant. Dislike, contempt, resentment: all, she had encountered. But she had also in these last days encountered a malicious violence aimed specifically at her in the destruction of her property, and now Gisbourne wielded words without a pretense to courtesy or prevarication, without implication, merely stated the ugly and unadorned truth as he saw it.

She watched him go, aware of a cold and dreadful hole in the pit of her stomach, of a reaction so strong she felt physically ill. To be so hated ... *I have made two enemies,* she thought with a cold clarity that astonished her. *And one of them could destroy me.*

Perhaps, in this cell, using parchment and pen in place of sword and knife, he already had.

"Begin, madame," Mercardier said.

She turned back abruptly, lacking all grace; turned away from Gisbourne's poison, from the too-watchful eyes of the mercenary, and began to inspect the tax rolls. Tears stung her eyes, but none of them fell.

William deLacey felt a welling up of anticipation almost sexual in nature as he rode into the cobbled bailey of Huntington Castle. He had disliked Robert of Locksley long and well for a number of reasons, but he found himself nearly as pleased to discommode Huntington himself. Earls were powerful men that sheriffs did well not to cross, but deLacey discovered within himself the appetite to kick fuel from Huntington's fire with a well-aimed and malicious boot toe. Nottinghamshire was *his* to administer, and so it should be for a man of good Norman blood; he needed no English nobleman to undermine his authority with a word here and there, the brief but autocratic gesture from a hand, a haughty glance down the bony, prominent nose. DeLacey had proof. DeLacey had the authority. DeLacey had the honor-bound *duty* to arrest a man who stole horses from other men.

The Lionheart was dead. John was king, and John had given the Lord High Sheriff of Nottinghamshire the order to do as he saw fit to secure the shire for the good of John's rule. Huntington had plotted against John before. DeLacey could not arrest the earl, but the son was his.

He reined in at the head of a small troop, but did not dismount at first. "Remember," he told Gisbourne in a low but steady voice, "tell the earl precisely what happened. Explain to him the outrage of having your horse stolen by Robert of Locksley, a fellow knight—"

"It *was* an outrage!"

"—and how such dishonorable behavior betrays all the codes and oaths King Richard held so dear. Do not permit the earl to cut you off, nor dismiss you. You are my steward, a knight, a man of honor, a husband and a father, dedicated to the preservation of the laws of England as codified by Henry the Second, Richard's own father, and you cannot permit such lawlessness to go unpunished. The law protects everyone equally, Gisbourne. If a man steals a horse—and in this instance, *two* horses—he must be punished for it."

"I do understand, my lord."

"Be certain of it, Gisbourne. No one shall stand in the way of our sworn duty." DeLacey glanced at his men, bade them follow but offer no threat beyond their presence unless he ordered it, then jumped down from his horse and strode up the stairs to the archivolted door. A peremptory gesture brought Gisbourne to heel. Behind the steward came the eight mailed and helmed soldiers.

The sheriff did not wait on ceremony. He caught the first servant who came within reach, demanded to know where the earl and his son were, and was told with only the merest hesitation. Smiling grimly, he went directly to the indicated chamber, trailing mailed and armed authority in his wake.

Ralph, the earl's steward, was in the corridor as deLacey arrived. Before the man could offer up the protest his shock delayed, the sheriff unlatched the door, shoved it open so widely and so firmly that it crashed against the wall, and marched straight in.

He stopped short even as the soldiers came in to flank him, because instead of one earl he confronted four.

William deLacey, silently, began to swear.

Gisbourne, not so silently, began his determined explanation of his misfortune and declaimed in loud, ringing tones the identity of the man who had stolen his horse.

In view of the exalted company bearing witness to this declamation, all the sheriff could do was think, *Not now, Gisbourne.*

Huntington, sitting stiffly in his high-backed chair, listened to the explanation and accusation without comment. There were no shocked gasps from him, no angry denials, no contempt. He merely listened, mouth crimped small and tight.

When Gisbourne was done, the earl looked directly at deLacey and said, "My son has been with me all this day."

"No, my lord!" Gisbourne cried. "He stole my horse but a matter of hours ago!"

The silence was deafening. And into it came the slightest sound of metal on metal: eight soldiers stood flanking the sheriff, prepared to aid in the arrest of the Earl of Huntington's son. And now he could not use them.

DeLacey flicked a glance at the others in the chamber. He knew them. Had met them. Had done their bidding five years before, when they had been robbed upon the road. The earls of Alnwick, Hereford, and Essex, three of the most powerful men in England. Geoffrey de Mandeville had been King Richard's Justiciar, had participated in Richard's coronation. His honor could not be impugned.

And yet he, as did the others, met now, once again, with the Earl of Huntington. Because, the sheriff knew, John was king. They were Arthur of Brittany's men, certainly. And they would offer no support to a man whose office and authority was held at John's behest.

Lastly, deLacey looked at the fifth man who stood apart from the others, not sitting with them as if in discussion or agreement, merely present. He once again wore fine clothing befitting an earl's heir and the natural confidence of a man born to rank and privilege, of a knight honed in battle, of a king's confidant. Of the Lionheart's friend.

His hair was damp, combed back somewhat severely from a face so often masked by apartness, by an inner ironic amusement. The architecture of the face was clearly visible instead of softened by shadow, by hair, made stark by a resolution, by a stillness deLacey equated with a man sworn to himself, to the dictates of his conscience no matter what the odds. He recalled seeing that face, that man, that resolution on a wagon bound for Lincoln, stealing money after a flurry of arrows had struck down every soldier. This was not a weak man, in spirit or commitment. He lacked the overwhelming hugeness of Little John, the bulk and power of Mercardier, but there was skill in him, and danger, and the promise, if cause were given, of violence.

"My lord," deLacey said to the earl, though he looked nowhere save at Locksley, "I am arresting your son."

Huntington inquired, almost idly, "Are you?"

Now he did look at the earl.

"Are you?" Huntington repeated in the same cool tone. "Do you name me a liar?"

"Not you, my lord, but—"

"Then I say again: my son was with me all the day."

He had brought soldiers for this. They waited for the order.

Geoffrey de Mandeville, earl of Essex, asked very quietly, "Shall you accuse each of us of lying?"

Eustace de Vesci, eyes alight with quiet mirth, hitched his shoulders in a slight shrug. "He was here all the day."

Henry Bohun merely looked at deLacey and nodded once.

The room held too much power, too much nobility. It festered like a wound, and would not bleed itself free of contagion unless he himself lanced it, which he would not, dared not do. William deLacey knew the stories of one hundred Gisbournes, no matter how heartfelt, no matter how true, would not win acknowledgment and aquiescence from these men. Not when the scope of their goals was the welfare of a realm and the service of a king.

One earl he would risk. But not four. Not together. John himself would not risk that, not at a time when he needed such men as this in the infancy of his sovereignty, and would disavow such precipitous action even if deLacey believed he might manage it.

Gisbourne glared at Locksley. "You stole it. A knight's horse, stolen by another knight. You *stole* it."

DeLacey saw and seized the opening. "Search the stables," he ordered his men. "If the horse is found, well . . ." He smiled kindly at Huntington, setting the barb. "Then I can only assume you are mistaken, and your son was not with you quite *all* the day."

The earl, trembling with outrage and increasing frailty, thrust himself to his feet. "You shall do no such thing!"

The voice was quiet. "Let him," Locksley said. "Let him search every stall, every paddock, every dovecote, kitchen, and midden, if it pleases him to do so. Let him search my very bedchamber—or even yours, my lord father."

By that, deLacey knew defeat. There was no horse to find.

"Where did you leave him?" Gisbourne demanded of Locksley. "What did you do with—"

The sheriff cut him off with a quick slashing gesture. He wasted no more breath on the earl or his son, made no threats or promises. He simply turned on his heel and marched from the room. With him came his soldiers, deprived of their duty even as he, once again, was deprived of his pride.

"My lord," Gisbourne said as he followed him through the hall, "what shall we do?"

"Go home," deLacey said sharply.

"But—"

"We go *home*, Gisbourne. We've lost this battle. For now. For today." In the bailey he retrieved his horse's reins. "But not for good."

Twenty-Three

The Earl of Huntington stared hard at his son as the door thumped closed behind the last of the sheriff's men. "Do not lie to *me*, Robert. Is it true you stole this horse?"

The answering smile was crooked. "Gisbourne may be a fool, but in this case he is a truthful fool."

"Why ever would you steal his horse?"

"Because *mine* was stolen, and I required one. Immediately. I needed to reach Locksley before the sheriff did, or as soon thereafter as possible."

The earl glared. "What does it matter that the sheriff is in Locksley?"

Robert wandered to a chair and collapsed upon it. His hair, nearly dry, loosened from its combing to fall against his shoulders. "It matters when he intends to arrest my friends."

Huntington scoffed. "Those peasants." He sat down again, clutching the arms of the chair as he lowered himself. "The horse is not here?"

A tilt of the head indicated direction. "I left him in a copse of trees on the hill behind."

"You *knew* deLacey would come?"

"I suspected he might."

"So," de Vesci observed with no little amount of irony, "you not only consort with outlaws, but you are yourself one."

"Nonsense!" Huntington snapped, rapping a fist on the chair arm.

"And have been," Robert confirmed easily, "when circumstances require it."

"Robert!"

His son was neither repentant nor reluctant to confess. "I have stolen coin for my king's ransom. I have stolen horses when haste was required. I have even stolen baubles and chains of office from the men in this chamber."

The others started, exchanging sharp glances. Henry Bohun, astounded, murmured, "That was *you?*"

"It was; the moment, which is too complicated to explain just now, required it. But so did Richard's ransom." He smiled briefly at their nonplussed expressions, then continued speaking to his father. "You may certainly name me outlaw and be perfectly truthful. But what I have done was done for good reasons, and is no more reprehensible than what all of you discuss here in this chamber. I have broken laws. I will break others, I do not doubt. But when you ask me to join you, when you invite me to support a conspiracy to remove John from the throne, you also invite me to commit treason."

The earl shifted in his chair. "Robert—"

"Tell me, my lord father, why I should accept your rebuke for my actions when what you advocate—and attempt to involve me in—might cost me my head?"

Geoffrey de Mandeville said quietly, "You risked your life on Crusade."

"That was war."

"So is this," de Vesci stated. "Perhaps not fought with swords and the invocations of priests before battle is joined, but it is war nonetheless. And this time we fight not for God, not for Jerusalem, not for Richard's kingly might, but for England herself. Because John will surely destroy her."

"We cannot be certain of that."

"Good God, Robert, how can you say such a thing?" Huntington demanded. "You know what manner of man John is. He is mad! When thwarted he throws himself into the rushes and foams at the mouth, like a diseased dog. And how many times did he attempt to overthrow King Henry, his own father? He conspired with Philip of France to keep his brother imprisoned in Germany! This is the man you wish to hold England?"

"Richard was none too kind a man, when the temper was on him," Robert replied quietly, face gone still. "I watched as he ordered nearly three thousand Saracens killed *after* we had won the city. Kings do what kings believe they must."

"As do we," Bohun said. "We are committed, Robert. You may join us, or not, but we shall go forward."

"And if there is another way?"

"What way?" de Vesci demanded curtly. "Shall we *ask* him, do you think, to treat England gently?" The bluff man shook his head in vigorous denial. "He bleeds her for coin, in the name of vanity."

"So did Richard, in the name of Crusade."

De Mandeville, who had known the Lionheart better than all in the chamber save one, frowned. "You were in his confidence, Robert. How can you betray his memory so?"

"Because my memory is untainted by hero worship and misguided zeal," Robert replied promptly. "Oh, my lords, do believe me in this: I loved the king. I worshipped the king. I killed for my king, and thanked him for it. But he was also a *man*, our Lionheart, one of the Devil's Brood just as John himself. And Richard was as prone to sins as anyone save a saint."

Bohun asked, "And you would serve John as you served his brother?"

Without hesitation Robert of Locksley vowed, "I will serve no man ever as I served the Lionheart, in battle or in peace. Certainly not John."

De Vesci leaned forward intently. "Then join us. Serve *us* in the name of Richard."

But Robert shook his head. "You don't need me."

Huntington felt the first glimmer of alarm. He had believed his son won. "Of course we need you."

The fine brows arched in delicate irony. "Why?"

"Because we are the heart of this realm," the earl declared. "Without us, John cannot rule. United, we shall overcome him. Divided, we shall fail."

With precise and measured emphasis, Robert declared, "But you don't need *me.*"

No one answered. No one stirred. No one looked at their host, only at his son.

Huntington saw it for the first time in the faces of the others. They wanted Robert. They needed Robert. They required the Earl of Huntington, with his inherent power and wealth. But Robert was the man they desired to *be* the earl.

It struck him like a blow. *They believe I am dying.*

He looked at them, read it in the careful blankness of the expressions, in the quietude of their bodies and the determination not to look at him lest they reveal their thoughts.

Men died. No matter how titled, no matter how wealthy, no matter how powerful. And when such men as he were involved in vital matters, men as could alter the future of a realm, continuation and stability were requisites.

From him, neither was certain. He was old. He was ill. Requisites no longer applied.

But even in Robert there was no promise of continuation, of stability.

He threatened to turn outlaw as the moment dictated. He threatened to wed a woman who could bear no children. He threatened to spurn a heritage other men might kill for. He had promised to be, and was, a son not even a father might command. Only a king, and that king was dead.

Huntington chafed, infuriated by infirmity. He needed *time*. Time to live. Time to retrain Robert, like a recalcitrant but valuable horse. Or time to train that horse's promising colt.

He needed time to die.

Huntington looked away from the men he called his friends to the man they wished to call fellow conspirator in the preservation of a realm. For the first time in his life he permitted his son to see the truth of his fear: that he might die alone, a man with no son to inherit the legacy he had worked long and hard to protect so that his life would count for something. "Join us," he said hoarsely. "Robert . . . please."

Marian, strained eyes aching with fatigue, allowed the parchment to roll itself up. She pressed fingers against both sockets and gently rubbed. "It won't be here," she said in weary frustration. "I know it. He has struck it off. Or has had the pertinent roll redrafted."

The mercenary's harsh voice rasped in the cell. "Then why search?"

She removed her hands and glared at him. "Because he is lying. Because I must. Because if I don't search, if I overlook any possibility, he will win."

The bisected eyebrow quirked. "Is it winning and losing that counts in the matter of taxes?"

Marian's throaty burst of laughter was rich with contempt. "Winning and losing counts in everything, Captain. Before God, *you* can ask such a thing? You fight for coin!"

"I am paid whether I win or lose."

"Precisely," she agreed. "You have no 'side,' and also no conception of what I confront." She studied his face, marking the hard, unkind bones, so very different from the finer architecture of Robin's features. "Have you land, Mercardier? A home? A wife? Children?"

His dark, pocked face was schooled to blankness. "None of those things."

Her own tone hardened. "Then you cannot comprehend what it is to have something you treasure threatened by another."

"Including my life, madame?"

She shook her head, examining his imposing person, his indefatigable posture. "I doubt your life is in danger, Mercardier. Ever."

He remained expressionless. Mute.

Marian took up the rolled parchment, smoothed its edges, pushed it back into the case and found another, uncapping it to slide out its contents. "He threatens me, does my lord sheriff. He has before, in small, quiet ways, but never was there anything of value he could take. Certainly not my pride, and my reputation was ruined long ago. But now there *is* something of value he may take. He has found the weapon, Captain. And be certain he will use it."

"So you said before. I invited you to explain. You have not yet begun."

She clutched the uncased parchment, hearing its crackle of protest against the tightness of her fingers. "Explain to you what lies between William deLacey and me that brings us to this war?"

"The whole of it, madame. You see, I have never known a man to declare war on a woman, nor a woman"—his gesture encompassed the cell—"so willing to take the field herself."

She looked into his cruel face, into the opaque eyes, and knew what he had not said. "You believe I am lying."

Mercardier did not reply.

She put a snap into her voice, as akin to command as she could. "Do you not?"

The faintest narrowing of his eyes indicated he recognized what she did. "Madame," he said in his accented voice, "he is the lord high sheriff of Nottingham. You are but a woman."

" 'But a woman,' " she echoed.

"And a woman others name whore."

Marian muttered a harsh, succinct phrase she had learned from Robin, who had been more than a little chagrined when she demanded a translation. It was an utterly vile vulgarity, couched in the Saracen language.

But she had forgotten Mercardier knew it as well.

"And with a viper's tongue in her head," he added.

"Woman's weapon, yes? So you said in the hall."

The mercenary crossed heavy arms across his mailed chest. The Crusader's cross high on his shoulder rippled as he moved. "Tell me the tale, madame. Convince me that what you claim is true: the lord high sheriff of Nottingham, charged with the welfare of the king's own shire, has joined battle with a woman."

Marian turned abruptly and swept the parchments and scroll cases tumbling from the table onto the floor. When it was clear she swung back and, despite the encumbrances of chemise, hitched herself up onto the tabletop. Perched there gracelessly, uncaring of propriety or decorum, she stabbed a rigid, commanding hand at the single chair. "Then perhaps you had best sit down, Sir Mercenary. This tale requires time. Even a man such as you may find it . . ." She swept a pointed glance around the cell. "Taxing."

Mercardier's level brows flew up beneath a ragged lock of near-black hair, then came down again. With no hint of amusement, he said, "I served as the Lionheart's personal bodyguard, madame. I am accustomed to standing."

She let him have that victory, but offered another pass in the lists. "And do you expect to find my tale *entertaining?*"

"I do not, madame. Locksley will tell you I find nothing entertaining."

Marian pondered that a moment. She thought perhaps he matched irony with irony. But she did not know him, and could not be certain.

And so she told him what had begun it all, this war between a man and a woman, between a lord high sheriff and a dead knight's daughter; explained with laudable brevity but also a clipped intensity why William deLacey's stance that Marian FitzWalter had not paid her taxes was merely the latest weapon he had found to levy against them all: knight's daughter, earl's son—and five men now sought without respite despite the Lionheart's pardon of them.

Robin knew they would come. He had seen it in their eyes, the careful examination of his words, tone, and intent. But he had expected all three to descend upon him, not merely one strolling casually up the path.

And they had chosen well.

He sat in idle reflection upon a bench within the walled kitchen gardens. He had emptied his mind of such things as earls and kings and countries, thinking instead of sons, of daughters, and the legacies of fathers looking along the years from infancy to the child's adulthood. When the shadow fell across the pathway before his feet, he nodded acknowledgment but did not look up.

The Earl of Essex said, "I helped crown Richard."

Inwardly, Robin winced.

"I helped Richard protect the laws of this land."

He made no reply.

"I helped raise the ransom to buy him back from German Henry— though I do confess I did not realize that a certain knight-turned-outlaw would increase my contribution." The faint dryness of the tone brought Robin's head up. He looked into Geoffrey de Mandeville's aging but still handsome face, into blue eyes fading but still capable of weighing a man's worth. "And I joined with other men to plan a way to prevent John from stealing his brother's throne while Richard was imprisoned."

"Richard was still king," Robin said quietly. "But now he is dead, John is king, and what you plan is treason."

"If we lose."

Robin looked at him more sharply. "That is twice I have heard such said. Does no one believe in the moral issue of right and wrong? Does only the winning count?"

"In this case, yes."

Belatedly, Robin shifted on the bench and gestured de Mandeville to be seated. Essex accepted the invitation, stretching out booted legs as he settled his spine against the wall. He did not speak again.

The silence was oddly companionable, for all that what lay between them was an offense that could cost them their heads. But Robin knew there was more.

De Mandeville offered it. "You said you believed there was another way."

Robin nodded. "John may be half a madman, if what they say of his fits is true, but he is not entirely a fool. He needs you, my lord. All of you. His reign is but days old, and there are unruly barons to think about, and Arthur of Brittany, and Arthur's mother, and even Arthur's grandmother. Eleanor never favored John. And if *she* should take Arthur's part, John may be relieved of his crown by his own relations."

De Mandeville's mouth twitched. "Thereby saving our heads?"

Robin sighed. "The tales told claim the Devil's Brood nearly killed one another one hundred times over when the old king still lived. What is to say it will not happen now?"

"And would you then support Arthur?"

He shut his eyes. "All I wish is to live in peace. Quietly. Away from court, away from kings, away from battle."

De Mandeville said gently, "And captivity."

His eyes snapped open. After a moment Robin managed a smile. "My lord, do you refer to the Turks? Or to my father?"

The earl laughed softly in appreciation. "It is difficult for heirs. Indeed, and I should know: I was one myself."

"But you were *born* to it, my lord. I was not. I was born a third and last son. Had my brothers lived, I might have been bound for the Church."

"And instead you served God on the field of battle in the Holy Land. God—and your king."

"My king," Robin agreed, "who named John his successor."

"Ah, but not in everything."

De Mandeville sounded too certain of himself. Robin went very still. "What do you mean, my lord?"

"It is true he left *England* to John. But he left the balance of his lands and all of his money to Arthur."

Robin, astounded, stared.

The earl crossed his arms and offered, "John is king in name only. All monies collected should go to Arthur."

He felt a chill of foreboding slip down his spine and sat up abruptly. "But that is sheerest folly!"

"It seems to be fixed in the blood," Essex observed mildly. "Old King Henry promised England to each of his sons many times over."

"But Richard became king."

"Because Richard was strong enough to take and keep her, Robin. Geoffrey was dead. John, too soft, too fickle. But Coeur de Lion was warrior enough to assert his claim. By dint of personality, he conquered England and won her people. Even you, *Sir* Robert, who rode to battle at his side."

"No," Robin said idly, "Mercardier rode at his side. I was somewhere behind him."

"Robert—"

He slid neatly past the reprimand, returning to the topic. "And now Richard echoes his father by parceling out his kingdom to more than one man."

"Arthur is a twelve-year-old boy. He cannot win on his own. But there are the Bretons, led by his mother—and there is Eleanor of Aquitaine."

"King in name," Robin murmured, staring thoughtfully into the distance.

"You said you believe there might be another way."

"Rather than risk treason and execution? I do."

"And all monies collected are to be sent to Arthur."

"So you have said."

"Do you expect John to permit that?"

Robin laughed. "Likely not! And I suspect the sheriff will be hard-pressed to get the money safely to John, once word goes out."

De Mandeville asked lightly, as if he inquired which vintage to drink, "Is it outlawry to take back from a thief that which belongs to another man?"

After a startled moment of perfect stillness, Robin released a breath of amusement. "John called it so. Richard pardoned it."

"Arthur, I daresay—or Arthur's grandmother, once he is king— would do the same."

Robin rose. Walked two paces away. Then turned back. "My lord of Essex, you are the second person who has counseled me to commit a crime for which I could be hanged."

Geoffrey de Mandeville, who had crowned a king of England, stretched his legs and made himself more comfortable upon the bench. "And if Arthur loses this family quarrel, the rest of us lose our heads. Dead, I should think, is dead."

"My father would disinherit me."

"If you are dead, does it matter?"

Robin cast him a scathing glance.

De Mandeville, smiling sweet as a babe, bent and plucked a wildflower from the path's edge, then inspected its blossom with deep consideration. "If you will not serve us by being the Earl of Huntington, serve us another way."

"What, by becoming an *outlaw?*"

The blue eyes were steady as he looked at Robin. "Judging by what the sheriff's man accused you of, and by what you yourself confessed to us regarding the missing horse and the theft of our 'baubles,' I should say you already are one."

"I stole the horses because circumstances demanded it—"

"Hors*es?*" de Mandeville emphasized in amazement. "There was more than one?"

"—and I stole your purses and chains of office to convince real outlaws I was one of them—"

"*That* is why?"

"—and I stole the tax shipment because it was meant for Richard's ransom and John was stealing it for himself," Robin finished. "There was purpose to all my actions."

"So a peasant might say who poaches the king's deer to feed his family," Essex argued without heat. "And if you believe there is no good purpose to preserving England, then your father would do well to disinherit you and go to his grave rejoicing that he sired no such son."

It took the breath from his body. When he had it back again he said, "You are formidable."

"We fight how and as we may," de Mandeville said simply. "We owe that much to England."

"I gave England two years of my life and the blood of my body."

"Pittance."

"Pittance?"

"How many years of his life did Hugh FitzWalter give England?"

Shocked anger boiled up. "Unfair, my lord! Marian's father has no part in this."

"But he might," de Mandeville said, "had he not died in the name of God, his king, and his country in the land of the Saracen."

Robin, who had witnessed that death, who had seen the head struck from the body, who had felt the hot spurt of Sir Hugh FitzWalter's blood upon his face, could find no answer among the swarm of words in his mouth. There were too many to speak, too many, and all of them offering evidence of his own shame.

Geoffrey de Mandeville rose, set a hand briefly on his shoulder, then walked away. Robin, shivering beneath the light of a cooler, kinder sun than that of the Holy Land, sank down onto the path and buried his face in his hands.

Marian studied the hard, dark face before her, looking for anything akin to comprehension, possibly compassion. There was none. Mercardier, formerly Coeur de Lion's captain of mercenaries, seemed neither appalled nor moved to sympathy by her summary of how she and William deLacey had come to such a pass.

She had been raised to care about others, to desire fairness in the world, to believe wrongs should be righted. Her own father had commited himself to the cause of God and his sovereign, eventually surrendering his life for that commitment. But she was coming to understand that many people believed such things as fairness and righted wrongs were impossible, not worth concern, and certainly not worth any effort. And here was proof before her even in the guise of a man who had gone on Crusade.

"Do you believe none of it?" she asked.

"It is not my place to believe or disbelieve."

"Then why did you *ask?*"

"To understand what would move you, a woman, to go to war against the sheriff."

She eyed him narrowly. "Surely it is my right to do so—even though I *am* a woman."

His tone was touched with only the faintest trace of scorn. "Have you no man to do your fighting for you?"

"My man," she said icily, "fought for his king. As you well know."

Mercardier held his silence, imperturbable.

Marian studied him. "Do you care about nothing, then? Nothing save coin, and the employer who pays you?"

Without irony, he said, "I am a mercenary, madame. What would you have me be other than a hired soldier?"

"And does that cross on your shoulder mean nothing?"

A still man always, he became akin to stone.

Marian prodded. "Well?"

In cold tones, he said, "I am a mercenary. Some answers must be paid for."

She slid off the table, yanking her chemise into order once again. "I begin to understand that you fight your *own* war, Captain."

"I, madame? Do you mean the taxes?"

"I do not. I mean your opinion of yourself."

For the first time Mercardier smiled, albeit it was a slight one. "My conscience is not battlefield."

"Have you one? I thought not." She paused. "Unless that be hired, too, perhaps."

He evinced mild surprise as she approached him in the open doorway. "Are you done inspecting, madame?"

"I am."

"You have not read all the rolls."

"I think it is impossible to do so. I would wager the roll that once contained my name is not even in this cell."

He moved aside, permitting her exit. "Then what shall you do?"

Marian slipped by him into the dungeon proper. "Find my own weapon."

"What weapon, madame?"

She paused near the cross-hatched grate in the floor before ascending the stairs. "Would I be foolish enough to tell the sheriff's man what weapon I might choose?"

It seemed somewhat to irritate. "I am the king's man, madame. Not the sheriff's."

"In all things?"

"In the matter of the taxes."

"Then you are the king's man *and* the sheriff's man, because deLacey is John's creature. He uses you, Captain. Be certain of that."

Mercardier opened his mouth to answer, but it was another voice entirely that she heard, thin and muffled. "Marian?" And again, from deep in the floor beneath her feet. *"Marian—?"*

"My God," she blurted, dropping to hands and knees beside the grate. *"Much!"* She peered down through the iron lattice, trying to see him, but the shadows were too deep and the nearest torch illuminated only a narrow portion of the pit. "Much—can you come into the light? Let me see you!"

She heard a rustle of musty straw, the shuffle of feet. The light was poor, but she made out a shape that was his. He turned his face up, though little was visible save a wan glint of dulled eyes and smears she recognized as blood.

"They beat—" Marian grabbed the bolt and attempted to wrench it back. The lock held firm, clanking against the iron. "I'll have you out, Much. I promise!" Still kneeling, thick braid dragging on the floor, she craned her head to look up at Mercardier. She did not plead, but ordered. "Get him out. Now."

"I have no key, madame."

"Then fetch the key from a guard. At once!"

Mercardier stolidly made no reply.

She sat back on her heels, hands befilthed with grime. "This is a boy, Captain! They have beaten him bloody, and for no cause!"

" 'No cause'?" Not Mercardier: the voice was different, the accent. She realized with a start of dismay it was William deLacey speaking as he descended the stairs. "I have every cause, Marian. He is a cutpurse. A poacher. An accomplice in the robbery of tax monies." Torchlight silvered the gray in his curling brown hair, limned the pleased amusement in his face as he reached the bottom of the staircase. "And he withholds information on other criminals."

She scrambled to her feet. "This is a travesty! You don't care about him—"

"Quite right."

"You only mean to use him!"

"Again, quite right. But he refuses to tell me what I wish to know."

"And so you *beat* him?"

"Perhaps you should note that he still has both hands, Marian. A bloodied nose is surely better than the alternative."

"He's a boy!"

"And thus the wrists are easier to sever." He still wore mail and spurs. There was a strange glitter in his eyes, an odd febrile tension in his body, as if he had been bested in a battle and badly needed to release the frustration of defeat. "Tell me, Marian, would you buy him?"

It astounded her. "Buy—?" But she dismissed the reaction because he desired it, because he sought to provoke. "With what?" she demanded. "With the money I lack because I paid my taxes?"

He struck a thoughtful pose. "Ah, but there is yet something of value you may use to buy this boy."

She laughed curtly. "Surely not my body!"

DeLacey's brows arched in mild surprise. "Indeed, surely not. Too well used, I fear." He said musingly, "No, not flesh."

And she knew.

Knew.

Comprehension sickened her. It took the breath from her lungs. It filled her heart with such wintry emptiness, her soul with such fierce pain, that she thought she might crack into a thousand pieces.

But a life was a *life.*

Marian did not flinch, nor did she hesitate. She knew she had to do it, and why, and that she would do it again and again if it preserved a life. "Yes."

"Yes?"

"For his life, yes."

"How do you know what this price is?"

"I know."

"Are you certain?"

"I am."

"Then declare it."

She gritted her teeth. "For the release of this boy—with no more violence visited upon him!—I will give you Ravenskeep."

DeLacey reached for the keys at his belt and unhooked the ring. "You are certain?"

"Yes."

Smiling calmly, he knelt, inserted the proper key, turned it. The lock fell open. "You are *quite* certain?"

"Yes."

He removed the lock and slid the bolt back. "Say so," he commanded.

With exquisite precision, leaving him no room for prevarication within, for reinterpretation of the terms, she declared, "For the release of this boy, *with no more violence visited upon him,* I will give you Ravenskeep."

DeLacey's expression was oddly serene. "He is a cutpurse, Marian. You yourself witnessed his attempt to steal *my* purse."

"Yes," she said. "Release him."

"He stole the tax shipment."

"Yes."

"You admit all this?"

"I admit also that he was pardoned by the king himself. Release him."

DeLacey peeled back the iron grate and paused, holding it upright. "But that king is dead."

"Fetch him out, Sheriff."

"In exchange for Ravenskeep."

"I said so. Yes."

"You are certain, Marian. Certain of your course. Certain of its worth."

"Yes!"

The sheriff said gently, "Then perhaps you should join him below."

She had expected no such ploy, even from deLacey. *"Join* him—?"

He dropped the grate back down with a crash even as Much cried out in incoherent despair. "You have just attempted to bribe an officer of the Crown, Lady Marian." DeLacey shot the bolt. "Moreover, the bribe offered is property that in a fortnight shall be forfeit to the same Crown." He locked the bolt and rose, looming over her. "They have completely corrupted you, have they not? Robin Hood and his men. You would do anything for them."

"And you would do anything *to* them!"

"But I am the king's man—the *living* king's man—and I have the authority." He smiled. "While you have nothing but a foul reputation as an outlaw's whore."

She understood at last what it was to be impotent, and weaponless, and utterly helpless, in the face of such provocation that would move even a saint to murder.

Even a woman.

"In a fortnight," he said, making certain his voice carried into the pit, "I shall plan a celebration. You may attend, if you wish, though I doubt you will do so. Because in fourteen days you shall forfeit Ravenskeep, and the boy below shall forfeit both hands."

Much's wailing shriek harrowed the soul. All the flesh rose on Marian's bones. "You *cannot.*"

DeLacey made no reply.

She could not believe him. Not in this. Not Much. Not Much's *hands.*

But she knew this man. He was obdurate. He was vengeful. And his expression victory incarnate.

From the dark pit below, Much's sobs were palpable.

Yet again, Marian dropped to her knees. She locked fingers into the cross-hatched iron. "We'll have you out, Much," she said over the sound of his anguish. "I vow it. I promise. Do you hear? *I promise.*"

DeLacey clamped a hand around her arm and jerked her to her feet. "Enough," he said. "My God, you are cruel . . . you feed the boy on false hope!" He steered her roughly toward the staircase even as Much sobbed below, then pushed her up the first three steps. "Go now, or I shall put you with him so you may weep and wail together."

She caught her balance upon the stairs as he released her. DeLacey had turned away; all she saw was his back. But she was aware of eyes, of dark, pitiless eyes, and raised her own to meet Mercardier's.

She was cold. Deadly cold. And well beyond anger. "Surely," she said, "the blood you spilled for King Richard was cleaner than this."

He was unruffled. "I spill no blood here."

"Swear it," she challenged, trembling, "by that cross on your shoulder. That you will spill no blood for this whoreson, nor abet him in revenge."

Mercardier said, "This is not my war."

"It will be," she told him. "That man will make it so."

Huntington, standing on the hall steps of his own castle, watched his son come up from the kitchen gardens. His head was slightly bowed, his posture tentative. The earl had not seen him so in years. Robert was nothing if not stubborn, and content within his body when declaiming his convictions.

It gave him hope. He cared not at all for the concerns his son might have, the regrets; if Robert joined them, his presence was well worth a bit of temper, even a certain petulance. That, the earl could deal with. It was the quiet implacability, the commitment to his unpredictably wayward conscience, that tested Huntington's patience.

But Geoffrey de Mandeville had gone to speak with him, and Huntington held great hope that at last his son had been made to see reason, to comprehend the need. Essex would convince him. Essex had exerted no small measure of control over the Lionheart.

Robert came up to the hall, deep in thought. The hair, now dried of its washing, fell loosely against his shoulders, and Huntington abruptly was put in mind of his late wife. There was nothing effeminate about Robert, but the same feyness, the same cool apartness, echoed what in his mother the earl had found incomprehensible. But the woman had borne him a trinity of healthy sons, and he had found it simpler to let her withdraw into her fancies and fantasies. When she took Robert with her, the earl at first protested, but he had never liked the boy; and William and Henry had been enough.

The earl saw himself noticed. Robert halted at once. His expression, oddly, was irresolute. "Well?" Huntington asked.

"My lord?"

"Has Essex made you see sense?"

"Sense?" His son's smile ghosted briefly across his face, was gone. "I think . . . yes."

"Ah." An upsurge of satisfaction lent a lilt to the earl's voice. "Then you will join us."

No answer was offered.

Alarm replaced satisfaction. "Robert—you *do* mean to join us!"

"I mean to marry," Robert said, "and where I desire."

This was not what the earl had expected. *"Her?"*

"Her."

"But—she has no role in this! We are speaking of England, of the future of a realm, of putting a boy upon the throne in place of a man, and you speak of marrying a whore?"

Robert sighed. "I came here to tell you my decision, as I promised. I mean to marry her."

"She can bear no children!"

"That is her grief," he said steadily, "and mine. And be certain it is genuine. But it does not concern you."

"Grandchildren," the earl snapped. "That is my concern. You deny me grandchildren." His chest ached as if a blade pierced his vitals. Futility, utter and absolute. "I should have disinherited you five years ago," he blurted hoarsely. "Indeed, I should have done so!"

Robert shut his eyes a moment. "I am going home," he said softly.

"This is your home!"

"It never was. Huntington Hall was my home. You razed it to build this monstrosity."

"Robert—"

"I am going home," he repeated. "To Ravenskeep."

"To *her* home."

"Yes."

"Robert." His throat ached with it. "Robert, I beg you—"

"No."

The tentativeness, the irresoluteness, was gone. In its place was the man the earl could not begin to fathom. Only the anger, the immense frustration, that he could not have the ordering of his own son.

"I shall do it," he said, as a roaring came into his ears. "I shall. And Ralph shall bear witness. No lands, no title, no money, no power. Nothing from me. Nothing from any of us who were your ancestors."

Robert said nothing.

"No honor. No respect. No peerage."

In silence, Robert bore it.

The pain was tangible, but he would not retreat. "I will have it known what you are: disinherited. *Attendre.*"

Beneath the white-blond hair, hazel eyes, fixed wide as if he scribed the words on his soul, were unblinking.

"I shall have Ralph write it up and deliver it to you at the whore's hall." He took pleasure in calling her that: *whore*. Because he and his son had gone beyond such things as even bland, false civilities. "You had best go now," Huntington said thickly. "Nothing here is yours, nor will anything of mine be at your behest. If you desire a horse, I suggest you retrieve the one you stole."

Robert made as if to mount the steps, to move past him. The earl's abrupt gesture stopped him short. "My clothing," he explained. "I will change out of these and take back what I came in."

A cough threatened to burst from the earl's chest. "No," he said with as much contempt as was in him to employ. "It is a parting gift I make you: keep what you wear in memory of your mother."

That pierced the armor as nothing else had. The flesh of the face thinned to translucency, went pale as fine-worked parchment. All the bones were visible in a stark, bitter bleakness.

And so he understands. Huntington said, "All that you knew, all that you had, is denied to you." And as Robert made to turn away, he asked, "What will you call yourself?"

Again, he stopped short. "My lord?"

"Robert of Huntington?—but no; I deny it you. Robert of Locksley?—but no; those lands, the village, the name, I also deny you, who gave them to you. So I ask, whom shall you be?"

In a sere tone of winter, the man said: "Ravenskeep."

Twenty-five

On the ride back Marian had cried tears of outrage, tears of futility. Her heart and spirit could no longer contain the bitter welter of emotions she refused to exhibit before deLacey and Mercardier. Now she was done with weeping, with all such things as grief, disbelief, denial. All that remained was to *do*, not to weep, not to wish things might be different. Because for all the wishes in the world, perhaps even prayers, nothing at all would be changed unless she herself changed it.

In Ravenskeep's courtyard Marian jumped down from her horse, pressed reins into Hal's hands, and took herself directly into her hall, her mind fixed on how best to proceed. But she was brought up short even as she entered. Tuck was back.

He sat hunched upon one of the benches at the trestle table, picking at food. That he had not already devoured what lay on his hard-crusted trencher, that he but played with food as if he could not eat, betrayed more of his state than any explanation.

Marian frowned. Tuck and the others had been sent away, sent to what they had supposed was safety at Locksley. But somehow they had fallen afoul of Adam Bell and his men, and Robin had gone to ransom them back. Questions piled one atop another: Why would Tuck be back at Ravenskeep when it was so dangerous; why would Tuck be alone at table when they should be celebrating their freedom; why would Tuck be in such obvious poor spirits? And where was Robin?

She asked sharply, "What has happened?"

He started, then heaved himself around on the bench to face her. "Lady!"

She felt a flicker of foreboding. "What has happened, Tuck?"

He told her. The whole of it.

It was astonishing. "Adam Bell took *Robin* captive?"

Tuck nodded. "He intended to, yes. Just as he did us."

"Then it was a ploy all along," she said bitterly. "He baited the trap with all of you to capture Robin, so they could demand ransom of the earl."

Tuck agreed. "Though the earl refuses to pay."

The world was turning too fast; she could not keep up with it. Robin taken by outlaws, Ravenskeep in peril, Much imprisoned in Nottingham Castle. She had to find a way to *stop* the world, to make it do her bidding instead of the sheriff's, the outlaws', or England's new king. "Where are the others?"

Tuck seemed puzzled. "Locksley Village, aren't they? 'Tis where they were bound. Bell only sent me to the Earl of Huntington."

Marian shook her head. "No. That's where the sheriff's men captured Much. They would be gone from there already."

Tuck was horrified. "*Much* is taken?"

"And will forfeit both hands in a fortnight if we don't find a way to free him." Her thoughts worked swiftly. "We need Robin," she said, "and we need the others. We know they were not taken or the sheriff would not have beaten Much for information. They will be in Sherwood." She nodded, then looked at Tuck. "Do you know where they would go?"

Tuck was crossing himself as he murmured a prayer for Much. "In Sherwood?" He shrugged heavy shoulders beneath black wool and shook his head.

"Away from Locksley," she said, thinking it through. "Too close to the sheriff. The only home they know—together—is Ravenskeep."

"But the sheriff would know that, too," Tuck protested.

"Oh, they won't come *here*," she said, "nor should you be here; it's far too dangerous." Though even as she said it, she thought it unlikely deLacey would come again looking for them. "But near here, yes. Somewhere close by, in Sherwood."

Tuck watched in startled amazement as she strode to the stairs. "Lady—?"

She paused with one foot on the bottom tread. "I must change clothes," she said. "And then we are going into Sherwood, you and I, to find the others, and then we shall find Robin and free him, and then we shall all of us go and rescue Much."

"But—you can't!" Tuck cried. "You dare not, Lady Marian! A woman alone in Sherwood?"

"I won't be alone, Tuck. You will be with me."

He gestured futility. "What aid am I?"

Marian smiled briefly. "As much as I need."

Tuck, refusing to be wooed, shook his head lugubriously. "Robin would never let you."

"Robin," Marian said dryly, "requires rescuing."

He scowled as much as he was capable of scowling, with his kind, gentle face. "If you mean to hide that you are a woman, I have told you before 'tisn't possible. And I told you *why*."

Indeed he had, and at some pains to explain that while he was himself supposedly inured to such things as a woman's appeal to a man's baser senses, he knew very well that no manner of masculine disguise would hide her gender.

She laughed at him. "I promise, I am not changing clothes in order to be a man. Only so I may *walk* like a man. You wear 'skirts' of a sort now, Brother Tuck, and once wore hosen—which garb would you recommend for wading through a forest?"

Tuck, giving up the battle, merely sighed, sat himself down upon the bench, and took up his meat-knife as Marian ran up the stairs.

The Earl of Huntington was not a man much given to religious observances, nor to prayer, nor to vouchsafing his welfare to an inchoate deity whose influence with kings, despite their posturing in His name, seemed decidedly absent. But neither did he altogether ignore his duty as a Christian; he tithed, allowed mendicant priests to take lodging in the castle from time to time, accorded the noble-born clergy their influential places in the ordering of the realm, and had even sent off his only remaining son to the Crusade in an effort to win back Jerusalem. Therefore he had certainly not skimped in having a chapel built even as the castle was built.

He went there now, for no reason he could discern save that no one would think to seek him in such a place.

Inside the door he halted, distractedly aware of soaring arches and ribs, vaults in place of columns, all designed to remove from the chapel the appearance of crypt, undercroft, or dungeon. The masons had done a fine job—apparently *they* were religious, even if he was not—and his eye could appreciate the symmetry of the chapel even if his soul saw no reason for it.

The altar beckoned. Huntington lingered in the doorway, body responding to the long-dormant urge to genuflect. After a moment he gave in, bent stiff and trembling knees, sketched a cross athwart his breast. He felt slightly ludicrous doing so, but the moment passed and he was himself again.

Himself, without an heir.

He did not go to the altar, to kneel before it, to pray, to seek solace or guidance. Instead, he made his way to the nearest bench, collapsed upon it, and stared unseeingly into the distance.

When he spoke, it was with the subtle rasp of vermin stirring in brittle rushes. "I have no son."

The Lord Christ, hanging upon his cross, gazed equally unseeing into his own death.

"I have no heir."

Nor did God; at least, an heir upon the earth in fleshly form.

"It began, and ends with me."

Alpha, and omega.

But he regretted no portion of the words he had spoken to Robert. Only that Henry and William had died. Only that his wife had ruined the youngest son. Only that such wealth and power as he had inherited, retained, and amplified through all the years of his life would, in lieu of living and legal heirs, revert to the Crown.

"Arthur," he said. "Let the boy in Brittany have it all. Let John have none of it."

Nor Robert. Sir Robert of—nothing.

The earl bowed his head. He did not pray.

He wept.

The horse borrowed from Gisbourne was missing—likely it had been found by one of Huntington's serfs and brought down to the castle—and so Robin walked to Locksley. Once there he called together the reeve and the couple who tended the hall, and explained that he was no longer their lord; that they now should look to the earl. All rents once again were payable to Huntington, in coin and such provender as could be raised, grown, and made in the year.

He saw startlement in them as well as dismay. It touched him, if distantly; he was numb just now to such things as how others felt, lest there be more pain than expected. But a lord was a lord; their lives would not change because he was gone from the village. Serfs and tenant farmers, peasants and yeomen had no such changeable portion of the world as lords, knights, and kings.

He answered their questions as best he could, but in no way informed them what had occasioned the change. He believed they knew, or would work it out. It had never been any secret that the earl and his only surviving son were not often in accord. In fact, Robin suspected the question asked most often would have nothing to do with why it had happened, and everything to do with wondering why it had not happened long before.

There were things he valued in the hall, but nothing he cherished as what his mother or Marian had given him, and those were at Ravenskeep. And so he remained outside, explaining matters, and did not go in again, not even to bid the hall farewell. It had been his, but never truly a home. Huntington Hall, razed for stone and wood, had held that place in his heart. The castle was his father's folly. Locksley Village had provided income and a measure of stature, but he had never been a man who needed the latter. As for the former, well . . .

It struck him then that he was entirely dependent on Marian.

As he stood there before the hall, before folk who had served the earl, then the earl's son, and now the earl again, he realized abruptly he was two men. One was truly free, unencumbered by the duties and expectations of childhood, adolescence, young adulthood, by the needs of a village working in his name. He was wholly himself at last. Wholly a man at last.

But there was also the disinherited man. The dishonored man. Shameful words to attach to a soul. They weighed much among other words, shackled a body with the knowledge of failure, of folly. Of a father's futility equal to his own, if for different reasons.

Disinheritance was his freedom. And yet he took no joy in it, no pleasure, no relief.

Perhaps tomorrow.

Or perhaps an hour from now.

Only himself to please. Only himself to serve. Only the dictates of a conscience now freed of the need for explanations to a man who could not, would not comprehend what lived in his son's soul, what whims and wishes stirred his heart to joy, to happiness, to deep satisfaction and commensurate contentment.

Still standing before the hall, before the reeve and the couple but hearing nothing they said, Robin knew himself reborn. No more a son living beneath his father's roof. No more a soldier earning the king's coin and confidence. No more a landowner living on the rents paid by tenant-farmers.

He was utterly penniless, powerless, and without prospects.

Except for outlawry, which the Earl of Essex supported in the name of Arthur of Brittany.

After all, the father embarked on actions that could be construed as treason, depending on who was king at the end of the dance. Why should the son not dally equally with thievery until the music stopped?

A spark of dry humor lit the darkness of his thoughts. Adam Bell styled himself King of Sherwood. Surely there was room enough left over for a lord.

Essex would approve, no doubt. But Robin abhorred politics, the conspiracies of his father and men like him, even the otherwise admirable de Mandeville himself. Certainly there was no need for him to turn to outlawry for any reason, now that the Lionheart was dead; there was no kidnapped king, no ransom requiring ruthless one-time methods. Huntington Castle was denied him, Locksley Village was again his father's holding, but there was still Ravenskeep. Still a home beneath Marian's roof.

Bestirring himself from reverie, Robin thanked the reeve, the couple who tended the hall, bid them farewell, and took himself off his father's lands. In such finery as he had not worn in five years, certainly not appropriate apparel for a man walking the road, Robin struck a pace that would have him home at Ravenskeep, with Marian, before sundown.

Marian strode out of the hall into the courtyard and was delighted to see how she stunned everyone there: Hal, Sim, Joan—even Tuck himself, who had known what she intended. But she supposed even imagining a thing was not so akin to truly seeing it; she might, she decided whimsically, be every bit as shocked if Robin appeared wearing one of her gowns.

She had assembled clothing from the motley of castoffs packed away throughout the hall. From Robin she had the oldest of his hosen, a time-faded greenish-gray, and the most worn of his tunics, summer-weight wool dyed the russet-brown of fall; from her brother's dusty trunk she had unearthed a stiff belt with a brass buckle, the leather badly in need of oiling; from her father's stores she had taken a leather hooded capelet. The scalloped shoulders were much too wide for her frame, but she had cut out a generous section and crudely whip-stitched the skirting back together again. The hood itself was still too large for her, but the cloak portion no longer overwhelmed her shoulders. It had not been vanity; as Tuck said, she was too feminine to be mistaken for a boy, so she had best not allow overly obvious men's clothing to illustrate what she was underneath.

She had chopped the bottom off the tunic; beneath it pulled the hosen up nearly to her breasts and knotted the laces, then bunched and belted everything around her waist, tugging fabric into some semblence of fair fit. Her hair she had braided as tightly as possible into one plait, then stuffed it down inside her tunic beneath the hooded capelet. But a man's boots, so costly he often wore them to ruin, merely having the cobbler restitch, patch, and resole as often as necessary, could not be remade for her, and so she wore her mother's old riding boots dating back more than three decades. Marian's feet were somewhat larger, and the mildewed leather pinched her toes, but they would do.

"*Jesu,*" Joan blurted, then crossed herself hastily with a sidelong glance at Tuck.

The Benedictine blinked astonishment, not bothering to rebuke her. Hal and Sim, who had, respectively, brought up two horses and Marian's bow and quiver, gaped like pimple-faced boys spying their first naked woman.

She smiled sweetly, spreading her arms so they might examine her more closely. "Do I make a comely lad?"

"*Jesu,*" Joan said again. " 'Tis your brother, when he was a boy."

Marian's smile departed so instantly she felt her face collapse.

"Aye," Hal said hoarsely, who had taught that brother to ride. Sim, clutching the bow and quiver, merely nodded, white of face.

She had not thought of any such thing. He had been dead too long, drowned in her childhood. Thirteen years had separated them—five dead babies between the living firstborn and the last—and she was too young when he died for her to recall him as anything but a young man, never a boy. She hadn't been old enough.

She did, so she had been told, resemble her mother. But that was expected of a girl of identical coloring: black hair, blue eyes, and white, white skin. Her brother claimed it also; but he was long dead by the time she was old enough to be considered a woman, and so they recalled the mother when they studied her, never the brother.

Until now.

First her brother, then her mother. Lastly her father, but five years before. And all those stillborn brothers and sisters.

She was the last. With her, the line ended.

And her own children lost before she even knew they existed.

Marian, as stiff in movement as the leather of belt and boots, looked at Tuck, then shook her head at Hal. "We walk," she said. "Horses invite thievery, and mark us different." Joan began to protest, but a glance silenced her. "We will be safer this way," Marian explained.

Tuck was no more happy than Hal or Sim, but he marked her expression, the tone of her voice, and agreed: they had best go afoot.

Monks did not ride, and Marian should not call attention to herself by riding a quality mount.

Not even, Hal asked hopefully, one of the plowhorses?

"If we go crashing through the forest aboard such a horse," she pointed out, "every outlaw within a league will come to spy out the noise."

" 'Tis near sundown," Sim observed with an overly careful lack of censure in his tone.

Marian had already noted the sun's position and the quality of light. "We have time," she said. "And no, I do not intend for us to spend the night beneath a tree in a bed of ferns . . . if we cannot find them before sunset, we shall return."

"To begin again in the morning." Joan did not ask it. She knew better.

"Of course," Marian said. "Until we find them."

"Pray then that they are found quickly," Joan said glumly.

Tuck smiled; that much he could endorse. "Yes, please. Do pray."

The woman was no more pleased that he sounded content. She raised her strong chin. "And if you don't come back?"

"We shall," Marian declared. "Joan, they cannot be far . . . we mean only to go across the road and into the edge of the forest. Not to search the heart of it."

"Black heart," Joan muttered. "Men die in Sherwood."

"Men die anywhere," Marian said sharply. "Even boys in castle dungeons."

As she intended, that shut Joan's mouth on further protest. Marian took the bow and quiver from Sim, then nodded at Tuck.

It was quite true: she did not intend to go far into Sherwood. Only far enough to find Will, and Alan, and Little John. And then Robin, followed by Much.

She needed to gather what providence and coincidence had conspired to make her family. They were all she would ever have.

Twenty-Six

William deLacey's shadow bloomed against the stone wall of the cell as he inspected the Exchequer cloth, the stacks of caskets full of coin, and the cases of rolled parchments. *Marian made a mess of things . . .* light flickered as movement guttered the torch; leather creaked, metal fittings chimed faintly. He glanced up briefly as a man entered the cell, prepared to order him out again. But it was Mercardier, and the sheriff did no such thing.

Anticipation kindled; Mercardier had been present as Marian inspected the tax rolls. "So," deLacey said, "was she as angry as I expected?"

The big mercenary shrugged. "Say, rather, unsurprised."

He laughed softly, resettling scroll cases before any could fall. "Marian is not stupid. Only a fool, betimes, in the man she takes to her bed."

Mercardier made no response to that. "Did she pay her taxes?"

DeLacey arched a brow. "Would it matter to you either way?"

"I am not paid to have a conscience, Sheriff, nor to care one way or the other. But if she did not, she should be made to do so for the sake of the king." He paused. "Or punished."

"As I intend," the sheriff said curtly, annoyed to be told how to do his job. "You heard me, Captain: if in fourteen days she has not paid the taxes, her manor and lands are forfeit."

"And if she has paid them?"

"Proof is here, if she has." DeLacey's quick gesture encompassed the cell. "All taxes come here, all accountings, all receipts, for all of Nottinghamshire. If she paid her taxes, the record is here." He smiled with delicate irony. "If there is no record, then naturally no proof exists."

Mercardier offered no comment.

DeLacey sought an indication of the mercenary's thoughts, but they were well shielded behind the implacable mask of the professional soldier. Still annoyed—did a mercenary presume to judge a sheriff?—he unlatched a casket and tipped the lid back. "This is war as well, Captain. The battlefield is entirely different, but the result is the same. In your sort of wars, you require weapons. Horses. Armor. Well, it is money that *buys* those things, Mercardier. Taxes. Do not for a moment consider what I do here less vital to England's welfare than what you did on the battlefield we know as the Holy Land."

"I do have some acquaintainceship with taxes." The tone was only slightly dry. "Money is what causes me to *take* the battlefield."

"Ah. Of course. For a moment I mistook you for a nobleman." DeLacey, frustrated by the man's immense self-control—he could not manipulate someone who gave no indication of weakness—permitted a trace of contempt to grace his tone. "What was it you wanted, Mercardier?"

"I inquire of you when I may escort the taxes to Lincoln, Lord Sheriff."

He slammed the casket closed. "When I am done collecting them, Captain. Nottinghamshire is large, and its people uncommon stubborn with regard to paying as they should. You need merely witness the farce presented by Marian FitzWalter."

"A headstrong woman," Mercardier observed.

It was the first time the man had offered an opinion. DeLacey, relatching the casket, laughed briefly. "Indeed."

The tone, despite the accent, was bland. "Such women are dangerous."

"Dangerous?" The sheriff considered the word. "I should say frustrating and impossibly infuriating, but hardly dangerous."

"The Duchess of Aquitaine," Mercardier elaborated. "Frustrating, *oui*. Infuriating, *ah, oui*. But also dangerous. Such women may convince kings to commit war, or halt it; to commence Holy Crusade, or even to carry home the very crown of heaven if she believed, out of vanity, it suited her brow."

DeLacey grinned, amused and pleased; finally something from the man that he might use. "Ah, but they do tell tales of our fair Eleanor, do they not?"

"And she has earned them all." Mercardier paused. "Have you her like in Nottinghamshire?"

"Her like . . ." DeLacey blinked. "Do you mean Marian FitzWalter?"

"I have said how a woman might be dangerous. Is she?"

"Good God, Mercardier! Marian?" He laughed in genuine amusement. "She is neither queen nor soldier, Captain; how could she be dangerous?"

"She sleeps with Sir Robert of Locksley."

The sheriff was completely baffled. "Should that matter?"

"He was," the mercenary said, "one of King Richard's most trusted men."

There was a hint of—*something*—behind the words. "And you did not approve."

"I hold him in no affection, nor ever did."

There was promise in this. The sheriff probed deeper. "You believe *him* dangerous."

"The king did not knight men lacking in skill and courage. And I saw him fight."

DeLacey nodded. "You believe she might convince him to defy me in the matter of the taxes."

"Despite suspect morals, Eleanor of Aquitaine married two kings, my lord. She was a most convincing woman."

He contemplated that, again seeking and again not finding an indication of Mercardier's thoughts in the plain, pocked face. "Let us say, then, that she does convince Locksley to take her part in this matter of the taxes. Would you defend me against him?"

"You, my lord? No. I would defend the taxes. That is my task."

The sheriff laughed softly; he began to understand. "So it is. But I see what stirs you to concern: you are aware Locksley stole a tax shipment five years ago."

"I had the tale of my lord king."

It was an illuminating thought, that even the Lionheart found amusement in the story of the sheriff's undoing, in Locksley's outlawry. But then, Richard had loved him, and pardoned him, and saw no harm in what had been done.

John was an entirely different sort of man.

"You disapprove," deLacey observed, interest increasing.

Something akin to irony softened Mercardier's expression. "Had the shipment been my responsibility, it would never have been stolen."

The shipment had been deLacey's responsibility. It was censure Mercardier levied, albeit unsaid, and likely something John himself had suggested he point out. Most annoying.

DeLacey scowled. "He claims he did it in Richard's name."

"Perhaps he did. He was most devout in Coeur de Lion's service. But my lord is dead. His brother rules. And my duty now is to protect these taxes against all threats."

The sheriff refolded the Exchequer cloth and dropped it onto the nearest pile of caskets. "Would you, Mercardier? *Could* you?" He paused, employing irony at his own expense. "That is, if he threatened the taxes."

"My lord?"

He no longer prevaricated. "Could you kill a man knighted by Coeur de Lion?" He studied the hard face. "Could you kill a man with whom you fought in the name of that king?"

There was no hesitation. "Should he threaten my duty, yes."

DeLacey smiled, contemplating discovery and an abrupt anticipation of a new kind of battle. Here was answer, here was weapon, here was ally in place of adversary. "Then we have much in common."

Though Mercardier was mute, the question was implicit.

An enemy, deLacey declared inwardly. But, "Taxes," was what he said aloud, "and their defense against threat." Now he weighted the words with potent implication. "Against *all* threat, offered by any man."

Robin, footsore and decidedly out of sorts when at last he reached Ravenskeep, was more than a little startled by the greeting offered him as he entered the hall. Joan, employed in the ordering of repairs to the damage done by the sheriff's men, turned at his entrance and promptly blurted, "But she went to *rescue* you!"

Robin limped to the nearest bench and collapsed upon it, levering up a leg so he might jerk the boot from his sore right foot. "Rescue me from what?"

"Outlaws!"

He gritted his teeth as he worked at the boot; flesh stung, which suggested blisters were bleeding. "I rescued myself."

"But she's gone after you!"

Complete comprehension arrived abruptly. Blisters no longer mattered. "Where did she go?"

"Sherwood."

"Sherwood!"

"I told her not to!" Joan cried. "We all did, my lord. But she's a stubborn head on her shoulders—"

"Alone?"

"With Tuck, my lord."

Discomfort was forgotten as he stood up. "By all the saints in heaven—"

"We *did* tell her, my lord. That she shouldn't go. We all did. But—"

"But, being Marian . . ." He sighed, stamping his foot back down into the boot and suppressing a wince. "A woman with a monk. No certainty of safety, that."

"She went as a man, my lord."

"She went . . ." He blinked. "As a man?"

"Yes, my lord."

He was visited by a brief and altogether ludicrous vision of Marian dressed as a man. He could not comprehend it. So he banished it. "Where in Sherwood did she go?"

"Across the road, she said. She said she'd be back by sunset."

He scowled. "It's nearly sunset now."

"Yes, my lord. But she was in some haste because of Much."

That brought him up short. "What about Much?"

"He's taken. The sheriff has him."

Robin swore in three languages. When he could speak in one again with something akin to civility, he asked for the story from start to finish.

Joan told him straightly enough, though near the end she rushed it so as to implore him to find Marian at once. "Because 'tis only my lady and Tuck out there in the forest, my lord, and you know what Sherwood is."

Oh, indeed, he knew what Sherwood was. And because he did, Robin bid Joan ask Hal for his horse, Sim for his bow and quiver, and ran in all haste up the stairs to the bedroom under the eaves so he might himself fetch his sword.

With more than a little trepidation, Marian peeled aside the encroaching branch threatening an eye. They had penetrated the fringes of the forest, and already she was aware of a heaviness in the place, the weight of oppression in its shadows. From the wheeze of Tuck's quickened breathing, she suspected he felt much the same.

And then she chided herself for falling prey to childish fancies. Sherwood was a *forest*, not a being, not a personality intent upon destruction. Its architecture was such that it favored men who hid, and so men hid in it; but it was men who were dangerous, not the forest itself.

She was no stranger to it. She had spent her life near its skirts. But now she was adult enough to realize the potential for danger, the possibility of harm, should men employ Sherwood to fulfill their own aims, such aims as were not acceptable under the king's law.

Marian grimaced. Under the Lionheart, law was one thing. Under John, as yet a cipher to his people beyond a reputation for temper tantrums and a lack of martial—and marital—prowess, it might well yet prove another.

Shouting would not do; it would undoubtedly bring down outlaws upon them. And yet what had seemed a fair idea originally—to skirt the fringes and find Alan, Will, and Little John, who should surely be nearby—

now seemed impossible, and impossibly dangerous. Either she took the risk of shouting for them anyway, or perhaps never find them. And she did not wish to stay in Sherwood any longer than necessary.

Marian continued to pick her way through vegetation, discovering pockets of darkness in ferns, beneath low-limbed trees, in hollows screened by vines, branches, immense and shattered trunks. A man might make Sherwood his demesne, had he need, to ward his welfare and withstand the sieges of men who lacked woodcraft; and she recalled that indeed Adam Bell had done such a thing, and most successfully. He had evaded capture for years.

Behind her, Tuck stopped. His breathing was audible. Yet when she turned back, fearing to find him stricken with apprehension or stilled by fatigue, she found him instead standing squarely with sandaled feet planted, a face of exaltation turned up to the living lattice arching against the sky.

"This," he said breathlessly, "this is God's cathedral!"

It was wholly unexpected. Marian merely stared.

Tuck closed his eyes and murmured in Latin, crossing himself twice before folding his hands in prayer. His expression was beatific.

Marian slowly lifted her gaze from the depths to the heights, marking how the upright trunks formed vaults and pillars of wood, not stone; how the canopy of limbs became living arches and archivolts; how a multiplicity of altars gathered around them in broken trunks and piled stone.

God's cathedral.

Trust Tuck to see Sherwood with the eyes of innocence, of trust and integrity, eyes that sought beauty in place of danger.

Tension broke, foreboding dissipated. Marian laughed, genuinely amused by the dichotomy of opinion. And even as Tuck fumbled for his absent rosary, a red-haired giant thrust himself into the open, leading two other prodigals not to the Promised Land, but surely to reunion.

Robin came upon them clustered near the road, gilded ocher and amber in the touch of a lowering sun. It was Little John he spied first, of course, red hair afire; and then Tuck of the rotund, cassocked silhouette. His mind registered the others according to shape and coloring as well: Will, posture stiff and truculent; Alan, negligent in the repose he had honed in high courts, with golden curls somewhat less than clean.

And Marian. It must be. She was the only one left. But even he, who knew her intimately, would never have taken her for a woman. Not from behind. A lad, yes; a slight boy more than twelve and less than eighteen. But never as the woman with whom he shared a bed.

When they did not immediately join him, he marched out again, grabbed Marian by the arm, and jerked her in after him.

This time they followed.

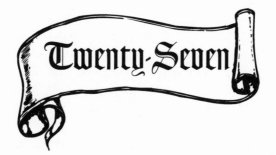

Twenty-Seven

DeLacey's daughter presented herself to him in the midst of his evening meal, which he shared with Mercardier. He considered telling her to depart at once lest she ruin his appetite, but forbore. Better to deal with her now and have it done with, than to anticipate it another time.

She had borne two children, but her body remained as narrow and sharp as before, except for a looser belly, as did expression and tongue. There was nothing soft about his youngest, least of all her temperament. In a man it might have been advantage; in a woman, in Eleanor particularly, it did nothing but plague him.

Eleanor never cared who in the hall heard what she had to say. She had learned deceit, but never circumspection. She utterly ignored Mercardier. "Gisbourne tells me you mean to have Ravenskeep for your own."

He drank down the last of the wine and motioned for more. A servant refilled the cup "Gisbourne speaks out of turn."

"He is my husband. He should speak to me of such matters."

"Gisbourne is, apparently, husband in name only." He smiled to see the color surge into her face; now she was very aware of Mercardier's presence. "You told me so yourself."

She stood very erect. "I want them. Her lands. I want them."

"And Gisbourne wants them *for* you."

That, she had not expected. It amused him to see the unshielded expression on her face, the open astonishment. Eleanor no doubt had heard from Gisbourne that he wanted Ravenskeep, and she acted merely to preempt that claim.

"Indeed," he continued. "He suggested you and the children might be more comfortable away from my hall."

Because relief was a tangible thing now that he saw them whole and unharmed, he could afford to be angry. And so he was, galloping up to them on a high-headed horse whom he barely contained, and let them see it in his face as he glared down upon them.

"Good Christ," he said as he reined in with no small vehemence, "have you entirely lost whatever wits you once possessed?"

It was not precisely the reception any of them expected. Certainly not Marian, who turned to him so sharply the hood slid off her head. And then there was no mistaking her for a lad, with a spray of loosened hair framing a potent femininity in the purity of her features.

It was Little John who found his voice first. "She said you were captured!"

Charlemagne, in his hasty halt, had dug up dirt from the track and sprayed them liberally. Marian swept a dollop from her face and spat grit, then scowled up at Robin. "He *was* captured. Or so Tuck told me."

The monk stared at them in alarm as they turned as one to him. "You heard Adam Bell! He said he intended to capture him!"

"He's here now, aye?" Scarlet said, smearing dirt across his brow with the scrape of a forearm.

"What are you doing on the road?" Robin demanded, forgoing explanation that he had indeed been Adam Bell's captive. "The high road to Nottingham, I remind you; do you *wish* to get yourself taken by the sheriff?"

Scarlet glared back. "If we're unpardoned, *you're* unpardoned. And you're on the road, aye? Ahorse!"

"Aye," Little John expostulated. "Easier to see on a horse."

Robin supposed they both of them had a point in that.

Alan of the Dales was smiling crookedly. "It was suggested we return to Ravenskeep."

"And I suggested they not do any such thing," Marian inserted. "DeLacey's been there once already."

"And that's why he won't be back," Little John declared vehemently. "Why search it twice?"

"The hall won't *survive* a second search," Marian retorted. Then she looked at Robin. "Does it matter whether we are in the road or in the forest? The sheriff has Much. *That* is what matters."

Robin jumped down from his horse and dragged the reins over Charlemagne's head. "Indeed, so it does. And there is much to discuss about it—but shall we do it elsewhere?" He marched by them then, leading the horse beyond the verge and into the forest.

"But—" Clearly, she was baffled. "I thought he wanted the lands for himself. To live *there*."

"Of course you did. But though Gisbourne would just as soon live apart from you—and, I presume, away from children who may not be his own—he never claimed Ravenskeep for himself. He asked it for you."

DeLacey watched her sort through the information, attempting to find a way to turn it to her advantage. In the end she settled for the simplicity of repeated demand. "I want the lands."

He sipped wine, settling back into his chair. "They would revert to the Crown, Eleanor."

"You know as well as I that John owes you," she retorted. "Ask him for them."

It was true, but he might have wished she be not so blatant before a man who served the king. Still, Mercardier might as well hear the truth of his new master. He had been Richard's man. "John may owe any number of men any number of things," he observed, "but such facts guarantee nothing. Indeed, if reminded of this 'duty,' he may see fit simply to destroy the one who does the reminding."

"John needs money," she said flatly. "He is king in name, but it is to the boy in Brittany Richard left his money. *Buy* the lands."

He was impressed by the extent of her knowledge. But then, Eleanor had always made a practice of listening at keyholes, of bribing servants to gain information.

"She will never find the coin in a fortnight," Eleanor said. "The lands are forfeit. Pay John a sum toward the taxes. He has all of England— a lesser Nottinghamshire manor could not possibly matter to him—but he needs money."

"And then I should give the lands to Gisbourne."

"To *me*."

"He means them for you."

"To me alone," she insisted. "I want something of my own."

He smiled. "You have what I have given you. This hall, this city, an entire shire. You are the daughter of the Lord High Sheriff."

"And heir to none of it," she retorted. "The title and castle go with the office, and that you purchased. If John takes a fancy to put another in your place, where does that leave me?"

He affected innocence. "With Gisbourne?"

Eleanor colored again. "If you are put out of your office, Gisbourne is put out of his. And I have children to think of."

The sheriff observed lazily, "It is true that a woman knows the children of her body, even if the man never knows who is the father."

He had shocked her at last. Her eyes slanted sharply in Mercardier's direction, and then she drew herself up, very white of face. "Give me the lands. I want a home apart from you, apart from Gisbourne. I want something *of my own.*"

DeLacey had never wanted the lands. He had wanted their lady. He no more desired them now even without their lady; he desired simply to take them from her. It did not matter to him if Gisbourne claimed them, or Eleanor, or even the King of England. The point was merely to relieve Marian of them.

"I shall consider it," he said. "Now, if you please, I intend to finish my supper."

"I want—"

"You have *said* what you want, Eleanor! Enough. You have my answer."

With acid sweetness she inquired, "And when will you have finished this considering?"

DeLacey smiled. "Well, I think I shall certainly know when the fortnight is ended. So take yourself away and consider whatever it is women consider until then."

She took herself away. The sheriff sighed, rubbed briefly at his brow, then cast a resigned glance in Mercardier's direction. "Have you children, Captain?"

"I have no wife," he answered. "Bastards, perhaps. If so, they live with their mothers."

"Ah." DeLacey nodded. "Possibly the wisest course of all. A man need not trouble himself about bastards."

"Unless," Mercardier said, "they are the sons of kings."

The sheriff grunted. "The world might be different if the Lionheart had sired a cub. Even a bastard one."

"And you might have no office."

DeLacey looked at him sharply. As usual, there was no indication of amusement or intent. Merely observation, without emphasis or implication.

He lifted his wine cup. "Somewhere, I do trust, I would have an office. One merely must have the money with which to buy it." He offered the big man a smile. "Perhaps I am as much a mercenary as you. Perhaps we all of us are, unless we be born kings."

Mercardier said simply, "Or serve out of honor."

DeLacey laughed. "Oh, honor. Indeed. Honor!"

"You disbelieve in honor?"

"Say, rather, I have little acquaintance with it. In these times, in the service of Henry's sons, it is a commodity rarely come by."

"My lord Lionheart," Mercardier said, "had honor in plenty."

DeLacey could not resist. "Perhaps he might have wielded his cock in honor's service, then, and given us an heir, instead of wasting himself in men . . . or in wasting those men *and* money on far Jerusalem. *Which,* I might add, remains in the hands of the Infidel." He gestured toward the mercenary. "What say you now in the Lionheart's defense?"

Mercardier, characteristically, said nothing at all. DeLacey, still smiling, drank to his small victory with a final gulp of wine.

Marian scowled. Robin looked remarkably comfortable with command as he seated himself upon a fallen tree, reins hooked casually through an elbow. His clothing was far finer than anything she'd seen him wear in years, his manner overly relaxed. She saw no tension in him, no apprehension, merely an overwhelming *competence,* as if he had accepted something in and about himself to which he had not before given full consideration.

Suspicion roused sluggishly; was fed by an uprush of startled fear. Was this what a man was, she wondered, when secure in the knowledge he would inherit wealth, title, power? Secure in the certainty he would be an earl, with no such concerns as a sheriff bent on ruining his hall or his holdings by lying about taxes?

She felt hollow abruptly, and chilled to the bone. She had given him the choice. Had insisted he had the choice. Obviously, he had made it.

Marian closed her eyes tightly, blinding herself, setting herself at distance, then opened them again. He looked no different, save for the clothing. But he *seemed* different, and not just because of the clothing.

The others had arranged themselves as students to a master. Marian, hugging herself, did not, nor did she sit. She stood in shadow, wishing she might hide herself from what she feared was the truth.

Robin looked straight at her out of hazel eyes gone opaque. And she recognized the mask. Knew that mask. It was the man he had been five years before, home from Crusade, from captivity, to tell her her father was dead. When he himself had been as dead, if only inside. "Tell me."

She did: how she had discovered Much in the pit; how he had been beaten for information; how the sheriff intended to cut off his hands in a fortnight.

The others had heard it already. Robin had heard part of it—she was sure Joan had explained—but now he heard the whole of it. Now he understood.

"How shall we do it?" she asked. "How shall he be freed?"

He averted his face, staring hard at the ground. One booted toe dug into soil, overturning stones and twigs. Charlemagne, bored, nibbled desultorily at Robin's fine silk-shot overtunic, who merely hitched the shoulder to shoo the horse away as if he were no more than an annoying insect.

At last he looked at Marian. "You should go home."

Unaccountably, tears threatened. She considered telling him that she might very soon have no hall to go home *to*.

"You," he said to Little John, "should hide yourself in Sherwood. And you"—he looked at Alan, Will, and Tuck—"should go to Nottingham."

They were astonished, and said so. Vociferously. Marian waited them out, watching Robin do the same.

"But you see," he said finally, when they gave him space to speak, "I doubt our zealous sheriff will wait those fourteen days. I think he will haul Much out into Market Square the moment the fancy strikes him."

She had not thought of that. Nor had any of them. Protests died abruptly as Robin continued.

"We must be in Nottingham," he said, "to rescue him."

"Rescue him how?" Scarlet demanded.

"However the moment strikes us," Robin answered. "We have longbows. We can shelter at distance, and from distance stop the proceedings."

"You'd have *us* in Nottingham?" Scarlet grumbled. "The lion's den, aye?"

"He will not look for us there," Robin explained. "At Ravenskeep, yes; he has. At Locksley, yes; he has—and nearly caught you there, even as he caught Much. We four may hide ourselves in Nottingham. John"—his gaze flicked to the giant—"is too big to hide anywhere in the city. Even in disguise."

Glumly, Little John nodded.

"Five," Marian murmured.

They shifted to look at her.

"Five," she repeated. "I have my own bow."

"But you can't," Scarlet blurted. "You're a woman."

"Did you know I was a woman when you first saw me like this?" She looked at Robin. "Did you?"

"Not from behind," he admitted.

"Nor does the bow know I am a woman. I can shoot as straight as any here, save you."

Alan's dolorous sigh was excessively exaggerated. "I do need my lute. This requires a ballad." He grimaced. "But my lute currently lends her lovely presence to Adam Bell and his men, who have no appreciation of her worth."

Robin looked like he wished to protest Marian's decision, to insist she go home, but did not go forward with it. Instead, he declared simply, "We will get Much back, and whole."

"He'll expect it," Little John warned. "And 'tisn't Much I mean."

"Then we shall give him what he expects," Robin said. "Once we permit him to see us in the city when he takes Much to the square, we shall then show ourselves in as many places as possible—without falling prey to soldiers, need I add?—and drive him to distraction. We shall be"—his smile was brief and fleeting—"midges he cannot *quite* reach to slap away."

Little John frowned. "And what if he hauls Much back into the castle to chop off his hands there?"

"That is a risk," Robin confirmed. "But we shall have to rescue him before that can be done."

Marian sat down at last, perching upon a stump. "William deLacey will want him seen by as many people as possible. He won't wish to punish him in secret, but to set an example for anyone who contemplates defying the Lord High Sheriff of Nottingham. And it isn't because Much filched purses, but because he is one of you."

" 'One of us'?" Alan questioned, eyebrows arching beneath a tangled coil of golden hair.

"You stole the tax shipment," she said. "He slit the throats of his own men for it, to make you seem worse than thieves and murderers, but butchers as well. He has no desire to cut off Much's hands in secret inside the castle, but to let everyone see the sheriff's justice. And to let *us* see what he intends if he ever catches us."

The minstrel smiled, quoting again. " 'Us'?"

"You were not there," Robin reminded her gently. "You were never a part of that theft."

"But I have harmed the sheriff far more deeply than any of you," she replied, "and he counts me as much an enemy now as he does you."

It was Robin who knew her best, and Robin who arrived at comprehension before the others. "Marian . . . what have you done?"

"I have looked him in the eye," she said, "and declared my own war."

His face tautened. "Why?"

She found her voice steadier than expected. "Because in fourteen days he will take my home."

The others were horrified, and said so. Only Robin was calm. Too calm. "How?"

Bitterness welled up. "I have not, he says, paid my taxes."

"You did."

"I did."

It was Tuck who said it first. "He altered the rolls," he blurted. The others stirred, staring at him. "The tax rolls," he amplified. "All the names are listed, you see. In all the shires. The accounting is taken to the Exchequer. The *taxes* are taken, aye?" He shrugged off their bafflement. "I was a clerk. I've inscribed rolls before myself. 'Tisn't difficult . . . likely he struck off her name."

"My name is nowhere," she affirmed. "Oh, indeed, I did look. Be certain of it. That is where I was earlier today, searching for my name. But as Gisbourne said: 'There is no record.' "

Little John was genuinely stricken. "Then what happens to you?"

"He takes my home," she said, "and turns me out of it. He has *promised* it."

"He won't," Scarlet declared emphatically. "We'll not let him, will we?"

"No," she said, "we won't. *I* won't. But first there is Much. I have a fortnight. He may have but a day." She nodded at Robin. "Do we go to Nottingham now?"

He did not answer at once. She saw something in his eyes, some indefinable emotion. But it was gone too soon; she could not name it, nor study it to comprehend it.

"In the morning," he answered. "For now we are going back to Ravenskeep—*all* of us," he said firmly as the others raised brows. "Because for this night the sheriff will not trouble us. He has Much, and he believes he has Marian's lands. He will do nothing before tomorrow, and likely not before afternoon."

Will Scarlet was incredulous. "How can you know that?"

"Because, as Marian said, he will want as many witnesses as possible. And tomorrow is Market Day. It will be midday, I'd wager, when the square will be crowded. And so I think we may sleep the night safely beneath Ravenskeep's roof." He looked at Marian. "But not for the last time. That, I promise."

She ventured it at last. "The word of an earl's heir?"

He opened his mouth to answer, but shut it again. In a moment of incongruity, he seemed to recall what he wore. He glanced down at the fine summer-weight hosen, the silk-shot overtunic, the good leather boots. Saw himself as she did, as they saw him; and she watched him register also that a nobleman's horse stood at his back, and the sword sheathed at the saddle was the blade of a knight who was also an earl's son.

The mask shattered as the breath went out of him in a sharp exhalation. She saw now what was in his mind. How the truth entered his eyes, crowded on his tongue, and threatened to offer proof of who he truly was instead of whom she had feared.

She felt tears in her own. "No," Marian said, knowing abruptly what he was thinking: to rid himself of what came of his father. "You would do better to go clothed than not; and the stallion will sire strong foals; and no man can afford to be rid of a good weapon when the Lord High Sheriff of Nottingham names him enemy."

No one spoke. No one could, as they stared at one another.

It was Charlemagne who broke the moment, shattering the tension. The horse pushed his muzzle into the back of Robin's neck, lipping at hair, and snorted wetly.

It was enough to allow Marian to smile, Robin to swear, and the others to laugh.

Shadows deepened. Time to go home, if only for the night. Marian led them there.

Twenty-Eight

Alan mourned his lost lute as they gathered in the hall to eat what Joan set before them, who waved Marian back down before she could rise to help. Will Scarlet suggested it was not a bad thing that Adam Bell and his men had relieved the minstrel of his instrument, as its absence meant they need not listen to his caterwauling; Alan affected elegant affrontedness. Yet there was no mistaking he truly did feel naked without his lute, nor that Tuck was not happy to lack his rosary. But it was Little John who banished thoughts and yearnings after lost things, when he reminded them what they lacked most was Much.

It silenced them all. Then the giant set back his bench and rose, saying he was for bed in the barn. Marian, startled, said he might have his place in the hall, but he shook his head and said he'd feel safer elsewhere, in a place affording a hasty escape. Scarlet considered that a sensible thing, and they departed together. Alan sighed again, clearly wishing to close the evening with music so he might ease his own apprehension, but got up without further comment and wandered out into the night. Tuck rather hastily finished his food and gulped down the last of his ale, then said *he* was bound for the oratory, where he had some discussing to do with God before they left for Nottingham to rescue Much.

And so they were gone, Will and John and Alan and Tuck, and Joan had shooed away the servants as well as herself, and Marian and Robin stared at one another across a table that resembled a battlefield of crockery, horn cups, pewter tankards, platters, and hard bread trenchers.

He was, in that moment, struck by the pallor of her face, the sharpness of bones beneath flesh thinned by tension. He rose, rounded the table, pulled her to her feet before she could frame an inquiry. He took her out of the hall, out of the courtyard, out to the stone wall beside the lane that edged the lower meadow where Little John's sheep settled in for the night. The sun was gone and they had neither torches nor lamps, but the moon, nearly full, flooded the landscape with illumination.

Robin lifted her, sat her upon the moss-clad wall. Behind her stretched the meadows, and wood copses, and serpentines of stone walls and hedgerows. Behind *him* lay the gates opening onto the courtyard where torches blazed; where every window in the hall was limned in candlelight.

"This is yours," he said. "All of it. And it shall remain so."

Tears glittered in the light, but they did not fall, and she did not brush them away.

"I will do what I must," he said. "This is yours."

Marian was silent, gazing beyond him. He knew what she saw. Everything her father had built. All that was left of him, of her mother, her brother. Everything that was *hers*.

"One moment," she murmured.

It puzzled him. "What?"

"You said: 'one moment.' And the world was unmade, turned upside down."

He nodded, remembering.

"It is a plague," she said, "of disaster. The king, dead; and now everything is gone wrong. Everything we had is threatened, everything we were is undone. We are like the world: unmade. And as men remake the world, they also remake us. Your father. The sheriff. They *steal* from us. Joy. Happiness. Contentment. The future." Marian closed her eyes. "I feel as if I am grown old in a single day."

He stood before her, felt the pressure of her knees against his body. He clasped his hands around her waist, slid them home to her hips. "If you are old, then I am ancient."

That won a smile, albeit brief. She opened her eyes. "Older than ancient. You are dust in the tomb."

"And your ghost wafting through it, ruffling it in your wake."

But her mind had turned away from wordplay. "What did he say, Robin?"

He knew whom she meant. He had known it would come. He had not expected it to hurt quite so much.

He stared hard into her face, though he did not focus on it. "The Earl of Huntington has no son."

She caught her breath on a quick inhalation. "Ah," she said, "no."

He did not repeat it. He did not deny it.

"So." Her voice was uneven. "It is done."

"Done," he echoed, though he had not meant to.

"Oh, Jesu," she said, and the tears fell at last. "I never wanted it. I wanted *you*, but I never wanted that. A son deserves a father—"

"That one?"

"Yes, even that one. He deserves to have a father of any ilk, to hope for a new beginning."

"Or to witness an ending." He sighed, staring past her now into the meadow. "We were naught but adversaries, ever. I could do no right in speech, in actions, in thought. I was hers entirely, though he might have blamed himself for that; and perhaps he did, when he realized he needed me after all." That brought him up short; it seemed his father had not after all required him. "There was nothing between us but enmity. The road led here from the day I was born."

Marian shook her head. "How he must hate me."

He looked at her sharply.

"Think on it," she said. "You say your mother stole you from him . . ."

"He gave me to her. He had my older brothers; there was no tolerance for a third son full of fey thoughts and fancies."

She went on as if he hadn't spoken. "And now when he most needs you, *I* steal you."

"You are," he agreed, "an outlaw." And then his heart closed up, and his throat. Outlaw was what he had been once, briefly, in the name of a king. Now what was he? That king was dead, and so was his past. So, perhaps, was his future.

Marian studied him for a long moment, marking the mask of his face, the burning dryness in his eyes. Then she parted her legs, leaned forward; set hands into his hair to cup his skull, and pulled him to her. With her upon the wall, their heads were on a level. She bent his against her shoulder, embraced it. Cradled him there, threading fingers through his hair. Murmured the sort of things a mother murmurs, or wife, wishing to ease a soul.

His soul was in need of ease. So, rather abruptly, was his body. She made it easy for him, with a knee against each hip. He moved close, caught her, lifted her from the wall with a thigh astride either hip. Hosen made it a simple matter to carry her this way, with no impedence of skirts.

Marian said, rather breathlessly, "Tuck is in the oratory, and the others are in the barn."

"We have a room," he answered, and proceeded to take her to it.

The earl shook his head at the servant. "No," he repeated. "Not even if I am dying."

"My lord." Ralph's voice was very calm. "My lord, I honor your decision; it was yours to make, and my place is not to dissuade you. But—"

Huntington cut him off, glaring. "Then why do you attempt to dissuade me now, in this?"

"My lord, give me leave to tell him, to send for him, should it be necessary. If you are dying, what does it matter?"

The earl lay propped against piled bolsters, sipping warm spiced wine as a bedtime posset. "Am I dying yet, Ralph?"

"No, my lord. Pray God you have years left. But you have been ill—"

"And I am old. Yes? Is that what you mean?"

"My lord, if you should take ill again, and it seems likely you may die—"

"I want him nowhere by me. Not now. Not when I'm dying. Not after I am dead."

"He is all there is left, my lord."

"I am alone, Ralph. Do you understand? There is *no one.*"

"If you are dying, my lord, would you not wish what remains of your family present?"

Huntington grimaced. "He was hers, never mine. Her I married. She was wife, not relative."

Ralph sighed faintly. "I shall ask you again another day."

"Another *year,*" the earl said belligerently. "Next year, when Arthur of Brittany becomes Arthur of England, and I can die knowing my work is not in vain. Ask me then, Ralph. But not before."

The steward bowed. "Good night, my lord."

Huntington scowled as the door was pulled to, the latch set. Then he drank off the remains of the posset, set the cup beside the bed, and slumped back against the bolsters to stare dry-eyed into the shadows.

One wife. Two sons. Dead. A third son as good as.

He was alone in the world. But it was a world he had had the making of, and he would not complain.

This union had been more urgent than most, if no less satisfying; indeed it was oddly more so, as if they sealed themselves to one another not as who they had been, but as what they had become: a woman in danger of losing her home; a man who had, in his pernicious principles, been stripped of everything. There was no knowledge in it of anything but that they had one another, that no one in the world might take that from them. It had provided ease for them both despite the storm that swept them up, a peace after turbulence that gave him sleep he might otherwise have lost in fretting; that gave her time to realize that for all she would fight for Ravenskeep even to the death, her home was with Robin. Wherever it might be.

The bed was narrow and sagged a bit in the middle, its frame weakened further by the violence visited upon it by the sheriff's soldiers but two days before. It crossed her mind, most incongruously, that the bed might actually collapse; but Robin, hearing that murmured into his ear in the midst of something other than discussion, merely laughed and suggested they could break it well enough even with *no* soldiers involved.

She had chided him in mock asperity for his vulgarity, then forgot the bed altogether.

Now she lay close, body set against the lean, warm length of him as he lay on his side. Her left arm was trapped beneath his neck, but she didn't care. The other she employed to sweep the hand from his shoulder to hip, though she did not touch him, merely outlined in the air the jut of shoulder, the hollow of the waist, the slight curve of a male hip. She had found it somewhat annoying to divest herself of hosen in place of skirts, since she had applied any number of strangenesses to hold the hosen up and the tunic down; *he* had found it most entertaining to merely remove her belt, unknot the thongs, and let the hosen drop. She was far more accustomed to doing that to him than to herself, but in the end clothing had been evenly dispersed. His lay somewhere, hers were elsewhere.

All unexpectedly her thoughts found and centered upon a certain thing, stopped there to linger, to taste like a butterfly the nectar of her mind. But this was bittersweet, unpalatable; no blossoms would come of it.

He stirred, seemingly aware of her not-touch, or perhaps attuned to the tension that had crept back into her heart. "What is it?"

His voice was not as sleepy as expected. Marian dropped her hand to his hip, took security in the touch. "I was wishing . . . wishing a thing with all that is in me to wish."

His head shifted slightly, moving upon her trapped arm. He waited.

"Wishing," she confessed, "that I could give you children."

He was very still. And then he turned, altering his posture to face her. They were close, too close for clarity of feature even if there was light beyond the moon sliding through cracks in the wall, but she could feel him, smell him, sense his heart.

He gathered her close, held her, set lips into her hair. "Marry me."

She stiffened, even in his arms.

And again, in a whisper, "Marry me."

She thought of all the arguments she could use, the disparagements of his choice, of his reasons. But he had stood firm before his father, paid that price, and she could no more dishonor him for that than she could conjure a child.

Overwhelmed, she was mute. She could find no words.

It alarmed him. She felt him tense, felt him tighten his embrace. "Marian—?"

"I will," she blurted, realizing he might misconstrue her silence; she had refused him more than once when he had asked before. "Oh, I will . . . as many times as you like!"

His breath, as he expelled it on a rush, warmed her ear. "Praise God." And in English, not Arabic.

She laughed. But, "Much first," she said. "And this question of the taxes must be settled."

"Of course."

"Perhaps," she said, "May Day?"

"Below in the hall," he agreed, "with feasting in the courtyard. We shall have to find Alan another lute; what would a wedding be without music?"

"So long as he promises not to sing those horrible verses he made up about us both."

Robin laughed. "I shall make him promise it."

Marian, of a sudden completely overcome with an exaltation and exhilaration she could not possibly describe, wrapped herself around him—heart, soul, spirit, and limbs—and clung. For the first time in days the unmade world and its perilous future seemed not so daunting.

And these tears were all for joy.

William deLacey, on the verge of sleep, was visited by an idea so sudden and altogether entertaining that it jolted him back into complete wakefulness. In his head he heard the *click-click-click!* of a plan coming together, and grinned into the darkness. As the last piece locked into place, he laughed aloud in sheer jubilation.

He tore back the covers, leaned over to the chest beside his bed, and took from its lid the striker and flint. By touch he employed them; heard the scrape, saw the spark, smelled the pungent tang. In a moment the spark set the candle wick aflame. Parchment lay there beside it, and a quill, and an ink pot. He had learned that often his best inspiration came as he fell asleep; had also learned not to begrudge the lost sleep, because invariably the idea that interrupted it proved intensely satisfying.

He swung his legs over the edge and sat there, drawing parchment to him even as he uncapped the ink. When the quill was properly weighted, he began to write in haste, smiling all the while.

When he was done, he read what he'd written, thought it through again, added a final line, then signed it with a flourish so exuberant the feather passed through the candle flame and caught fire. DeLacey swore, dropped the quill to the floor, then leaped out of bed to make certain the burning feather would not set his coverlet afire. Satisfied it was put out at last, if burned and curled into a malodorous stump, he folded the parchment, sealed it closed, then got back into bed. The stench of crisped quill annoyed him, but as he thought again on his plan irritation faded.

Still smiling, he blew out the candle, slid beneath the covers, and went to sleep at once.

*   *   *

He lay very still beside her, aware of every inch of her body. How the skin met his, how the curves fit his own, how the hair, come loose of its braid, wound itself around him as if to make certain he would not leave. But he had no intention of it. He was where he most wanted to be.

She slept deeply, spent at last of labors both physical and emotional, unaware that he was awake. He did not disturb her. He merely lay there, content. There were tasks that lay ahead—Much's rescue, the sorting out of the taxes—but in this moment, having settled at last the question of whether they would marry or continue to live in sin, such tasks were distant. *This* time she had said yes. *This* time she had agreed.

It was astonishing how so simple a thing could kindle such happiness.

And ironic, he felt, that now, when she assented, he could offer her nothing at all. Nothing but himself.

With Marian beside him he lay in the darkness, staring at the roof, and swore then that he if he could offer her nothing of his own, he would do whatever was necessary to see that what was already hers remained so. Regardless of such men as earls and sheriffs. Even such men as kings.

Twenty-Nine

They gathered in the courtyard, longbows at hand and quivers at their belts, save for Tuck, who bore neither. Marian was clad again in her borrowed men's clothing, hair braided tightly and stuffed down the back of her tunic, hidden beneath the hooded capelet. She agreed with Robin that she did not make an overly convincing boy, but she believed it possible to draw no attention: a bit of dirt smeared on her face to alter the lines even while hooded; eyes kept mostly downcast; nails pared back nearly to the quick and dirt worked into the cuticles; strides lengthened and posture roughened; a stain upon her chin that mimicked a blemish and drew the eye away from the rest of her face.

Her part was not to go into alehouses, but to find quiet places near the castle gates, lingering idly, moving from time to time so as not to draw attention. It was Alan and Will who would go into the alehouses to learn news of the sheriff's activities and if he had any imminent plans for a public punishment, and Robin who would remain near the stocks and the block, where Much most likely would be taken.

She was confident she could manage the subterfuge. No one would expect Lady Marian of Ravenskeep to be clad as a boy, carrying bow and quiver. Often people saw only what they expected to see. She would not withstand scrutiny, but there was no reason anyone should examine her so long as she did not draw the attention of the castle guards.

She saw Robin examining each of them, as if he weighed their worth. But she knew him; it wasn't that he doubted them. He worried now that he led them into a battle, that he risked their lives, that they put faith in his ability to see them through such risk. He was what her father had been: a natural leader whose mind worked in such a way that he was first to comprehend, first to offer suggestions for resolutions. Such men, regardless of birth, eventually were looked to by others as deliverance, if such was needed.

This time it was Much's deliverance. They none of them would shirk it. But neither would Robin merely fling them at the enemy with no thought to their fate.

She caught his eye then. For a moment he was as serious as she had ever seen him, thinking of the task; and then he marked that it was she, remembered what he had asked in their bed the night before, and what she had answered.

Unable to help herself, Marian smiled. Robin smiled back. It was a fleeting moment of intense privacy, of a shared past and future. It left a warm glow in her soul.

He looked again at the others. The plan was simple, Robin said. Alan and Will were to find out what they could, then, like him, stay near the Square. When Much was brought out, Robin would, at an opportune moment—and from a distance—confront the sheriff and order the boy released. If he was not released—and Robin did not believe the sheriff would simply acquiesce—they would do what was necessary.

" 'Necessary'?" Alan asked warily.

Robin looked at him. Mildly he said, "That is why we carry longbows."

The minstrel rubbed one palm against his hosen, as if ridding it of sweat—or, Marian thought, wishing for his lute. He was musician, not mercenary.

"Here," Scarlet said roughly, " 'tis only Normans we'll be shooting."

Alan cast him a baleful glance even as Tuck blanched. "I would as lief not shoot anyone," the minstrel declared.

"We've done this before," Robin said calmly, still not pressing.

"Five years ago," Little John muttered.

"Here," Scarlet said again, "you'll be in the forest. What have *you* to think on?"

"The sheriff killed those men," Marian said flatly, making herself the target so Robin wouldn't be. Accordingly they shifted to look at her. "You shot them to wound, yes? But he cut their throats."

"We *tried* only to wound," Little John agreed. "But some died of our arrows."

"Then try to wound again, if necessary," Robin said, shedding diffidence. "I won't ask you to kill. But be certain the sheriff shall do more than merely *try* to chop off Much's hands." It succeeded in silencing additional protests, and he continued. "It is Market Day. In the confusion, in the aftermath, Tuck's cassock and tonsure will buy him a moment or two to spirit Much away. Any man, even a Norman soldier, will hold a killing stroke at first sight of a monk. It should be enough time, particularly in the crowd."

Tuck's face was pallid. "One does pray so."

Scarlet's tone was uninflected. "What about the sheriff?"

They knew what he asked, and why, but no one offered an answer. He leaned and spat, then nodded to himself. "So be it. He's mine."

"Will," Robin said, "our task is to get Much to safety."

"Aye, and so we will. But if, in this 'confusion' and 'aftermath' you speak about, an arrow finds that bastard's black heart, who's to complain?"

"We want you alive," Marian said with no little vehemence.

Scarlet looked at her sharply, startled. Then he hitched a shoulder. "I'm not dying, am I? Just shooting."

"I'd advise against shooting *him*," Robin said dryly. "It would complicate matters even more." He glanced at the others. "Find rooftops. Find anything with height—and a clear means of escape—and go there. If we are fortunate, the threat of our presence will be enough. We'll meet in the forest near the road, where we met last night." He looked hard at Marian, no longer smiling, no longer conjuring between them the warmth of memory. "Keep yourself safe."

He meant her not to shoot, not to put herself in harm's way. She looked at the others one by one, men who had faced danger, men who had, in the name of a king, been the cause of other men's deaths. Tuck was troubled, as she expected. Little John was grim-faced, unhappy at being sentenced to hide in Sherwood even if he had no taste for killing. Alan's elegant hands gripped the bow with none of the delicacy he tendered his lute. Scarlet, being Scarlet, wore no expression at all, though his eyes were dark with malice. Thinking, she did not doubt, of his poor dead wife, murdered by Norman soldiers.

She thought of what they risked, and why, and for whom. "I saw Much," she said quietly. "The sheriff beat him. Himself. He took his own hand to him, and he *beat him bloody*—and then told him he'd chop off both his hands. All because Much wouldn't tell him where any of you were."

It was as much for Robin as for the others. And there was no more talk of keeping safe, of not shooting, of shooting only to wound.

Tuck said, with startling simplicity, "God will see. God will hear. God will provide." He crossed himself. "And God *will* forgive."

Huntington broke the seal and shook away wax fragments as he unfolded the parchment. He was aware of Ralph remaining next to the bed, lingering to see if there was business for him to conduct on his lord's behalf. The earl had considered telling Ralph to hold the letter until later, but curiosity had caused him to give it his attention. He and the Sheriff of Nottingham had parted on civil but unproductive terms, and he could think of no good cause why deLacey would be writing him so soon.

Unless it be to mend a wall he sees as broken . . . Huntington flattened the crackling letter and turned it into the light so he might better read it.

"My lord?"

He was staring. He realized it. Staring into space.

"My lord?"

He refolded the letter upon its creases and considered the import of the news, its implication, and the ramifications if he went forward with the carefully couched suggestion.

"My lord earl?"

Huntington smiled briefly and extended the letter to Ralph. "See to this," he ordered. "Carry it out at once."

"My lord." Ralph accepted the parchment and bowed himself out of the room.

William deLacey calmly finished his watered wine as guards brought up the prisoner from the dungeon. He was somewhat startled to see how the eyes had blackened, how swollen was the face; apparently his blow had broken the boy's nose. Much had contrived to wash himself, such as he could manage, but it served merely to point up the contrast between pallid flesh and purpling bruises.

The soldiers brought him into the hall. When Much saw whom he faced, he recoiled visibly. Wrist manacles chimed. A throttled sound caught in his throat. DeLacey thought it was perhaps a whimper, poorly suppressed. "*I* shall not strike you again," he promised comfortingly. "The next blow you feel will be the ax taking your hands."

The whimper became a wail. Much fought briefly, was subdued at once. When he realized there would be no escape, the boy sagged, trembling. His face was bloodless.

DeLacey heard the scrape of wood against stone: Mercardier, still seated at the table, shifting on the bench to have a better view. Smiling, the sheriff answered the incipient question. "It shall be today, you see," he said. "Not a fortnight from now. He has friends, this boy, men who fancy themselves his defenders. I will give them no opportunity to put a plan in motion for rescue. This shall be done now."

Though Mercardier's tone was uninflected, deLacey read disbelief into it. "You think Locksley would risk himself for this boy?"

"I do," he answered flatly. "He is a fool for such things as *he* interprets as just and righteous. His morals are entirely flexible. But this boy is a thief, an unrepentant cutpurse, as anyone in Nottingham may attest, and he participated in a heinous crime when he, with the others, stole a tax shipment intended for Prince John. Twelve of my men died in that theft. This punishment is not only merited, but overdue."

"Intended for Prince John?" Mercardier echoed.

Inwardly deLacey chided himself. "Intended for the Exchequer," he clarified with careful intonation. "Prince John was in Lincoln on behalf of the king, awaiting the shipment. But it was stolen by Locksley—calling himself Robin Hood, as if that would shield him against discovery—and his companions." He smiled grimly. "I was present, Captain. I do assure you I am intimately familiar with what happened. In fact, I was the only survivor."

"How fortunate for you," Mercardier said with no evidence of irony.

The chains chimed. "For Lionheart!" Much cried. "For the ransom! Robin said!"

"*Robin*," deLacey observed, mocking the diminutive, "is as much a thief as you." He gestured sharply at the guards. "Take him outside and wait for me. I'll accompany you to the Square."

*　*　*

Marian watched as Alan, Tuck, and Will Scarlet disappeared through the city gate into Nottingham's populace. It took no longer than a moment for them to become anonymous, merely bodies like any other. Alan and Scarlet, with longbows and quivers, would be taken for yeomen, even as she and Robin would be. Tuck was what he was, judged merely by cassock and tonsure; she did not doubt Robin was correct when he said the sheriff's soldiers would not immediately attempt to stop Tuck or harm him, particularly before a crowd. As for Robin himself, she did not fear for his ability to remain safe; he had survived the Crusade, even captivity. He had fought—and killed—before.

He stood with her now beside the city gate, bent over, ostensibly digging a stone out of his shoe. The hood shielded his face and pale hair. She kept her own face downturned, meeting no one's glance.

"Will you stay here?" he asked in a low voice, meaning outside the city where she would be safe. Not involved.

She had known it would come. "You are three," she said, counting only those with weapons; Tuck could do nothing from a distance. "You need me."

"You have never shot a man."

Marian gripped her bow, aware of the weight of the arrow-laden quiver over one shoulder. "And I hope not to do so now," she pointed out. "I have a good eye. I can shoot *beside* them. The warning should be enough. You said so yourself."

"I said I *hoped* it would be enough." He glanced up, hazel eyes serious. "Marian—"

"I know," she interrupted. "I shall be careful, I swear it. But so must you."

He nodded at the gate. "Wherever you go, make certain you have an escape. Stay away from unfamiliar alleys and lanes. Allow yourself room to run. If they catch you—"

"I know," she said again. "I do know, Robin."

He lingered, tense as a bowstring. Clearly he wanted to kiss her, to touch her, but would not, lest it draw unwanted attention. "Go," he said.

She drew a breath so deep it fair made her lungs creak, then turned on her heel and strode toward the city gate.

Behind her, markedly altering his accent from nobility to peasantry, Robin called out that he'd meet her in the tavern called The Lion's Heart. First, he explained loudly, he had to take a piss.

Shrouded by the hood, Marian winced. Then she raised her hand in a brief gesture denoting agreement, and went on through the gate.

Thirty

Nottingham was always busy on Market Day, thronged with residents and merchants as well as peasants and tenant-farmers from the outlying regions. Robin used the crowd to hide himself among folk as he would among Sherwood's trees.

He had put off the fine clothing he'd donned at his father's castle in deference to the earl's insistence, though he had been glad enough to strip out of mud-laden tunic and hosen and put on dry again. Now he wore a plain gray summer-weight wool tunic, hosen with buskins cross-gartered to his knees, leather bracers, and the hooded capelet. He was hardly alone in the latter; it was not unusual to hear someone described as the "hooded man" or "the man in the hood." The only risk he ran was if he came face-to-face with one of the sheriff's men, and only if that man knew him by sight. Otherwise, he was merely a yeoman in Nottingham on Market Day, very like perhaps a fifth of the current population.

Of course, once Much was rescued, the risks increased significantly.

Robin's mind was fixed upon that task as once it fixed upon the needs of war, the requirements of a man's mind, soul, and body that permitted him to kill another man.

He had never enjoyed war, not as the Lionheart relished it. He did not enjoy this. But he accepted both as his duty, to take lives, if necessary, in the pursuit of an honorable goal: to win back Jerusalem from the Infidel, and to keep Much from being maimed in the private battle Robin of Locksley—no, *Robin Hood*—now fought with the Sheriff of Nottingham.

He could see neither Will nor Alan, nor Tuck, nor even Marian. Robin supposed that was good, for if he could pick them immediately out of the crowd they were too obvious. But it made him uneasy that Marian was absent, or as like to invisible as an outlaw in Sherwood Forest, mere shadow in the wood. He would far rather know where she was, so he could keep an eye on her and be certain she was safe.

Have faith, he chided himself. They were none of them fools, nor careless with their skins.

But Marian's skin was more precious to him than his own.

Have faith, he repeated, because if he divided his concentration with concern for Marian, he risked everyone's life, including hers.

Robin shook off the nagging worry and reconnoitered several alleys, lanes, and closes near the open square hosting stalls and wagons as well as the stocks, whipping post, and the block where limbs were struck off. He considered renting a room at an inn, an upstairs room with a window overlooking the square. But swift escape would be hindered by such things as narrow stairs, ladders, or even people who might prove loyal to the sheriff. Much *was* a thief; Robin did not doubt someone might attempt to stop him once the deed was done.

And then he recalled Abraham the Jew, a money-lender with whom he had conducted business years before in the name of King Richard. The Jewish Quarter was not close enough to the Square to be ideally situated for his needs, but other buildings were. And a fair share of people who lived and worked in other buildings owed debts to Abraham.

Robin wasted no time. He ran.

In short order Marian discovered she had better chance than expected of remaining anonymous and unremarkable even near the castle gates. She was dressed like a great many others, and a great many others thronged the lanes and alleys as well as the square itself, browsing booths, stalls, carts, wagons, even cloths spread on the ground. Men and women shouted out their wares as others bargained with raised voices. A street minstrel, whose poor voice and lute skills would appall Alan, had attracted a clutch of young women who seemed inured to sour notes and wandering pitch. Not far from the gates stood the smithy, where the broad, sweating man before its open doors pounded hot iron against an anvil. Not far from him was a tinker's wagon, where pots were mended; nearby a pack of street dogs fought noisily over a bitch apparently in season.

Marian felt some of the tension spill out of her shoulders. She had focused solely on the danger, on the idea of what they risked despite the goal and her willingness; she had forgotten how noisy and crowded Market Day was. While the sheriff might find the audience he desired to see his justice meted out, they, too, could use the audience to shield them from the sheriff.

Feeling better, Marian began drifting from stall to booth, from wagon to cart, keeping an eye on the castle gates. The castle was surrounded by a curtain-walled bailey with a sentry-walk atop it. But the walls were in turn surrounded by streets and alleys tangled up like skeins of yarn. It was small task to find a narrow, winding lane at one corner of the castle wall that gave out into the square even as it led away into the depths of the city itself, bisected by countless others. There was even a water barrel to catch runoff from the wall, and a bench, both providing reason to linger. She could slouch there at the corner unobtrusively with escape at her back, and a clear view of the castle gates from which the sheriff and his soldiers would issue with Much in their midst. Meanwhile, she could wander; deLacey would, as Robin noted, wish to parade his prisoner. There was time for her to take up her post at the wall.

She nodded absently, then leaned the longbow against her shoulder as she wiped a damp-palmed hand against the hem of her tunic. Much deserved this. They would not fail him. But she would be a liar if she denied a measure of apprehension and anxiety.

Get up, Robin had said. Find a high place, for the angle and the chance for escape. Well, she lacked the high place as well as significant height. But the castle gates were tall, and the sound of an arrow loosed from an English longbow, whining through the air and thunking into wood, was unmistakable no matter where it struck.

She took the bow grip into her hand once again, and with the other checked the seating of the quiver over her shoulder. Robin had lessoned her well in five years, and she had wasted no time rehoning her eye after deLacey had come to her hall. Let him reap what he had sowed.

DeLacey set Gisbourne the task of gathering up a small troop of castle guards and going out into the city to cry the announcement of the upcoming punishment of a notorious thief. Once the introductions were made so that as large a crowd as possible was ready to witness the moment, the sheriff and another clutch of soldiers would escort Much to Market Square and to the block, where he would be chained down and his hands struck off. But only *after* deLacey had recounted the boy's sins and crimes, not the least of which was helping "Robin Hood" rob the tax shipment of monies gathered from the citizens themselves.

He knew there had been widespread laughter and jests with regard to Locksley stealing the shipment quite literally from under the sheriff's own nose; the auxiliary tax collection had been most unpopular, and many believed the robbery poetic justice, especially since Locksley foolishly had Abraham the Jew distribute the money among the poor before it was reclaimed by the Crown. Even King Richard, newly ransomed, had been amused by the audacity of the robbery and subsequent distribution, and pardoned the act rather than punished it. But the wealthy merchants of the city had been neither pleased nor amused, and the only reason deLacey had not been able to arrest Locksley and the others was that the Lionheart was home again, and all of England rejoiced. It would have been politically foolish to arrest the son of a powerful earl when that man was also a Crusader knighted personally by the immensely popular king.

Times were different now. There would be no pardon for such acts as thievery, and Much was known as an expert pickpocket. DeLacey had simple-minded Much dead to rights.

Meanwhile, Robert of Locksley was disinherited; Marian was on the verge of losing her manor and lands; Alan of the Dales was cut off from his former life among the gentry, forced to make silver pennies in roadhouses instead of silver marks in the halls of lords; and Tuck was denied an opportunity to join the priesthood and rise through the ranks of the Church. DeLacey had begun his revenge, however slowly it progressed, and he did not doubt eventually he would have them all destroyed.

Robin ran lightly up the narrow stairs to the room under the eaves, secure in the knowledge no one in the building would hinder him. Abraham's note had given him the freedom to come and go at need, and the door to the street would not be immediately unbarred should soldiers arrive demanding to be let in, which would give him a chance to escape.

The room huddled beneath a steeply pitched roof, the angle so extreme that Robin had to duck his head to avoid cracking open his skull. A single window illuminated the tiny room. A broken cot was shoved against the wall beneath the window; Robin pushed it out of the way with a scrape of wood on wood, then unlatched the lopsided shutter. Leather hinges were stiff and unwieldy, but he tamed the shutter's temper and set it against the wall. A narrow opening, but tall enough for him to perch himself in it so long as he sat upon the sill. Below the window extended the thatched overhang shielding the street door from rain. Robin worked his body into the unshuttered frame and settled his rump upon the sill, one foot outside dug into the thatching for support, one bracing himself from the inside. The building fronted the portion of the Square in front of the castle gates; he had a clear and unobstructed view of the pillory, the stocks, and the block. From here, an archer with an English longbow could punch an arrow through plate armor, let alone through mail.

Robin stripped off the quiver, leaned down into the room, and set it against the wall. He could not shoot from this position—the bow was too long for the opening—but he had two options: to slide back into the room, take up one arrow after another, nock, aim, and let fly through the window; or to stand up on the thatched overhang and shoot from the open.

He nodded. And waited.

Marian's head jerked up as she heard the call: *"Oyez! Oyez!"* It was quickly followed by the shouted announcement that all citizens of Nottingham were to gather in the square to witness the punishment of a known pickpocket.

A chill swept her bones, setting the hairs to rising on her flesh. She saw the gates pushed open, saw the troop of soldiers, saw Gisbourne at their head. They wore mail, blue surcoats, Norman helms, broadswords, and carried shields and crossbows. The latter disturbed her; crossbows were limited in distance and accuracy compared to longbows, but nonetheless afforded the soldiers better offense against archers than swords. It gave them more latitude to stop the rescue, to wound or possibly kill Robin and the others.

Or even me . . . But she shook that off at once, concentrating instead on sliding through the crowd to take up her position near the corner of the wall, beside the bench and barrel. When a taller man stepped in front of her, it was a wholly natural response for her to climb up onto the bench, not in the least unusual. The added height gave her a better view of the gates and the soldiers and allowed her room to shoot over the crowd, but she was not so tall that she was markedly obvious. Robin had been right to send Little John into Sherwood; the giant would have been noticed immediately, and targeted by deLacey's men.

She was aware of an almost painful emptiness in the pit of her stomach. Tension bled back into her shoulders. Her breath ran shallow, as if she could not pull in enough air to fill her lungs. Marian wrenched her eyes from the soldiers and looked about swiftly, searching for Robin, Tuck, Scarlet, and Alan. Tuck she knew had to be somewhere in the crowd, somewhere near the block, but the others would be up if possible, stationed at a high vantage point. No one on the ground would have opportunity to shoot through the crowd without the risk of hitting an innocent bystander.

Her quick search found no familiar faces. She supposed that was good; if even she, knowing they were somewhere in the square, couldn't find them, neither could the soldiers.

Gisbourne and the sheriff's men cleared a passage through the gathering crowd, opening room around the block. She heard hawkers cursing Gisbourne; all customers now turned their attention to him instead of continuing to bargain. But after a few moments even the vendors grew interested. Some of them threw cloths over their wares and shinnied up the stall posts to balance atop their shelves or to cling precariously to awning supports. The crowd was in two layers now: those on the ground, and those climbing up on whatever they might—stalls, wagons, benches, even the pillory and stocks—to find a better view. People gathered in ground-floor doorways and second-story windows. Fathers snatched children up onto their shoulders, bidding them not to miss the show.

"*Oyez! Oyez!*"

The crowd was pushed back further by Gisbourne and his troop of soldiery, while other onlookers were ordered down from the stocks and pillory. Marian assessed the opening in the crowd, noting how much room surrounded the area where Much would be brought. Into that space, if necessary, she had to carefully place her arrows so as to warn away the soldiers, while harming no one.

A full listing of Much's crimes was shouted above the noise. And then a second troop of soldiers exited the castle, a clutch of men on foot surrounding the boy, moving awkwardly in his chains. Behind them, mounted, rode William deLacey.

Those nearest the bench upon which Marian stood surged forward, moving into the Square proper. Marian still needed the extra height to see over the crowd, but no one stood beside her. No one stood behind her. Everyone was thronging into the square, trying to see and hear what was about to happen.

One well-placed arrow, and deLacey was dead.

The very thing that Will Scarlet desired.

Marian's breath ran raggedly through a constricted throat. Somewhere in the crowd, somewhere above the crowd, Scarlet drew his bowstring. She knew it. *Knew* it. And cursed him for it.

"Don't," she murmured. "Will—don't."

Much was the object. Not the sheriff's death.

Thirty-One

DeLacey was pleased by the number of people thronging Market Square. It proved there was always interest in justice, despite the occasional complaints from the peasantry that they were not treated fairly. But a thief was a thief; whereas poachers engendered sympathy among those who lacked food, cutpurses did not. Cutpurses stole from everyone, and in an offensively personal manner.

Gisbourne's troop had done a good job clearing the crowd from the immediate vicinity of the block. The sheriff wanted to make sure any attempt at rescue would require Robin and the others to cross unshielded space, where they would be easily spotted by his men. Gisbourne's mounted troop now took up equidistant stations within the interior perimeter of the crowd; people feared and respected horses even if they were willing to challenge men.

Gisbourne himself had dismounted, handed his horse off, and now stood near the brazier next to the block. Mature coals burned within, brought over from the smithy; a length of iron had been thrust into the heat for use in cautery once each hand was struck off. There was no sense in letting the boy bleed to death. The point was to set a visible example, a reminder people would see every time they saw Much.

And as much a reminder to Robert of Locksley that no one was inviolable.

The boy was taken directly to the block, but was not immediately chained down. He was made to stand beside it, between the block and the pungent coals, where, deLacey was satisfied to see, he trembled uncontrollably. The face was corpse-candle pale save where bruises purpled it. A fitting vision of imminent justice for other cutpurses and malcontents.

Still mounted, deLacey had a good view of the crowd. Hundreds of faces stared at him expectantly, some fearful, some appalled, some plainly fascinated by what was about to happen. It never failed to pique the sheriff's curiosity that public punishments and executions brought out such perversely avid interest.

DeLacey thrust a hand into the air. It took a few minutes for the waves of sound to die down as the serried ranks of people were hushed by their neighbors. When all was quiet save for the squall of an infant or the piping question of a child, the background complaints of livestock brought in for Market Day, he lowered the arm. He pitched his voice to carry over the crowd.

"This boy," he said. "This boy, this miller's son you know as Much, is a thief. He steals hard-earned money from everyone here, be you merchant, yeoman, gentlewife, or even, much as it pains me to say it, the Sheriff of Nottingham." He paused for the tittering and laughter to die down, allowing them their amusement at his expense. "You know this boy. You know who he is, *what* he is, and what he has done. For every purse cut, for every ware snatched from wagons and stalls, you need only look upon him to see the face of the thief who stole it."

"Every purse?" someone called skeptically. "That busy, then, is he?"

DeLacey overrode the challenge and the scattered laughter it provoked. "When next you bring complaints to me of such things, recall what you see this day. Remember it. And know that I *will* punish every thief caught. For it is my duty as High Sheriff of Nottinghamshire to see that justice is served, that the king's law is obeyed. I swear to you this day that *no* man—and no woman—is above the law. Justice sees no stations, only actions. So let it be known by all gathered here today— wealthy merchant, innkeeper, goodwife, yeoman, men of the cloth, *even the thieves themselves*—that none shall go unpunished." As he intended, the crowd cheered lustily. He smiled, raised his arm again. "I promise you this day—"

But that promise remained unmade. Before he could finish, an arrow sped into the ground at his horse's hooves. That one was still quivering as another and another and yet a fourth sliced through the air to stand upright from the ground.

"*Hold!*" someone shouted.

Three more arrows flew down from the heavens, striking the block, the stocks, even the pillory. A fourth found a home in one soldier's mailed shoulder, and he cried out in shock and pain as he bent over in his saddle, clasping the shaft.

DeLacey's first thought was of disbelief; how could they have known he would act so quickly when he had promised them a fortnight? But there was no time for questions; as his plan collapsed, he roared at his soldiers to find the archers. "It's Locksley!" he shouted, gesticulating. "Look for him—look for the earl's son, and the giant, the minstrel, Will Scarlet . . ." The arrows had come *down*. "Gisbourne—look for them up high, on roofs, in the windows—"

His horse shifted uneasily. He reined it in sharply, annoyed—and then the animal abruptly staggered and began to collapse.

Robin, having balanced atop the thatched overhang to shoot, twitched slightly in startlement as the arrow struck deLacey's horse. It was not his shaft, nor would it have been his choice to drop the sheriff to the ground, for there deLacey would make a far more difficult target; unless, of course, Will Scarlet had intended the sheriff as his target and shot the horse by mistake.

He grimaced as the horse went down, wishing he had impressed upon Scarlet with more vigor that killing deLacey would do them considerable harm. Tuck had gotten Much away with greater alacrity than expected, and the crowd had swallowed both boy and Benedictine. But there were no guarantees of safety; deLacey had his share of supporters among the wealthier citizenry, and Much could still be recaptured before he and Tuck ever reached Sherwood. Rescuing a cutpurse from maiming was one thing. Robin doubted anyone save Much's victims would care. Killing the Lord High Sheriff of Nottinghamshire, however, would invite the scrutiny and fury of King John himself. Even the Lionheart could not forgive the outright murder of a sheriff. John, who had favored deLacey on more than one occasion, would see them all executed.

Of course, that was only if the sheriff *were* killed, and if they *were* caught—and if he didn't kill Scarlet himself before anyone else reached him.

In Arabic, Robin muttered maledictions. Then he returned his attention to the matter at hand: making certain Much and Tuck were not immediately pursued.

The very instant she had loosed the arrow, Marian saw it coming, saw what was happening; *knew* what would happen.

Her sore hand spasmed into a cramp, flaring in sudden pain as she released the bowstring. Instead of planting itself in the ground, the arrow found a living target.

This was not at all what she had intended. Only to shoot *near* the horse, to control the sheriff's actions. Precisely as she had done twice before. No one, neither man nor beast, was supposed to be struck. No one was to be harmed.

But the horse had gone down, was dying—and it was her fault.

Hers alone.

She recoiled upon the bench, curling back abruptly against the castle wall to slam her spine and the back of her skull into stone. The bow was heavy in her hand. She wanted nothing more than to hurl it away, to strip out of the quiver, to take back what she had done and make it all *un*done. Frantically she rubbed the cramp out of her hand, cursing herself for weakness.

And then movement caught her eye. She jerked her head sideways, saw the mailed man in the lane behind her, a tall, dark, bull of a man, staring straight at her.

In that instant she comprehended what the disguise meant. It was safety of a sort, but also danger. She was not Marian of Ravenskeep. She was merely the hooded stranger, presumably male, who had shot at the sheriff, had brought down his horse. And so she would be treated.

She responded without thought. Despite the residual pain in her hand, the arrow was nocked, the bow raised, the string drawn back to her chin in an effortless series of motions, precisely as Robin had taught her. No more did she wish to discard the weapon. It was now deliverance.

He had, she marked, a broadsword, but sheathed, and no crossbow. To reach her, to threaten her, to kill her, he would have to cross the distance dividing them. And in such time as that required, she could drive an arrow through his body.

That much he knew. And halted.

Her hand trembled, and so did the bow. Marian eased herself down from the bench. She backed up with infinite care, making certain her feet had decent purchase on the packed and rutted lane. If she tripped he would be on her; and any shot she attempted would go awry.

When enough space lay between them that he could neither kill nor capture her, Marian released the tension of the string without releasing the arrow. She turned. She ran.

As his mount went down, deLacey caught a glimpse of a feathered shaft standing out from the horse's ribs in front of his right leg, then threw himself away from the dying animal so he would not be trapped as he had been trapped once before in similar circumstances. He rolled awkwardly, blindly aware of screams, shouts, cries of shock. But there was also a surging, powerful undercurrent of abrupt and avid interest:

they were not the targets, not the good folk of Nottingham. He was. The king's man. Sheriff. The *Norman* sheriff.

DeLacey struggled up to his knees. "Find them! Find them, I say—" An arrow whizzed by his head from behind. He flinched and remained kneeling so as to present a smaller target. "Gisbourne—"

But Gisbourne, on foot, stood near the crowd, both hands held stiffly away from his body in an eloquent statement of obedience to the enemy's shouted order. In utter disbelief, deLacey stared at his men and saw them standing down. Each of them was armed, but no one moved to defend him. They were clearly nonplussed by the attack, uneasily aware they were at a disadvantage. The man who had been shot still bent forward in his saddle, cursing noisily in Norman French, but no one moved to his aid, lest they become targets as well.

DeLacey realized then the boy was gone. In the confusion, as his men looked at their wounded comrade, the boy had escaped. Or been rescued.

"Are you soldiers?" he roared, infuriated. "Or cowards? In the name of King John, I order you to do your duty! Find that boy! Find Locksley and the others!"

"Sheriff!" called the voice he now recognized as that he most despised. "Your soldiers are wise men. I urge you to be the same."

DeLacey hung there on his knees, not testing Locksley's resolve. But he addressed the audience, not the men who meant to stop him. Much was missing, swallowed by the crowd. And he knew he needed that crowd if his men were to find the boy. "He is a *thief!*" he shouted. "Will you give him up to murderers and rapists? To men who steal your coin?"

"Taxes!" Locksley shouted. "Taxes collected from people who have no money with which to pay, and yet are *made* to pay. Again and again! How many of you paid your taxes five years ago, and then again, and then donated to the ransom for the Lionheart?"

A massed shout went up from the crowd, followed by muttered commentary. At last a few of the soldiers were lifting crossbows, preparing to span them.

Locksley called, "And how many of you were given some of your money *back* from that additional collection when it was taken back from King John, who wanted it for himself?"

This time the shout was a roar of triumph. The soldiers aimed their crossbows not toward Locksley's voice, but at the crowd.

DeLacey swore under his breath. He was winning them, was Locksley. While they feared the sheriff and his men, they were malleable. But fear

was clearly fading; his men had been slow to act, and the crowd was fast becoming a mob, spurred on by Locksley's appeal. DeLacey hastily waved at his men to hold and made another attempt to recapture the spectators. "But how many times has that boy stolen for *him*self? How many times has your precious coin gone for a sweetmeat stuffed into his mouth, when you meant it for something else?"

"And how many times have the tax collectors sent out by William deLacey threatened you and your families?" Locksley countered. "No one is safe. Only a matter of days ago the sheriff set his men on Lady Marian FitzWalter's manor, turning the livestock loose and destroying furniture. If he is willing to do that to a knight's daughter, how can *you* stand against him? He has set himself up as lord of Nottinghamshire, taking your money in the name of the king!"

Thirty-Two

Robin slid back in the narrow window and caught up his quiver, slipping it over one shoulder. He had no time to linger; best to make his escape now, to get out of Nottingham and back into Sherwood, where soldiers would find it difficult to track him and the others. He trusted Tuck to bring Much to the meeting place, and the others to make their ways as well. But his mind was on Marian even as he ran back down the crude staircase. He knew she was neither a fool nor a coward, but neither was she accustomed to being hunted. It changed a man, made a man think differently, to anticipate the actions and threats of others and respond accordingly. To be willing to do whatever was necessary. He had no doubt she could find her way to the meeting place, but she still needed to get out of Nottingham without being discovered or caught.

"Taxes are necessary!" deLacey shouted. "Without taxes England will fail. How else do you suppose Crusades are mounted?"

"*Fair* taxes," Locksley agreed. "Collected by fair men. Is there anyon in Nottingham who has not been victim to an overzealous officer of the king

The crowd roared denial.

"Is there anyone in Nottingham who sees his family suffer so he might pay the taxes?"

This time the crowd affirmed it.

"It is the law!" deLacey shouted. "The boy must pay for his crimes. *Give him back!*"

But it was too late. Much was gone, perhaps shielded by the crowd, perhaps spirited away to a building, or an alley, or hidden within one of the stalls. DeLacey drew in a breath to order his men to commence a search, and then realized it was futile. The crowd was clearly on Locksley's side, thanks to his discourse about taxes. Horses could break through easily enough by virtue of trampling people, soldiers could even shoot various spectators, but either the mass of people would obstruct the search by the expedient of simple stolid numbers, or would panic into flight if soldiers began loosing crossbow quarrels or hacking bodies with broadswords.

Panic could kill. He had seen it happen before. And the memory of the day would not be the sheriff's attempt to carry out a lawful punishment of a lone boy cutpurse, thwarted by outlaws, but that William deLacey's overzealous actions had caused the deaths of men, women, and children, killed by Norman soldiers.

He had not survived in office this long by permitting wounded pride and fury to overcome political pragmatism. He had himself been a soldier, once. He understood the complex geography that lay between true defeat and strategic retreat.

DeLacey climbed to his feet, glad to be off his knees. To an archer in the crowd, on the same level, he was no longer a target, but he knew full well Locksley and the others could kill him easily from their elevated positions; he knew also that they themselves knew it and were secure in that knowledge. With precise, deliberate movements, the sheriff gripped his sword hilt with his off hand and drew it. He dangled it from his fingers, then released. The weapon thudded to the ground.

"Stand down," he called, so that his men—and Locksley—could hear.

Let Locksley have the day, have the boy. There would be another opportunity, and time for another plan.

Marian tugged the hood forward to make certain it didn't slide back in her flight. No one seeing her hasten by would name her a woman, merely a young man clad as a yeoman and carrying bow and quiver; but all knew the sheriff and his soldiers had been stymied by hooded archers,

a known cutpurse rescued. Anyone who had been robbed would be likely to stop her if possible, to turn her over to the sheriff. Anyone who supported the sheriff—and she knew there were many in the merchant class and nobility—would assume the worst of her.

She went into the crowd at once, however, knowing her best chance lay in losing herself among hundreds. Young man or not, yeoman or not, she was hardly the only one. If the sheriff meant to arrest everyone who wore a hood or carried a longbow, he would have to round up a fair portion of the populace.

The spectators themselves were entertained by the rescue. As she moved through the crowd, she heard laughter and jests and sly commentary on the sheriff's failure to carry out his duty, how Norman soldiers when faced with good English archers could only throw down their weapons and give way. The poorer folk had never been robbed by anyone other than the king's tax collectors and deLacey's obsessive attention to detail in the collections; they would applaud the rescue rather than decry it.

Marian slid through a knot of men, then paused. Deepening her voice, she clipped off the syllables. "W'at 'appened?"

"W'at?" someone asked. "Did 'ee miss it, then?"

"Jus' got 'ere, aye?" she muttered.

In a tumble of words, laughter, and vulgarity, she was told by several what had happened: how the sheriff had been made a right proper fool of by Robin Hood, who had once before helped the poor of Nottinghamshire.

A hand came down on her shoulder. Marian tensed into stiffness. "Aye," a man said lightly in high good humor. "Good English archers as are better'n Norman soldiers! And 'tis our taxes as pay for 'em!"

"Taxes," Marian rasped, then spat at the ground. This occasioned the same response from others; as they spat and cursed the sheriff, the king, and all tax collectors, she eased herself away from them and slipped through the crowd again.

William deLacey had neither time nor patience with the cursing soldier who yet bore an arrow buried in his shoulder. The wound was unlikely to kill him; he was therefore living testament to the troop's incompetence.

DeLacey stomped back through the gates, ordered his dead horse to be disposed of, then bellowed for Gisbourne to attend him. Gisbourne arrived at a run, helm clasped under one arm. The sheriff eyed him blackly a moment, then gestured for the others to be gone. It left him with his seneschal, who was looking more than a little trepidatious.

"Gisbourne," deLacey said silkily, "what just happened?"

"Happened, my lord?"

"What just happened, Gisbourne?" He waved an arm. "Out there?"

Color stole up Gisbourne's neck and into his face. "We lost our prisoner, sir."

"Had him *stolen,* Gisbourne! From under our noses!"

"Yes, my lord."

"Not a man of yours made any attempt to stop the outlaws."

"Sir—there was some concern that you might be killed."

"Some concern that *you* might be killed," deLacey snapped. "Do you think I don't know the face of a coward when I see one?"

The suspect's face was stiff with tension. "My lord—it seemed a wiser course to protect you."

"Protect *me!* Me, Gisbourne? I had my horse shot out from under me!"

"Well," Gisbourne ventured. "Better the horse than you. My lord."

DeLacey shut his eyes a long moment. When he opened them again, he had regained some measure of self-control. "Gisbourne, you are to gather your soldiers immediately. Divide them into three troops. Send one to Locksley Village. Send another to Ravenskeep. And the third, Gisbourne, the third you shall lead yourself—into Sherwood Forest."

Gisbourne was plainly astonished. "Into Sherwood, sir? But—"

" 'But' nothing," deLacey said. "That was Sir Robert of Locksley, Gisbourne. Or perhaps he has given that up in favor of a new name, one 'Robin Hood.' He has proven himself before all of Nottingham to be nothing more than an outlaw, and I will have him caught. All of them, Gisbourne. Your task now is to find them, arrest them, and bring them to me."

"All of them, my lord?"

"All of them," deLacey declared. "I was willing to let the boy go with the forfeiture of his hands, but this crime cannot be tolerated. Locksley is no longer the heir of a powerful earl, Gisbourne, but a disinherited outlaw, subject to the laws of the land. No pardons will be given by *this* king, Gisbourne. Therefore it is your task to catch him—to catch them all—and bring them to me."

"Will you execute them, my lord?"

A new voice intruded, explaining matter-of-factly, "That shall be for the king to decide."

DeLacey snapped his head around, primed to upbraid the individual who dared interrupt the sheriff's business. Then he recognized the man. "Captain," he acknowledged grimly.

Mercardier inclined his head briefly, but he looked at Gisbourne.

"Do as the sheriff commands you," he said simply. "Bring them in, every man. But their disposal shall be the king's desire."

"You saw what they did," deLacey said sharply.

"Indeed," Mercardier agreed. "They disgraced you, Lord Sheriff, disgraced your authority and the authority of the king, by whose whim you hold your office. I am certain you shall have your execution, but such determination is the king's to make. Your task is merely to catch them." The mercenary gestured briefly. "Redeem yourself, Lord Sheriff. Prove to the king you deserve his confidence."

Outrage boiled into deLacey's throat like bile. "It was the *former* king who pardoned them!"

Mercardier said, without inflection, "But I think this king is nothing like his brother."

The sheriff contemplated that statement a moment, seeking clues to implication. But the mercenary was impossible to read.

And Mercardier continued, speaking to Gisbourne. "I saw the archer who shot the sheriff's horse. He is not tall, and is markedly slight, very like a boy."

DeLacey was astonished. "You *saw* him shoot my horse?"

"No, my lord. I followed the path of the arrow, and sought the archer. I found him."

"Yet you stand before me with no prisoner," deLacey said with exquisite contempt. "Am I then to assume this archer escaped? From *you*, Captain? The Lionheart's infamous mercenary, scourge of the Infidel?"

Mercardier said simply, "For the Lionheart I would gladly have died. But not, I think, for you."

With great effort, deLacey suppressed his fury. Pointedly he observed, "You knew Locksley before this. Fought with him on Crusade." There was no need to be more explicit. Mercardier would understand.

Mercardier did. "Lord Sheriff, please recall I *am* a mercenary. I am not paid for, nor can afford complications of the heart. Should the present king wish my former comrade-in-arms to be executed for what he has done, be certain I shall carry out the command." For the first time since the mercenary had arrived, deLacey recognized the dryness in his tone as irony. "You see, no man may accuse me of having a conscience."

DeLacey ground his teeth. King John had sent this man; he could not afford to antagonize him further. Not yet. Not until he had secured some promise from John that he, deLacey, would not be punished for what had happened this day. And he could not write him with a complaint of Mercardier until Locksley and the others were captured.

"Perhaps," the sheriff said, "I should have you ride out with Gisbourne. Who better to set a trap for an outlaw than one who knows how he thinks?"

Mercardier did not so much as blink. "Were I hired by you, Lord Sheriff, be certain I would do so. Were I sent by the king to serve you in this, be certain I should do so. But I was not hired by you, and the king sent me to guard his tax shipment. Not to go into the forest looking for outlaws cleverer than you."

DeLacey glared. "And if I should prevail upon the king to have you aid me in this?"

The mercenary hitched one broad shoulder in a casual shrug. "Then I would catch him, this outlaw you fear, as well as his companions. And I daresay I should keep them."

The sheriff decided then and there the day was a total failure. He had lost his incomparable example for other city pickpockets, had lost face before the citizenry of Nottingham, had lost a battle of wits with Robert of Locksley, and now even a humorless paid soldier bested him. It was time, he believed, he went back into the castle and called for wine. As much as he could drink.

But there was one matter of business to finish first. To Gisbourne, he said, "Take the men. Go. Find Locksley. Find them all. Bring them here. Do not show your face within these walls until that is accomplished." He paused, aware of Gisbourne's quick glance at Mercardier. "Do I make myself clear, Gisbourne? Because I pay *your* keep and thus have the ordering of *you* even if I do not claim this mercenary's service."

The seneschal's eyes snapped back. He colored. "Yes, my lord."

"Go."

Gisbourne went.

Robin struck a steady trot at the verge between road and forest. His ears were attuned to pursuit, but for the moment there was none. His goal was to move quickly without impediment for as long as he could, and then go into the trees. He longed briefly for Charlemagne, but he had left the horse back in the forest where they were to meet. Such was Sherwood's architecture that a man on foot stood better chance of flight through its depths than a man on horseback. It was hard to be quiet when a mount crashed through all manner of foliage, leaving obvious spoor in the detritus of his motion. A man might slip into the trees and leave no sign such as a soldier might find, particularly a Norman lacking woodcraft.

The soldiers would be angry, Robin knew, stung by deLacey's insults and their own bruised pride. Their goal would be to find Much and the men who rescued him as quickly as possible, to placate the furious sheriff as well as redeeming their own failure. But such anger and haste would increase incompetence; it was stealth that might catch their quarry, not sheer numbers and might.

Robin smiled grimly. Four more strides—and then he ducked off the verge into the trees, taking care to move quietly and carefully, leaving no sign, as he crossed into the depths. Let them try to find him. Let them crash through on horseback, alerting him to their presence. Let them curse their Norman curses, serve their Norman lords, ride their Norman horses, while an Englishman bred of English bone led them a merry chase through the heart of an English forest.

He found a deer track leading in the proper direction. It wound around through the trees, took him over fallen logs and across streambeds, but all the better. He began to jog again, finding a comfortable rhythm that put distance between him and the road, between him and any pursuit.

Marian slipped into a deep-cut doorway near the gates leading out of the city to the road beyond. It was a poorer part of town, with ramshackle lean-tos doubling as shelter, and top-heavy, sagging buildings slumping toward one another across filthy lanes fouled with refuse. Children wandered by, shouting epithets as they pelted one another with stones and horse droppings; two women followed, clad in layers of shapeless skirts and tunics and tattered shawls. Marian reached beneath her own tunic and felt the locket there. Her spirit quailed from the thought—Robin had given the necklace to her—but she removed it regardless.

When another woman came down through the lane, Marian whistled her over. She displayed the silver locket briefly, then shut it away in her hand.

The woman was curious, but equally suspicious. She stopped out of reach, studying Marian from red-rimmed eyes. Then she grinned, displaying a misery of poor teeth. " 'Tisn't a whore, this'un," she said, "not for a stripling boy!"

Even a woman took her for a lad. Marian nearly laughed through her blush, but gulped it back down. She was careful with her accent. "Your skirt," she said, "and your shawl."

"Skirt, is it?" the woman cried. "And leave me naked?"

"You're wearing two," Marian pointed out; she had made certain of that.

" 'Tis cold in winter!"

She matched the intonation. " 'Tis near summer!"

The woman gestured with her chin. "What's that bauble worth?"

"More'n *your* skirt and shawl. But never you mind, then, I'll find sommat else."

"Wait!" the woman cried as Marian made to move. She glanced around furtively. "You'll be givin' me that bauble for a skirt and a shawl?"

Marian drew breath and commenced the tale. "My husband beats me," she said. "I'm off clad as a boy, but won't hold, will it? Once I'm out of Nottingham—I'm Lincoln-bound, aye?—I'll change back to women's clothing."

"My man beats *me*," the woman responded, unconvinced. "No cause to run from that. Better a man than none."

Marian took a gamble. "Then come with me. We'll both go to Lincoln."

"Lincoln! Me!" The woman laughed and tossed her head. "Na, na, Nottingham's me home. I'll be stayin'." She eyed the locket again. "But I'll give up me shawl and skirt, I will, for that, aye? 'Twill buy me sommat better."

The exchange was made. Once the woman was gone, tucking the locket into her bosom, Marian immediately pulled the skirt on over her trews, tugged it down to cover her ankles, slipped the hood to her shoulder. Then she unstrung the bow, looped the string around her waist, wrapped the shawl around her head and shoulders to hide the quiver and her face, and took up the bow again. The wood was curved from its service, but she tied a torn strip of grimy homespun around the grip, then affected to lean on the unstrung bow as if she had a bad foot or leg. With exquisite care and equally precise subterfuge, she limped down the lane toward the city gates.

Thirty-Three

After three large goblets of unwatered wine, William deLacey felt somewhat better. But not as well as he preferred to feel under the circumstances; and so he ordered food, more wine, and eventually lost himself in contemplation as he sat deep in the chair upon the hall dais, booted feet propped up on the table.

He hid from no part of the day's events. He had attempted to disarm the potential threat against him and his plan to punish the boy by announcing that said punishment would be undertaken in a fortnight. His intent was to lop off Much's hands before any of his outlaw friends might know about it, so that the deed, already done, would drive them to fury, and fury into a mistake that would lead to their capture.

Instead, Locksley had anticipated the misinformation. He had anticipated the sheriff's actions. He had prepared his battle, waged it, and won.

Mercardier had claimed Locksley cleverer than the sheriff. DeLacey neither feared nor believed that, so the insult did not strike a blow to his heart to form a permanent canker the way it might with another man. Oh, he granted Locksey was indeed a clever man; he had never believed otherwise. But cleverer than he? Indeed, he thought not. It was merely a matter of adjusting his thinking to fit the facts at hand: that Locksley had the wit and mettle to challenge his enemy. That ability should come as no surprise in a man who had fought the Infidel on Crusade, who had been knighted by the king for his valor in the field.

But Sir Robert of Locksley had also been *caught*. Disarmed and dishonored in the field, captured in the field, imprisoned by the Infidel until ransomed by Coeur de Lion.

Now it was deLacey's task to have him caught again. Only this time there would be no ransom paid. And John would not be seduced by the honor in a man, the valor in a soldier, a fall of white-blond hair and the clever hazel eyes.

Meanwhile—deLacey drank wine again, drowning the taste of gall— *there is the problem of Mercardier and the taxes.*

Robin was most pleased to find Charlemagne where he'd left him. That hadn't been a given; there were outlaws aplenty in Sherwood, and a fine horse such as Charlemagne would fetch a good price at the Lincoln horsefair. There were people in the world who would not care that neither pedigree nor provenance was offered. A good horse was a good horse.

He held a one-sided conversation with that good horse, explaining their current difficulties and why he was not stabled at home in Ravenskeep's barn, with straw bedding underfoot, fresh hay for fodder, oats, and apples for treats. Not to mention that his mares were missing as well; the big animal took his position as herd sire seriously. By the time Robin was done discussing matters with Charlemagne, Alan of the Dales came bursting breathlessly into the clearing, golden curls festooned with bits of tattered leaves, strung bow clutched in one hand. Not far behind him was Scarlet.

"Will," Robin said brightly, with false joviality. Then took three long strides across the small clearing and loosed a blow from his fist that knocked the other down. He forbore to swear only with great effort when the impact set up a complaint in his hand, and loomed over the man. "I said you were not to kill the sheriff."

From his less than impressive position on the ground, Scarlet glared up at him. "Didn't, did I?"

"I also said you were not to *try* to kill the sheriff. Do you remember that? Shoot to warn, I said. It wasn't folly, Will. I had good reason for insisting on restraint."

Scarlet hitched himself up on his elbows, scowling fiercely. "The only man I shot was a soldier, and in the shoulder, not the almighty sheriff. And if 'twas me, I wouldn't have hit the horse!"

Frowning, Robin looked at Alan. He would not expect it of the minstrel, but— "Was it you who shot his horse?"

"No!" Alan cried, aghast. "Why would I?"

"Perhaps by mistake," Robin said. "*Someone* shot the horse."

"What do you care about the horse?" Scarlet asked belligerently.

"Other than had we intended the sheriff to be a target, and it is difficult to make a man a target when he's on the ground instead of on horseback, I don't," Robin replied. "But had deLacey been killed, we would be wanted for murder, not the rescue of a boy." He paused. "I hardly think Tuck shot the horse."

"No," said a voice. "*I* shot the horse." And Marian was there, coming out of the shadows.

Robin, stunned, was utterly bereft of speech. It was Alan who blurted, "You?"

Scarlet, thus exonerated, spat out a curse intended for men who struck before they knew the truth, and got to his feet. "There," he said, "will you hit her now?"

"I didn't mean to shoot the horse," Marian declared, leaning her bow against a tree to unwind the shawl from her head and shoulders.

Alan blinked. "What, you intended to kill the sheriff? You?"

"No, I did not intend to kill the sheriff. I did not intend to kill the horse. My intent was to shoot at the ground, as I'd done before. But— my hand. The shot went awry." She stared down at the left hand, palm still wrapped to ward the still-new cautery scar. She looked forlornly first at Charlemagne, then at Robin. "I didn't *mean* to," she insisted, and then burst into tears.

The storm did not last long. Marian was ashamed of it—the last thing she had expected was that she would horrify them and embarrass herself by weeping—but Robin did not appear to be horrified, or particularly surprised. With a quiet word to the others about keeping an eye open for Tuck and Much, and Little John, he caught her elbow and guided her out of the clearing. He found a fallen tree and sat her down upon the trunk, then took up position beside her.

Marian yet clutched the soiled shawl. She wiped at her face, sniffed noisily, then heaved a heavy sigh. "Why," she began in bewilderment, "am I so upset about the sheriff's horse when I nearly killed a *man?*"

"Because the horse is innocent."

She thought he might be joking. She slanted him a sideways glance and saw he was not. "You mean that."

"Of course I do. The horse is not our enemy. William deLacey is."

"But I didn't intend to shoot *him,* either!"

He grimaced. "Well, no. But as you say, the shot went awry. An innocent animal who has no choice in his days or his duties died because of your mistake. Anyone would feel bad."

Marian disagreed. "A man would not."

"Some men would."

"Scarlet would not."

"I said 'some men,' Marian. And yes, it is an accepted battle tactic: there are times when the only way to defeat the enemy is to unhorse him."

She winced, seeing again the horrible vision of deLacey's horse collapsing; imagining horses dying by the hundreds on battlefields. "They have no choice ever, the horses, do they?"

"No. But—sometimes neither do we. Particularly in war. And there are many small moments seemingly innocent, often unintended, that grow to become a war."

Marian began to pick at the frayed shawl. "And was this a war, what we undertook today?"

Robin smiled crookedly. "Rather, a skirmish."

"And we won."

"We gained our objective, yes: we rescued Much."

"And deLacey? How will he view it?"

"A supreme annoyance," Robin said dryly.

She studied him a moment. "But there is more. I can see it in your eyes."

He nodded, pale hair stirring. "Before, we were male dogs across the road from one another, tails stiff, hackles raised, posturing for effect. There were occasional attempts at dominance. But now . . ." He sighed, smiled faintly. "Well, I have intentionally crossed that road and entered his territory. There is no greater challenge."

"And so you shall fight."

"Until one of us rolls over to expose his throat and belly."

Marian knew better. "Neither of you will do that."

He did not reply.

Tension was a hard knot in her throat and belly. "There was another man, Robin. A man who came and found me, after I shot the horse. Who knew what I'd done. But—I didn't hesitate. I saw him, and I counted him as the enemy, and I prepared to shoot him. And I think—I think I would have. In that moment. Had he come for me." Tears welled up again, as did a painful desperation. "What am I, that I can in one moment be horrified that I killed a horse, and the next prepare to kill a *man?*"

He sat very close to her but did not touch her, did not wrap an arm around her, nor grasp a hand. He gave her the space to sort out her feelings without trying to take them into himself. "A survivor," he said at last.

"A what?"

"Survivor," he repeated. "Marian—it is never easy to kill a man. At the moment, that very moment when you realize that he must die *because* he is the enemy, and *because* he will kill you or countless others, you do one of three things." His voice was very quiet. "You hesitate, and die. You run away, and die inside because of the shame. Or you strike your own blow first. And survive."

"Mercardier," she said.

He was very still.

"Mercardier," she repeated. "That was the man. He came to me. He might have stopped me. Caught me. I didn't hesitate. I didn't run away. I nocked an arrow and raised the bow, prepared to strike my own blow first, just as you said—and *then* I ran away." She paused. "Walked."

"Marian." His tone now was peculiar. "You escaped *Mercardier?*"

She nodded, though she did not know if she would characterize running—or walking—away as escaping so much as cowardice.

Then she said, feeling oddly distant, "I cannot stop shaking . . ." And put out her hands to display the trembling.

Now he did touch her. Now he gripped her hands in his own and stilled them. "Marian. What you feel is natural."

She shivered, felt something hard and hot well up in her chest, then creep to engulf her throat.

"What you faced today, what you accepted with all good intentions, was the willingness to take responsibility for Much's life—but also two other things. First, you acted at great risk to yourself."

"But *I* didn't matter! It was Much!"

"Hush," he said with mock severity, then went on. "When you accept the risk on another's behalf, it is easy to forget the danger. But once the goal is accomplished, the blindness of dedication falls away. You understand what *might* have happened to you, had things gone wrong."

Marian stared hard at the ground.

"The second is that you had the ordering of a man's future. You might have killed William deLacey today."

"Yes," she said numbly, lips and hands icy. "I was angry enough to." She looked at him sharply. "What if it wasn't my hand so much as hatred that sent that shot awry?"

"When you kill a man," he said evenly, "everything changes. You are never the same. And when you realize you *might* have killed a man, that you held that power over him for the time it took to nock and loose an arrow, you realize why man is mortal. We are not fit to be God. No man—or woman—should be God. But sometimes, sometimes, there is no choice."

"And then everything changes," she murmured dazedly.

"Yes."

Marian swallowed heavily, painfully. "I do not wish," she began with careful clarity, "ever, *ever*, to make that choice again. Not even by mistake. Nor by necessity, to survive. I want him stopped, oh, yes. But killed? By me?" She shuddered, then looked at him. Gazed at him, at the beloved face that shared her anguish, because, she realized, he had felt it, too. His own rite of passage, when first he had gone to war. "You knew it would be like this. When I said I would go with you, would do my part in rescuing Much."

He held his silence a moment. Then, "You believed you could make a difference. It was not my place to rob you of that."

Bitterly she said, "I nearly killed a man. And I played God with Mercardier's life."

"A kinder God that man has never known."

She thought that an odd statement, and said so.

"You offered him mercy," Robin said. "That is more than he has ever offered himself." Then, as if abruptly overcome, he wrapped his arms around her, drew her against his chest, and set his face into her braided hair. He murmured a prayer of thanksgiving, of gratitude, of overwhelming relief that she was alive and unharmed, and kissed her fervently.

Then he remarked that the shawl stank, and now so did she.

It was incongruous and wholly unexpected. Shocked, Marian would have protested, but a voice called out Robin's name and then the others were there. Scarlet, Alan. Tuck. And another.

She jumped to her feet. "Much!"

"There's a problem," Alan declared grimly. "We have no key for his shackles."

"Ah," Robin said. "Well, then, I shall have to go and fetch an ax, or a hammer and chisel."

"Fetch them?" Scarlet echoed. "From where?"

"Ravenskeep," Marian said decisively, glad to have a goal instead of memories and fears. As one, they stared at her; was she playing God again? But, "Where else?" she asked. "You all know where such things are kept, there."

Tuck was deeply worried. "But won't the sheriff go to Ravenskeep?"

"Or send soldiers?" Alan agreed vigorously.

"I doubt he will go there himself," Robin said. "I think he would prefer not to show himself quite so soon after losing Much; the people might laugh. Rather, he will send men. This time."

"You'd risk it?" Scarlet asked.

Marian said promptly, "I will go."

"No, you will not," Robin countered lightly. "You have no gift of stealth; nor should you, the way you were raised."

"Stealth? In my own home?"

"Marian, either you return to Ravenskeep as chatelaine and risk being arrested—"

"The sheriff doesn't know I took part in Much's rescue!"

"—and interrogated," Robin went on, ignoring the interruption, "so the sheriff might discover where we are hiding; or you must *steal* the tools. And there are those of us better fit for such activity."

"Aye," Scarlet agreed morosely. "The one most fit for it is the one who has need of the tools!"

Marian looked at Much. His face was pale and grimy, and deeply bruised. Heavy shackles linked by iron chain weighted arms and ankles. "Then go," she said abruptly. "One of you. All of you. Just hasten. We need to get Much free."

"I'll go at once," Robin agreed.

"No." It was Alan, unaccountably. "Let me. Robin—if you were caught, you would pay the highest price."

"And you wouldn't?" Scarlet asked.

"Everyone knows it was Robin who challenged the sheriff in his own city," the minstrel explained. "They saw no one else. I have not been near Nottingham for two years; no one would expect me, and no one would necessarily recognize me. You, Will, are wanted for murder; the soldiers would likely kill you before taking you back." He shrugged. "I would rather have all of you free to rescue *me,* than Robin caught and in need of us to rescue him. Wouldn't you?"

Frowning uneasily, Marian glanced into shadows. "Where is John?"

"Hiding?" Tuck asked.

Scarlet scowled. "Still?"

"Never mind John," Alan said. "He'll be well enough. But Much needs these shackles cut off." He glanced at Robin. "I'll be back before sundown."

They watched as the minstrel slipped back into the trees. Scarlet shook his head. "I'd never have thought it of him."

Tuck merely smiled. "God provides courage when it is most needed."

"Courage?" Scarlet asked skeptically. "Sweet Mary in Heaven, I'd call it stupidity!"

Much held his arms out. "*Off,*" he said, with simple desperation.

Even Will Scarlet had the grace to look abashed.

Thirty-four

DeLacey was roused from his contemplative reverie with the arrival of one of his tax collectors. In view of the day's events, in view of all the wine, he might otherwise have looked on this interruption with disfavor. But money had arrived, and an accounting was always satisfying. This cheered him immensely.

The sheriff personally escorted the man down to the cell, where he stationed two guards for the duration. There he spread the Exchequer cloth and beckoned the tax collector to begin doling out the bags of coins and the various receipt markers. The procedure required time and repetition, but it served to take his mind off Robin Hood.

Until Mercardier arrived.

The mercenary did nothing more than station himself in the doorway, thick arms folded. He said no word, made no sound, merely stood there, like massive statuary. DeLacey found it intensely annoying, and eventually accepted that his concentration was completely destroyed. He excused the tax collector, then glared balefully at the captain. "What is it?"

"Taxes," Mercardier said briefly. "Was this the last of the collections? May I expect to escort the shipment to the king very soon?"

DeLacey opened his mouth to snap that no, it was not the last of the collections; that the captain had best not expect to go anywhere very soon—but almost immediately changed tack. Perhaps this was the opportunity he had begun hoping for.

"I must have the accounting in order," he said instead, keeping his tone light, "which requires me to inventory what has just arrived and add it to the rest. This will take time. But I think it possible you may expect to leave tomorrow. Will that satisfy you?"

"It is for my lord king to be satisfied."

"Of course," the sheriff acknowledged, making a supreme effort to remain agreeable. "And I am certain he shall be. This will be a positive way to begin his reign, I should think." With precision he realigned the markers in the Receipt square on the painted cloth. "Tomorrow, Captain. Now, may I return to my work? Delays here will of course delay your departure."

Mercardier's expression remained characteristically implacable. He inclined his head slightly in a passable imitation of civility, then turned and left the cell. DeLacey listened to the receding footsteps.

When he was alone again, surrounded by stacks of chests, sealed scrolls, and the table bearing cloth, markers, and payment, he smiled. There was no humor in it. Only grim satisfaction. "By all means," he said. "Tomorrow."

Then he began to muster in his mind the men he believed most capable of undertaking and completing the task, the plan he had developed while sitting at the table drinking too much wine, with too much time to think about desperate kings and clever outlaws and unmanipulable mercenaries, all of whom plagued his life beyond the extremes of tolerance.

John would have his taxes. John would be pleased. John would be assured William deLacey was the only man for the office in Nottinghamshire.

John would *not* be pleased to learn that his late brother's prized captain of mercenaries was incompetent.

As they took up various places to await Alan's return, Marian realized that Robin had the right of it: the borrowed—or, rather, "purchased"—skirt and shawl had imparted a pungent and unpleasant odor to her hair, tunic, and hosen. In the tension of escape she hadn't noticed; now she could notice nothing else. She shed both skirt and shawl with alacrity, caring little that it was in the middle of the clearing in front of everyone else—after all, she still wore hosen, tunic, and hooded capelet—and hooked both upon the broken ends of tree limbs. Then she took herself as far from the stench as possible.

"Better they be burnt," she muttered, "had we a fire."

Will Scarlet, leaning against a downed trunk with legs outstretched, snorted. "There's many I know as would be grateful for such clothing."

Marian wrinkled her nose. "And welcome to them!"

He shrugged. "Peasants wear what they can. Smell don't matter, does it, when 'tis warmth you're after."

She opened her mouth to retort, then realized she had none.

"Aye," Scarlet said knowingly. " 'Tis hard for a lady to understand."

"Well," Robin said lightly, as he leaned against the saddle and pad he had taken from Charlemagne's back, "I was raised an earl's son, and there were times when *I* stank."

"When?" Will challenged. "You, with serfs to clean and mend your tunics?"

"In the Holy Land," Robin said, "there was sun without surcease. Water, when we found it, was for drinking. Most of the army was ill much of the time with the flux, and other things even the physicians didn't recognize. The Germans ate a spiced food they called *sausage*, the entrails of pigs stuffed with ground meat and—other things. They hung them from their saddlebows and carved off chunks as they went. In armor, leather, and mail, we never stopped sweating. It ran from our faces, down our spines, chafed our thighs. After a battle, there was the blood. And worse." He shrugged. "I daresay none of you would have desired to be anywhere near me then. Certainly the first thing the Turks did when they took me was have me bathed."

Scarlet's mouth dropped open. *"Bathed?"*

Tuck, seated next to Much, looked baffled. "The enemy had you bathed?"

"They believe in it daily."

Scarlet was horrified. "They *bathe* every day?"

"Why not? They pray five times a day."

"To their Infidel god!" Scarlet expostulated.

"Allah," Robin said. *"Insh'Allah.* 'In Allah's—God's—name.' "

"Allah," Much mimicked.

"Don't teach him that," Tuck said, scandalized. "Let the boy pray to *our* God, the Christian God!"

But Scarlet was far less concerned with religion. "Whyever would they bathe you?"

"They said I stank. At least, at the time I assumed that was what they meant, since I was dumped into a tiled pool almost immediately upon reaching the city. Later I learned the words for it."

By his expression, Will still could not comprehend why the enemy would bathe a prisoner. Marian, amused, sat down next to Robin. "I imagine men in battle pray to God more than five times a day."

"Five times an *hour,"* Robin agreed, reaching out to rub her back, "once battle is joined. It was part of the din . . . every man praying to his own God in his own language—and therefore begging the same thing at any given moment."

"Same thing?" Tuck asked skeptically. "Christians and Saracens?"

"English, Norman, German, French, Moslem and Christian. We prayed for the things all soldiers pray for: glory, bravery, victory—and worthiness." He shrugged. "If we die worthy, then there is release into a better world. For Christians it's Heaven. For the Moslems, Paradise."

Scarlet grunted. "What's this Paradise like? Full of people bathing?"

Robin smiled. "How would I know, Will? I'm a thrice-damned Christian pig."

Marian laughed, luxuriating in his touch.

Tuck, however, was horrified. "Don't say such a thing!"

"To *them,"* Robin clarified dryly, eyes alight. "Do you know, we have the same name for one another? 'Infidel.' To us, they are the Infidel. To them, we are."

"Oh, I have a name for 'em," Scarlet said vehemently, but never got a chance to announce what it was as Robin sat bolt upright and gestured him into silence.

They were all on their feet as the crashing sound approached, grabbing up bows and nocking arrows. But there was no need for defense: the noisy arrival was no enemy, but Little John.

"Soldiers," he said succinctly, out of breath. "On the road just outside of Nottingham. Gisbourne leads them."

"Did they see you?" Robin asked.

The red-haired giant shook his head. "I hid myself."

"How many?"

Little John told them. "But they're well behind me. Gisbourne had them all halted in the road, telling which lot to go where."

Robin nodded. "They'll divide. Some for Locksley Village, no doubt. Some Ravenskeep. The rest likely for Sherwood."

"Makes sense," Scarlet agreed. "And easier for us. Fewer in the forest."

Little John looked at Marian, then dug a pouch from under his belt. "Here," he said diffidently, and put it into her hands.

She stared down at it, feeling the weight. "John—what is it?"

Under the tangled ruddy thatch hanging over blue eyes, his face colored. "For you," he said. "For your taxes."

"Taxes!" She unloosened the thong, then upended the pouch into her palm. Coins chimed against flesh.

"Not much," John said with regret. " 'Twas all he had."

Marian looked at him. "All *who* had?"

"The peddler."

"Peddler!"

Will Scarlet let out a shout of laughter. "You robbed a peddler?"

Little John looked only at her. "We'll not let you lose your home to the sheriff."

It took her breath away. Rendered her speechless. All she could do was stare, like a lackwit.

Scarlet grinned. "Stealing's easier than earning it, aye?"

"John," Robin said mildly, "was he a wealthy peddler?"

The big man shrugged. "Wealthy as a peddler can be, I guess, from the look of his wagon and horse. No sense in robbing a poor one, is there? No money to be had."

"Indeed," Robin murmured. He had removed the arrow from the bow. Now he set the broadhead against the back of his neck and began idly to scratch—gently—beneath his hair. He smiled at Marian, lopsidedly. "You yourself suggested the answer once. You and a man who was once Justiciar of England. We had to stop King John, you said, you and the Earl of Essex. To take the tax shipments from deLacey so that John would not have the money to pay his lapdogs, such as our beloved sheriff. Do you recall, Marian?"

She recalled it. She had said it. She had not known someone else had suggested the same. But today they had committed themselves to outlawry in front of all of Nottingham, and such things as she had suggested on impulse in the depths of a night now were tangible. Had been acted on. It stunned her into silence.

"You said," Robin continued, "that as he would likely hang me anyway, I may as well give him reason."

"I would just as soon you *didn't* hang," she said sharply, finding her tongue again. "But that had nothing to do with peddlers. I never meant you should rob innocent people of their wages, only deLacey of the taxes."

"And the king," he said dryly.

Marian flushed as the others laughed.

"You did say it."

"I said it," she affirmed. "I was angry with the sheriff, after what he did to Ravenskeep. I wanted to hurt him. And to stop King John from taxing us all to death."

"*We* are angry with the sheriff," Little John pointed out.

Scarlet nodded. "And *we* would like to hurt him." Then he added casually, "And you already shot his horse."

That stung. "The horse was an accident!"

He shrugged. "How do you know he wouldn't hang you for killing his horse? Because you're a woman? Last time he meant to have you burned as a witch just because you wouldn't marry him."

Tuck nodded. "And he took your name off the tax rolls."

"And near destroyed your manor." That from Little John.

Much said softly, startling them all, "No friend to you."

No. He was not. Nor had been for years.

The world, she realized with a jolt of painful clarity, had changed for them forever. Because a man who was king had died. And such things as this moment, this comprehension of it, changed them further, even as happenstance and tragedy formed endings and beginnings for a man who knew how to seize them, to shape them in his image to further his own goals.

A chill coursed over her flesh. "He has been waiting for this," she said aloud. "This, or something like. For opportunity."

"Probably," Tuck agreed, who had worked for the sheriff, albeit reluctantly. "He is a patient man."

"I am also thinking," Robin went on, intent, she realized, on a wholly different beginning, "that soldiers will be entering Sherwood in search of us, and that they cannot possibly remain bunched together because of the terrain, but will end up separating from one another."

"Lone targets," Scarlet observed, "make better targets."

It was decided, she knew. Without her. Because of her. In spite of her. Nothing she said would alter it.

Little John nodded. "One by one. We'll have their swords, *and* their money."

"Better soldiers than innocent men," Robin said lightly, slanting a glance at Marian.

"Like peddlers?" she retorted, wanting to shock them into common sense instead of dangerous fancy. And yet she understood. She knew why it appealed.

"A *wealthy* peddler," Little John shot back. " 'Twouldn't do to steal from a poor one."

Will Scathlocke, now known as Scarlet, laughed. "That makes it all right, then, aye? Steal only from the wealthy, never from the poor."

"But it still makes you outlaws," Marian said dryly. "Merely discriminating."

Robin's glance was level. "We were outlaws five years ago. We became so again the day Richard died."

She meant to protest that, to deny it to them all; surely not the *very* day King Richard died. But something entirely different issued from her mouth: Recognition. Acknowledgment. Even acceptance. "And today we reaffirmed it before all of Nottingham."

Scarlet grunted. "Should have killed the sheriff, lady, instead of his horse."

"No," Robin declared. "We will not kill William deLacey. Why should we? Making him look the incompetent fool and getting him dismissed from office is far more effective a punishment than killing the man. Because if he is dead, he cannot be made to suffer the public humiliation we shall bestow upon him. He is a king's toady. Being dismissed by the king would ruin his ambition, and in turn destroy his life." He looked at Marian. "Would that suffice you, lady? To embarrass him, humiliate him, and have him turned out of office? So that he could not strike off any names from the tax rolls ever again?"

"Nor make it possible for peasants to be taxed to death," Tuck declared stoutly.

Little John said, looking at Much, at the battered, still-swollen face, "Nor ever threaten children with the loss of their hands."

They all of them had suffered for so little reason. She could not name all the things deLacey had done to them, nor to so many others. She looked at Robin, Tuck, Scarlet, Little John, and Much, aware of a sudden lessening of the tension in her body. It bled out of her. Diminished entirely. Fear was gone. Reluctance was relinquished. Determination supplanted all other emotions.

William deLacey had destroyed the lives they knew. He deserved the same.

"Would it suffice?" Marian asked. "I should think: barely."

DeLacey, lingering at the table, still relaxing in the great chair from which he governed the shire, waved the servant in when the man paused, fearful of intruding. He accepted the proffered parchment, noting the fine hand, the seal set in ruby-colored wax.

The sheriff felt a jab of anticipation. He sat upright, broke the wax, unfolded the letter, and read with great absorption.

When finished, he stared down the hall into the distance, contemplating the successful courtship of opportunity and its consummation; the flavor of revenge, of pride restored, of a plan bearing fruition.

The sound of his laughter echoed in the hall.

Thirty-Five

Well before sundown, Alan returned with hammer and chisel. No one, he said, had seen him, though he did not doubt at some point the theft would be discovered. "Sim or Hal," he predicted.

"John," Robin said, "you are best for it." And then he told Much what the boy was to do, as the giant took the hammer and chisel from Alan.

Much sat down atop the huge fallen tree, astride the trunk as if he rode a horse. He leaned forward, offering one hand, and Robin settled the right shackle against the wood, taking care to turn it so that the lock was exposed. Little John, muttering of challenges, knelt beside the trunk.

"There," Robin said, indicating where the chisel point should go. He took it from John, set the point himself, then clamped both hands around the iron. He smiled at Much. "If he misses, he strikes us both." But the glance he shot at Little John was far less sanguine.

No one spoke. All watched with transfixed expressions. Much bit deeply into his lower lip, leaching the color away; Robin held the chisel steady in both hands. *Strike well, John.*

The hammer was crude, made for driving bolts and poles, not nails. But the haft in Little John's huge hand seemed slender as a reed. The giant eyed the chisel's flattened end closely a moment, judging its size, then tapped gently with the hammer. Once. Twice. Thrice. The way a blacksmith bounced his hammer against anvil as he worked hot metal.

"Steady, lad," the big man said, almost whispering.

Once. Twice. No more than practice strikes, judging weight and distance. Little John glanced at Robin, who nodded. And then he raised and brought the hammer down, crushing its crude head into the end of the chisel.

Robin felt the vibration run up his wrists and through his arms. Much cried out. But the lock split.

John threw down the hammer as Robin lifted away the chisel, and yanked the shackle apart with massive freckled hands. "There, lad!" he cried. "You're half free!"

Scarlet, watching, grunted. "And still a hand attached."

"One more," Robin murmured, and helped settle the other shackled hand upon the trunk, adjusting the chain. "This time you know what to expect," he told Much. Then, "John?"

Once again the chisel bit was set. Once again Little John tapped with the hammer to make certain of weight, distance, and aim.

"Almost," Little John murmured, raising the hammer. He struck once. Sharply.

Hastily Robin tossed the chisel aside and peeled the shackle apart as the lock dropped off. He saw the chafing and bruises ringing the thin wrists. He had worn iron himself, and understood the humiliation as well as the pain. "You did well," he told Much firmly. "As well as any man might do, even the Lionheart."

Much's swollen mouth twitched into a brief smile. He lifted his hands into the air, turning them this way and that. So close, Robin knew, to losing them that he dared not truly believe he still claimed them.

And he knew that feeling, too. "Marian," he said quietly, "there's a creek just yonder. Could you fetch some water?"

In a matter of minutes the wrists were bathed and wrapped in strips of homespun torn from the odorous shawl. But this time no one remarked on the stench.

Robin pressed Much's shoulder. "You'll do," he said with casual comfort. "And now I need you to remain here, with Tuck and Marian. The rest of us have a task to perform."

"What task?" Alan asked.

"Killing Norman soldiers." Scarlet said.

"No." Robin shook his head. "Killing them is not necessary. As I said, they shall be divided by the forest. We'll be hidden in the trees, shielded by vegetation. It's a simple matter for us to take them by surprise, rob them, then disappear again."

Alan was astonished. *"Rob* them? Soldiers? The ones seeking us?"

"Aye," Scarlet said dryly. "Ask John how 'tis done."

The minstrel stared at Little John. "You robbed a soldier?"

"I robbed a *peddler."*

Alan was utterly baffled. "Why did you rob a peddler?"

Scarlet rolled his eyes. "To get his money, lackwit!"

"Wait," Tuck said sharply. "There is something I must say." He waited until he had their attention. "I think," he said carefully, "if we are to do this, there should be rules."

Scarlet nearly gaped. *"Rules?"*

Little John frowned. "How can there be rules in robbery?"

Tuck squared his heavy shoulders. "You want this money for Marian, for the taxes, so she doesn't lose her manor. Fair enough. But what about the poor? *They* haven't anyone helping them, have they?" He fixed them all with a steady gaze. "If we take enough from the soldiers to pay Marian's taxes, and there is coin left over, we shouldn't keep it for ourselves."

Scarlet pointedly wanted to know why not.

Tuck scowled at him. "Because we should use the money for good, Will! If we steal money for ourselves, we are no better than outlaws."

"We *are* outlaws," Alan reminded him with pronounced irony.

"We snatched the boy right away from the sheriff's 'justice,' " Scarlet pointed out. "We'll be wanted for that—not that we weren't wanted already, since the pardon's revoked. The sheriff'll likely put silver on our heads. If they mean to make money off us, why shouldn't we make it off them?"

But the monk was uncommonly stubborn. "We should do *some* good with it! Think of it, Will . . . what about the poor folk who can never pay all their taxes? What about in years where the harvest is poor? They pay in seed corn, and flour. But without seed corn to plant, without flour for bread, how are they to live? You said yourself that peasants are grateful for anything, even filthy rags to wear in winter. Well? If we help them with their taxes, then they'll have seed corn to plant and wheat to mill and bread to bake. They can *live*, Will, like human beings instead of animals!"

"We'll need to live, too," Alan said.

Tuck nodded vigorously. "Some for us, yes. But the rest for the poor."

Idly, Robin said, "We stole that shipment for Richard's ransom. We didn't need it after all, as Richard came home—but neither did we keep it."

Tuck spread his hands. "We gave to those in need. 'Twas never for us."

"And when my taxes are paid twice over?" Marian shook her head. "There is no need to continue stealing. The point is to disgrace deLacey, to have him turned out of office. So long as no one learns who is responsible for the thieving, you may all come home to Ravenskeep. We'll live as before."

As one, they looked at her. No one seemed willing to speak, until Robin did. "Marian," he said, hating himself for the truth, "it may be that none of us but you can return to Ravenskeep."

The color bled out of her face.

"King Richard pardoned us for stealing the tax shipment, but King Richard is dead. John rules now, and the pardon is revoked. All of us, save you, are now wanted for something." He shrugged, smiling wryly. "I stole two horses myself only a matter of days ago, and deLacey came after me for *one* of them. He might have arrested me then, but my father and the others provided protection. That is over now."

Marian nodded determination. "And when deLacey is turned out of office—"

"We will likely still be wanted," he said steadily, shirking no part of the truth. "Circumstances will be different, yes, and we might hope for the best. It is even possible the new sheriff will have other matters to keep him busy for a fair amount of time, and he will lack the personal desire to have us caught and hanged, but we shall still be considered outlaws. Certainly by King John, who wants these taxes so badly."

"Unless John isn't king anymore," she observed pointedly. "You told me yourself the barons want him replaced."

He saw again the earls gathered with his father, heard again de Mandeville suggesting he steal the shipments so the money would not go to John, who needed it badly if he was to hold England. If Arthur of Brittany became king, Robin trusted de Mandeville to see to it they were pardoned once again. The man had promised it. There was hope. Some small hope. With deLacey dismissed *and* John overthrown, they might indeed return to Ravenskeep.

"That may be," he agreed cautiously. "But *until* John is dethroned, we must assume we will be hunted."

Despite her beauty, the bones were stark beneath flesh grown too pale, too taut. "Then why," she said, "do we do this? Why save Ravenskeep if none of you will be there?"

Tuck was shocked. " 'Tis your home!"

"It is only home," she said flatly, "when all of you are there."

That prompted sidelong glances, abashed color in their faces; they had none of them expected her to state it so baldly, no matter what they believed, or hoped to believe, about her feelings for them.

"Ravenskeep is your birthright," Robin said gently. "We shall see that you keep it."

Her anger was obvious. "Huntington was *yours*. The earldom was yours. You gave it up, Robin. All of it. For me." She glanced at the others in a scouring bitterness he hated to see. "Well, perhaps *I* should give up Ravenskeep for all of you!"

"If we don't steal enough to pay your taxes—again—you won't have to give anything up," Little John declared, clearly discomfited by her emotion. "The sheriff'll simply take it."

Robin nodded. "So he will."

Alan sighed. "There really is no choice. We can't live as we did, not now. Those days are ended—at least, for the time being. Even *I* recognize that." He looked at Marian. "All I ever wanted to be was a minstrel, playing in noblemen's halls, kissing their wives, their daughters." He smiled ruefully. " 'Tis my misfortune that I was caught kissing deLacey's daughter—though she was the seducer, not I—but it might have been anyone. And had it not been for Robin, I would already be dead." He shrugged. "This is at least a worthy cause."

Scarlet caught up his bow, shouldered his quiver. "We should be at it," he said gruffly. "If 'tis Gisbourne leading them, they'll be easy enough to stop."

Tuck startled them all by clamping a hand on Robin's wrist. "For Marian," he said. "But for the *poor,* as well. Tell them, Robin. They'll listen to you."

Robin met the brown eyes he usually viewed as placid, and saw the strength of purpose there. He smiled, then glanced at the others. "When we come back," he said, "we'll pour our takings into Marian's hood and divide everything up. Some for her, a little for us, but the rest for the poor."

"We're poor," Scarlet grumbled, but bobbed his head in agreement.

Little John looked at Marian. " 'Tis a good plan, lady."

Alan sighed deeply. "It wants my lute," he mourned.

All of them were gone, save for herself, the monk, and the boy. Marian stood stiffly, arms wrapped around herself in a tight hug, and stared fixedly into the trees dividing the clearing from the road. Emotions frayed the logic of her mind, yet the logic still attempted comprehension, control. She feared to lose Ravenskeep, could not bear to lose her father's lands, the manor gifted to her entirely by King Richard. But in that fear, in the fury that drove her to challenge deLacey to a battle of sheer will over the manor and lands, she had never once considered that the others might not be there.

Five years. She had grown accustomed to them all. They were as much a part of her life as Ravenskeep itself. *I cannot imagine living at Ravenskeep without them. Nor do I wish to!*

Tuck, who seemed to know her thoughts, said with characteristic diffidence, "Alan has the right of it. Our former lives are over. We are different people now. Even me. Do you believe I have a future in the Church?" He smiled sadly. "The sheriff will have seen to it my career is ended."

He sounded so secure in his decision. But Marian sensed an underlying apprehension. "Then we shall see to it the sheriff's career is ended," she said. *With all good speed and dedication.*

"We shall harry him," Tuck agreed, echoing her thought. "Steal from the wealthy, take the tax shipments, make it impossible for him to stop us. And when the merchants and noblemen scream about the sheriff's

incompetence, and King John realizes he gets no taxes from Nottinghamshire, deLacey shall lose his position."

"And if John loses his?"

"With the lad from Brittany put in his place?" Tuck shrugged thoughtfully. "If he were made king in John's place, there might be a pardon for
us."

"Might."

"A new king might look kindly on men who made the old king's life
a living hell."

Marian smiled. "Might."

"Sins are forgiven," Tuck said without equivocation, "when sinners
confess before God and ask for absolution. Why should a new king be
different when these 'sinners' have aided his cause?"

"By harming John's." Marian nodded, beginning to feel a little better.
"It is possible, Tuck. But we must be very careful not to harm anyone.
Our goal is to undermine the sheriff's authority, to undermine John's
ability to rule. If we harm anyone while taking their money, no one will
pardon us. Ever." She cast him a sidelong glance. "Do you realize how
odd it sounds for a *monk* to be advocating robbery?"

"God will see what we are doing, and God will know why we do
it," Tuck said. "Oh, 'tis a sin; I don't dispute that! But do you really think
God wishes to punish the man who poaches to feed his family, who would
otherwise starve?"

"God may not punish him," Marian said darkly, looking at Much,
"but the sheriff does." And then she thrust up a silencing hand as she
turned swiftly toward the road. It was not visible behind the friezework
of trees and vegetation, but sound carried clearly. Mounted men were on
the road, riding swiftly. She heard the faint clink of bits and fittings, the
snorting of the horses, the pounding of the hooves.

The pace was too steady. There was no hesitation, no slowing, no
outcries to halt or turn aside. Marian felt safe in working her way carefully,
quietly, through the trees, nearly to the verge between forest and road.
Much came with her, and Tuck, melting into shadows, until they could
see through a gauze of green fern.

Soldiers.

Tuck waited until they were gone, only dust marking their passing.
Then he knelt ponderously beside Marian, who crouched in the brush.
"Bound for Ravenskeep," he said quietly. " 'Tis a good thing we stayed
here in Sherwood."

Marian stared after the sifting dust. "Gisbourne wasn't with them."

Tuck shifted beside her, crackling brush. "Little John said Gisbourne was dividing up his men. Some to Locksley, some into the forest, some to Ravenskeep. Gisbourne either went to Locksley, or into Sherwood."

"There is no one at Locksley," she murmured, "and no one at Ravenskeep. Gisbourne and his troop will never expect to be *robbed* by the others; they'll be searching for men in hiding."

"Aye, lady. Should make it a simple thing for Robin and the others to take them one by one when the forest separates them. Likely they'll take the horses, too, so the soldiers are afoot."

"Slow them down." She nodded. "Keep them from going for help immediately." She sighed, glanced at the monk, then found a more comfortable position. "We'll wait here for these men to return from Ravenskeep. And then I shall go there."

"To Ravenskeep?" Tuck was shocked. "But, lady, what if—"

"What if they leave men behind?" She shrugged. "Robin said I was not trained for stealth, but I daresay I could sneak back undetected. I am somewhat familiar with my own home! We need food, Tuck, and blankets. Our goal was to rescue Much, but there is more to it than that. Now we must find a way to survive in the forest."

"But 'tis dangerous—"

"I will go," she said firmly. "I want to see if they have destroyed the hall again. I want to let Joan and the others know we are all right, that Much is rescued. I want to make certain the outlaws I count as friends have food and blankets, so they need not poach quite yet." She smiled to see the concern in his face. "I promise you, I shall be careful. I have no wish to be a hero."

"Me," Much said.

"*You* wish to be a hero?" Marian asked, amused.

"I go with you," he said. "To get in. Get out. No one will see."

"Robin will not be pleased," Tuck warned her. "He wanted you to stay here."

She found that oddly amusing. "Ah, well. I do not ask Robin's permission for my actions any more than he asks mine for his. Because if he did, I would never have let him go to rob Gisbourne." She smiled at Much. "I shall be glad of the company."

Thirty-Six

Arrow nocked, Robin stood very still behind a fat-bolled tree, screened by vine and hip-high fern. The lone soldier's horse crashed on by him, flushing birds in a whirring of wings and very helpfully shredding limbs and greenery that might otherwise ruin his shot. *Gisbourne,* Robin noted with amusement. *How appropriate.* Then he slid out of the shadows, drew the bowstring, and pitched his voice to carry over the sound of the horse's passage.

"Were I you," he called, "I should halt. Because from here I could put a clothyard arrow completely through your spine and out the other side. In fact, if there were another man before you, I daresay the same arrow would kill him as well."

He read Gisbourne easily, even from behind. The tension in the line of shoulders, the stiffening of his spine, spoke of incipient motion, not compliance. He meant to set spurs to the horse and leap out of range. Accordingly, Robin sped the arrow into the tree within a foot of Gisbourne's head.

"*Now* do you believe me?" He grinned; the tension in Gisbourne was abruptly entirely different. Brittle stillness had replaced intent to move. "Dismount," Robin commanded, nocking another arrow. "Come here toward me. Don't fret about the horse; we'll send him home presently."

Gisbourne stepped down from his horse, but he did not move toward Robin. Instead, he yanked at the reins and attempted to swing the horse sideways, shielding himself behind the animal. But Robin, not in the least surprised, lowered the angle of the arrow and loosed. The shaft flew true beneath the horse's belly and planted itself in the ground immediately next to Gisbourne's foot.

"Do try me," Robin invited. "Next time I shall not be so discriminating with my aim. The sheriff lost his horse to an arrow; shall you lose yours?"

Gisbourne, at last recognizing his assailant, cried out in incoherent fury. The loose horse, nonplussed by the arrow and shouting, crabbed away, intending to run, until its trailing reins caught on a tree limb and brought it up short.

"I did warn you." With elegant economy of motion, Robin drew a third arrow from the quiver over his shoulder and nocked it. "Now," he said, "unsheath your sword and throw it—carefully!—toward me." He gestured. "Here."

"You shall hang for this!" Gisbourne cried, white-faced in outrage.

"Only if you catch me. And just now, I have caught *you.*" Robin jerked his chin sideways. "Your sword."

Gisbourne cursed him in Norman French until he ran out of breath, but complied. The two-handed broadsword, flung stiffly, landed with a heavy thump one pace away from Robin.

"My thanks," he said gravely, bending to pick it up. He rattled the arrow back home in its quiver and settled the bow slantwise across shoulder and chest. Then he unhooked the reins of the trapped horse, knotted them high on the animal's neck, and brought the flat of the blade down in a noisy slap across the wide rump. Given its leave in so rude a fashion, the horse promptly bolted. "And now," Robin said, "you are to reach under your surcoat and untie the purse attached to your belt."

Gisbourne blurted another vile oath. "You stole my horse, and now you steal my purse?"

"Be accurate, Gisbourne: I stole your horse a number of days ago, yes, but not *this* horse. And why the shock? Am I not living down to your expectations? You and the sheriff have determined I am an outlaw, subject to punishment. Including, you say, hanging."

Gisbourne was livid. "You have in the past few weeks stolen two horses—now three!—delayed a royal messenger, taken a boy from the sheriff's lawful custody, and now you *rob* me? What else are we to do with you? Thank you?"

Robin laughed, giving him that. "But it seems I have no choice now but to be what you have made me. I am disinherited, have no roof-tree above my head, no means for earning a living, and the pardon is revoked. What else would you have me be?"

"A prisoner," Gisbourne spat. "In the dungeon!"

"Ah. Well, I should prefer otherwise. Now, your purse." But Gisbourne didn't move. "Come, come," Robin said in mild rebuke, then explained in elaborate detail how he had learned various creative ways of torturing a man from the Infidel Turks themselves. That earned him a blanch of Gisbourne's saturnine face, who knew Robin had indeed cohabited with Turks, and a purse tossed at his feet. "Better." He retrieved and tucked the purse behind his belt.

"What do you mean to do with me?" Gisbourne demanded.

"Well," Robin said lightly, "we are not friends, so I doubt I shall invite you for a meal and a cup of wine." He pondered it a moment. "Kneel."

It startled him. "Kneel?"

"Pretend to pray."

Slowly, stiffly, Gisbourne lowered himself to his knees, head slightly inclined.

"Remove your helm."

Gisbourne did so with shaking hands, eyes furious. Robin moved until he stood behind the kneeling man. Then he struck a blow at the base of Gisbourne's skull with the wheel-pommel of the sword.

Robin gazed down upon the unconscious man, aware that he had committed himself utterly—and possibly irrevocably—to an entirely different future than he had ever envisioned. But it was done. And the campaign against William deLacey was begun in earnest.

Robin saluted the prone Gisbourne, then balanced the blade atop his right shoulder as it were a prime pole intended for fishing, and took himself away into the forest.

As the sun sank down to spend itself in a haze of gold and gilt along the darkening, tree-fringed horizon, the soldiers came back along the road from Ravenskeep, bound now, Marian assumed, for Nottingham. She and Much skirted the road, crossed it, came in across the sheep meadow along the stone wall, and slipped through a postern gate near the kitchens. She did not see any soldiers stationed to keep watch, but dared not make assumptions. Instead, she and Much made it into the barn and hid there in the shadows.

"If we wait a bit," she said very quietly, "Hal will come to feed the horses."

And so Hal did, who was surprised nearly unto death when he discovered Marian and Much. Once he had recovered sufficiently to speak again without wheezing in shock, he expressed his relief at finding them whole. Particularly Much.

Then he looked at Marian. "Soldiers were here."

"I know. That is why we did not simply walk in. Did they leave a man here?"

Hal shook his head. "But they may have made him wait elsewhere along the road, so we wouldn't know."

Marian contemplated that, realizing they would have to be very careful on the way back. "Hal, we need food and blankets. Can you go up to the house and have Joan pack us whatever she can?"

He was startled. "You're not coming back?"

"Not tonight," she said, refusing to admit aloud that the others might not come back at all. "We'll stay in Sherwood until we're certain it is safe. Oh—and Much has something for you."

On cue, the boy presented the older man with the hammer and chisel. Hal evinced surprise. "*You* had them! I thought I had gone mad, lady—couldn't find them earlier."

"We needed them for Much," she explained. "For the shackles. Alan came and got them." She looked beyond Hal to the open barn door. "Take Much with you—here, Much, put this on—" She slipped out of the hooded capelet and helped him into it; if anyone was watching, Much would not be immediately recognizable. "Go tell Joan we're here, then bring back whatever you can. We need to go before it is too dark to find our way back."

But Hal did not go just yet. "Lady Marian, you will come home? Soon?"

She told him the precise truth. "As soon as I may."

That sufficed. He gestured at Much, and the two of them went out into the sunset.

Marian, left alone, converted barn to oratory. "Dear God," she prayed aloud, "let none of us be killed in this. Let all of us survive, so we may come home."

William deLacey was ensconced in his private solar with his castellan, Philip de la Barre, when Gisbourne shouted a request for entry and, without waiting for permission, unlatched the door and crashed it open against the wall. The man stomped in, somewhat disheveled and entirely out of sorts. "We must kill him," he announced without preamble, then winced and felt at the back of his head.

DeLacey, prepared to reprimand his steward for such crude behavior, withheld the vicious words in view of Gisbourne's obvious fury. Gisbourne only rarely showed so much naked emotion. Interesting. "Kill whom?"

"Locksley," Gisbourne declared. *"Robin Hood."*

"Ah." *Most* interesting; and Gisbourne was clearly in pain. "I take it you return here without his company?"

"Without his company, without my sword, my horse, and my purse," Gisbourne elucidated, color high in his face. "He took them all."

"All?"

"And not just I was treated so harshly . . . six more of my men as well."

That brought deLacey to his feet. "Six others? *Seven* of you were accosted by Locksley?"

"Not all by him," Gisbourne answered sullenly, as if sorry he could not blame everything on Robert of Locksley. "The others as well. Little John. Will Scarlet. Even the minstrel."

"Minstrel," deLacey echoed, at a loss.

"Alan of the Dales," Gisbourne explained. "The man who violated Eleanor."

That minstrel. DeLacey had given him up years ago. "He is back?"

"Yes, my lord. I saw Locksley myself; the other descriptions match." He closed his eyes a moment and swayed on his feet before collecting himself again. "I daresay the monk and the simpleton were involved, as well," he said in more muted tones.

"Gisbourne—did you say these men *robbed* all of you? Seven of you?"

"Yes. My lord."

DeLacey was baffled. Why would men seeking to escape soldiers show themselves and actually rob them? It made no sense.

"I want him killed," Gisbourne repeated, though with much less vehemence. He was looking ill now, deLacey noted.

The sheriff seated himself again, thoughts working swiftly. For some strange reason the news did not make him angry. It was startling, puzzling, and annoying, but it did not make him angry. And it should.

But then the pieces began to come together, and he understood why he was not angry. This offense, embarrassing and infuriating as it was, actually provided an ideal opportunity.

"You may go," he told Gisbourne.

The steward blinked. "Go?"

"Go. Elsewhere." DeLacey waved his hand. "Rest, Gisbourne. Leave this to me."

But Gisbourne did not dismiss so easily. "My lord, I am your seneschal—"

"And Philip, here, is my castellan. I am consulting him with regard to other measures we may take regarding Locksley and the others. Now, you may go." He paused, marked the hue of Gisbourne's face. "And I suggest you do it *before* you collapse at my feet in a pool of your own vomit."

The imagery was enough. This time Gisbourne acquiesced and took his leave, calling for a servant as he wobbled out of the hall. DeLacey, pondering opportunity again, glanced across the table at the castellan. De la Barre had done him a service five years before, and repayment had been in the form of promotion. Now let the man earn his place again.

"I think," deLacey said, "we have been given a sign."

De la Barre, dark-haired, dark-eyed, and young for his position, raised his eyebrows. "A sign, my lord?"

"Robin Hood now robs with impunity. The roads are threatened, as are lives. It would be a miracle if a tax shipment could get through. Even one escorted by the infamous Mercardier."

A glint in de la Barre's eye told deLacey all he needed to know. The young man had always been a quick study, and willing to undertake any kind of service the sheriff might ask of him.

"You understand," deLacey said, "that such a robbery would infuriate the king."

"Indeed," de la Barre murmured.

"And the man who recaptured the tax shipment from outlaws would be granted a royal boon, incurring the king's trust and gratitude."

"A most generous man, the king," the castellan noted, smiling.

"See to it," the sheriff said. "As I have described to you."

Philip de la Barre inclined his head.

Robin, arriving not long before sundown at the clearing that had become an impromptu camp, was gratified to find Alan, Scarlet, and Little John already present, and safe. They were in high good spirits, intoxicated on success: a practiced bow and flourish from the minstrel indicated a pile of Norman swords. Grinning, Robin tossed his own contributions down to chime atop the blades; in addition to Gisbourne's, he had liberated sword and purse from one other soldier.

"And?" Tuck asked archly, seated on the ground with a cassocked lap full of coin. "We must divide it all up, as agreed."

In the act of drawing two purses from his belt, Robin froze. "Where is Marian?"

The monk's expression altered. "She and Much went to Ravenskeep."

"*Why?* I told them to remain here."

Tuck began, "She said we—"

"—needed food and blankets," Marian finished for him, slipping out of the shadows. She carried a basket hooked over one arm, and hugged a large bundle to her chest. Behind her, Much came in with a second bundle strapped to his back, and a third clutched in his arms. "And we do," she said, dumping her bundle to the ground. "If someone will gather kindling and wood, I also have flint and steel."

"Is that wise?" Alan asked. "The woodsmoke will give us away."

Marian shook her head. "There are other outlaws scattered throughout Sherwood who light fires—we could see the haze along the treetops from Ravenskeep—and charcoal burners aplenty. Can't you smell them? I doubt one more fire will make a difference."

Robin nodded. "Were we to help ourselves to the king's deer tonight, we might bring them down upon us. But we'll save that for another night, when we are deeper in the forest. A small fire will do." He knelt to begin unwrapping the bundle Marian had put down. "You should have stayed here, Marian, but—"

"But now that I am back safely, you are glad to have the supplies?" She grinned. "I know. So am I."

"I'll get wood," Scarlet said, and turned back into the trees.

Tuck and Little John fell to opening Much's bundles, sorting out the contents, while Alan gathered up stones to build a fire ring. In a short amount of time they had a fire laid and burning, blankets and cloaks made up into pallets and coverlets, and food shared out: cheese and bread and salted meat, early fruit, flasks of ale. It was a supremely simple meal, but nonetheless delicious in view of the day's events. Much in particular looked blissfully dazed. He fell asleep with a crust of bread still clutched in one hand, head lolling against a tree trunk.

"Poor lad," Tuck murmured, leaning to drape a blanket across the boy.

Robin nodded. "A long day for him."

"But a pleasing conclusion." Alan hooked bedraggled golden curls behind his ears.

The clearing was small, tree- and brush-hemmed, made cozy by the fire, food, and a company contented with what they had wrought. Shadows loomed large, crowding in among them. The latticework of branches high overhead screened out the moon- and starlight, so that the only dependable illumination was that given off by the modest fire. It was cruel to Scarlet's face, Robin noted absently, whose flesh bore the marks of hardship, grief, and ill humor, but kind to Marian's. She sat close beside him, leaning against his left shoulder as she chewed a small hard apple. A warm and decorous blanket covered his legs and hers, which were entwined at the ankles.

Little John, seated on the other side of the fire, stared into the flames, beard glowing ruddy-gold. Alan, inspecting his fingers for bow-born blisters that might interfere with his luteplaying, was humming beneath his breath. Tuck had gathered up three of the stolen pouches and separated out the coin: one pouch for Marian's taxes, one for the poor, and the smallest amount for them. Joan had sent along enough provender and plenishings to get them through a few days, but they would need more.

A full belly and freedom, for the moment, from the need to think, the awareness of pursuit, left Robin feeling oddly calm and detached. They had accomplished their goal of rescuing Much, and had done it without getting themselves hurt or captured. As for what they would do now, well, what lay ahead immediately was to gather enough money for Marian's taxes—Robin believed one more fat purse or two might accomplish that—and then consider what they would do afterward.

At least, Robin would allow the others to consider what they would do. He already knew what *he* intended to do.

The Earl of Essex had given him the key, that day in the garden at Huntington. To overthrow John, one need only replace him with Arthur of Brittany, who would prove generous to all who aided his goal of claiming England for himself, and in his forgiveness of certain sins. Their role in such doings was infinitely simple: to steal from John the financial means to support his kingship. He needed taxes for that. And this session's collection, currently residing in Nottingham under the sheriff's authority, was due to be shipped within a few weeks.

Thieves they had become. Thieves they would be.

For as long as necessary.

Marian shifted against him, sighing. He crooked his left arm around her shoulders so he might smooth the hair from her face. "We shall get through this," he murmured.

She settled her skull beneath his chin. "I know it."

"We may be on short rations for a time, and badly in need of washing, but there is game and water aplenty."

"And plenty of victims to rob," she said dryly.

He grinned, rubbing his chin against her hair. He needed to shave; already the bristles caught. Or perhaps he would simply forgo shaving altogether and grow a beard. "We'll rob the ones who deserve it."

"How will you know that?"

"Merchants," he said, "who overcharge customers; have I not lived near Nottingham all of my life to know who is fair and who is not? Clerics who have forgotten their vows of poverty; my father entertains far too many, so I am acquainted with those as well. And lords who keep their tenants living in hovels, with not enough to eat."

"And tax shipments?"

He smiled. "Most especially those."

"Be grateful," she said suddenly, with one of her lightning shifts of mood.

He blinked. "Grateful?"

"That it is spring, not fall. Sherwood would be unkind in winter."

He grunted acknowledgment. "By winter, if all is well, we shall have a new sheriff. And possibly a new king."

"And a new pardon?"

He kissed the top of her head. "Let us hope."

"Let us *pray*," Tuck clarified.

Robin stared into the flames. He was not himself certain prayer was effective; he had given up on prayers while a captive of the Turks.

Then again, he *had* survived. He *had* been ransomed. He *was* home safe, and whole. Perhaps some prayers simply took longer in the answering.

Before winter, he suggested, aiming it at the skies. *If You would be so kind.*

Thirty-Seven

The Earl of Huntington abhorred showing personal weakness of any kind, lest an adversary find opportunity in it. The men he joined outside in the fog-shrouded bailey to bid farewell were confidants, not adversaries, but he found it galling nonetheless that they should see him so weakened by the malady that would not depart despite chest plasters, possets, and bleedings. Coughing had weakened him further, turning his voice into a ruin. Breath rattled in his aching lungs. He found it difficult now to stand upright, even to breathe in the fog, which weighted his chest even more. His steward, Ralph, waited close by, prepared to offer physical support if necessary.

Huntington was determined it should not be necessary.

He had marked it before in the faces of his companions, and marked it again now as they waited for horseboys to bring up their mounts: the opinion that he was dying. Eustace de Vesci, of supremely robust health and temperament, was made most uneasy by his host's condition. Henry

Bohun, more schooled to tact than de Vesci, gave little away in expression. And in Geoffrey de Mandeville's eyes, of them all a friend as well as a man of like opinion in the ordering of the realm, there was empathy and compassion.

"We shall see it done," Huntington said, mustering as much vigor as possible. "The boy put in John's place."

"As soon as may be," Bohun agreed.

De Vesci, uncomfortable, hooked thumbs into his belt. Fingers drummed on leather; he was eager to be gone.

"You have done more than your share," de Mandeville said quietly. "Leave the rest to us."

Kind words, a friend's reassurance, but plainly they believed he would die before their plans bore fruit. They expected and desired no more of him now, lest he leave something undone.

He had left nothing undone.

The horses were brought. De Vesci, clearly relieved, swung up at once, sweeping his cloak aside with eloquent expertise as he settled into the saddle. Bohun took the moment to touch Huntington's shoulder briefly, thanked him for his hospitality and advice, then turned to his own mount. It left Geoffrey de Mandeville, the Earl of Essex, formerly Richard's Justiciar and once one of the most powerful men in England, still unmounted.

His eyes were kind. "You set a fine example, my lord, of a dedicated man prepared to sacrifice all for his country."

"So should we all," Huntington said testily.

A smile flirted with the corners of de Mandeville's mouth. "Indeed. But there is yet one more thing . . ."

"Yes?"

"Forgive him, my friend. He shares your pride, your stubbornness, your determination. When employed for the proper goals, all of those things are invaluable."

Huntington glared.

"England requires your son, as she has required you."

"I have no son," Huntington declared.

De Mandeville seemed on the verge of saying more on the subject, but withheld it. He moved forward, clasped Huntington's shoulders briefly, then turned away to his mount.

Ralph was close beside him. "My lord, allow me to assist you into the castle."

Huntington put out a hand to halt him. It would not do to permit the others to see such weakness. He stood as straight as possible, fog dampening his wispy hair, and watched the three men ride out of the bailey toward the road beyond.

Abruptly he repeated, "I have no son." Ralph supported him now, taking much of the earl's weight onto himself as he turned him toward the castle. "No son," he said, "no heir. It should revert to the Crown, the title, the lands, the money. But I will make a different accommodation. Soon."

Ralph held his silence as he guided the earl to his bedchamber. He removed the heavy outer robe, then helped him to climb into bed. When Huntington was settled against bolsters and pillows, buried beneath mounds of covers, his steward put into his hand a cup of warmed and well-watered wine, mixed with herbs that would allow him to rest. It was as the earl gave over the last of his tightly hoarded strength that the steward finally spoke.

"My lord, you are dying."

He supposed he was. And how odd that he felt no stirrings of anger at Ralph's bald speech.

"My lord, allow me to send for your son."

He stared into the distance, through the shadows of the chamber. "I have no son."

"You have a fine son, my lord."

He managed a thin smile. "Arthur of Brittany shall have it all, Ralph, even if he is not king in name yet. John has coveted and feared this castle since first he ever saw it. Let him continue to covet it. Let him continue to fear it. Let him know that all of my wealth and power, which he needs so desperately, shall be delivered on my death to the boy in Brittany."

"You did not have this castle built for Arthur, my lord."

No. Not for any king, living or dead, nor for a boy in far-off Brittany. But for a boy who believed himself a man, capable of self-government, now living in the forest.

Let Sherwood be his castle. Let outlawry be his legacy.

"Let me send for him, my lord."

He was very tired. "So he may witness my death, and rejoice?"

"He will not rejoice, my lord. Trust me in this."

Huntington closed his eyes. "He was never the son I wished for. I believed, when Henry and William died, he might be made to understand what he must become. But he did not. He refused."

"My lord, he is your only surviving child. Your immortality. Forgive him the failings you believe to be his."

He was not so near death he could not parse out careful phraseology. " 'Believe to be his,' " he echoed. Ralph's way of saying Robert had failed in nothing, only his father in accepting his differences. Huntington considered chastising his steward for such frankness. But just now he hadn't the strength.

I have no son.

His sons were dead. The only one remaining belonged wholly to his mother, equally dead.

How perverse of God to take the sons he needed, and leave behind the one he could not countenance.

Ralph disapproved.

Let him. He was not the earl. Only the earl's steward.

It came to him then that he should make provision for the man who had served him so many years. Even if Ralph did believe there was worth in Robert.

But then, Robert had always had a way about him that attracted others, enabled them to forgive him all his sins and failings. He had won Ralph. Even the Earl of Essex. All men, it seemed, save his father. And the Sheriff of Nottingham.

Knighted, but disinherited. He was an outlaw now. But the Earl of Huntington believed, with sour acknowledgment, it was entirely possible his fey, fanciful son was capable of winning forgiveness even for that. Again.

He plucked ineffectually at covers, was relieved when Ralph resettled them for him. *I was not strict enough with Robert. I should have beaten the fancies out of him.*

He had tried. But obviously not hard enough.

Morning fog lay low along the ground, dampening hair and clothing. "Bird calls," Robin said.

Marian blinked. She was not quite wholly awake, seated on a pallet of folded blankets with a cloak wrapped tightly around her to keep out the chill. "Bird calls?"

He smiled. "Like this." And proceeded to run through a series of whistles and hootings Marian could not distinguish from the actual fowl.

"How can you *do* all that?" she asked, astonished; he had never before demonstrated such ability.

He shrugged; a tendril of fog peeled away from a shoulder. "As a boy I spent many hours tracking and mimicking birds. I pretended to be them."

Little John was taken aback. "To be *birds?* An earl's son? Whatever for?"

Marian thought about it. "I never pretended to be a bird. I pretended to be a horse, galloping across the meadow." She could see it again in her mind's eye, feel the choppy rhythm of her pretend canter.

"I was never the horse," Robin said. "I was always *on* the horse. A destrier, in fact, riding to the lists."

"And winning?"

"Of course, winning! Would I imagine losing?"

Will Scarlet, gnawing on hard-crusted bread, grunted through a mouthful. "*I* imagined eating a whole meal."

"Tedious," Alan remarked. "I, on the other hand, pretended to be Queen Eleanor's most favorite jongleur."

"Well," Little John said slyly, "you *were* Eleanor's favorite jongleur. But she wasn't the queen, was she? Only the sheriff's daughter."

Alan promptly tossed the remains of a loaf at Little John, who batted it away.

"Here!" Scarlet bestirred himself to fetch the loaf out of the new-laid fire, brushing it free of soot. "You never wanted for food, did you, any of you?"

"I was always fat," Tuck said resignedly, adding wood to the fire. "No one, looking at me, would ever think *I* wanted for food."

"Bird calls," Robin said sternly. "Let me hear them."

"Why?" Marian asked.

"For signals," he explained. "Far better than shouting names across the road at one another as we're preparing to rob people."

"I can do a duck," she said, and blew firmly through pursed lips into the hollow of a fist. She mitigated the volume and intonation by opening and closing her fingers.

"A decent duck, that," Tuck observed judiciously.

"Except ducks are in lakes and ponds, not hiding in the forest," Scarlet pointed out. "No one will believe a lone duck is calling to others along the Nottingham road."

"It doesn't matter," Robin said. "Marian goes back to Ravenskeep today."

She stiffened. "I do?"

"You do. We are embarking on outlawry—well, more than what we did yesterday, or five years ago—and it's best if you go home."

"Yesterday you believed it wasn't safe for me to go home."

"Yes. Yesterday. But the soldiers have been there now."

"They could come again."

"And if you remain gone, it will be far too suspicious."

"You were the one who said the sheriff might arrest me and take me to Nottingham to make me tell him where you are."

"Yesterday you knew where we were. Today you will not."

It shocked her. "You intend to hide from *me?*"

"It is safest."

"For you?"

"For you."

Almost as one the others got to their feet, murmuring identically about returning in a moment—Scarlet was frank enough to declare he needed a piss—and disappeared into the fog, crashing through vegetation. Even Much went, when Tuck tugged him to his feet.

Marian watched the mass defection with interest. "They believe we are going to fight."

"There is that possibility," he agreed. "If you refuse to go."

She knew that tone, that tilt of the head. He was amused, but serious. "Explain it to me, then," she invited. "Why should I go back to Ravenskeep while all of you are hiding in the forest?"

Employing his meat-knife, he carved off a sliver of cheese from the chunk in his hand. "Because the sheriff knows it was us—me, Little John, Tuck, Will, and Alan—in Nottingham yesterday, rescuing Much. He does *not* know you were there. Best to leave it that way." He ate the cheese, and carved another bite. "You are already in his bad graces."

"So you will send me back home to wait and worry." She scowled at him, noting absently the stippling of white-blond stubble along his jaw. Would he grow a beard now that he hid in Sherwood? "I have told you before how much I detest that. Women sent along home to wonder in ignorance what is becoming of their men."

He continued to carve the cheese into pieces with all due seriousness, as if nothing else in the world mattered but his breakfast. "If you leave Ravenskeep now, you tell the sheriff he's won. You forfeit possession."

Her head came up sharply.

"Marian," he said, "outlawry is hard. It is not a life any man chooses for himself. Why would he choose it for the woman he loves?"

"Perhaps she will choose it for herself." But the protest was half-hearted. Robin was right. She could not absent herself from the manor while the sheriff plotted to take it. "If I go," she said, surrendering, "how will I find you?"

He smiled; he never gloated in victory, for which she was grateful.

Otherwise she would have to smack him. "Ride along the road. If you hear a plethora of bird calls, likely it is us."

"Robin—"

But he cut her off. "I have thought it through, Marian. When added to what Little John took from the peddler, within a day, possibly two, we should have enough coin to cover your taxes. I will have it delivered to deLacey, and a proper receipt executed in front of witnesses."

"Who shall deliver it? You? You would walk into the castle and risk arrest?"

"Abraham the Jew," he told her. "DeLacey dares not arrest Abraham, not for this. He will be safe. And then the taxes shall be paid, and Ravenskeep will no longer be at risk."

"But you'll still be in Sherwood. Robbing people."

"Until deLacey is dismissed, yes. But if we rob enough people and steal all the taxes, make it impossible for him to properly govern the shire, he shall be gone in short order."

"And until then?"

"Until then, you will be home safe in Ravenskeep—"

Dryly she interrupted, "While you and the others pretend to be birds."

"But not a duck," he said, feeding her the last piece of cheese to silence further protest.

From behind them in the trees came a rude cacophony of very poor bird calls.

DeLacey ran lightly down the steps of the castle into the inner bailey. The fog had lifted and he felt ineffably young this day, buoyant with high hopes and good spirits. He smiled at Mercardier, standing by the wagon.

"Well?" the sheriff asked. "Does it meet with your approval?"

"I am not a horse," the mercenary declaimed, "to know if the wagon is loaded properly or not."

DeLacey wondered if ever the man said a word that could not be construed as criticism, or failed to imply the question he answered was foolish. "Oh, the loading has been handled properly." He walked around the wagon, tugging at the canvas covering the chests, checking ropes and knots. "I inquire as to whether you approve of my escort arrangement."

Two soldiers sat on the wagon seat. A dozen others ranged on horseback in the bailey, waiting for departure. Only two men meant to accompany the shipment were not yet mounted: Mercardier himself, and Philip de la Barre.

"It appears suitable," the mercenary answered. "Though I am not convinced you need to dispatch quite so many men. It becomes obvious, my lord."

"It *is* obvious," deLacey agreed. "It is what it is, Mercardier: every coin in taxes collected from the shire so far this session. Were outlaws to steal it, we would all of us be most discommoded." In fact, many of them would likely be dismissed from their service, including himself. Discommoded, he felt, lent the moment a touch of understatement.

"You are expecting an attempt?" Mercardier inquired.

DeLacey permitted himself a brief and genuine laugh. "You ask that after what occurred yesterday?"

"They rescued a boy," the mercenary said. "I am not convinced they would attempt to steal taxes."

"Is there anything you *are* convinced of?" But the question was purely rhetorical; deLacey continued without waiting for a reply. "Perhaps I have attached too many men to the duty. But I had rather be certain the shipment arrived where and when it is intended. Better to be a careful fool than a poor one." He paused. "Or a dead one."

Mercardier studied him a long moment from beneath heavy dark brows. Then he seemed to arrive at a conclusion, for he turned away from the sheriff to signal for his mount. A horseboy brought the animal forward, even as the castellan asked for his. Within moments the wagon was surrounded by armed and armored soldiers.

Two on the wagon seat. Fourteen to ride alongside. Any outlaws who attempted to take the taxes would face certain defeat.

Mercardier, now helmed, looked down upon deLacey from his huge horse. "Lord Sheriff," he said, "I thank you for your hospitality. Be certain I shall tell the king of your assistance and thoughtfulness."

A pretty speech. DeLacey repressed the impulse to ask if that truly were Mercardier behind the helm. "I serve the king in all things."

"Indeed." Which sounded altogether like Mercardier again.

DeLacey caught the eye of his castellan. "Philip," he said, "guard this wagon with your life."

The young man inclined his head. "Of course, my lord. It is my honor."

"*Allez, allez,*" Mercardier said impatiently, and signaled the wagon forward.

DeLacey watched the taxes roll out of the inner bailey into the outer. When the gate was shut, he turned and ran back up the stairs.

With a stab of mild surprise, he realized he was humming.

Thirty-Eight

Marian, clean again, clad as a woman again, reacquainted herself with Ravenskeep. This time she saw it through eyes grown cynical, eyes that understood the motivations of men, not merely the eyes of a girl grown to womanhood, the eyes of a chatelaine. There yet remained damage from the sheriff's men, but Joan and the others had taken care to repair and put back what they could. Somewhat battered, but still her hall. Still her home.

But empty of those men she had come to care for.

She felt herself divided, become two people. One had the ordering of the manor, was busily sorting through what they had and what was needed, counting bags of flour, how much salt was left; did the roof require new shingles yet again; how many lambs had been born, and which old ewes should be slaughtered. The other person, the other Marian, was not beneath a roof at all, but out among the trees with a longbow in her hand and bird calls echoing.

He would come home again. They all would.

When deLacey was no longer sheriff.

But deLacey had been sheriff for as long as she could remember. He had begun in Old King Henry's time, before her birth; continued through King Richard's ten-year reign, twice buying his office; and now served John. She could not speak for his habits when Henry was king—she had been too young to know of such things—but he and her father had been friends. He had certainly been kind to her as a child. Nor would Sir Hugh FitzWalter, before the battle that killed him, have told Sir Robert of Locksley should anything happen to him, his daughter was to consider a marriage with William deLacey—unless he believed deLacey would treat her well.

Perhaps once he might have. The sheriff had been a decent man, she knew, a man her father respected. But no one could apply that description to William deLacey now. Surely her father would abhor what he had become, would never suggest his daughter consider his suit.

When had it happened, then, and *what* had happened that caused a man to change so significantly?

In her own experience she knew men who had changed, had *been* changed, because of circumstances. Will Scarlet, formerly Scathlocke, had come home to his peasant's hovel one day to find his wife so badly violated by Norman soldiers that she died of it, bleeding to death in his arms. He had sought the men and killed four of them before he was captured. Grief and the need for revenge had changed him into a murderer, had left him bitter and angry and violent. He had found a measure of peace at Ravenskeep in the past five years, but there was a part of him none of them knew, that he kept locked away. A part of him wholly unpredictable, and equally dangerous.

And Robin himself, for that matter. She had known him slightly in her youth, had worshipped him in burgeoning womanhood, but he had gone away to war. Like Will he had killed, but in the name of his God and his king, in the name of Jerusalem, not in revenge or in grief. Yet he had been altered by the war despite its righteousness, and captivity had changed him even more. There were nights when he woke her crying out, striking out; nights when he woke her by leaving the bed entirely, and when she sought him she found him downstairs by the fire, eyes transfixed by memories and waking visions he would not share.

But these men had reason. A wife, violated by men and weapons until she died. A soldier imprisoned a year by the enemy after months of brutal battles. What had William deLacey encountered that had altered him? That would cause him to plot to trick her into a sham ceremony to force a genuine marriage; to name her a witch with manufactured evidence and coerced witnesses; to set his men to tearing apart her hall; to strike her name from the tax rolls so that he might claim her manor and turn her out of it?

But she was no longer a child, no longer innocent. She understood the things that some men needed. Craved.

Power. Ambition. Politics.

Not offenses of the body, the ravages of emotions, but desires of the mind.

William deLacey could never be a king who was born of such things as power, ambition, and politics, whose royal parents wed and conceived children solely for the sake of holding or gaining realms. He could never be a lord born to wealth and privilege, only a man appointed to office by the king, finding identity in it, defining himself by power, and the ambition for more. A man utterly dependent on the king's whim; and John was notorious for the fickleness of his whims.

Politics.

John had wanted England when his brother ruled it in absentia. DeLacey's little kingdom, the shire of Nottingham, was therefore threatened. He had judged John most likely to be the victor, and thus took his part. But John had lost the battle for the throne when Richard came home from captivity, ransomed by nobles and poor alike through auxilliary tax collections. DeLacey had then bought back the office Richard might have stripped from him; the warrior-king needed money to continue his battles, and he was not averse to allowing men to remain in office if they would pay for it. But now Richard was dead, John was king, and deLacey, King of Nottinghamshire, once again was firmly in John's camp.

Power. Ambition. Politics.

Marian, in the midst of the buttery counting how many crocks remained whole, and full, spread her left palm and looked at the cautery scar. It had caused her to miss her shot, to kill the sheriff's horse when she had meant only to warn, to contain the man. But it was done; she had committed herself. She, too, had changed: had made herself an outlaw in the name of a justice deLacey refused to condone. The only reason she was here while Robin and the others hid in Sherwood, intending to steal money so her taxes might be paid, so the poor might be fed, so Arthur of Brittany might be aided to the throne and they could be pardoned again, was because no one knew she had been there in Nottingham, helping to rescue Much.

One moment, one birth or death, could alter the world.

A wife's murder changed Will Scarlet. War and captivity changed Robin. The Lord High Sheriff of Nottingham changed Hugh FitzWalter's daughter.

Marian closed her hand on the scar. Aloud she said, "He sowed the crop five years ago, after my father's death. Let him reap it now, and know the blame for his own."

She left the buttery then, left the counting of crocks undone. She went upstairs to the room under the eaves she shared—*had* shared—with Robin, and began to pack warm clothes and necessaries into a bundle. She would tell Joan what else was needed, and Hal as well. She would tell them also that possibly, if necessary, she might take up residence in Sherwood for a time until all was settled.

When a life could be changed of a moment, it was best to be prepared.

* * *

They had moved their little encampment from near Ravenskeep to a small clearing between Huntington and Nottingham, covering supplies with brush and deadfall leaves. Robin, perched upon a tree stump in desultory conversation about which bird calls would mean what, and how they might deploy themselves depending on circumstances—they had done this very thing when stealing the tax shipment five years before—glanced up sharply as an owl hooted from nearby. Within moments the owl resolved itself into Much slipping out of the trees into the tiny clearing cradled by fallen trees.

He squatted. "Lords."

"You're certain?" Robin asked.

"Fine horses. *Fine* clothes." Much nodded. "Lords."

"How many?" Scarlet asked. "And what kind of escort?"

Much spread three fingers.

"The escort," Alan urged.

"Three lords," the boy insisted.

Scarlet shook his head. "Lords don't ride unescorted, do they?"

"Some do," Robin said thoughtfully, "when they are meeting in secret."

Little John, sitting cross-legged on the ground, looked at him sharply. "Meeting with who? What for?"

"Meeting with my father." Robin rubbed idly at the roughening stubble along his jaw. "To plot the overthrow of a king."

" 'Tis treason!" Tuck cried.

Robin agreed. "They could lose their heads for it. Just as we could be hanged for outlawry." A wry smile twisted his mouth. "What a fine family tradition *that* would be for the earls of Huntington: one executed for treason, the other hanged for thievery."

"You mean for us to rob men meeting with your father?" Alan asked, startled.

"Best to rob men with money."

Little John was puzzled. "Yes, but—if they mean to overthrow King John, then we are on the same side."

Robin said gently, "Outlaws have no sides."

"Coming soon," Much reminded.

"Well, then." Robin stood up, brushed debris from his hosen. "Shall we put to the test the methods we've just discussed?"

"Now?" Scarlet demanded.

"Indeed, now. 'Coming soon,' Much says."

Tuck was alarmed. "What do you mean to do?"

"Invite them for ale and a bite of bread," Robin explained. "And then they can ransom their freedom by giving us their coin."

Little John was patently unconvinced. "And what if they go to the sheriff?"

"I believe they will not," Robin said mildly.

Now Scarlet was unconvinced. "How can you say that? How can you know?"

"Because they invited me to join them," Robin explained, "when it was thought I should be heir to my father's title. To risk my head as they risked theirs. When peers of the realm undertake treason, they rarely complain to a sheriff of minor matters such as outlaws along the road. Particularly to a sheriff who supports the very king they mean to replace."

"Coming," Much said urgently.

Robin picked up his bow, hooked the quiver over one shoulder. "Do as I described, and it should fall out properly. Tuck, remain here . . . uncover the food and ale and set a 'table,' if you would. We'll have guests for a midday meal."

He sent himself and the others into the trees along the road, hoping they would do as asked, as he had explained. It was not so different from what they had done to rescue Much: one stopped men on horseback with the threat of arrows from cover, then told them what to do. If they could not see who stopped them, how many there were, and where they hid, they were far less likely to protest. Everyone in England knew the power and accuracy of a longbow. And anyone in Nottingham the day before had witnessed or heard of how arrows had been used to control the sheriff.

Robin reflected a reputation might be useful. Certainly it had benefitted the Crusaders: every man of all nations knew the Lionheart's reputation for brilliance in the field and personal ability, his gift for inspiring men, not to mention his cheerful but unflagging ruthlessness. Even Saladin had respected Richard. Such things as reputations could be employed as tools themselves.

But he rather thought a reputation would take care of itself, if they robbed enough people.

The lords approached, coming into view from around a tight curve. They were indeed the men Robin anticipated: the earls of Alnwick, Hereford, and Essex. A few quiet but scattered bird calls told him the others were in place. Grinning, Robin pulled up his hood, settled it in place, then stepped out onto the road.

"Hold," he commanded.

Then he raised his hand, and the arrows flew.

The lords, as expected, reined in sharply as the shafts stood up from the ground in a rough semicircle.

Robin raised his voice. "Swords, if you please."

Eustace de Vesci, well in character as his face grew red, blustered immediately. "Who are you? What is the meaning of this?"

"A robbery," Robin replied. "Swords, if you please." He did not alter his accent, his voice, or his phraseology as he had five years before in a similar confrontation. The times were different now, the cause, and his committment.

"By God!" de Vesci cried. "Again? *Again?* I cannot but think the road to Nottingham has become a den of thieves!"

"Bad luck," Robin observed gravely. "My lords, if you please—your swords. Now."

Bohun already had his sword unsheathed, dangling from gloved fingers. De Mandeville was eyeing Robin with something akin to speculation, though nothing of his person bespoke a reluctance to follow orders. He, too, unsheathed his sword. "Eustace," he said mildly, "this man is not alone. He did not shoot five arrows at once, did he?"

Robin grinned. "I shot none of them."

De Vesci jerked his sword from his sheath and tossed it down before his horse. Bohun and de Mandeville followed suit.

"Much," Robin said.

The boy darted out into the roadway, collected the weapons deftly, and disappeared on the other side of the road.

"Dismount," Robin suggested. "Come six steps toward me."

De Vesci was horrified. "Do you mean to take our *horses?*"

This time Henry Bohun was less willing to follow orders. "We'll just toss down our purses and ride on, shall we? There is no need to leave us afoot."

Robin gestured. "Down," he said. "Leave them there. Come here to me, as I have said."

De Mandeville dismounted and released his reins, doing as told. After a moment Bohun did the same. De Vesci, muttering imprecations beneath his breath, jumped down from his horse and took three long paces forward that put him alongside his companions.

"Much," Robin said, "take the horses to Tuck."

The boy came back out into the road, *sans* swords, took up the dangling reins, and led the horses into the trees. They crashed after him through thick vegetation.

Robin, still several strides away from the earls, slipped his hood, smiling. "The past repeats. But at least this time none of you swears I have no right to my sword."

"By God!" de Vesci cried, face reddening once more. "It *is* 'again'!"

Bohun blinked. "Robert?"

Geoffrey de Mandeville nodded to himself, as if a question had been answered.

"We have food and ale," Robin said. "Do join us for a meal." He whistled a low but carrying call. "Will, Alan, Little John—escort our guests, if you please."

One by one the men materialized out of the forest on either side of the road, longbows in hand but no arrows nocked. Robin watched as the earls took the measure of them, paying particular attention to the towering size of Little John and the hard-eyed attitude of Will Scarlet, no man's fool.

"Why are you doing this?" Bohun inquired. De Vesci, baffled, merely scowled.

Robin glanced at the Earl of Essex. Geoffrey de Mandeville sighed, lifting shoulders in a slight apologetic shrug. "I had no chance to tell them what we discussed in the garden."

"Ah. Well, I suppose it would do best coming from me." He gestured the others forward. "Go," he suggested, as Alan fell in before the lords and Will and John behind. They went single-file, trailing slowly into the forest.

Robin went to where Much had left the swords, gathered them up, and followed his men.

His men.

His army. Such as it was.

He was not Richard the Lionheart, and they were not Crusaders. But he did not see that it mattered who they were or what they were called, so long as what they undertook was for the good of England.

Robin sighed and resettled the swords in his arms. *I am become my father after all.*

Thirty-Nine

DeLacey was more than a little shocked when he was admitted to see the Earl of Huntington. He had known the man was ill and growing frail, but now he was wasting away. There was little of him left, only the dull blaze in his faded eyes, the ascetic repressiveness of his thin face. Somewhere beneath the covers the body lay, but the sheriff could see none of it save gnarled hands extruding from bedrobe sleeves and a head crowned with wispy white hair.

It came as a shock. *He is dying.*

All men died. But the earl had been old for decades, somehow frozen in time. Only now did he seem vulnerable. Only now was the decisive and difficult spirit dimmed by physical weakness.

DeLacey inclined his head swiftly to hide his expression. "My lord," he said, betraying no startlement.

"My steward tells me this is a matter of business." The whispery tone was like parchment tearing.

The sheriff in that moment wanted nothing so much as to depart. At once. To hide from the final, fatal truth that all men confronted, far easier to ignore when one was not brought face to face with mortality. *I will grow old one day.*

"Indeed," he said, withdrawing a folded parchment from his sleeve. "But, my lord—it may wait."

"Business rarely waits." A palsied hand gestured. "Tell me."

DeLacey unfolded the parchment. "This is a letter explaining matters to Marian FitzWalter," he said. "It is best left to me to tell her, my lord, that you have assumed her tax debt. It is I as sheriff who must account for such matters, and arrange them; men such as yourself need not trouble themselves with evictions."

A white brow arched. "You will evict her?"

"Indeed, my lord. You own the manor now. Unless you wish her to remain." He gestured, trying not to lead the man too blatantly. The earl was old and ill, but deLacey knew it extremely unlikely the man had lost his wits. "You perhaps may wish her to act as chatelaine, to keep the tenants in order."

"Leave her overseeing the management of a manor that once was hers? To pay rents to the man who would not permit his son to marry her?" The earl's cracked lips moved into a faint, wintry smile. "You are cruel, William."

"But efficient."

"Oh, efficient. Always." The earl coughed, spasming against the pillows, but he waved deLacey away when he made as if to offer assistance. "No. I will not have her stay. I shall make a different provision for the management of the manor. My steward has been a loyal man, and I intend to reward him for it. My title, lands, and wealth shall pass to the Crown upon my death, and likely Ralph will eventually be dismissed as the king chooses his own man. One day the king will no doubt give some favored family or courtier my title as a reward. Therefore I shall have it written that upon my death my steward shall inherit the FitzWalter manor. And I doubt he will have need of that woman running his household."

It took deLacey's breath away. That Huntington would give the hall and manor to his *steward!* He himself was dependent on his office for a roof over his head; now Ralph of Huntington, a mere servant, would own his own lands, his own hall. All because he had served a stubborn old man for more than two decades, while William deLacey had served an entire shire for thirty years.

But he kept all of it from his face. He would still have the pleasure of turning Marian out, and that in itself was worth any price.

"I shall have this letter delivered to her," the sheriff explained. "It is a straightforward document, plain in speech. She has forfeited the manor for want of the proper tax payments. You are now the owner. Therefore she must depart."

"She is of no moment," the earl said breathlessly. "But I wish my son to understand what he has given up. An earldom, Huntington Castle, Locksley Village, and now even the girl's hall. He must see what it is to be alone in the world as a poor man, no better than a peasant, no richer than a serf. He must know what it is to be *destitute.*" His hand trembled as he wiped at damp lips. "Do you know how many men in England would beg for such an inheritance as I intended to leave him?"

William deLacey had a very good idea indeed.

"And yet he rejects what I have done for him. What I have *built* for him." The earl's grimace was a rigid spasm. "He is an ungrateful son."

DeLacey was not certain if he should agree—it was one thing for a father to defame his son, quite another for someone else to do so—and thus he held his tongue.

Then the earl waved a hand. "But he is not my son anymore."

"My lord—"

Huntington closed his eyes. "I have no son."

The sheriff could think of nothing else to say, and the earl appeared to have fallen asleep. So he refolded the parchment, slipped it back inside his sleeve, inclined his head briefly to the old man—just in case—and took himself from the room.

Downstairs, before the main door, he met Ralph, who brought his summer-weight cloak. The now infamous Ralph, loyal, helpful, faithful Ralph. Who surely must know soon what the earl had decided, if not already.

But deLacey merely looked grave and accepted Ralph's aid in the donning of his cloak. "I did not realize the earl had taken so ill." Which was perfectly true, even if intended merely as overture.

"He has worsened over the last few days," Ralph said in a subdued tone.

"He has been a good master to you."

"I could not have wished for a better one."

"And what of Robert, his son? Do you feel as strongly as the earl does, that the boy should remain disinherited?"

Something flickered in Ralph's eyes before he smoothed the servant's mask back into place.

"Ah." The man need say nothing; it was clear he cared very deeply for Robert of Locksley. Likely Ralph had helped raise the boy to manhood. This made it simpler. "I myself believe the earl is being too harsh. One cannot excuse the follies of youth, of course, and it is quite true that discipline is necessary, but disinheritance? Extreme, I should think."

Emboldened by a like opinion, Ralph succumbed to frank speech. "My lord and his son have often been at odds. It is most distressing. They are both proud and stubborn men, unwilling to admit when the other may be correct."

"But should a father be so stubborn when he is dying? When he has so much tradition to pass on to his son? Surely he could forgive him."

"I pray for it, Lord Sheriff. Every night."

Prayer. Well. DeLacey did not believe in the efficacy of such. Best a man do what he himself could, rather than begging God for such things as wealth and power.

"Would he come, do you think?" DeLacey asked, as if he had only just been struck by the idea. "You say they are often at odds . . . but should a son not be at his father's bedside when death approaches? Even if the father disapproves?"

"My lord, *I* believe so. And I have told the earl. Let me send for him, I have asked. Repeatedly. But the earl says I may not go."

"But would he come?"

"Robin?" The telling slip into the familiarity of a long-time servant was unmarked by Ralph, but significant to the sheriff. "Oh, I do believe so. If he knew his father was dying, I believe he would."

"And so he should." DeLacey rested a hand on the steward's shoulder. "You are a good man, Ralph. One any man should be glad to have in his service. Let us pray you may yet convince the earl to send for his son. Perhaps—tomorrow?"

Ralph was perplexed. "My lord?"

"And perhaps it should be done no matter what the earl desires." DeLacey squeezed the shoulder bracingly. "He is a stubborn man, my lord earl, as you have said . . . he may indeed wish for his son to be here, yet cannot bring himself to ask for his presence after insisting against it. But if you were to go on your own . . ." He arched suggestive brows.

Ralph frowned. "I could not go against my lord's wishes."

"In nothing else, of course not. But he is *dying*, Ralph! Would you deny him a chance to see his son a final time, to deny that son the chance to ask forgiveness for so much misbehavior? It may be the final opportunity for them to reconcile."

But Ralph was as yet unconvinced.

DeLacey knew when not to press a man. "Well, it may be moot regardless. He could die tonight, I daresay—and there is no time for you to send for Robert today. Perhaps, if he lives the night . . . well, you may feel differently in the morning. Even the earl may. Perhaps you might ask him again tomorrow, when there is time for you to fetch Robert." He paused. "To fetch Robert *home*, Ralph, where he belongs." He resettled his cloak, hooking brooches. "Prayer will help. Give God the opportunity to know what is in your heart. Pray tonight, Ralph, and ask the earl again tomorrow—he would send *you*, would he not, so faithful and trusted a man?—and perhaps you may bring the prodigal home again."

Ralph seemed encouraged. "I will indeed pray tonight, my lord, and see what the earl says in the morning. Thank you for your confidence."

DeLacey strode out of the hall into the late afternoon, resolving to station a man to report when Ralph rode out of Huntington. *Plenty of time,* he reflected. The earl and his steward did not know Locksley had taken to hiding in Sherwood. Ralph would go all the way to Ravenskeep to fetch the son home to his dying father, and that would give deLacey time to arrive at Huntington with his soldiers to offer Locksley an appropriate reception.

He smiled as he waited for his horse. Everything was coming together so nicely, and all at the same time. Efficiency incarnate.

Or perhaps God did not like outlaws, even nobly born ones, any more than William deLacey did.

Now *that* was a deity he would willingly pray to. One who punished outlaws. It would certainly save the sheriff a lot of time and aggravation.

"And so that is why," Robin finished, leaning against a tree trunk.

Eustace de Vesci, a flask of ale clutched in one hand, stared uncomprehendingly at Geoffrey de Mandeville. *"You* told him to rob us?"

"Well, not precisely rob *us,"* Essex replied. "I suggested he serve us— and Arthur—by keeping the taxes from John. He has no money, no treasury, merely the title. A king cannot keep his crown if he has no money for the ordering of the realm."

Henry Bohun was less offended than de Vesci. "But was it necessary to carry out the charade there in the road? You might have identified yourself before taking our swords and making us dismount."

"Practice," Robin said succinctly. "I was not raised to this, you see."

De Mandeville smiled, genuinely amused. De Vesci glowered and said, "You've adapted well enough."

Robin looked at them one by one. The three of them sat in a row along a log, like birds upon a limb. Alan, Will, and Little John, bows in hand, ranged behind them casually. "What is to complain of, my lords? We have fed you, given you ale, kept you company."

"You have *delayed* us," de Vesci explained. "We meant to make Lincoln by nightfall."

"And you still may. I don't intend to keep your horses, or even your swords." Robin shrugged. "Only your purses and rings."

After a moment of stricken silence, de Vesci boomed out a hearty gust of laughter. "By God, you learn fast! I almost believe you."

"Do," Robin suggested. "You may all of you go as soon as the toll is paid."

Bohun understood more quickly than de Vesci, eyes narrowing. De Mandeville did not bother to hide his startlement. "Robert?"

"Or you may stay the night here," Robin said quietly. "Perhaps in the morning you will feel more generous."

Will Scarlet prodded the stunned de Vesci in the spine with his longbow. "Pay the toll, aye? Then 'tis Lincoln-bound you'll be."

Robin smiled at them companionably. "Fear not. The coin and baubles are not for us. We will take a percentage—I think that is only fair, considering the risk—but I'll send most along to Arthur."

"*We* can send money along to Arthur!" de Vesci cried, now almost purple with rage. "And he has no need of our jewels!"

De Mandeville was frowning. "Robert, I must protest—"

"*You* cannot be seen to send money to Brittany. *You* cannot be seen to support him in any way. You certainly cannot be seen to steal taxes from deLacey. I am already outlawed—a small matter of a pardon revoked, a brace of borrowed horses, the rescue of a cutpurse from under the sheriff's nose—and disinherited. Surely I am beyond hope. Surely I can no longer embarrass my father. Surely I may convince you I mean what I say."

"Robert, there is no *need*—" de Mandeville began.

"A sacrifice," Robin overrode him, "for the good of the realm. Such things are often asked, and as often offered." He lifted his brows. "Surely *you*, my lords, comprehend the need." He took an empty leather pouch from his belt and tossed it to land on the ground at de Vesci's booted feet. "Please put your rings in that. Your purses you may donate to Little John as he takes you to your horses."

De Mandeville stiffened. "This is not what I intended when we discussed this in the garden."

Robin nodded sympathetically. "I know. But one must consider this a war, my lord. Wars are not won by undertaking the simple things. Wars are not won by undertaking the *friendly* things. Wars are won by undertaking what is necessary. No matter what others may think."

"War is honorable!" de Vesci bellowed. "By God, would the Lionheart countenance this?"

"The Lionheart," Robin said very quietly, "did whatever was necessary. What he *perceived* to be necessary. I was there, you see, when he ordered executed nearly three thousand of Acre's citizens after the city was won. Even women, my lords."

That did not sit well with the three earls. They shifted uncomfortably on the log and exchanged concerned glances.

"But—robbing *us*?" Bohun asked. "We are on the same side!"

"Outlaws have no sides." Robin grinned, scratching again at stubble. "And we do intend to rob many folk. You are not the only ones."

De Mandeville sighed deeply. "I suppose we should be grateful you are not other outlaws. They would keep the coin for themselves."

Scarlet declared pointedly, "Other outlaws might even kill you."

De Mandeville began methodically to strip off his gloves. Rings followed. He bent, took up the pouch Robin had tossed down, dropped the rings into it. Then he handed the pouch to Bohun with a murmured comment, "The sooner done, the sooner we may go."

With an expression of taut displeasure, Hereford repeated the process with his own rings. But de Vesci, when he was given the pouch in turn, merely threw it to the ground. "This is travesty!"

Robin shrugged. "This is robbery."

Scarlet prodded the man in the spine again. "Give over," he suggested. "You can't win this war, aye?"

Robin looked at Alan and Little John. "Much is with the horses. Escort my lords of Hereford and Essex to them. Collect their purses. Then see them to the road, and return their swords. As for my lord of Alnwick"—he looked now at Eustace de Vesci—"we shall, it seems, share his company overnight."

De Vesci leaped to his feet. "You *dare* to threaten me?"

Robin folded arms across his chest and stretched out his legs in a posture of relaxation, crossing them at the ankles. "I would not construe eating our bread, drinking our ale, and sharing our company as a *threat*, my lord. Rather, it is hospitality. This is our home, you see." His gesture encompassed the forest. "I would be remiss as a host if I did not fête you properly."

De Mandeville was grave. "Robert, do take care. I understand what you are doing—and I suppose I should share some of the blame!—but you risk making enemies here."

Robin ran out of patience. "Good, my lords, I have been disinherited. Outlawed. I may be *hanged* for my actions. I have nothing to lose by doing what I do here, but very much to gain, as my lord of Essex pointed out a matter of days ago in my father's garden." He paused. "And Arthur of Brittany, because of what I and my companions do here today and in the days to come, may become King of England."

It struck them all to silence. Henry Bohun looked thoughtful. Geoffrey de Mandeville was resigned. "My brilliant idea," he murmured ruefully.

Eustace de Vesci, face aflame with choler, jerked the rings off his fingers and tossed them to the ground. "For Arthur, then," he declared forcefully, as if it would defray the embarrassment. "But I will not excuse you for't!"

"Nor should you, my lord of Alnwick. This is indeed an outrage." Robin nodded at Scarlet and the others to gather up the noble chicks. "And I will freely submit to any discipline you wish to mete out . . . once Arthur is on the throne."

De Vesci turned on his heel and snapped an order at Scarlet to show him to his horse. Henry Bohun went with him, escorted by Alan.

It left only Geoffrey de Mandeville. Little John stood behind him, waiting in silence. "A dangerous gamble, Robert."

"One you have taken as well."

"But not to the same degree." The older man's expression was compassionate. "If our efforts fail, and John remains on the throne . . ." He gestured futility.

"We shall hang," Robin said simply. "But first they must catch us. Here in Sherwood, that is not so easily done."

De Mandeville glanced around at the encroaching trees and vegetation. He nodded slightly, then extended his arm to Robin. His gaze was steady. "Your father is a fool."

Smiling, Robin gripped the arm. "But consistent in his convictions. In a world of kings, crowns, and power, that is all too rare."

Forty

Marian was startled when Joan came running up the stairs, breathlessly announcing *'that Norman'* was back again. Even after close questioning the woman could not identify the visitor better than that, so Marian left off packing her bundle and went downstairs, mentally prepared to face anyone. But she was not expecting Mercardier.

The perverse part of her that preferred accuracy in all things, even things that did not truly matter in the ordering of the world—it was her besetting and most annoying flaw, Robin had explained in exasperation on several occasions—very nearly informed Joan he was not Norman, but from the duchy of Aquitaine, or so Robin had explained. But she restrained the impulse. His birthplace was hardly at issue, nor had bearing on the moment.

He stood just inside the door, seemingly ill at ease. She thought perhaps he was a man more comfortable—and best suited to—being out of doors, or in castles and tents discussing war strategy with kings and high lords, not for lingering within halls intended for civilian habitation.

She nearly missed a step as she approached, abruptly and vividly recalling that it had been he at the business end of her nocked arrow the day before in Nottingham. Had he recognized her after all?

But Marian thought not: she wore a woman's chemise again, and her hair had been taken from the tight braid and washed, left loose to dry. Even now it spilled over her shoulders to her knees. There was nothing about her that recalled the lad in yeoman's clothing.

"Madame," he said in his accented English, "I am in need of a horse."

Neither tact nor courtesy were his gifts. But Marian looked more closely at him. He carried his helm in the crook of his elbow, yet his gray-threaded dark hair bore no signs of compression. In fact, his hair was entirely disordered. Dirt floured his surcoat. "You appear to be in need of more than that," she observed. "Have you been in a fight?"

Color abruptly stained the saturnine face, surprising her with its intensity. It was an entirely different Mercardier who gazed back at her, clearly discomfited despite attempts to hide it.

"You have," she said in discovery. "What happened?"

Beneath the high color, the pocked face was rigid as stone. "May I borrow a horse, madame? Be certain I shall have it returned safely."

"What happened to *your* horse?" In view of who he was and whom he served, it mattered. "I cannot in good conscience lend you a horse if there may be danger to it."

Color remained in his face. "Madame, as surely you must know, there has been a robbery."

"As surely I must know?" she echoed, truly startled. "Why must *I* know, Captain?"

He barely moved his mouth, merely issued the words in a harsh monotone that nonetheless expressed his fury more eloquently than shouting. "Because in all likelihood it was Locksley and his men who did it."

"Locksley and his men." Already it had begun. And yet she could not hide the note of puzzlement in her tone. "Forgive me, Captain—but are you accusing Robin of robbing you?"

"Of robbing the king, madame."

"The *king?*"

"He and his men have stolen the taxes."

Genuinely taken aback, Marian clapped both hands over her mouth.

Mercardier's eyes narrowed. "Feigned shock, madame? Is this studied response because you knew this was to happen?"

*"Un*feigned," she said through parted fingers. "And unstudied. This response is pure astonishment, Captain."

He scoffed. *"Ah, oui.* Astonishment, *certes."* He glared; this was an indeed entirely new Mercardier, to be so extravagant with emotions. "I am to believe you did not know? Come, madame—I may be a mercenary, but not a stupid one."

"I did not know," she answered forcefully, with the weight of truth in the words; because it *was* true. "Nor am I convinced it was Robin. There are many outlaws in Sherwood." She had of course known they intended to steal the taxes, but not when. Not so soon. Certainly not today. It was weeks early for the shipment; Robin and the others would never have been prepared to undertake such an effort without time to plan carefully.

Mercardier scowled at her. "If you continue to delay me with prevarication, I have no choice but to believe you knew what they intended."

"A telling point," she acceded, "but untrue. Though I realize there is no way to convince you." Marian, frowning, studied him. "Are you injured, Captain?"

The color flooded back into his face, which had grown uncharacteristically pale. "We were set upon, madame, and quite overpowered." His mouth thinned. "Briefly."

She very nearly laughed; clearly it deeply hurt his pride to confess defeat. Perhaps he had never known it before. "Briefly?"

He gritted his teeth so hard muscles jerked in his jaw. "The others rode after the outlaws."

"The others? Oh, you must mean the soldiers accompanying you; surely not even you would have been expected to be the sole escort." Marian blinked, affecting ingenuous discovery. "Do you mean then that you were left behind? You did *not* ride after the outlaws?"

"I was rendered unconscious," he said grimly, "and fell from my horse." Absently he touched a mailed hand to the back of his head, as if recalling the blow. "My horse was not present when I roused."

It was not truly amusing—he was obviously in discomfort—but he was so desperately offended that she wanted badly to laugh. Instead, she smothered it and settled for delicate, dry irony, Robin's most devastating weapon. "Perhaps the horse went after the outlaws as well."

And very clearly the mercenary recognized the progenitor of that irony. He took a sharp step forward as if he meant to grab her arm, but aborted the movement with a wince. Marian believed it more likely that pain curbed his temper rather than manners. She was grateful nonetheless; Mercardier was not a man for gentleness. If he touched her, even in mild rebuke, she would very probably bruise. "If you like, I can put a cold compress on your head," she said, "and offer you a bed."

Mercardier glared at her sourly. "And keep me from reporting this theft to the sheriff?"

"Ah. Of course you would believe that." She shrugged acknowledgment. "Then I rescind the offer. Yes, you may borrow a horse." She turned to Joan. "Show him to the barn. Hal will see to it he is given a mount." She looked again at the angry man. "Do see that *this* horse does not run into the woods chasing outlaws, if you please."

Will Scarlet, accompanied by Little John, Much, and Alan, came back laughing from escorting the earls to their horses. "Yon lords are most discommoded," he announced, briefly attempting a noble accent before dropping back into his own peasant speech. "I think the beefy gent would hang you himself."

Robin, squatting next to Tuck, who sat on the ground with the contents of several pouches spread across his cassocked lap, shrugged. "De Vesci, Earl of Alnwick. He has always been disposed to excitability."

Alan shook his head. "And you say the one suggested you turn thief?"

"The Earl of Essex. He did, yes. For Arthur's sake, he said; but I think he truly had not realized what the task entails."

Little John nodded. "They should try it themselves, aye?"

Scarlet scoffed. "Not them. Never dirty their hands, would they?" He spat in contempt. *"Lords."*

Alan arched golden brows in mock startlement. "Are you forgetting our very own Robin was once a lord himself?"

"Aye, but not anymore, is he?" Scarlet countered cheerfully. "Just an outlaw like the rest of us, groveling in the dirt."

Robin, observing Tuck's treasure from his position in the dirt and deadfall, nodded sagely. "I came to my senses. This is a much better life than living in a fine hall with fine clothing to wear and fine food to eat and a true bed to sleep in." Coins and rings glinted against black Benedictine wool in tree-latticed sunlight. The others gathered around, peering down at the riches.

"How much?" Little John asked.

"Enough for Marian's taxes," Tuck answered primly, "thanks to our friends the earls. Not so much for Arthur of Brittany—we'll send him the rings, as we can hardly pay taxes with them—and very little for the poor."

Alan leaned closer. "What about us?"

"Naught for us," Tuck said.

"Naught?" Scarlet was outraged. "How can there be naught for us?"

"Because we come last," Robin explained.

"Last! Why last? 'Tis us doing the thieving!"

Tuck began dividing the coins and rings into separate pouches, carefully counting them out.

Robin glanced up. The others all loomed over him wearing various expressions ranging from Will Scarlet's hostile affrontedness and Alan's speculative smile. But the minstrel had always been an observer, using what he saw as fodder for his ballads. "Because we are not doing this for ourselves."

Scarlet was scandalized. "Of course we are!"

"Not *first*," Little John told him. "We come last. Marian, Arthur of Brittany, the poor, and then us."

It did not mollify. "None o' them are living here with us, are they? I still say we should come first."

Robin stood. "Will, when your wife was alive, who ate first?"

It baffled Scarlet entirely. "Meggie served me first."

"Did you eat?"

"I waited for her." He shrugged. "Only fair."

"But you might argue that you were more deserving, having worked in the fields all day."

"Maybe."

"But you, being a fair man—you have just said so—wished to share the meal with her."

Scarlet shook his head. "What are you getting at?"

Alan laughed softly. "He's getting at that we may be more deserving, having worked to steal the money, but 'tis more fair to share it with others first."

"Will," Robin said quietly. "We need you. *I* need you. But you are a free man. You may go, if you prefer."

"And rob by myself?"

Little John made a sound of derision. "We're not known through all of England, are we?"

"You are," Alan observed, smiling cheerily. "The Hathersage Giant."

The Hathersage Giant shot the minstrel a quelling glance and went on. "You could go down to London if you liked, look for work there. 'Tis a big city; they'd likely not know you at all. No need to be an outlaw there."

"I *am* an outlaw. I murdered Norman soldiers. I've silver pennies on my head, like a wolf."

"You were pardoned once," Robin said. "We all of us were."

"But King Richard is dead," Tuck pointed out.

Robin nodded. "So long as John is king in his place, we are outlaws. Yes. But if we aid Arthur, there may be a pardon in it."

" 'May,' " Alan emphasized.

"We stole the taxes before with no expectation of a pardon," Robin observed mildly. He looked at Will. "Are you with us in this?"

Scarlet ducked his head, kicking at leaves as if to excavate each one. When he looked up again, his eyes were less hostile. "They'll hang you, too, aye?"

"Me?" Robin nodded. "Of course. I am, as you say, an outlaw like the rest of you, groveling in the dirt."

"Even being an earl's son."

He very nearly laughed. "Oh, I imagine it is possible they would do me the honor of chopping off my head with an ax instead of hanging me, but I believe I would still be dead."

"Well, then." Will Scarlet nodded. "We're all wolf's-heads, aren't we?"

Much tipped his head back and howled.

Alan sighed. "Thank you, Will. He'll be doing that for days."

Robin reached over and planted a hand on Much's mouth, cutting off the howl. "Birds," he said sternly. "Not wolves. Birds." He glanced at Tuck as he released the grinning boy. "I'll take the pouches with Marian's taxes, Arthur's money, and what is meant for the poor, and deliver them to Abraham the Jew."

Little John was startled. "In Nottingham?"

"They'll not expect me there," Robin told him. "Abraham will see to it Marian's taxes are paid, and that Arthur's money is sent on and the portion for the poor is distributed." He received the pouches from Tuck. "When I return, we'll need to discuss what to do when the sheriff sends the tax shipment. It won't be for a few weeks yet. But we must be ready." He hooked the pouches through his belt.

"You'll be wanting your bow," Scarlet reminded him as he turned to go.

"No. Too obvious." He dropped his hand to the sword at his hip. "But I have this. In fact, you *all* have swords, with thanks to the soldiers we robbed yesterday. I suggest you set about learning how to use them."

"Swords?" Little John asked doubtfully.

Scarlet nodded. "Lords use swords."

"Then consider yourselves lords in Sherwood. Lords *of* Sherwood." Robin, laughing, made an elegant leg in tribute, then took his leave to fetch his horse.

Behind him, Alan began a song about parfait gentil knights wielding swords on the field of battle, seeking glory and honor and entry into Heaven, even as the others set up a chorus of groans.

"Well," Robin murmured, striding toward Charlemagne, "somewhat better than wolves."

Somewhat.

DeLacey, in the inner bailey, was in the midst of assigning a man to report at once should the earl's steward ride out of Huntington Castle at any time, when Mercardier arrived in a flurry of iron horseshoes ringing on the cobbles. Everything about the mercenary's tight, jerky motions bespoke his anger; deLacey repressed a smile and prepared to be outraged.

As Mercardier dismounted—he said something in a quick aside to the horseboy—he stripped off his helm and thrust it into the crook of his elbow. His strides were long and militant, sharply clipped in the sound of their mailed tread. One hand gripped the hilt of his sword, as if it needed to be doing something to feel competent.

With carefully measured amazement, deLacey demanded, "What are you doing here?"

Mercardier drew himself up. His mouth was compressed into a taut, angry line, and his color was somewhere between the red of rage and the sweaty pallor of injury. Dark eyes glittered with a feverish intensity; Mercardier, the sheriff realized, was very, very angry.

And hideously embarrassed.

Oh, but this is sweeter than I envisioned. "Yes?" he asked in feigned alarm. "What has happened?"

"Robbery." It was ground out between clenched teeth.

It played out so well that deLacey was not even remotely at pains to sound genuine; it was all too easy to imagine it real. Because if the taxes *had* been stolen, it would certainly spell his ruin. He tapped the outrage easily. "The taxes? The *taxes?*"

Mercardier nodded once.

DeLacey did not shout. He spoke with exceeding gentleness. "Where are my men, Captain?"

"Chasing outlaws."

He permitted contempt to grace his tone. "Then why are *you* here? Should you not be out with them? Should you not be doing your duty? The command was *yours,* Captain. And you did assure me, most assiduously, that the shipment would be safe with you. It was, in fact, why the king sent you: you were the most able man for the job." With quiet pleasure, he saw the words strike home. "I think I shall send *you* to inform the king of this travesty."

The color had completely fled Mercardier's face. "It is my duty, Lord Sheriff."

"Your duty, and your downfall! God in Heaven, Captain, but do you realize what this means? This is disastrous!" He wiped a trembling hand over his face. "My God, my God . . . we are both ruined, Captain— *both* ruined by this!"

"Lord Sheriff—"

"How did this happen? Explain to me how this happened. How this *could* happen, with you as escort!"

Mercardier drew breath, composed himself, then began in soldierly fashion to report what had occurred. How arrows had sprung out of the trees on either side of the road; how they had been ordered to halt and stand down, or die where they stood; how he had been struck a terrible blow on the head by one of the outlaws. He had roused, he said, to find the wagon gone, the soldiers gone, and his horse missing.

"Then you don't *know* where the taxes are. You don't *know* where my men are."

Mercardier allowed as how he did not, not with any certainty.

"Who was it?" deLacey snapped. "Did you see anyone you might recognize?"

The hard face did not flinch. "I was not to see many before I was rendered unconscious."

"*Anyone,* Mercardier?"

"They wore hoods," he said briefly. "Six of them. One was quite tall; another remarkably stout. Yet a third was slight and quick, like a boy."

"And?"

A muscle jumped in the dark-stubbled jaw. "I believe it was the men who rescued the cutpurse."

He made it statement, not inquiry. "Robert of Locksley."

The thick neck was unbent, the head unbowed. "My lord."

DeLacey turned his back on Mercardier. Let the mercenary interpret the motion as outrage, as disgust; but he was hard-pressed not to smile.

And then he heard shouting and the sound of many horses, the rattle of iron-rimmed cartwheels and hooves against the cobbled outer bailey. "Lord Sheriff!"

DeLacey swung sharply back, even as Mercardier turned. Coming through the gates into the inner bailey was a wagon, and mounted soldiers. And Philip de la Barre.

"Lord Sheriff!" The wagon was halted at de la Barre's gestured order. "We have the taxes, my lord!"

"You *have* them?" DeLacey sprinted toward the wagon. "God in Heaven, swear it, de la Barre!"

"We have them. I swear it." De la Barre reached down to the wagon, gestured for one of the small chests to be handed up, and carried it to the sheriff. He leaned down from the saddle. "There, my lord. Will you be certain of it?"

As Mercardier came up, deLacey unhooked the latch and lifted back the lid. Inside lay a pile of coins spilled from their careful stacks. He looked hard at the mercenary, then displayed the contents. "And so we are redeemed."

White-faced, Mercardier nodded once.

"Did you see them, Philip?"

"Not all of them, I regret, not to attach names; they know the forest well, my lord—better than we, I am ashamed to confess. But the one who mattered, yes: 'twas Locksley, my lord."

"You captured none of them?"

"My concern was for the taxes. I did dispatch four men to hunt the outlaws in the forest and, if possible, come back with their location. But the rest of us returned so as to safeguard the wagon."

"Well done." Satisfied, deLacey closed and latched the lid, then handed the small chest back to de la Barre. "Thank you, Philip. You have saved us all." He flicked a glance at Mercardier, then looked back at his castellan. "Have the wagon unloaded and the chests placed back in the dungeon cell. I think it best that we do not immediately send the shipment off again; why tempt fate a second time? It is early yet in any event; we shall wait a few weeks." He turned now to Mercardier. "Captain, you will forgive me, I am sure, if I do not ask you to oversee the transfer. You have been injured, that is plain to see, and should rest."

Mercardier, clutching his helm in rigid fingers, jaw muscles jumping, inclined his head.

"And now, if you will excuse me, I must contemplate how best to capture Locksley and his men." DeLacey turned on his heel and departed.

Marian, after supper, wandered listlessly up the stairs to the room under the eaves. Her bundle was mostly finished; she added a handful of items to it, then tied it up into a pack with rope and leather thongs. Still listless, she lay down on the bed, propped her head upon the bundle, and thought about Ravenskeep as the sun went down. About Robin. About the others: Tuck, Much, Scarlet, Alan, and Little John. About men whom she admired—and the one man she loved—but who would nonetheless be hanged if captured.

She could not bear the idea of losing the manor. But there was something far more important to her than lands and a hall. Something for which she had been willing to trade Ravenskeep to the sheriff, and would again.

Marian closed her eyes. Put both hands over her face, shutting out the sunset, hiding in self-imposed darkness, and said her prayers. "Don't let them die. Don't let any of them die. Don't ever let them be caught." And then, very softly, *"Please."*

Forty-One

He found the weight oppressive. Attempts to dislodge it failed. He lay trapped, unable to move, breathing painfully.

"My lord?"

That voice. Ralph? He opened his eyes. Indeed. Ralph.

"My lord." Ralph bent down over the edge of the bed. "My lord, if you please—shall I go and fetch your son?"

His son. He had three, did he not?

"May I go and fetch Robert, my lord?"

Ah. That son. The youngest. The weakest.

"My lord. Can you hear me?"

There was nothing wrong with his ears.

"My lord, I think he should like to see you."

He closed his eyes again.

"Please, my lord. May I go?"

He had no strength for speaking.

"My lord . . . you may dismiss me, if you like, but I am going to fetch Robin home."

Robin? Oh. Robert. The youngest. The weakest. The one his wife had ruined.

"Forgive me, my lord."

The door shut behind Ralph.

DeLacey was smiling broadly when Philip de la Barre came into the hall, passing a small, stooped man on his way out. The castellan glanced at the elderly man casually, frowned briefly, then approached the dais as deLacey motioned him forward.

"Who was that, my lord? Do I know him?"

The sheriff raised his brows. "Has it become my business to be aware of whom you know?"

De la Barre had the grace to blush. "No, my lord. My apologies."

"I daresay if you have borrowed money from the Jews, you may well know him. He is a money-lender. Just now, a very unhappy money-lender; his mission has failed." He straightened in the chair, noting how the other's color deepened yet again; perhaps he *had* borrowed money from the Jews. So many Christians did. "Now, Philip, what business have we?"

"I have received word that the steward has left Huntington Castle, my lord."

DeLacey laughed. "Splendid news!" He glanced at the hour candle burning upon the table where he conducted the business of the shire, then looked again at de la Barre. "It will take time for him to ride all the way to Ravenskeep, and for Marian to lead him to Locksley. Give it until midday, Philip. Your men are ready?"

"They are, my lord."

"Good. Reacquaint them with our goal. In a matter of hours we shall be taking up residence in Huntington Castle for as long as necessary, though I suspect the response will come today. Collect Gisbourne—I daresay he will enjoy this—and I will join you later."

"Yes, my lord. Shall I ask the king's mercenary to accompany us?"

He snickered. "Alas, the captain is in my bad graces, as well as suffering from the headache. We shall leave him behind, I think." DeLacey scooted down in the chair again, stretching booted legs out as he indicated with a gesture his castellan was to leave. As de la Barre bowed and departed, the sheriff permitted himself an intense pleased glow of anticipation. "I do believe this is the most *delicious* day I have enjoyed in some time."

Marian was cutting roses for her table—taking far more care than when she had sliced open her hand, so as not to repeat the experience— when the man rode in at a gallop. Dust drifted; she waved it away in irritation as it settled on hair and clothing, then went immediately to learn the man's business. He was down from his horse by the time she reached him, clearly intent upon entering the hall even as Sim, come up from the pigs, remonstrated with him.

She gestured thanks and the servant fell silent. "What is it?" she asked the stranger.

He turned sharply, hair disheveled, clothing disordered, his spirits clearly as agitated as the horse whose reins he clutched. The animal dripped foam from a bit he chewed steadily. She smelled the salty pungency of the lather streaking the animal's chest and flanks. "Lady Marian?— *yes*, thank God in Heaven! I am here for Robin. He must come home at once."

"Home?" she echoed, startled.

"To Huntington." He seemed well cognizant of what he said, by the expression of his face. "Lady, I beg you . . . is he here?"

And so it is come. Marian slipped the pruning scissors into the pocket of her loose overdress and folded her hands together, straightening her shoulders. Indeed, it had come. "Who sent you?"

"No one—that is, I came myself." Color stood high in his face. "The earl would not say I should, but I felt it necessary." His eyes implored her. "He is dying."

She felt extraordinarily calm, strangely serene. It was her game to win or lose, and a man's life in her hands. Without compunction, without hesitation, she accepted the weight of that responsibility. "The earl is dying?"

"Indeed, yes." He gestured helplessly. "He may even be dead as we speak."

"And so you wish Robin to go back."

"Yes, lady—"

"He is disinherited."

"Yes, of course, but—"

"The earl, you say, did not send you."

"No, lady, but—"

"This is a trap," she said crisply.

He stared at her, mouth agape in unfeigned shock. She realized abruptly she knew who he was: the earl's own steward. "A trap? Lady— *no*, it is no trap! Why should it be a trap?"

"To catch an outlaw."

But Ralph flung out a dismissive hand as if the last thing in the world that mattered was what the sheriff called Robin. And perhaps it was; no guilt graced his face and eyes. "Lady—" He was desperate. "Shall I stay here, then? As surety? Will you give him the message and let *him* decide?"

Marian looked hard at Ralph, assessing the language of his body, the expression of face and eyes. If there was truth in what he said, she had no right to keep the news from Robin. But neither did she have the right to lead him into a trap if Ralph played her false.

She turned to Sim, waiting in case she needed the stranger taken away. "Bring me a horse, if you please."

Sim disapproved. Clearly. But he nodded and went off to the barn.

"We shall take a ride," she told Ralph, "and if we are fortunate, perhaps we shall be found where the birds are most active. But I promise nothing."

It utterly baffled the steward. "Please, Lady Marian . . . he *must* come home. There must be a final chance for each of them to forgive the other. For reconciliation."

There was equal truth in that. But, *Am I doing the right thing?* "Wait here," she told him curtly, "there is something I must do."

While Ralph waited with his mettlesome horse, as Sim grudgingly brought up a mount for her, Marian went into the hall to retrieve her bundle and her bow, and to say farewell to Joan and the others. Temporarily.

She hoped. She prayed.

Robin allowed Charlemagne to crash through vegetation, then put him over a downed tree. The horse answered gamely, landed easily. Robin whistled. He heard bird calls echoing in answer and smiled grimly; they had learned the lessons. But the smile faded quickly. As he burst into the clearing on the snorting horse, he swung down out of the saddle, gave the reins over to a startled Much, and reached to scoop up a flask of ale. Drinking would delay the explanation and allow him to regain some self-control.

Little John had been supervising an ungainly mock sword battle between Will Scarlet and Alan. But weapons clutched in rigid and untrained hands were tossed aside as they gathered to face Robin, alarmed by his demeanor.

"What is it?" Tuck asked.

Four swallows of ale had not made him feel more in control. He wiped his mouth with the back of his hand, then pushed the words out past the swelling anger in his throat. "He sold it."

"Sold it?" Tuck echoed.

"The manor. The lands. For the tax-debt. So he told Abraham." Robin abruptly hurled the flask into the trees. "He sold it *to my father!*"

His sword was half drawn; Little John caught him before he could do more violence. "Robin—Robin, wait. Hold."

"Let me go—" He struggled briefly, but John was unforgiving. And it was this man who had at first meeting beaten him at quarterstaffs and knocked him into the river.

"Hold," the giant repeated, containing him easily. "You'll harm yourself—or one of us, aye?"

He released the sword hilt. "Do you understand?" He did not believe they could, nor would. It was too painful, too excruciatingly infuriating. *"He sold Ravenskeep to my father."*

Scarlet shook his head. "Bastard."

"Whoreson," Alan muttered, exchanging shocked glances with Tuck.

Much stood there clinging to Charlemagne's reins. "Gone?" he asked. "Our home?"

"John, let me go—" This time Robin jerked free, because Little John allowed it. He turned to the boy, still half blind with rage, viciously tugging his tunic back into order. "Gone," he affirmed bitterly. "Oh, the manor is still there . . . but it belongs to the Earl of Huntington."

And then he sat down all of a sudden, collapsing onto a stump. He bent over crossed arms, hugging himself, breathing through clenched teeth—and rocking slightly at the waist because he could not sit still, not at all, not for one moment. He had never, not once in all of his life, been so angry. When Abraham had told him, the shock had stunned him into frozen silence. But the ride back gave him time, time to think about the ramifications, the magnitude of the betrayal.

And to think about Marian, whose home was lost.

"How?" Alan asked.

Tuck crossed himself, murmured a prayer. "The tax-debt," he said. "If the taxes are not paid, the sheriff may sell the property to whomever will pay the debt."

"She had *fourteen days,*" Alan declared.

Tuck shrugged. "Do you believe anything deLacey says?"

Scarlet frowned. "Wouldn't the king want it? The manor?"

"He gets the money," Tuck explained. "That is what matters to John."

Little John shook his head, frowning. "But Marian already paid her taxes."

The monk nodded. "I'll wager—though not really, because 'tis a sin—that our sheriff kept the earl's money for himself."

"You won't wager because 'tis a sin," Scarlet said in disbelief, "but you'll rob people?"

"Never mind." Robin stopped rocking. "*Insh'Allah*, I could kill him. Send him directly to hell."

Alan arched brows. "Your father?"

Robin cast him a scorching glance. "Oh, *he* will go to hell, that I promise. But I meant the sheriff. The bloody whoreson bastard—"And the anger welled up again, swamped him, spilled over, demanding release. He proceeded to fill the air with invective couched in a polyglot of three tongues. Tuck, who understood two of them, blushed in mortification, while the others marveled at his facility with languages.

"What talk is that?" Little John asked with interest.

Alan grinned. "French."

"No, that other one. Not the French one."

"Likely Infidel," Scarlet ventured, then blinked. "Spits a lot with it, aye?"

A new target. Robin broke off his maledictions. "Do you find this amusing?"

"No," Alan answered before volatile Scarlet could reply in kind, and possibly start a fight. "I think we are all of us willing to kill the sheriff. We're waiting for you to tell us when and how."

"Christ," Robin said, stripping hair back from his face with two doubled fists. "Oh, good Christ—how do I tell Marian?"

Much, staring past them, abruptly thrust the reins of Robin's horse into Tuck's hands. He disappeared into the trees before anyone could ask him what he was doing.

"Was that a duck call?" Scarlet inquired.

A moment later they heard Much shout a name. And it was none of theirs.

"Well," Little John said to Robin with genuine regret, "you'll be telling her now, aye?"

Robin shut his eyes a moment, then stood and stared blankly into the trees where Much had gone. The road lay beyond, shielded from view by vegetation. He felt ill, and old, and entirely, utterly helpless. Not since the Saracens captured him had he felt such dread and despair. "I think this shall be the hardest thing I have ever done."

And then Much was back, followed by Marian crashing through on horseback. He was startled to see she was dressed for working in the hall, not for traveling; and her kirtle showed the effects of her ride through trees and underbrush. Sherwood was a vigorous forest, unkind and occasionally hostile to those not prepared for its encroachments. Marian's hair had been pulled loose of its braids to straggle over her shoulders. He marked again the contrast between white skin and black hair, the richness of blue eyes. And wanted more than ever for the nightmare to end.

Tightness filled his throat. *How do I tell her?*

Behind him, Charlemagne nickered a greeting. Marian's horse answered. And then Robin saw the second rider coming through after Marian. His mind registered astonishment—why would Marian bring anyone to their camp?—before recognizing the man. And then he knew him.

Ralph flung himself out of his saddle. "My lord!" He let go of the reins and forced his way through a tangle of blackberry bush, unmindful of obstruction. "Robin!"

Ralph only rarely lapsed into familiarity.

And then the steward was there before him, eyes frantic, breathing hard and helplessly, opening and closing his mouth as if there were too many words to choose from.

Robin saw the pallor of shock, the trembling of great emotion, the taut impatience of anxiety. The steward drew breath to speak. "Come home," Ralph said; it was command, not suggestion, as if in that moment he had banished a lifetime of servitude and the courtesies of his calling. "Your father is dying."

He felt rather than heard the stirring of shock among the others.

Illogically he thought, *Did I not just promise my father would go to hell?*

Ralph reached out and gripped his arm. "I beg you. Come home. Let him die with his son at his side."

There was nothing in him but emptiness. An absence of emotion. He felt cold and old and bespelled into silence.

Then Marian broke it. "Could it be a trap?"

But he had seen Ralph's face and eyes. Heard the ravages of grief in the shaking voice. Ralph had served his father for more than twenty years. Had helped raise the third son, the fey, fanciful, rebellious son, seeing to it he was fed even when the earl said he should have no meal; salving the wounds and bruises of the earl's punishments. Ralph was his father by default, and both of them knew it.

No, it was not a trap.

And then he was gathering Charlemagne's reins and a handful of mane, one foot in the stirrup, his mind ranging far ahead, gone from the clearing in the forest to a room in a castle where an old man resided, a bitter bastard of a man whose only inclination was to control those around him. To kill a wife's soul with indifference, to wrack a young son with self-doubts, to put a king off his throne because the earl preferred another.

Robin pulled himself up, swung a leg over, settled into the saddle, hooked the other stirrup with his right foot. He looked at Marian. There was a great and terrible grief building inside his soul to couple with the anger, but it had nothing to do with his father.

Tuck of them all was the one who understood. "Go," he said. "I will tell her."

For that, too, he cursed his father. Robin let the anger carry him. He dug heels into Charlemagne's flanks and departed in a flurry of leaves and soil.

Marian was absently aware of Ralph leaping to his horse, of swinging up and reining the horse's head around sharply. She neither rode after Robin nor dismounted. She knew him; he desired no one to be with him. Ralph would see that.

"Tell me what?" she asked Tuck.

Behind her Ralph went crashing after Robin.

"Tell me what?" she repeated.

"If his father's not dead already," Scarlet drawled, "Robin'll likely kill him."

They all knew something. Something she did not. Something that had moved Robin to speak of business with his father when his father was dying. Something that had moved Will Scarlet to speak in jest of a man's murder when that man was already dying.

And abruptly she knew: Robin's grief had been for *her*.

"The money-lender went to see the sheriff about your tax-debt," Tuck explained quietly. "We had enough, you see. But the sheriff told him the debt was already paid." His eyes were compassionate. "By the earl."

"The earl! Paid *my* tax-debt?" It was inconceivable. "But why? He has no love for me; quite the opposite! And he disinherited Robin. Why would he do such a thing?"

Scarlet said bluntly, "To take your home from you."

Forty-Two

Tuck was shocked by Will's comment, telling him sharply to hold his tongue. Little John cuffed him over one ear, cursing him casually. But Marian merely sat upon the horse, slack in the saddle. She was aware that her mind registered a cluster of granite boulders, a small campsite with belongings set out, a fire laid but not lit, longbows, swords, and full quivers leaning against trees. And faces. Their faces. Expectant, worried faces, waiting to hear what she would say.

She listened again to the words in her mind. *'To take your home from you.'*

Alan was at her stirrup. "Come down."

Marian stared at him.

He reached out a hand. "Come down, Marian. Come sit by the fire—Much is lighting it now—and have some ale, a bit of bread, some salted meat."

Why should she be thirsty? Why should she be hungry?

She made as if to turn the horse away, toward the road—perhaps she should go after Robin—but Alan's hand was on the reins. "No," he said. "Let Robin say what must be said to the earl. You did not see him when he returned from Nottingham—there is nothing you might say to the earl that could possibly be more devastating than whatever Robin will tell him."

Scarlet grunted. "Oh, I daresay 'twill be hot in that room!"

And then Little John was there, clasping her waist in his big freckled hands. There was no choice anymore; he lifted her down, steadied her on her feet, then guided her to the fire as if she were an errant child. Tuck hastily tossed a folded blanket over a boulder as John urged her to sit.

"We'll get it back, aye?" Little John said. "We'll pay the taxes again. You won't lose Ravenskeep, lady. We'll see to it."

The words meant nothing. She heard them, but they made no sense.

She realized she was shaking uncontrollably. She wanted to scream, weep, shout, shriek, howl. But all her body would do was sit there like a lump of suet. Trembling.

"My home," she said numbly; her mouth was sluggish at forming words. "My father—my father was given Ravenskeep by Old King Henry more than thirty years ago. I was born there. My brother died there. My *mother* died there. And my father's sword—all that came home from Crusade—is with them both, down in the crypt." She looked up into the red-bearded, sorrowful face. "How can he take my home?"

Little John shook his head.

"Robin will get it back," Tuck said with certainty.

She wanted to be angry, but all she could feel spreading within her was a cold, quivering hollowness. Her bones had all gone brittle, fragile as glass.

And then something within her broke. The glass shattered to pieces. Marian began to weep.

It was Alan who came to her and knelt, who placed graceful hands on either side of her head and gently cradled her skull. He said nothing, merely offered comfort. She reached up, caught his wrists, clung, then bent forward. He took her weight against him, guided her brow against his shoulder, and let her cry herself out even as Tuck prayed for her.

When she was done she pulled away from Alan with a watery smile and a grateful pat on his shoulder. She was aware of their eyes watching her as she straightened upon the boulder, wondering what next she would do. Scream? Shriek?

But Marian felt strangely calm now. Strong. The shock, the storm, had passed. There were things to do.

She shook her head. "I should have killed deLacey instead of his poor horse."

"Ah," Scarlet said with comfortable affection, "there's our lass!"

Much brought her ale in a mug. Marian thanked him, drank half of it down—she was thirsty after all—and wiped the residue from her upper lip. She was clear-headed now, certain of her course.

"I brought some things," she said. "The pack is on the horse. Would someone get it down?" As Little John turned to do so, she looked at the others. "We shall wait for Robin. When he is back, we will decide what to do."

"What do you *want* to do?" Alan asked with some trepidation.

"I want to punish William deLacey," she said grimly. "I want him to be dismissed, as we discussed. And *I* want to be a part of it." She stopped short. "Did you steal the tax shipment yesterday?"

They looked blank. Tuck shook his head.

"We had guests," Alan said. "A parcel of lords." He smiled, taking a seat upon a thick log. "And none too pleased to be here."

" 'Tis how we had enough to pay your taxes," Scarlet explained, then had the grace to look abashed for bringing it up again.

Little John brought back her bundle as Much began to unsaddle her horse. "Robin took the money in to Abraham the Jew," the giant said as he set her bundle down beside the boulder. " 'Twas to go for your taxes, for Arthur of Brittany, and the poor."

Marian leaned down and began to untie her bundle, peeling back layers so she could rummage through it. "Mercardier came and said he'd been robbed . . . that you had stolen the taxes."

"No," Tuck said firmly. "We did no such thing."

She frowned. *"Someone* stole the taxes. They bashed him over the head. The soldiers went off after the outlaws and left Mercardier lying in the road."

Scarlet smirked. "Likely he deserved it."

"Could it have been Adam Bell?"

Little John was frowning as he sat down beside the fire, fetching an ale flask from the motley collection near the rocks. "Does it matter?"

"It might," Marian answered. "Mercardier believes you did it. I'm sure he's told the sheriff so by now."

Alan released a long, low whistle. "He'll be harrying the countryside for us."

"Nor will he stop till he finds us," she said. "We must be ready for him." She began dragging clothing out of the pack.

"What are you doing?" Little John asked.

She paused, one hand full of hosen. "Changing clothes," she replied. "I cannot very well live in Sherwood dressed like this."

"Live in Sherwood?" Scarlet echoed.

Marian draped hosen, tunic, and belt over one arm as she rose. "Where else am I to go?"

They exchanged startled glances. But no one offered an answer.

She grabbed up the blanket as well, intending to hang a privacy screen upon an appropriate—and appropriately distant—tree. "When I come back," she said, "I want someone to teach me how to hold a sword."

Tuck was astonished. "Why?"

Alan's expression was oddly blank, as if he feared to offend her. "Do you believe you could handle a sword?"

Marian remembered the weight of Mercardier's in her hands. "No," she replied truthfully. "But I need to know how a man handles a sword, so I may learn how to disarm him."

"See?" Will Scarlet gleefully nudged Little John's rump with a booted toe. "Didn't I say she was our lass?"

DeLacey and his men had spent the afternoon gathered in the room across the corridor from the earl's bedchamber. Plans were in place. What was required to set them in motion was the mouse to step into the trap. So when Gisbourne finally came up to say Locksley and the steward had just ridden into the castle courtyard, deLacey heaved a sigh of relief coupled with a spurt of anticipation. He shot a glance at Philip de la Barre, who nodded back; the castellan moved smoothly to the wall beside the closed door, gripping an iron fireplace poker. Other men had swords unsheathed and at the ready, waiting quietly with the look of avid predators on their faces. DeLacey himself did not draw his sword, nor take up anything that might be used as a weapon. He merely waited beside the door, which he had left slightly ajar. From here he could see the earl's closed door directly across the hall; if he extended his head beyond the jamb he could also see the end of the corridor where the staircase began. But he did not extend his head. It was a simple matter to hear the footsteps and voices as two men hurried up the stairs; he did not need to see them.

DeLacey closed one hand around the iron door handle. The left he raised to hold Philip de la Barre in place until such time as he gave the signal and jerked the door open, allowing the castellan to move.

"What am *I* to do?" Gisbourne asked.

DeLacey shot him a murderous glare. Locksley and the steward were at the top of the stairs. "Take the steward," he whispered, keeping an eye on the earl's door. "Don't let him interfere." He gestured Gisbourne to back up, fingers tightening on the handle.

Footsteps. The steward was saying something. Locksley made no answer. DeLacey tensed.

Locksley was at the earl's door: unlatching, pushing it open, and stepping across the threshold all in one motion.

Now—

DeLacey jerked the door open wide and sharply gestured de la Barre through.

* * *

Robin lengthened his stride as he approached his father's bedchamber, moving ahead of Ralph. He was aware of a strange complement of emotions: nervousness, childish apprehension, a trace of fear—would he find his father dead?—a touch of the old resentment; even a desire not to be here at all, to depart immediately so as not to involve himself—if he did not see his father dead, the earl would never truly *be* dead—and the certainty that the world was about to change again.

But he wanted to know. *Needed* to know. Badly.

Drawing a breath, he unlatched the door, pushed it open, and stepped across the threshold.

The first impression was of the sour scent of illness and agedness, of spiced wine left sitting too long, of the mustiness of a room with its window shuttered. He saw his father slumped back against pillows and bolsters, eyes closed, mouth parted; heard the thin rasp of shallow inhalations. *Not dead yet.*

There was movement behind him; likely Ralph entering. He took another stride into the room—

—and something hard and heavy slammed across the backs of his knees, dropping him sharply to the floor before he could even cry out. He heard the dull clanging thump of iron landing on carpeted floor; and then hands were on him. His sword was drawn and tossed aside. An arm closed around his throat as he knelt there, raising and twisting his jaw so the throat was bared, arching his spine backward. He felt the cold kiss of edged steel: knife. A quick slice or puncture would open his jugular.

So quickly. So polished. So well planned.

Marian had asked if it might be a trap. And he had dismissed it in the face of Ralph's genuine fear and anxiousness. Ralph had not lied; indeed, his father *was* dying. It was obvious when one looked upon him. And neither had Ralph arranged this trap. More likely he had merely been used to set and bait it by someone who understood very few could dissemble well enough to fool a man prepared for such.

Clever, clever trap. Truth used. Opportunity found. Men manipulated who were too distracted by an old man's dying to consider the consequences of a clever sheriff driven to finding a way to capture a man he could not otherwise catch by ordinary means. Who understood that the best trap of all let the prey put itself in it.

Inwardly, Robin shook his head. Beautifully played. Almost he could admire it, save he was the prey. And well and truly caught.

His arms hung heavily from his shoulders, slightly outstretched away from his body. He was not a coward, but neither was he a fool. At the moment there was no opportunity save the chance to live. He did not move. Did not so much as twitch.

"My lord!" his captor said sharply.

And then there was commotion in the hall; Ralph was saying something in a raised voice, asking what business they had. The room was abruptly filled with men, armed men, mailed men, helmed soldiers all. Blades were unsheathed. Ralph's voice rose yet again, outraged, desperate.

The man who held Robin captive stretched his spine another inch, cranked his jaw up another notch. Robin gritted his teeth, the tension of his throat so taut he could barely swallow. He was fully aware of the vulnerability of the position. His arms were free; he might reach for his captor. But not before the knife would enter his throat. Not before any number of soldiers might introduce the points of their broadswords into his belly and chest.

William deLacey entered his line of vision. Iron dripped from gloved hands: shackles and chains.

"Thank you, Philip," he said lightly, then looked at Robin. "I should welcome you home, save this is not home anymore, is it? The earl told me he has no son, that his title, castle, estates, and wealth shall revert to the Crown. One would not believe the Earl of Huntington should give anything over to John, but there you are. Better to the king than to an outlaw, yes?" He turned slightly toward the corridor and held out the chains, dangling them idly. Shackles clashed. He raised his voice. "Would you care to do the honors, Gisbourne?"

From out in the corridor Ralph was demanding to be allowed into the room, to see to the earl. And swearing to Robin desperately, whom he could not see, that he hadn't known it *was* a trap. By God in Heaven. And so he continued to swear until his voice was abruptly cut off.

Then Gisbourne was before Robin, seizing the shackles and chains from the sheriff's hands. His dark eyes were avid with malice. "Hold him," Gisbourne said sharply, then with great precision and ceremony set the heavy iron shackles around each wrist and locked them into place. The key was returned to deLacey.

Robin, feeling the weight, the pressure, the finality, was grateful he wore leather bracers. They would protect his flesh.

"And lo, how the knight is fallen," deLacey remarked dryly. "Crusader, is it? Coeur de Lion's well-loved man? But also, as I recall, captive of the Saracen for a year or more. A man who did not die properly in battle serving his king, but a man who *yielded* to the enemy. A man whose weapons were taken from him. A man who was imprisoned by the Infidel, and yet survived." He paused. "Tell me, what did you have to do for them in order to buy your life?"

He had learned among the Saracens how to hold his silence. How to offer nothing to those who would demand it. How to lose himself inside his head. Even when his captor took the knife away and released his throat, albeit only to sink a fist deep into hair and lock his head into place, Robin said nothing.

The Saracens had been dangerously devious in their punishments. Normans such as deLacey were simply brutal.

Brutality he could survive.

DeLacey smiled. "You father should see this, I think." He turned toward the bed, toward the man buried in covers. "My lord? My lord earl?"

Had he any breath left to lose, the outrage would have taken it away. Robin stared in disbelief as the sheriff approached the bed. Soldiers moved away, expressions indifferent. There was no noise at all from the corridor.

Ralph, he thought, was unconscious. Or possibly dead.

Clever, clever trap. But he had time. His disposition was not in deLacey's hands. It was for the king to say. John would have to be told; it would require days for a messenger to find him, possibly days for John to receive him. And time for John to make his decision; Robin could hope the king remembered Locksley as the Earl of Huntington's son. Days for the messenger to return with the king's answer. Time for him to think, time for Marian and the others to contrive a plan.

But "accidents" did occur, especially to prisoners.

"My lord earl, I beg you to waken. There is something you should see."

Robin had learned to go away inside himself when he was prey, and prisoner. But this was his father deLacey dallied with. An old, ill, dying man. *"Leave him,"* he ordered, as if on the battlefield.

It resulted in a fist tightened in his hair, a head held stiffly motionless, and amusement from deLacey. "But I understood from Ralph you and your father were often at odds. Stubborn men, he called you. Why should you care what this man sees? It was he who bought Ravenskeep away from Marian. He who cast you out. He who is responsible for your straights."

Robin held his silence.

DeLacey turned back to the bed. "My lord earl. There is something you should see." He leaned over the bed, put a hand on a shoulder buried in mounds of bedrobe. "Do look, my lord."

Breath hissed between Robin's clenched teeth and stiff lips. "*Leave him!*"

"No," deLacey answered sharply, and grasped the earl by both shoulders. "Wake up, my lord, and witness the downfall of your son."

Still on his knees, Robin surged upward, chains ringing, locked shackles clanking. But the man who held him slammed him down again, once more locking a forearm around his throat. Robin raised his chained arms, thrusting them up into the air as if he might grasp for his captor, but Gisbourne was there, Gisbourne who held an iron poker. Gisbourne who planted it deep in Robin's abdomen.

Breath whooshed out on a throttled and involuntary outcry. He could not breathe, could not *breathe*, just hung there with an arm around his throat, body spasming against the outrage of the absence of air.

"Nicely done," deLacey observed. "Good my lord, do look!"

Robin, fighting merely to recapture breath, saw nothing. But he heard the rasp of a voice ruined by coughing, a querulous and broken demand for Ralph's attendance.

"Do look at your son, my lord," deLacey urged. "It may be the last chance you have to see him. I am quite certain the king shall wish him executed."

Gone inward, wholly consumed with thawing frozen lungs, Robin saw nothing. But he heard the voice, heard the effort made to question, to understand. And then the thin-voiced, breathless question. "What are you doing to my son?"

"Ah, but you told me yourself you had no son. This is merely an outlaw, my lord. A man who steals from others. A man destined to hang."

Breath was coming back in unpredictable increments. When at last Robin forced his abdomen to expand so that air could get through, he began to see again. And saw his father, fighting to sit upright, to peel back the covers, to exit the bed, his mouth drawn back in a rictus of effort.

"Leave him," the earl said, in a weak echo of Robin's own order.

"I think not," deLacey replied. "He is dungeon-bound, this man, to await the king's pleasure. Be certain I shall acquaint the king with the fact of your disinheritance as well as the exploits of this man: how he stole a prisoner from me, stole horses, delayed a royal messenger, robbed innocent people. In fact, he stole the tax shipment only yesterday; it was our good fortune that we got it back again."

Tax shipment? Robin's glance went sharply to deLacey.

"My lord earl, you are well rid of this man. You need no part of your memory, your proud name, tainted by this man. We shall remove him from your sight."

At a signal Robin's captor heaved him to his feet. Soldiers closed in around him. Hands were on him. He was pushed and prodded from the chamber, knees and abdomen protesting the abuse they had suffered.

He would have protested none of it, having learned never to give satisfaction that way. But his father . . . Robin wrenched away, half turned, caught a glimpse of the gray face, the gasping mouth, and then was heaved bodily from the room. He nearly tripped over a man lying on the floor: Ralph. He saw no blood. But that meant nothing.

In the chamber, the earl was attempting to give orders. William deLacey laughed, then appeared in the doorway. At his nod, Robin was dragged away.

Behind him, the earl's trembling voice called weakly for Ralph.

Huntington swam up from the depths, clutched at covers, pushed them aside. The room had emptied. He was alone.

"Ralph?"

Distantly he heard the sound of mailed men tramping away, descending stairs.

"Ralph?"

DeLacey was here. DeLacey had his son. DeLacey had Robert. Meant to *execute* Robert.

He would permit no such thing.

"Ralph!"

The earl pulled his legs out from under the covers. His body was slowed, but his mind continued to work. He could not permit deLacey to shame his name, to shame his house. There was a way . . . he had nothing drafted yet.

"He is my heir," he rasped. "All of my land . . . all of my wealth . . . *he shall be Huntington"*— Where was Ralph? It wanted Ralph. Ralph would write the documents.

Robert would be heir, Robert would be earl, Robert would be too powerful for small men such as deLacey to plot against. Sheriffs did not dare to conspire against earls.

"Ralph . . ." He won free of the bed at last. The robe straggled from his frail shoulders, slipped down to his elbows. *I shall have the document written . . . he shall be my heir . . . I will have the world back the way it was . . .*

But the world did not wait on such men as were dying. The world moved on, ruthless and cruel, bearing no empathy even for men who were fathers, men who were earls, recanting of their whims.

"—let him marry the girl—"

But the world would not wait, would not even pause.

Ralph—

But Ralph did not answer. Only Death.

Marian was very nearly done braiding her hair into one tight plait when Alan announced they should move camp. That prompted rude comments from Will Scarlet, and questions from Tuck and Little John.

"Besides," Little John said, "Robin will look for us here."

"Robin likely won't be back tonight," Alan pointed out. "If his father's that ill, he'll stay."

"Unless the earl throws him out again," Scarlet muttered.

"And he'd find us anyway," the minstrel went on. "This is one of the reasons we've got our bird calls worked out, so we can find one another."

"*I* heard none," Marian put in acerbically. "I rode very quietly, and very carefully, and no one made any bird calls at all. It wasn't until I imitated a duck that anyone bothered to find me, and that took Much." She sent an approving glance at the boy. "But perhaps Alan is right. Didn't you say you brought prisoners here yesterday?"

"Guests," Little John clarified. "And we did that, aye. We gave them food and drink, made them pay a toll, and sent them on their way."

"Then they would know how to find you again," she observed, amused by the description.

Scarlet grunted. "Not likely to. They want that lad in Brittany to be king, and Robin says we're helping."

"That's where some of the money is going," Tuck explained.

"The one was most unhappy," Alan said. "But 'tisn't a bad plan, anyway, to move frequently. 'Twill make it harder for the sheriff to find us."

Marian tied off her braid, then bent down and began to gather up belongings. "I think we should go. It will be dark in two hours. Best to move now, while we can see."

"And go where?" Scarlet asked.

Alan was picking up blankets. "Deeper into the forest. Well away from the road, so we can lay a larger fire. I've a taste for the king's venison tonight."

"That's poaching!" Tuck cried. "They can cut off our hands for that!"

Little John cast him an amused glance. "Before or after they hang us?"

Much grabbed up his bow and quiver. "I'll go."

"You?" Scarlet demanded.

"His hands are better than yours, Will," Alan pointed out. "And his eyes are younger, too." He shot a glance at Much. "All right, lad, but see to it you bring us home a deer big enough to feed all of us."

"Bring back two," Little John suggested. "I'll eat one all by myself."

Grinning, Much darted off into the forest.

"Think he can?" Scarlet asked.

"I do." Marian had seen the boy shoot. "And now, Will, if you please—get your rump off that blanket and give us a hand."

"Oh-*ho!*" Scarlet grinned. "I see we're still the high lady despite the lad's clothing!"

"Marian," Tuck offered archly, "would be a lady anywhere."

She laughed, appreciating the defense. But amusement died away. Alan was right; Robin likely would under the circumstances stay the night in Huntington. But until he was back, she would worry regardless. "Tomorrow," she murmured, tying up her bundle, "midmorning. If he's not back by then, I'll go to Huntington myself."

Amazement, deLacey decided, best summed up the reaction of the populace. They could not believe what they witnessed: the son of an earl, though dressed like a yeoman, wrists shackled with iron, being made to walk steadily through the streets of Nottingham, striking a fair pace lest he be jerked off his feet and dragged behind the horse. The sheriff had briefly considered taking him in through the city a shorter way, but decided it was best to let the people see him. They knew Robert of Locksley, now Robin Hood, had engineered the rescue of the cutpurse on Market Day;

let them comprehend what such actions reaped. *Even the son of an earl* was subject to the sheriff's justice, and the king's pleasure.

At the moment, however, it was all deLacey's pleasure.

He rode calmly at the head of the phalanx of mounted guards. Robin was at the rear, save for the two men riding behind him: Philip de le Barre and Guy of Gisbourne. Their task was to see to it no one approached the prisoner. DeLacey supposed an archer might take them all easily enough, but he was certain none in Nottingham at this moment would attempt it. The trap had been too well constructed, too secretive. None of Locksley's men knew he was taken. And the sheriff had no intention of bringing him out into Market Square for punishment. He would remain in the castle until King John sent word how he wished the execution to proceed; and, unlike with the boy, this time it would be handled in private, behind the castle walls.

Unless, of course, the king desired Locksley be sent to London, where he might be beheaded at Tower Green. Though deLacey rather hoped he would hang, because death took longer at the end of a rope unless the neck was broken; and the sheriff would bribe the hangman to botch the drop.

Smiling, deLacey turned in the saddle, looking over a shoulder. There he was, Sir Robert of Locksley, Crusader knight, king's hero, tied to a horse by virtue of a rope connected to his chains. He walked steadily with no sign of a limp, but deLacey did not doubt it took effort; de la Barre had struck him a hard blow behind the knees. Yet nothing in his expression divulged his thoughts.

The loose fair hair shielded some of his face, but deLacey, riding in front, could see him clearly. Pale gold stubble defined jaw and cheekbones, pointing up the aristocratic cast of his features. Hazel eyes were quietly fixed on the horse before him, judging the pace, marking if the animal might trip or shy, either of which could prove disastrous for him. His mouth was set in a grim line, but there was no fear in his face. Only a calm mask that deLacey had witnessed five years before, when Locksley was just returned from captivity. He had been strange then, withdrawn and mostly mute, given, when he spoke, to unpredictability in temperament and conversation. The years since had aged him—what boyishness had been left after war and captivity was now gone—but it merely underscored a certain ruthless competency in his features.

A bad enemy, deLacey did not doubt. But now merely a prisoner, and incapable of troubling the sheriff ever again.

Through Market Square among shocked stares, whispers, murmurings, and the occasional shout. If Locksley were aware of them, he gave no notice. The castle gates stood open. DeLacey rode through, lifting a hand to the men who stood at attention, amidst the ringing clop of iron-shod hooves against cobblestones. Through the outer bailey and into the inner, to stop before the entrance . . . there he gave the order for the prisoner to be loosed from the horse. The rope was undone. The men, dismounting, fell into place around Locksley. DeLacey stepped off his own horse, gave the reins to the waiting boy, and led the procession into the hall.

Mercardier, seated at the table for an early supper, glanced up in mild interest, meat-knife in one hand. But that turned to startlement as he looked upon the procession, marking the men and their prisoner. He thrust himself to his feet even as his meat-knife clattered against the hardwood table. For the first time the mercenary was unmasked; his expression was a mingling of shock and, as that passed, speculation.

DeLacey unhelmed and passed it to a servant who came forward to aid him. He slipped the mail coif to his shoulders and peeled off his gloves, handing them over even as he walked, smiling faintly at Mercardier. He could not have asked for a better tableau.

"You see," he said calmly, "we have caught the man responsible for stealing the taxes. The man who proved himself more able in robbery than you in defense, despite the king's trust. Perhaps that is why you have never liked Locksley; might he be better than you in all things? Is that it, Captain?" He paused. "Did the Lionheart love him better?"

But Mercardier had donned the mask again. One hand rested lightly against the table. His dark, opaque eyes followed the guard contingent without expression as the prisoner was led the length of the hall.

"Perhaps you can visit," the sheriff commented. "Just now Robin Hood must inspect his private lodgings, but I believe it will be possible for him to receive you tomorrow."

Mercardier flicked a glance at deLacey. With a slight jerk of his lips—was that truly a smile?—he sat down again and returned to his meal.

Inwardly deLacey laughed. Oh, indeed. He could not have dreamed a better moment.

It was, Robin supposed, a humiliating spectacle, the procession through Nottingham. But he went deep inside himself, detaching himself from the world. His body was aware it moved—his knees ached, for instance, and his abdomen was sore—but felt little beyond the repetition of step after step after step. His mind marked the movements of the horse, watching for a misstep, but even that was done from a distance. His awareness was a kernel within the flesh, warding itself against the predations of pride, of shame, of mortification. He had survived the Saracens. Had withstood the beating meted out by Norman soldiers ostensibly his compatriots. This, too, he would endure.

Onward through the castle gates . . . through the baileys, where the rope was removed and his arms could drop down again, still heavy with iron but no longer stretched taut and subject to the motion of the horse. Still he built walls around his senses, distancing himself from the stares of the sheriff's men and servants. It was not until they entered the hall and he heard the scrape of a bench against the floor, the clatter of a knife, did he take note of anything beyond what was required to go where he was taken. And then he saw Mercardier, and detachment shredded.

Especially when deLacey asked, " 'Did the Lionheart love him better?' "

There was more. But he burned with anger. It took all he had to meet Mercardier's eyes without giving away his emotions. And those eyes were as usual shielded behind a barrier even Robin had never been able to penetrate with the irony and edged witticisms that pierced so many men. It had been learned in the years with his father, though kept internal. As a soldier on Crusade, among the king's favorites, he said what he wished, albeit not in obvious ways, and made enemies for it. It had amused Richard. Mercardier abhorred it.

There were many, Robin knew, who would relish this moment.

But the moment passed. DeLacey had him taken down into the dungeon. There the sheriff himself peeled back an iron grate, and motioned to the others.

A ladder was brought. But before it was put in place, before Locksley had so much as a glimpse of the pit below, a hand was planted in his spine and he was shoved forward over the lip.

He fell, twisting in midair, landing on hip and shoulder, braced hands pushing against the floor as he rolled to take some of the weight. There was straw beneath him, and soil beneath that. Above him, the grate was dropped down. He heard the sound of the bolt shot home, the heavy click of a lock. There was no light save what crept down through the cross-hatched iron. He pushed up to one knee, determined not to let deLacey see him lying on the floor, and stared upward. He could make out nothing but colors, shapes, and movement through the iron lattice.

He expected the sheriff to offer a comment. But nothing was said. The torches were carried away. Footsteps receded, ascended stairs. In the distance a door thumped closed. He was left in darkness and the squalor of the pit.

Robin released a hissing breath. Now he felt the aches, smelled the tang of nervous perspiration, knew the tremor of humiliation inside. But there was more to think about, even as he rolled his shoulders in an attempt to loosen overtensed muscles. There was his father, dead or dying. He had wanted nothing more than to confront the man about his acquisition of Ravenskeep, but in the moment of discovery, of seeing him so drawn and frail within the massive tester bed, anger had dispersed beneath the onslaught of shock. And then there had been no time for anything as he was attacked from behind.

Now there was time. Plenty of time. To see again in his mind's eye the man who had sired him and always regretted it, grown ancient but no less selfish and autocratic; and to know he was dying even as the sheriff acquainted him with his son's latest failings. To see again Ralph's desperation, to hear the steward's pleading for him to come home to Huntington. But Huntington Castle had never been his home. His home, Huntington Hall, had been razed years before.

He was not his father's heir. That had been made clear. But the task of having the earl's body, upon his death, interred within the Huntington crypt was likely his to do.

Except, ironically, it was now entirely possible that the son might die before the father.

Robin closed his eyes a moment, composing himself, then peered upward. Somewhere above a torch yet burned; the faintest trace of wan light made its way into the pit, though it illuminated no more than a dim patch upon the floor. Everything else was blackness.

He began to kick over the straw, digging through the loose scattering on top to the crusted layers below, down to time- and filth-packed earth. It was foul in the pit, rank with the stench of ordure and travail. There was likely a slops bucket somewhere, but from the pungent sting of urine issuing from one area he believed an inhabitant prior to himself had forgone that small token of civilization. He overturned the straw not to uncover things best left hidden for want of exercise or curiosity, but because he did not wish to sit in or, if he managed it, to sleep in waste and vermin nests.

When he had groomed one area as well as possible, kicking loose straw back over old, he sat down and leaned carefully against the wall. He assimilated the chill of raw stone until he could stand it without his flesh jumping, then drew up his knees and began to knead the undersides with his hands, shackles clanking, trying to bleed away the knots and tenderness.

He would endure captivity. He had before.

Much indeed brought back a deer, albeit small, and only one. Nonetheless it was more than enough for those who had not tasted its like before. Such meat was not permitted anyone lacking a writ of *vert and venison*—official permission from the king to kill and consume royal deer—and thus the peasantry, unless they turned to poaching, were denied the privilege reserved for select noblemen such as the Earl of Huntington.

Hung and drawn for a hasty bleeding, then skinned and pierced with a tree limb for crude spit-roasting over the fire, the deer proved most tasty. Marian, leaning against a log, did not even mind the grease dribbling down her chin. A corner of blanket proved up to the task of imitating table linen, and she occasionally dabbed at her face. But mostly she ate. With a belly full of venison and the last of the ale—they would have to steal more, Scarlet suggested; Tuck said they could buy it—she was sleepily replete under the rising moon.

"Alan," she said, contemplating the last of her bread as she heaved a happy sigh, "sing something."

He was perched upon a stump. "I haven't my lute."

"Sing without the lute."

Alan licked his fingers one by one, then wiped them against a quilted doublet that once had been rather fine. But its green velvet now was compressed and shiny with soiling, and there was one sizable tear along a seam coyly displaying the stuffing that formed its padded shape. They were all of them filthy now, save for Marian, who had bathed two days before. She was only mildly grimy.

"I could," he said finally, "if I did not despair of being shouted down by those who refuse to appreciate my talent."

"*I* appreciate it," Marian replied. "And if any of them complain, they can wash up the dishes." Joan had packed a handful of wooden bowls and two badly dented pewter platters along with several equally dented mugs. Keepsakes, Marian believed, of the sheriff's destructive visit.

"If he sings," Scarlet said, "*you* can wash up the dishes."

"He sings very well," she retorted.

"He does," Tuck agreed, soaking up the last of the blood and fat in his bowl with a crust of bread.

Firelight shone off the film of grease on Much's face. "Sing about Robin."

Alan was startled. "Robin?"

Scarlet grunted. "He's got no songs about Robin, lad."

"Oh, I think he does." Marian had a very clear memory of certain nonsensical verses she had heard years before. "And appropriate, methinks, in Robin's absence."

Little John was skeptical. "Have you one, then?"

Much scooted forward eagerly to sit at the minstrel's feet. Alan smiled faintly. There was no lute to aide him, but he did the best he could.

> *Lithe and listen, gentlemen,*
> *That be of free-born blood;*
> *I shall you tell of a good yeoman,*
> *His name was Robin Hood.*

* * *

DeLacey, ensconced within his cushioned chair upon the dais, permitted a servant to refill his goblet. In very good spirits—he had dined already, and this was his third cup of unwatered wine—he smiled upon Mercardier. The mercenary had said no word since being summoned to the hall. He merely waited stolidly, helm tucked under one arm, as he stood before the dais.

"You do understand that it shall save time and effort," the sheriff said. "You may explain to the king what became of his taxes—albeit briefly, by the grace of God!—*and* tell him that we now have in custody the man responsible for robbing you. I shall have my clerk write it all down, of course, but I am quite certain the king will request a verbal report as well."

Mercardier said, "I understand."

"Contained in the report of your misapprehension regarding your ability to guard the shipment will be detailed information of Robert of Locksley's behavior these past weeks. My lord king will recall, I am certain, that it was Locksley who stole the shipment five years ago. Clearly he has returned to his old habits; worse, he has extended them. But he resides in the dungeon now, awaiting the king's pleasure. When the king so desires, he may inform me as to his wishes with regard to the prisoner's disposal."

Something flared in dark eyes—pleasure, perhaps?—though the tone was without inflection. "And so you mean to kill him."

"*I* mean nothing, Captain! It may be my duty to have him executed, but it is not my decision." He waved a dismissive hand. "I shall have my clerk write the letter tomorrow. Expect to leave in the afternoon, yes?"

Mercardier inclined his head. "Yes."

No *'my lord.'* DeLacey might call him on the crude informality. But he was too pleased with the ordering of his world, just now, and the promise of his future. He let the slip go as the Lionheart's captain of mercenaries took his leave.

Besides, within a matter of days Mercardier's mouth would be filled to choking with honorifics and obsequious words, as he admitted before the king that he had failed.

After a while Robin stopped kneading his legs. With knees still drawn up he crossed his arms over his chest, tucking shackled wrists beneath armpits—the chain was long enough for that—let his skull rest against the wall, and closed his eyes.

Marian and the others would eventually realize he was captured, likely tomorrow. But he did not believe there was anything they could do about it. His future, if there was to be one, depended entirely upon the pleasure of King John.

Who once had wished Sir Robert of Locksley to marry his daughter. Bastard daughter, withal, but still of royal seed.

In the darkness, surrounded by the stench of dead men's waste, Robin smiled. It was a hard, twisted, self-deprecating smile, composed of very little humor. DeLacey himself had said it: *And lo, how the knight has fallen.*

Low indeed.

Forty-Four

Marian had never ridden so fast, so recklessly, that she endangered her life, but she did so as she returned from Huntington Castle—and didn't care. She had no time to care, merely to plan; to realize that another man had died and, in that dying, the world had once again been turned upside down.

She heard the bird calls in Sherwood, but made no answer. They knew her; they merely warned one another. And when she ducked under the last tree limb and threw herself out of the saddle, all of them had gathered.

"Trouble?" Tuck asked.

"The worst," she said breathlessly. "The sheriff has taken Robin."

" '*Twas* a trap!" Little John cried, as Scarlet cursed.

"Not initially." Marian let Much take her horse, but asked that the animal remain saddled. She went at once to her possessions and found shift and chemise. "The servant said deLacey and his men came after Ralph left. When Robin got there, they took him. He's in Nottingham Castle already."

"What about the earl?" Little John asked.

She shook out shift and chemise, gathered up long girdle. "Dead; he truly *was* dying. And Ralph was badly injured protesting the sheriff's intentions."

"What are you doing?" Alan asked.

"Changing back," she answered shortly. "I mean to go see deLacey." She glanced at Tuck. "Would you wrap my bow for me, make it look like a walking stick?"

Mystified, he nodded.

"We're going, too," Scarlet declared. "You'll not leave us behind."

Marian grabbed a blanket and flung it over the nearest tree; if it was not enough, they could turn their backs. "I know. I want you there. I need you to steal a wagon and put it near the castle gates, in Market Square."

"And do what?" Little John asked.

"Wait. Be ready." She slipped behind the screening blanket.

"Wait for what?" Alan asked, voice somewhat muffled.

Marian unfastened the belt that held tunic and hosen in place. "For us to come out."

"Who's 'us'?" That was Scarlet.

"Me. Robin." She jerked the hooded capelet and tunic off over her head, then folded them into a compact package and stuffed it into the back side of her hosen, belting both into place.

Little John was astonished. "And how d'ye mean to get him out of the castle?"

"I'll find a way."

"And if you don't?" Alan asked sharply.

"Then I shall be in the dungeon, too, and you'll have to rescue us both." She yanked shift and chemise over her head, flailing and digging for sleeves. "I am the only one of us who can confront William deLacey in person, so I shall."

"Confront him!" Scarlet echoed.

Little John was appalled. "And do what *then?*"

She tugged shift and chemise down over breasts and hips. "Find out what he wants."

"He's *got* what he wants!" Alan declared. "Robin!"

Marian double-wrapped the girdle low around her waist atop the tunic and capelet, then tugged at the skirts to make sure the hosen and boots were covered. "William deLacey is a man who will always want more. I intend to find out what it is."

Scarlet sounded dubious. "What if 'tis something you can do nothing about?"

"Then I'll find another way. But at least I shall be inside the castle." She snatched the blanket aside, striding back into the camp where she asked Alan for arrows. "Not many," she said. "Four."

"Arrows?"

"Arrows."

He handed four to her. She hiked up her skirts, ignoring various expressions of male startlement, and tucked the shafts inside her right boot. The broadheads rubbed her ankle, but she believed the hosen would provide some protection. With a thong borrowed from her bundle, Marian tied the arrows to her thigh beneath the fletchings. She could not bend her knee, but she did not need to. "Tuck?"

Silently, he handed her the coiled bowstring. He understood. Marian cast him a grateful glance and tucked the bowstring inside her other boot. Then she turned to her horse.

Scarlet did not understand. "You can't even walk, can you?"

She could stand well enough on the arrow-splinted leg. She slid her left boot toe into the stirrup, then smiled as she felt Little John's hands spanning her waist. He boosted her, and she swung the stiffened right leg with no little awkwardness across the horse's rump. She could not use that stirrup; she let the leg hang, canting herself slightly to the right.

Tuck was there to hand up the bow. He had wrapped it carefully in a bit of sacking, rope, and leather, altering its silhouette.

"Come into Nottingham one at a time," she said. "Steal that wagon. Be ready. And pray to God that I can get him out of the castle."

"That," Tuck said, "is what I am best at. Praying."

Marian nodded at them, absently noting frowns of concern, but she

But he knew it was Mercardier. He peered upward, squinting. "The torch," Mercardier said. Light flared, spilled down through the cross-hatched iron. Robin saw silhouettes. And then Mercardier squatted to get a closer look. "Ah, I see him now. Oh, indeed. Most fitting." His tone, usually so emotionless, took on a trace of contempt. "Do you know what you have cost me? Do you know you have given the sheriff opportunity to complain of my abilities?" The mercenary shifted slightly. "No one has *ever* had that chance."

That, Robin knew. Mercardier had been highly respected for his competence, though he was not known as a man of great wit. But his military prowess was legendary. He and King Richard had made a formidable pair.

"I will be dismissed," he went on, "and sent home in disgrace. *I*, Mercardier. Coeur de Lion's captain of mercenaries!"

Robin considered saying someone else would surely hire him. But he forebore; the mercenary was clearly angry. He had never seen him angry. Mercardier was a man of immense self-control.

But not just now. He rose. He stood atop the grate. There was movement. "You are a piss-poor excuse for a knight and Crusader," the captain said harshly in his ruined voice, "and so I piss on you."

The stream of urine rained down. Robin, realizing what it was a moment before it arrived, cursed and leaped awkwardly out of its path, chains ringing.

"Rot in hell," Mercardier said as Gisbourne laughed.

Robin turned his back. He stared hard at the wall, trembling with anger. With humiliation.

Eventually they left, and the light left with them.

DeLacey, frowning over parchment, glanced up in surprise as he recognized the voice echoing in the hall. He had not expected this, but it brought him great pleasure.

He pushed aside the pile of parchments—writs for this, complaints of that—set down the goosefeather quill, and made himself comfortable in the massive chair. "Marian! How do you fare?" And then he marked the walking stick she clung to, the pronounced hitch in her gait. "Not well, I take it. What happened?"

She waved away a servant who offered assistance. The chemise was a clear, brilliant blue that brought out the hue of her eyes, which were fixed on him with wintry determination. The stick was as tall as she was, slightly curved, knobby and wrapped with leather to guard her delicate

had no more time. She smacked her horse with the "walking stick" a͏ͅ
headed back toward the Nottingham road.

Robin had no idea when he might be fed, or even if he migh
Certainly nothing had been brought the night before, and nothing y͏ͅ
this morning. His belly was audibly displeased.

He had been awake for some time, having not slept well, and wa
aware of a sense of general dullness and vague soreness. It was trul͏ͅ
amazing, he reflected, how the body grew accustomed to specific bedding
He had spent several nights in Sherwood and now a night in the dungeon,
and his body made it known it preferred the bed in Ravenskeep.

Of course, that bed included Marian. This bed included rats.

He had paced out the pit earlier and knew its shape and size. Walking
had reacquainted him with the ache behind his knees, so he walked
steadily; a body grew stiff otherwise. But when he heard the sound of a
door creaking open in the distance and men's voices, he stopped moving
altogether. He stood in the faint patch of cross-hatched torchlight and
stared up at the grate, listening closely.

Three men, he judged, sorting through the descending footsteps and
voices. One was Gisbourne. Another he did not know. The third man
was—Mercardier? But why?

He heard the clank of keys. Hope surged; did they mean to bring
him out of the pit? But though the voices grew close, close enough he
knew they were not far from the iron grille, no one approached. Voices
receded somewhat. Gisbourne was complaining about something, though
Robin could not distinguish the topic. The light above was better, albeit
jumped and danced. The third man must be a guard carrying a torch.

And then Mercardier's raised voice carried clearly into the pit.
"Indeed, I insist; it remains my duty to see that the taxes are safe."

Gisbourne's tone, though the words were unclear, suggested ridicule.

Mercardier's answer was distinct and typically emotionless. "Until
the king himself relieves me of this duty, it is mine. Open the door."

Robin heard the sound of keys again, and a bolt shot back. More
conversation, though no words he could distinguish. Eventually he heard
the cell door swing closed, the bolt, and the clank of a lock relocked. Keys
chimed. Footsteps approached.

"Exactly as I left it," Mercardier said in a strange kind of satisfaction.
"Now, where is Locksley?"

"There." Gisbourne must have pointed at the pit.

"Down there?—*ah, oui.*"Someone stopped beside the grate. As before,
Robin could not make out identities, only shapes, color, and movement.

hands. But he was startled to see that her waist had thickened somewhat; was she breeding? *No wonder she is here to plead for her lover.*

"My horse fell," she replied curtly. "She broke her leg, and very nearly broke mine."

"So sorry," he murmured, seeing the stain of embarrassment in her face. "Perhaps you should have remained at home and sent a messenger."

"This I wish to address in person." She limped the length of the hall. "And I suspect you know very well what I've come for."

He felt a curl of pleasure deep in his belly. "Do apprise me."

She halted before the dais. "Robin."

He smiled with delight. "Indeed."

Marian said abruptly, "You and my father were friends."

"So we were."

"You watched me grow up."

"I watched you grow from childhood into beauty." He arched his brows. "But what has this to do with Robin Hood?"

"I would ask that you recall the days you and my father were friends, and how we hosted you at Ravenskeep. My mother, my brother. Even I was told to give you good welcome."

"Which you did most prettily," he agreed, "when your lady mother could convince you to stand still long enough to finish a sentence." He smiled. "You were always more interested in boys' things, then. I recall it was a struggle even to keep you in skirts. Though you have learned to wear them with surpassing grace." He shifted in the chair. "And now that you have reminded me that I have known your family since before you were born and thus should feel some softness for you, say what you've come to say. Plead his case, Marian."

Color rose in her face. "He did not steal the taxes. None of them did."

"Mercardier said they did."

"Mercardier is wrong."

"My castellan said they did."

"Your castellan is wrong."

"And the other men guarding the shipment?"

"If those men say Robin did it, those men, too, are wrong. He did not. *They* did not."

"But they have sworn they saw him."

"Others," she said coolly, "will swear Robin was elsewhere."

"Elsewhere?" He sat upright.

"Robin and the others were in Sherwood—"

"This occurred in Sherwood, along the Nottingham road."

"—robbing *others,*" she finished. "Mercardier and your castellan un-doubtedly saw what they expected to see: outlaws. But there *are* other outlaws in Sherwood. Robin did not rob this shipment."

She seemed quite certain. DeLacey contemplated that, chewing idly on a hangnail. "Have you witnesses?"

"Not here."

"Peasants?" He allowed a trace of contempt to underscore the word; peasants he could contend with. Peasants could disappear.

"Lords," she replied. "The earls of Alnwick, Hereford, and Essex."

His belly clenched. Those earls had indeed been at Huntington. He had seen them himself. But he managed a smile. "You are telling me these men were robbed by Locksley? And did not come to me to report this?"

She hitched a shoulder. "If they had, you would know very well Robin is innocent."

DeLacey glared. This was growing more complicated by the moment. He needed time.

And he had it. With a negligent shrug he settled again in the chair. "We have opposing witnesses, it seems. Most confusing. But nothing may be done until the king is informed."

"Something may be done. You may release him."

"Preposterous! Release the man who stole the taxes five years ago—"

"And was pardoned."

"—and stole two horses—"

"And returned them both."

"—delayed a royal messenger—"

"But the messenger got through."

"—and stole a known and sentenced cutpurse from just punishment?"

"Much is a *boy,*" she said, "and he is simple. I agree cutting purses should not be tolerated, but Much is not like other boys. He doesn't understand. Anyone who knows him realizes that." She drew herself up, then winced as if it jarred her leg. "I would be willing to assume responsibil-ity for him. Should he steal again, I would make good the loss."

This was highly amusing. "With what? You haven't the coin to pay your taxes!"

Now she was angry. "I paid them. You *know* I paid them."

He spread his hands in a gesture of helplessness. "Again, we have evidence that suggests otherwise."

Marian gripped the stick with both hands. "My lord sheriff," she said, "the king may well wish not to antagonize the Earl of Huntington by keeping his son imprisoned."

He displayed teeth in a grin. "The Earl of Huntington disinherited that son."

"And if he *re*inherits him?"

"Difficult," deLacey observed, "for a dead man."

Clearly she had hoped he did not know. The color fled her face.

"A nice attempt," he said kindly. "I do admire your courage and creativity. And I freely admit there *is* a chance the king will grant him mercy—he was after all a holy Crusader and a compatriot of his brother the late king—but until the current king's will is known, I cannot release the prisoner."

"And if I brought forward the earls to swear he was with them?"

Calmly he said, "It is for the king to decide."

Tears glistened in her eyes, but did not spill over. "Why," she began, "do you hate him so?"

DeLacey laughed. "He makes it easy." He sat upright then, grasping a folded parchment. With great attention he unfolded it, smoothed it against the tabletop, and offered it. "I intended to send this to you. But as you are here . . ." He waved it. "Take it, Marian."

"What is it?"

"Notification that the earl has acquired Ravenskeep, and that you are to leave."

She clutched her stick more tightly. "The earl is dead."

"Then his title and estates pass to the Crown, as he has no heir." He waved the sheet again. "Perhaps you should go to London and beg John for your manor back. If you are very good to him—in bed, of course—he may even grant it."

Unfortunately he was unable to see her reaction; one of his clerks arrived with three parchment sheets filled with crabbed writing. "My lord, the report you requested. For the king."

"Ah!" DeLacey put down the eviction notice and accepted the fresh sheets, looked through them briefly. "All seems in order. Yes, I shall give this to Mercardier." He nodded dismissal, and set the parchments on the table. He favored Marian with a distracted smile. "I'm sorry—have we further business? If not, you may go."

"No," she said tightly. "We have no further business."

Bemusedly, he watched her turn and begin the slow, limping journey back down the hall. Then he took up the clerk's report again and began to read through it, relishing the portions that underscored Mercardier's incompetence and Locksley's outlawry.

DeLacey grinned. He did not believe the king would grant anything other than execution to Robert of Locksley.

Once out of the hall proper—and out of the sheriff's sight—Marian grabbed the first male servant she saw. With a hand pressed rigidly against her abdomen, she adopted an expression of supreme distress. "Garderobe! *Please*—"

The servant, helpless in the face of potential female problems, immediately took her to the nearest garderobe. Marian thanked him hastily, jerked open the door and, emitting a piteous groan, stepped inside. Then she listened at the closed door even as she continued to make soft noises of distress, and was rewarded to hear steps receding quickly.

The garderobe was a tiny, noisome closet with a hole carved through the stone bench, leading below to the castle sewer. Quickly Marian leaned the wrapped bow against the door, untied her girdle and dropped it down the hole, then began working the chemise and shift off over her head. Those, too, went down the hole, though not without a wince of regret. Then she unwrapped the rolled tunic and hooded capelet and tugged both on, belting tunic and hosen into place. From the left boot she took the coiled bowstring and unrolled it, making sure there were neither knots nor twists. She put it between her teeth and began unwrapping the bow, discarding leather and sacking down the garderobe hole. When the bow was unencumbered once again she bent and strung it, smacking an elbow against the door. The belly of the bow scraped the wall.

She drew a deep breath, closing her eyes a moment. Her heart pounded. There was so little time, and so much yet to do.

Marian released the breath noisily, bleeding tension away, and reached down to untie the thong around her thigh. She pulled the arrows from her boot and thrust three of them through the back of her belt. The fourth one she nocked, but did not draw the bow. A finger hooked over the shaft at the grip and a little tension kept the arrow in place, though it would require adjustment when she drew the string back.

Now. Time to pray that she could reach the dungeon without being stopped; and additional prayer that one of the guards in the dungeon would have the keys to the cell.

She pressed an ear against the door. She heard nothing. Marian stuffed the braid down the back of her tunic underneath the capelet and drew the hood up. Softly she murmured, "Time to do this thing."

DeLacey was carefully folding the three-page report to the king when Mercardier, heeding a summons, appeared. The sheriff continued to fold the parchment, then with all deliberation took up a green taper and dripped wax upon the outer sheet. He pressed the signet ring of Nottinghamshire into the emerald globule, allowed it to cool, tied a ribbon around the packet, then extended it to Mercardier.

"There," he said. "You may now depart. I trust you will see to it this reaches the king with all speed." Naturally there was a copy; naturally a second messenger would be sent.

Mercardier inclined his head slightly, took one stride to the dais and accepted the packet. "As my duty to the king requires, Lord Sheriff."

"I do hope he shan't be too hard on you," deLacey said kindly. "The king can be—unpredictable."

The pocked face was implacable. "I failed in my duty."

"With no small thanks to Robin Hood." DeLacey smiled broadly. "Though I understand from Gisbourne, you paid appropriate tribute to that worthy earlier."

The mercenary said nothing.

DeLacey studied him. He had never known any man so self-controlled. "You are a difficult man to read, Mercardier. But I daresay in this I am right: you do not much admire Robert of Locksley."

A muscle jumped in the shadowed jaw. "What has he done that is admirable? It is true he was a sound fighter—and for it he was knighted—but he was disarmed and captured by the enemy." Clearly that was a supreme sin to the captain of mercenaries. Better a man die than give up his arms or person. "He did not ransom himself," Mercardier continued; and now deLacey heard the contempt. "Nor did he ask his father the earl to do so, but expected it of Coeur de Lion; and it is not for a king to do, to ransom a mere knight!" A second very great sin; the harsh voice now was laden with emotion. At last deLacey had found the key. "Then he returns to England and steals the taxes. *Twice.*"

The sheriff smothered laughter. "Indeed!"

High color underlay the pockmarks. "I say again he is a piss-poor excuse for a knight and Crusader, and I would piss on him at every opportunity."

An idea occurred. Casually deLacey said, "It is very likely you shall never see Robert of Locksley again. Would you wish to say farewell? Perhaps make it extremely plain how seriously he has erred? Surely the Lionheart would be ashamed that a man he knighted, a man he himself ransomed, a man he loved so well, should dishonor his memory in such a despicable fashion."

Something moved through the dark eyes. A spark of light, of an intensity so vivid it stunned the sheriff. No more was Mercardier the dutiful hired soldier taking no interest in anything other than money. There was something personal here.

DeLacey tapped fingers upon the table. "You once said you have no conscience."

"I am a mercenary. My conscience is hired. Currently it belongs to King John."

"Then I will make you a gift," the sheriff said. "The opportunity to undertake one thing that is for yourself, Captain. Entirely for yourself."

Mercardier frowned.

DeLacey took the ring of keys off his belt and tossed them onto the table. "Explain to Robert of Locksley how very, very much he has dishonored Coeur de Lion. No one will interrupt you."

Robin, sitting against the wall, heard the sound of the door again. This time there were no voices, merely quiet footsteps. It was difficult to distinguish how many men might be approaching; but he had learned there were two guards stationed in the dungeon near the line of cells extending away from the pit. He thought it unlikely they were present for him—he was heavily chained and there was no way out of the pit. Probably their task was to guard the cell containing the gathered taxes.

He stood, canting his head back to stare up at the grille. The light remained wan, no more than what was offered by a single bracketed torch near the pit. Whoever came down the stairs carried neither lamp nor torch.

Robin listened closely for some indication of the visitor's business. There was the grit of bootsole on stone, but nothing more. His belly clenched. Every fiber in his body, every corner of his soul, came alive with anticipation.

Movement. Someone was near the grate. Someone who bent down, unlocked it, then slid the bolt back. The iron lattice was peeled away, allowed to thump down against the stone floor.

Robin saw Mercardier standing at the rim, staring into the pit.

It registered instantly. Someone had given the mercenary the keys. And Mercardier despised him.

Chains chimed as he stiffened and moved back out of the patch of light into the darkness of the pit. He had no weapon. He lacked even the ability to use his hands freely. And there was certainly no escape, no opportunity to hide, no chance to avoid what Mercardier planned.

This bore the mark of William deLacey.

Inside his head, Robin swore. A beating, no doubt. Possibly even murder.

The mercenary sat down upon the stone floor and dangled his legs over the rim of the pit. It was an altogether incongruous posture for Mercardier, Robin thought. It spoke of casual companionship, of relaxation, neither of which he had known in the man.

"When one is a mercenary," Mercardier began, "one is subject to the whims of one's patron. But as mercenaries are only hired when that patron wishes things done he himself has no desire to do, and cannot trust servants to do for him, generally the mercenary's duty is one of enforcement. He guards, he fights, he kills. He also murders, if so ordered. He does not argue against such a thing, does not object to the individual he is hired to kill; he rarely cares what the dispute is about, or who the subject is. He is hired for his skills, not his opinions. And never for his conscience, which is nonexistent."

Robin, standing below in the shadows, felt a chill in his flesh. "You will forgive me, I pray, if I am not particularly interested in the nature of being a mercenary."

"But you should be," Mercardier said with profound satisfaction. "I am your judge, you see."

Gisbourne presented himself in the hall. DeLacey, who had not sent for him, raised an eloquent eyebrow. His seneschal was scowling. "I thought you sent Mercardier on his way with a report to the king."

"So I have."

"Then why did you permit him entrée to the taxes again?"

"I did not."

"But I saw him going to the dungeon."

"There is more in the dungeon than taxes, Gisbourne."

"There is only Robert of Locksley, my lord. What business has Mercardier with him?"

"The king's business," deLacey answered smoothly. "My business. Your business. The business of the shire. The business of making certain an outlaw may not escape, or be rescued, or be deemed unimportant by a king with other concerns on his mind."

Gisbourne's eyes widened as he grasped the implication. "But, my lord—"

DeLacey cut him off. "In fact, I think I should like to witness the demise. To be certain, you see. To be very, very certain." He rose. "You may go, Gisbourne. This is not your concern."

Robin nodded, though mostly to himself. It was a tidy solution for all concerned. Why wait upon the king's whim when one might very easily make the problem go away? All it required was a man willing to murder another. A man who had done such before, who had no opinion, no objection. No conscience.

It was impossible to rescue a dead man. And a dead man never escaped.

"A competent mercenary is, by nature, a good judge of character," Mercardier continued. "If one is not, one will not succeed. And when one is the king's captain of mercenaries, privy to the private matters of high lords and in the king's confidence, one must be even more vigilant. So that day I first saw you, I studied you. And I knew then you were nothing like the king. He was garrulous and passionate; you were closed. Quiet. He was unstinting in his opinion of men, be they friend or foe; you kept your own counsel even among men who might favor it. When he was angry, you were cold. When he was joyous, you were restrained. He was a great tree of a man, a bulwark upon which nations are built; you were a stripling boy, weighing little more than my sword. Yet for all the differences between the two of you, there was one likeness: *you fought the war to win it.*"

Perplexed, Robin stared up at the man. "What other reason is there to fight a war? Not to lose, surely."

"Not to lose, no. But for many men war is merely an opportunity, a path to reward. They have little interest in the war itself, merely in victory. They forget that victory must be earned. Victory must be paid for in rivers of blood. But it must never be their own."

Robin had witnessed those rivers of blood. He had killed, had spilled his share. The enemy's. His own.

"A mercenary," Mercardier continued inexorably, "serves as he is hired to serve. A season with this patron, a season with that. A skirmish here, a battle there. When one job is completed, he hopes for another.

If he is good enough, he has no lack of opportunity; the patrons often will bid for his services."

"Mercardier—"

"But now and again a patron becomes more than a patron. Now and again the mercenary realizes he has no other wish in the world but to serve this patron. Then it is not a job, not a service, not even a duty. But *honor*. As it was for me to serve Coeur de Lion."

Mercardier rose. Moved away. Robin frowned.

There was the scrape of wood against stone, and then the narrow ladder was shoved over the edge. It slid down, landed in straw. Leaned there, offering exit.

"Come up," Mercardier said.

Robin very nearly laughed. "I think not."

Mercardier's expression did not change. Then he disappeared from the rim of the pit. Robin heard the sound of something being dragged. A moment later a slack arm dropped over the edge, and the body quickly followed. When it landed, Robin saw it was one of the guards. Blood bloomed on his surcoat. He was clearly dead.

"Come up," Mercardier repeated. "Do you wish more proof than that?"

Robin did not move. *"Why?"*

"Coeur de Lion loved you well. Enough to ransom you from the Infidel, when he did no such thing for anyone else. It was not his duty to do so; he was the *king*, for the love of God! But he did it. And so, in his memory, I do this."

Marian, hiding in the shadows behind a massive pillar, saw the sheriff striding down the corridor leading to the dungeon. It crossed her mind then that it would be a simple task to kill him; she need only loose the arrow and watch him die. But she could not. No more now than in Market Square, when she nearly shot him by mistake. And she was cursed with the imagination to comprehend what would follow: oh, indeed, she might win Robin free, but they would be hunted far more vigilantly for the murder of the sheriff than for simple robbery.

And yet DeLacey was going to the dungeon. Going to Robin, she did not doubt.

And the sheriff had the keys.

Disbelief flickered to life along with fresh hope. There had to be more. But Robin knew better than to make assumptions. "Keys," he said sharply.

The ring was dropped down, chiming into straw. Robin scrabbled quickly after it, grabbed it, and began the process of fitting keys into the locks on his shackles.

"Allez, allez," Mercardier urged.

But none of the keys fit. He felt the sickening clench of his belly, the reestablished certainty that this was deLacey's idea of a jest.

He threw the key ring into a corner of the pit and glared up at Mercardier.

"No?" the man asked. Then, murmuring imprecations in French beneath his breath, he disappeared. Robin put one foot upon the bottom rung of the ladder, considering trying anyway. But Mercardier was back, dropping down another set of keys. "From the other guard, *oui?"*

Hands trembling, Robin tried the keys one by one. The fourth one unlocked the left shackle. Quickly he stripped it off, then unlocked the other. The sense of relief was profound as the iron fell to the straw.

"Allez," Mercardier said.

Robin climbed the ladder. Once over the edge, once free of the pit, once standing on the floor of the dungeon again, he said, "There is more to it than the Lionheart's memory. We were never friends, Mercardier; the dislike was mutual. I am turned thief; even I admit it. And you believe I stole this shipment. Why, then? This places you at risk."

A spark of anger burned in the dark eyes. "The sheriff is a subtle man," the mercenary said, "but he made a bad mistake. If one intends a man to believe he has been robbed by outlaws, it is best not to have a soldier who masquerades as an outlaw then appear before the very man who was robbed." He gestured. "When they brought you in yesterday, I saw two of them. One very tall man. Another short and slight. It gave me pause, and I looked more closely. These two I had seen, before being rendered unconscious." He shrugged. "I do not doubt the others were present as well, though I did not see them. But no more was necessary. The pieces existed; I put them together. And it all became very clear."

Breath gusted out of Robin. "Then deLacey stole his *own* tax shipment!"

"Oh, I think nothing was stolen. I think only one chest among the many on the wagon contained coin. Because when I entered the cell earlier, it was obvious to me none of the other chests had been moved."

"To make me look guilty," Robin said.

"And to discredit me," Mercardier added. "I interfere with his plans, with his private little kingdom. But it is of no matter now; I intended to withdraw from the king's service when I returned to Court. This John, he is nothing like his brother. Richard was . . ." He spread his hands, at a loss for words. "Richard was—"

"Richard," Robin finished, smiling wryly.

"He was a king," Mercardier said, "for whom it was a pleasure to serve. It was my honor for more than ten years. I would have done it for no payment."

That, Robin supposed, was the highest form of flattery a mercenary could offer. But . . . "Why the piss?"

The grim mouth twitched into a fleeting smile. "Most convincing, *oui?* Such hatred, such contempt for you displayed before witnesses, including the sheriff's seneschal. I knew deLacey would permit me to return. And so, I am here. And you are free." But there was no friendliness in the dark eyes. Enmity remained. There never had been, nor never would be companionship between them. "I suggest you go." Something in his face altered slightly. Briefly. "Go to that woman who would die for you."

Robin nodded, prepared to accept his freedom without further explanation. "What will you do? Hire on with someone else?"

"Perhaps. But first I am going home to Aquitaine. I have been too long away."

In the distance, a door opened. Robin froze.

"Mercardier?" It was deLacey's voice. "Have you quite incapacitated him?"

Robin looked sharply at the mercenary, whose expression assured him this interruption had not been planned. Grimly he indicated the dead guard, lying two paces away, and gestured. "The sword."

Mercardier went to the guard, drew the sword, and tossed it to Robin even as he unsheathed his own. His voice was a harsh whisper as he said what Robin was thinking. "So we fight, *oui?*"

"*Ah, oui,*" Robin answered grimly. It was the only way to convince the sheriff no complicity existed.

"Captain?" deLacey called.

Mercardier answered by attacking Robin.

Forty-Six

DeLacey heard the clash of blades as he descended the stairs. It froze him a moment; then he quickened his pace. He was nearly down when the combatants came into view, rounding the wide, arched entrance to the wing of cells.

Mercardier. And Locksley.

Something had gone wrong.

His hand grasped convulsively for his own sword. But he wore none. He was in his own hall, tending his own business. One did not wear a sword when at home.

But one had a knife. It would not do against a sword, but if Mercardier retained Locksley's attention there might be an opportunity.

Perhaps.

Then again, Mercardier had been King Richard's finest fighting man. He might neither need nor appreciate such assistance.

DeLacey halted there, four steps from the bottom. It provided him with an unobstructed view, a view worth watching. He had never seen two finer swordsmen. It brought to mind the memory that *he* had defeated Sir Robert of Locksley; though a perverse part of him also recalled that the dais steps and chair had impeded Locksley, forcing a slip, and had he not fallen, the fight might easily—and probably would have—gone the other way. Then King Richard had arrived . . . and Marian had broken the sheriff's arm with a blow from Gisbourne's crutch.

DeLacey swore. Had he succeeded in killing Locksley then, his life would have been much different.

The fight was almost too fast to properly watch. It was a brutal dance of death: attack, parry, break, thrust, parry, chop, parry, attack-attack-attack, feet constantly moving, bodies striking classic and improvised postures, finding ways to maintain balance, to unweight as necessary, to turn and twist and duck, to slide and lean, to back up, then plunge forward; and also a song: the clash of steel on steel, the subtle harmonies of the blade dependent on placement, be it near the hilt or the tip. Quillons caught, were entrapped, wrenched apart. Steel tapped, scraped, chimed, slid. No subtlety in broadswords, no edge on the tips: they were not for piercing and stabbing, but meant to slash, to smash, to hack and to shatter; to sunder flesh and bone, to scythe limb from trunk and head from shoulders.

They panted now, the opponents. Sweat ran freely, bathing grim faces, the rictuses of effort. Mercardier's damp dark hair clung to his head, hugging his skull like a steel cap. Locksley's longer, fairer hair mimicked pale spray as he moved, slapping his shoulders and back, swinging forward to curtain his jaw. They watched each other's eyes, judged movement by what was seen, was anticipated; stopped the expected offense, turned it to advantage, or reacted in time to recover from an unexpected ploy.

There was joy in it, deLacey knew, a wholly unimaginable and entirely inexplicable exaltation in the dance: of effort expended, of skill engaged, of the unflagging determination to *win*. To defeat the enemy.

These men had once, together, danced this dance against the Infidel in the name of God, of Jerusalem, and of Richard, King of the English. They had survived. They had killed. One of them had been knighted.

Now they fought one another. And one of them would die.

Neither spoke. They gasped. Grunted. Neither swore. They breathed. Concentrated. Occasionally deLacey saw one mouth something, as if in conversation with himself. Exhorting himself. Making promises to himself, or perhaps issuing prayers. Nothing else in the world existed for either of them but the movement, the moment, and the opponent.

They reeled close to the staircase. DeLacey backed up, gripping his knife. His own breath ran ragged and choppy, as if he, too, fought. He was tensed to move; he *needed* to move.

Torchlight glanced off steel; steel splashed flashes against the walls. The sheriff, poised five steps above the action, drew his knife. Mercardier need only force Locksley to the stairs, and up, and the knife would prevail over the sword.

But it was Mercardier whose back was to the stairs. Mercardier who was forced up them. And Mercardier who went down, sprawled there at deLacey's feet. One hand gripped his blade, but it was out of play. Locksley's blade was at Mercardier's throat.

"Yield," he gasped.

Mercardier said nothing, merely breathed noisily.

"Yield."

DeLacey, now four steps above, contemplated throwing the knife.

But it was a meat-knife, no more, utterly lacking in balance, and if he missed . . .

Locksley flipped the grip neatly in his hands, now holding the sword in a vertical position. All he had to do was drive it down and slam the blade through Mercardier's heaving chest. *"Yield."*

Mercardier's sword clattered to the floor. His voice was harsh. "I yield me."

DeLacey raised the knife, clasping it by the blade tip.

"No," a woman said. "Unless the lord sheriff *wishes* an arrow shot entirely through his heart."

Locksley looked up. And grinned.

Marian had heard the sound of swords as she crept to the door leading to the dungeon stairs. At first she could not begin to understand what it might mean. And then hope surged. There was no reason for men to be fighting in the dungeon, unless a prisoner had escaped.

A quick glance over her shoulder—no one approached—and she opened the door with care. A torch in a wall bracket lighted the staircase. Halfway down it turned, then turned again; she had been here before. Twice. She knew the staircase, knew the dungeon. Intimately.

Down the steps . . . moving silently. Torchlight flickered. The sound of blade on blade was clearer. There were no outcries, no way for her to tell who was fighting. And no deLacey, either. She thought he must be one of the swordsmen.

And then the staircase turned, and turned again, and the tableau lay before her. The sheriff, poised partway from the bottom, knife in hand. Mercardier, sprawled across the steps. And Robin, demanding he yield.

Marian halted . . . adjusted the arrow, fitting it more securely upon the string. Drew it. Told the sheriff what would happen if he threw the knife.

DeLacey twitched in surprise.

"Drop it," she said, aware of Robin's upturned face. She wanted to tell him to watch Mercardier—what if the man came surging up from the stairs?—but did not. She would not break her own concentration, not for a moment.

DeLacey's shock was plain in his voice. "Marian?"

"Drop it, Sheriff! It was I who killed your horse; do you truly wish to test me from range such as this?"

He dropped the knife.

Robin picked his way around Mercardier. He was smiling, she

thought. He stopped before the sheriff, two steps down, and silently gestured for him to turn around.

DeLacey did so. He now looked at Marian. Stared at Marian. His eyes were malignant.

Robin stepped close behind the sheriff. He set his left arm around deLacey's throat, shoving his jaw upward, and placed the swordblade against fragile flesh. "Climb," he said.

Marian glanced briefly beyond them both. "What about Mercardier?"

"He yielded." Robin was still smiling. "He won't trouble us."

Movement. She flicked her glance back at Mercardier, saw in horror that he was rising, had picked up his sword. "Hold!" she said sharply.

He stared up at her. She knew what he saw: a slight boy in yeoman's garb, until she shook back the hood. It settled on her shoulders. Best not to obstruct her peripheral vision. "You," he said, and she saw, to her shock, a certain amused satisfaction glinting briefly in his eyes. He knew her now; knew whom he had faced in the lane.

"He yielded," Robin repeated, when she did not avert the arrow.

Mercardier glared. "I *yielded,* madame."

It meant something to them, clearly. Something bound them now, though she could not discern what. Not friendship, certainly. Nor enmity; or at least not enough that would bring a man to fight. It was—what it was.

Marian swallowed. Her throat hurt. She felt tight as wire all over, and close to trembling so hard she likely would shoot Mercardier if she loosed, rather than deLacey. She chose to do as Robin apparently wished her to do, from the gesturing fingers. She backed up the stairs. At the door, she paused.

"Turn," Robin said. "There is the hall to get through, and the baileys. Be ready."

Marian turned. Leaned a shoulder against the door. Pushed. Robin, she knew, had his sword at the sheriff's throat. If anyone attacked, he could easily kill deLacey. But she doubted he wished to; that would destroy their advantage. It was up to her to lead them through the hall, to lead them through the baileys. And through the main gates beneath the sentry-walk.

Four arrows. She could expend three.

Behind her, she heard deLacey's harsh breathing. He would see her hang for this.

And so I am become an outlaw.

With no pretense to logic, Marian wondered what Alan, forever concocting ballads, would make of that.

Robin knew she was frightened. He had seen it in her posture, in her face, heard it in her voice. And yet she was in that moment as courageous as any *man* he had known, even hardened soldiers. Even mercenaries. True courage lay in accepting one's fear, not denying it, in doing what was necessary despite that fear.

He had never *not* been afraid, in war.

Even now.

She opened the door and stepped through, shoving it wide to crash against the wall. She was through, moving steadily and carefully into the hall, arrow nocked, bowstring drawn.

He knew it was possible they might both die in this.

And then, as he moved through the door and Mercardier followed, he heard the mercenary's familiar battlefield bellow.

"Stand aside! Let no man come near! Do not risk your sheriff's life!"

It succeeded in bringing soldiers and servants running into the hall. Mailed hands went to sword hilts. Bare hands flew to mouths.

"Stand down!" Mercardier roared. "He will surely kill your lord!"

Marian advanced. Robin marked how she selected one man as her target, pinning him in place until she moved farther and selected another. Wisely done. In trying to take aim at any number of soldiers even as she moved, therefore threatening all, she lessened her chances of accuracy and improved their chances of attacking her without risking injury. In threatening one, she promised at least one death. And no individual soldier wished to take that risk.

So long as they had only swords, not crossbows, he believed she was safe.

"My lord!" It was Gisbourne, come into the hall at a run. He stopped short, hand on hilt.

Robin turned the edge of his blade into deLacey's throat. "Is there something you wish to say to him?"

"Hold," the sheriff croaked. Then, more loudly, "Stand down, Gisbourne!"

"But—my lord!" Then he noticed Mercardier, eyes widening. "*Do* something, Captain!"

"He yielded," Marian explained, and Robin noted with a faint stab of amusement that Gisbourne had become her latest target.

It enraged the steward. "You won't shoot me! You haven't the stomach for it!"

DeLacey's voice rose in alarm. "Gis*bourne*—"

"She won't," Gisbourne said, and drew his sword.

Marian loosed. The broadhead punched through his right shoulder, front and back, before the arrow lodged in flesh. Only the fletching was visible against Gisbourne's tunic; the shaft had nearly gone completely through him.

With no wasted motion she caught another arrow out of her belt and nocked it, drawing smoothly and swiftly, before any man could move.

Gisbourne was down. He writhed on the floor, whimpering, left hand clamped to the meat of his shoulder. No one approached to aid him.

Robin's breath stirred deLacey's hair. "Move, if you please."

Through the hall and out of it, aware of eyes upon them, angry eyes, startled eyes, fascinated eyes . . . Mercardier walked behind him, seemingly unaware that he blocked Robin from a rear attack. Marian moved before him, still poised to shoot; and she had proved beyond doubt she had the stomach to do it as well as the skill.

"In the bailey you might be a bit more forthcoming with regard to warning off your soldiers," Robin suggested. "See what it earned poor Gisbourne?"

"Murder," deLacey rasped.

"That wasn't a death-wound, as you very well know. Unless you plan to kill him yourself and blame it on us. I recall you did so before, when you slit the throats of twelve of your own men."

They were at the threshold of hall and front stairs. "Stand down!" Mercardier roared from close behind; it took every ounce of self-control for Robin not to start. "Let them pass, lest your lord be killed!"

"How kind of him to ward your life so well," Robin murmured into deLacey's ear. "Without his assistance, you could be dead. Be certain to reward him—should you survive."

"If *I* were behind you, you would be dead. Even had I yielded!"

"That is because you have no honor. And *imagine* such a thing: one of King John's most loyal supporters lacking honor! How could it be possible?"

"Locksley—"

Robin cut it off with increased pressure on the blade against deLacey's throat. "We are in the bailey now. Hadn't you better ask your soldiers not to make it necessary for me to kill you?"

Breath hissed in the sheriff's throat. "Hold!" he shouted. "Stand down!"

"Better." Robin urged him onward. "Nearly into the outer bailey . . . is Marian not magnificent?"

"Marian's neck will be stretched even as yours is! Is she truly willing to lose her life because of you? Are you willing to risk her?"

"She has nothing left to lose *but* her life, Lord Sheriff. You and my father saw to that." He shrugged slightly. "And we shall let her determine what is and is not worth dying for, shall we? She answers to no man."

"She answers to your bidding."

"Ah, but this was all her own."

"Stay back!" Mercardier shouted; they were in the outer bailey. Men upon the wall, armed with crossbows, lined the sentry-walk. One bolt was all it required to strike Marian down.

"Tell them," Robin commanded.

DeLacey said nothing.

A bit more pressure, and blood flowed.

"Stand down!" deLacey choked. Then, as Robin moved the sword slightly to facilitate speech, "I said, *stand down! Hold!* Any man who shoots will be disciplined!"

"Better," Robin murmured.

They neared the gates. Were through. And then Marian shouted for aid even as a wagon careened toward them, and Robin had the fleeting impression of a red-haired giant upon the driver's seat.

From dwellings across the street, arrows flew in warning, thunking into the gates. Soldiers ducked.

"Well fought," Mercardier said abruptly. "And *your* victory, Locksley. Richard was right: you have honor, heart, and skill."

But there was no time for response . . . Marian threw her bow into the back of the wagon as it lurched to an awkward halt. Robin, giving way to nerves at last, spun deLacey back the other way and brought the wheel-pommel down against the back of the sheriff's skull.

"Hurry!" Marian was in the wagon, gripping the sideboards. *"Robin—"*

In two leaps he was at the wagon even as Little John yanked on reins to turn the horses, roaring at them to run. It lurched from under Robin, nearly upending him into the street. Swearing, he lost the sword entirely as he grabbed for the sideboards. He barked one shin, fell flat on his face, then pulled himself up and turned around so he sat facing backward, staring at the castle gates.

DeLacey was down in the dirt of the street, one hand clasping the back of his head. Mercardier stood over him. The sun was going down behind the castle; the mercenary, in silhouette, was a broad bulk of a mailed, man-shaped wall, features indistinguishable.

"*Merci,*" Robin murmured. Then he thrust a victorious fist into the air. "For the Lionheart!"

Marian's arms closed tightly around his neck as the wagon bounced and shuddered. "For Robin Hood," she said.

And kissed him soundly.

Epilogue

The priest concluded his prayers before the modest altar and rose, wincing slightly as his knees creaked. With each season he grew a bit more stiff, a bit more slow, but God did not mind if his servants were not as nimble as in their youth. God required the heart and soul, not the body.

He turned, his mind on a bite of bread, and stopped short. A man stood in the open door, silhouetted against the sunlight. "Father?"

Perhaps the bread would wait a bit. "Yes, my son?"

The man came into the small church. Now the candlelight fell clearly on his face: he was young, handsome, slim, with riotous golden curls. His clothing was a bit tattered, but clearly once had been fine. He had the manners and accent of a lord, yet the priest felt both were affected, not natural. "Father, I have a cart just outside. May I trouble you to accompany me on a short journey?"

This was not an unusual request. There were ill and injured people who could not come into Nottingham; he made it his practice to go where he was needed. "Of course, my son. Shall we be gone long?"

"No, Father, I'll have you back before sunset. And we shall feed you well, that I promise!" He indicated the door with a graceful gesture. "May we go?"

The priest appreciated the fine manners and charm, though he might chide the young man for veniality; pride of appearance and manners should never come before God.

Outside there was another man with the cart. His clothing was not so fine, nor his expression, nor certainly his manners. "Coming, then, are we?"

The fair-haired man pressed a light hand into the priest's back, urging him forward. His tone was mild, but the words were odd. "Will—we would do better not to be seen together."

The other shrugged. "Won't be here long enough, will we? Oh—I found you this." He reached into the back of the cart and pulled out a lute. "The fool with it was caterwauling terribly; 'twill be better as yours, you being a minstrel."

The priest was shocked. "You *stole* this lute?"

The other man—Will?—shrugged. "You can absolve me later, Father. For now—let's get you in the cart, aye?"

"But—"

"Please, Father." The charming man was at his elbow. "Let us not tarry. Nottingham is not always kind to our sort."

"Not if you steal *lutes,*" the priest said sharply, but obligingly allowed himself to be helped into the back of the crude cart. The sin would be mitigated with confession and absolution, and God would of course forgive.

Will handed the suspect lute to him, then climbed up on the seat behind the sharp-hipped piebald horse. The minstrel got in beside the priest and humbly asked if he might see the instrument.

The priest gave it to him. "You have fine hands," he remarked, as they embraced the instrument. Indeed, minstrel's hands.

"Ah," the young man said on a sigh, "it has been too long." But he did not play, merely grasped the lute with careful, covetous hands, and smiled unceasingly.

"Where are we going?" the priest inquired as the the cart jolted into motion.

The driver hitched a shoulder. "Bit outside the city. Not far. Just down the road, aye?"

They were through the gates in short order. Outside the city, not far, just down the road, Sherwood Forest began. The priest eyed the trees uneasily. *"How* far?" Outlaws inhabited Sherwood.

"Oh, not to worry," the driver declared offhandedly. "You're with us."

Unease increased. "We're going into Sherwood?"

The lute-player was amused. "Do you think then that God should discriminate?"

"Of course not! But—" He scowled. " 'Tis dangerous in Sherwood."

"Betimes," the driver agreed. "But not today."

"Why not today?"

The minstrel grinned. " 'Tis a *celebration,* not cause for concern."

The priest opened his mouth to demand further explanation, but just then the driver turned the horse off the road onto a narrow, overgrown track. Wheels creaked, thumped, and rattled; the old man caught hold of the sideboards, lest his bones fall out of his flesh.

He smelled woodsmoke, and roasting meat. "How much far—" But the question remained unfinished as the cart was halted.

The minstrel climbed out, one hand wrapped around the neck of the lute; the other he extended to aid the priest. "Come, Father."

The priest did not disdain the help, nor did he fail to thank the young man. But he was displeased, and knew they saw it. Precisely as he intended.

The driver was down from the seat. He cupped hands to his mouth and emitted a series of bird calls.

A moment later a boy burst out of the bushes, grinning maniacally. "Hurry!"

The driver scowled at him. "Where was the call, Much?"

"No more birds!" the boy said. "They're *waiting.*"

"Waiting, is it?" Will pushed his way past the boy, parting vegetation. "Come along, Father."

The priest found himself hemmed by the driver, the boy, and the man with the lute. They were casual about it, and not unkind, but he had the distinct impression he was not so much a guest as a captive. Then he pulled up short. "I smell venison!"

"Venison, ale, wine, fruit, bread—and anything else that somehow made its way here," the minstrel said. "Keep moving, Father, I beg you."

"We can't eat venison! 'Tis the *king's* deer! 'Tis *poaching!*"

And then they were through vegetation into a small clearing, where pine garlands and berry wreaths had been hung, and flowers tucked into hollows, and a crude table cobbled together of rough planks and tree-limb tripods. There was ale and wine as promised, and also bowls of fruit and platters of bread. But in the center of the clearing was a spit and a fire, and a fine deer was roasting.

"Poaching!" the priest repeated.

A very large man stood beside the table. No, a *giant* stood beside the table, presiding over the ale by sampling it. Beyond him was another, tending the meat. The priest was shocked speechless when he saw the tonsure and cassock.

The Benedictine had the grace to look mildly ashamed. "Forgive us, Father. But we had no choice. I am only a monk, you see, and this requires a priest."

Testily he demanded, *"What* requires a priest?"

Another man stepped into the clearing. He was slim but tall, and broad through the shoulders, with hair so fair as to be nearly white. He wore a fine green-and-gold checkered silk tunic, though it was far from new. "The wedding," he replied. He flicked a wry glance at the others. "I suggest we begin. The bride is growing impatient."

"Can't have *that*," the giant declared, grinning.

"Father, if you please . . ." The minstrel guided him toward a bulwark of lichen-clad granite, then turned him to face the clearing. "Stand here, I beg you." He looked at the others. "Do something other than hang about like lackwits; perhaps you might gather as if this meant something to you?" He nodded as they hurried to obey. "Very well, I shall play in the bride. Robin?"

"She's bringing herself," the other said. "I'm to wait with the priest."

A woman's voice said clearly, "Hurry *up*."

The man in the fine tunic looked imploringly at the priest. "If you please, Father?"

The priest sighed and gave himself over to the moment. He was here, was he not, and could not very well walk himself out of Sherwood and back to Nottingham. He was old. He tired easily. Better to be taken, as he'd been brought. The price was small enough; he'd have their confessions before he departed.

He glanced at the lute-player. "Begin."

Grinning beatifically, the man obligingly brought the first notes forth. They were distinctly out of tune. The minstrel was horrified. *"Oh, Jesu!"*

"Just play," someone muttered.

"But—"

The priest gaped as a woman stepped out from behind a cluster of bushes. She wore a somewhat wrinkled and soiled red chemise, ungirdled, a golden fillet on her brow to tame the loose black hair, and clutched a spray of flowers in her hand. Yet for all her loveliness, her expression was decidedly cross. "With *or without* music," she said.

Meekly, the minstrel began to play again. The notes remained out of tune, but no one had the bad manners to comment on it.

The bride, however, did not appear to notice. Or else she did not care. A smile replaced the scowl. Beauty bloomed. The priest very nearly crossed himself.

And then she was coming, the smile in place, with her eyes locked on the fair-haired man in the checkered silk tunic, and the priest forgot all about stolen lutes and poached deer, the dangers of Sherwood's outlaws. A wedding was a wedding.

But the lute truly was decidedly out of tune.

"*Jesu,*" the minstrel muttered.

"Hush," the priest rebuked, "and, if it please you, cease taking our Lord's name in vain!" Reprimand given—and heeded—he then bestowed a kindly smile upon the bride and groom, who now stood before him.

Sherwood, despite the arching of trees toward Heaven, was not a church. But God was everywhere.

And even outlaws could be forgiven.

In solid content together they lived,
With all their yeoman gay;
They lived by their hands, without any lands,
And so they did many a day.

But now to conclude an end I will make,
In time as I think it good;
For the people that live in the North can tell
Of Marian and bold Robin Hood.

—from *Robin Hood and Maid Marian*
(a later ballad)

AUTHOR'S NOTE

Lady of Sherwood is a historical novel; that is to say, a work of fiction in which the author has made up huge chunks of a story that never happened. History, however, offers writers fascinating and compelling glimpses of actual people—kings, queens, and commoners—whose lives were often documented, and we weave these actual incidents together with those springing from our imaginations. But as with any journalistic endeavor, the annals of the times cannot always be trusted for accuracy; the closest thing to the media in the twelfth century were generally clerics, men requested by their patrons to keep track of things for various reasons. Patronage often results in creative interpretation, then and now, which is why contemporary historians disagree with regard to the characters and actions of yesterday's heroes and villains as reported by chroniclers of the times. (For instance, scholars are *still* arguing over whether Richard III or Henry VII had the Princes in the Tower murdered.)

Employing the storyteller's license, I have significantly compressed and rearranged the events following King Richard's death. He did indeed die laying siege to a nonexistent treasure at Châlus, killed by a minor wound that turned gangrenous. There was great consternation when Richard, lacking heirs of the body, decided his brother, John, the Count of Mortain, and Arthur, Duke of Brittany, his middle brother's son, had equal claim to England. But there were no codified inheritance traditions in place at the time, and thus no one was certain who had better claim: the youngest son of Henry II, or Henry's grandson. Richard apparently decided "may the best man win" was the most feasible approach to determining who would succeed. But acceptance of the claimant was actually determined by the most influential men of the land; hence, what the English barons thought of John vs. Arthur mattered a very great deal. It was William Marshal, one of the most powerful men in England, who, in debate with Archbishop Hubert Walter of Canterbury after Richard's death, declared John should be king, and thus gave John the endorsement that won over many of the English barons. The Archbishop of Canterbury, however, had grave doubts, as shown by his response: *'So be it, but mark my words, Marshal, you will never regret anything in life as much as this.'*

Ironically, John was visiting his nephew in Brittany when word of Richard's death arrived. He immediately rode for Chinon where the Angevin treasury was kept; money was the key to all. But Arthur's mother, Constance of Brittany, made her son's claim all the stronger by entrusting the care of the twelve-year-old boy to Philip of France. The Bretons and French formally accepted Arthur as the rightful successor; John ended up in Normandy where he had himself named Duke, as the Normans wanted nothing to do with the Bretons. There he had his mother, Eleanor of Aquitaine, bring up Richard's mercenaries, under the command of Mercardier, to control things on the Continent, while he hastened to England to be crowned king in Westminster Abbey approximately one month after Richard's death.

After a few years of a contested reign, John eventually realized that if Arthur, whom he had taken hostage in 1202, remained alive, a threat to his rule would always exist. Reports indicate John sent men to blind and castrate Arthur, though it was not done. For a while there were rumors of Arthur's death, though others swore he was alive. Eventually the truth came out, reported by the chroniclers of William de Briouze, one of John's most loyal companions, who wrote that in 1203 King John himself personally murdered his nephew:

> *After King John captured Arthur and kept him in prison for some time, at length, in the castle of Rouen, after dinner on the Thursday before Easter, when he* [John] *was drunk and possessed by the devil* (ebrius et daemonio plenus), *he slew him* [Arthur] *with his own hand, and tying a heavy stone to the body cast it into the Seine. It was discovered by a fisherman in his net, and being dragged to the bank and recognized, was taken for secret burial, in fear of the tyrant, to the priory of Bec called Nôtre Dame des Pres.*

John kept Arthur's sister, Eleanor, hostage as well, though she lived in luxury until a natural death in 1214.

Controversy over who should rule after the death of a popular monarch always provides fodder for novelists, and so I selected the turbulent days immediately following the Lionheart's demise for the focus of *Lady of Sherwood*. But even in fiction a logical progression of events provides a vital underpinning for the story arc, so I developed my own extrapolation of what might have happened to the central characters of the classic Robin Hood ballads, following events in my earlier novel, *Lady of the Forest*. The concept of robbing from the rich to give to the poor is central to the Robin Hood legend, as is the feud between Robin and the Sheriff of Nottingham and conflict over taxation policies, but even as I told the tale of how such seemingly disparate parties as peasants, a knight's daughter, and the son of an earl might come to be co-conspiritors in *Lady of the Forest*, I chose to depict the resultant activities in the sequel as an outgrowth of the very real political conflict between John and Arthur. In the interests of accuracy, it should perhaps be noted that while Mercardier truly was captain of the Lionheart's mercenaries, for my own purposes I transported him from France to England and made him central to this version.

The story of Robin Hood, Marian, and the others, regardless of interpretation, remains a vital and viable part of contemporary society, one of the few universals in literature, and I am certain they shall continue to inspire novelists and screenwriters for centuries to come.

A NOTE ON REFERENCE MATERIALS

When undertaking to write any historical novel, an author relies on an infinite number of sources for information and documentation. Sometimes only one small kernel of information is mined from a fat reference work; other times there are whole chapters that inspire much of the resultant novel. With this in mind, I must say that, as usual, I am indebted to numerous reference materials. The primary sources I consulted for this novel include W.L. Warren's *King John;* Elizabeth Hallam's *The Plantagenet Chronicles; The Ballads of Robin Hood,* edited by Jim Lees; *Longbow: A Social and Military History* by Robert Hardy; and *Swords and Hilt Weapons,* by various contributing authors.

ABOUT THE AUTHOR

Since 1984, Jennifer Roberson has published twenty-one novels. In addition to historicals *Lady of the Forest*, a prequel to this novel, and *Lady of the Glen*, the story of seventeenth-century Scotland's Massacre of Glencoe, she has written two bestselling fantasy series: *The Chronicles of the Cheysuli*, and the *Sword-Dancer* saga. A collaboration with fantasy authors Melanie Rawn and Kate Elliott resulted in *The Golden Key*, a historical fantasy nominated for the World Fantasy Award in 1997. She has also contributed short stories to collections, anthologies, and magazines, and has edited three original fantasy anthologies. Her works have appeared in translation in Germany, Japan, France, Russia, Poland, Italy, China, Sweden, the Czech Republic, and Israel.

Jennifer Roberson has a Bachelor of Science degree in journalism from Northern Arizona University, with an extended major in British history. Her primary hobby now is the breeding, training, and exhibition of Cardigan Welsh Corgis and Labrador retrievers in the conformation, obedience, and agility rings of AKC dog shows and trials. She lives near Phoenix with (currently) seven dogs and three cats.

The author may be reached via her website at: *www.cheysuli.com*